José Raúl Bernardo

Scribner Paperback Fiction
Published by Simon & Schuster

The Secret of the Bulls

A NOVEL

SCRIBNER PAPERBACK FICTION
Simon & Schuster Inc.
Rockefeller Center
1230 Avenue of the Americas
New York, NY 10020

This book is a work of fiction. Names, characters, places, and incidents either are products of the author's imagination or are used fictitiously. Any resemblance to actual events or locales or persons, living or dead, is entirely coincidental.

First Scribner Paperback Fiction edition 1997
SCRIBNER PAPERBACK FICTION and design are trademarks of Simon & Schuster Inc.

Designed by Levavi and Levavi
Manufactured in the United States of America

1 3 5 7 9 10 8 6 4 2

Library of Congress Cataloging-in-Publication is available.
ISBN 0-684-81817-5
0-684-83137-6 (Pbk)

To my parents

Εὐχαριστῶ

. . . for the path to happiness is freedom
and the path to freedom
a fearless heart

THUCYDIDES

Prologue

MAXIMILIANO KEEPS in his old leather wallet a sepia photograph of Dolores, now partly faded and badly dog-eared, taken in a professional studio in 1913, when Dolores was eighteen.

Wearing a three-quarter sleeve ankle-length dress made of a white gauzy delicate fabric, Dolores stands facing the camera, looking radiantly beautiful as she leans against a high-back wicker chair in front of an old and badly wrinkled painted Victorian photographer's drop, a medal of the Virgin Mary hanging from her neck atop the high-neck dress, a bracelet on her left arm. She has abundant shiny black hair, parted in the center, that falls in loose waves and frames her oval face where her large shiny black eyes sparkle with life as her mouth rehearses a smile.

That smile is the most intriguing part of the photograph.

Dolores is trying to be serious—at the time people had to pose for a long time to have that kind of a studio photograph taken, so they were told not to smile—but she managed a smile nonetheless. The smile tries to be serious, but it has more than a touch of mischief.

This is the woman the young Maximiliano meets.

On top of the chiffonier in the bedroom she shares with Maximiliano, Dolores keeps, next to a tiny cameo photograph of the mother she never knew, a photograph of Maximiliano—dated June 6, 1911—taken around the time he and Dolores first met, when Maximiliano was in his early twenties. This photograph was taken in the swamps near Batabanó, the small Cuban village with an Indian name where he and Dolores were born.

Naked from the waist up, his hairless muscular torso and his thick neck glistening with sweat, Maximiliano stands facing the camera, backed by the Cuban jungle, a bandanna tied around his forehead, his legs spread wide apart. He is wearing loose-fitting mud-covered pants tied tight around the waist with a thick belt and inserted inside heavily stained knee-high leather boots, partly hidden in the swampy waters.

He is so deeply suntanned that he looks like a mulatto, except for his blond and bristly short hair, which shimmers like a golden halo around his head; and for his eyes, which are very pale and very bright, staring at the camera almost defiantly as he grins ear to ear.

He is holding in his tense bare outstretched powerful arms a Cuban *caimán*—a kind of large alligator peculiar to Cuba—which must have been alive and kicking, because it is out of focus in the old sepia photograph. He is grabbing the *caimán*'s thick strong tail with his left hand and is forcing the *caimán*'s mouth shut tight with his right hand in a Herculean display of raw power, his vigorous muscles about to burst.

This is the man the young Dolores meets.

DOLORES COMES FROM a well-read and well-educated family of wealthy landowners who descend from the first viceroy of the Indies and who arrived in Cuba more than four centuries ago.

But once Dolores met Maximiliano, the butcher, she eloped with him, and her family disowned her for life.

Part One

Guajiros 1911–1926

1

It is an early summer morning in the Cuba of 1911.

The light turquoise tropical sky is cloudless and clear; and the fragrant breezes coming up the Batabanó hill, where Dolores's house is located, smell strongly of *guarapo*—the fermented juice of the sweet sugarcane—and of the spiced salty ocean water, which is barely visible in the far distance.

One of the girls working in Dolores's large country estate has taken ill, and Dolores, who has just come back home from La Habana where she was in a boarding school, volunteers to go to town to buy the medicines the girl needs—accompanied by a chaperone, of course, Aunt Ausencia, an old maiden aunt who has remained living in the old family home.

Dolores's criollo-style home closely resembles a two-thousand-year-old model that originated in Rome: A square donut of a house where a series of rooms surround and open into a central square atrium, what Cubans call a patio. Except that Dolores's house, unlike most criollo-style houses, is not one story high, but two; its thick walls are made not of brick, stuccoed outside and plastered inside, but of stones; and the rooms are not tiny and crowded against each other, but enormous. Dolores's house is not a criollo-style house but a criollo-style mansion, built in the late 1600s with the sweat of hundreds of slaves, many of whom died while building it.

And yet, despite its age, which is beginning to show, the house is as impressive now as it was then.

It is approached by a long straight cobblestone drive lined by a *guardarraya:* a series of tall and slender royal palm trees, equally spaced along each side of the drive. This drive begins downhill at the bronze gates with the coat of arms of the first viceroy of the Indies located at the entrance fence and terminates uphill by drawing a wide circle in front of the main entrance to the house, which is accessible by a rise of six wide steps, each step made of a single thick slab of honed granite.

A deep veranda, supported by a two-story arcade of heavy stone columns, runs around both floors of the house, shading them from the hot Cuban sun and guarding them from the heavy rains Cuba gets six months out of a year; and the huge central patio, covered with large thick square slabs of white marble—now badly pitted and grayed by the years—houses a spring-fed fountain where the water is always heard gurgling, singing to the rhythmic swaying of the palms as they swish and dance in the gentle breezes.

The lower level has heavily ornamented twelve-foot-high coffered ceilings and houses the public rooms of the mansion. On the right side of the entrance hall is the large living room—what the family calls the ballroom—which opens totally on one side to the deep veranda and on the other side to the central patio, making it feel more like a pavilion than a room in a house. On the left side of the entrance hall there's first a small room—small by the house's standards—called the office, where Dolores's father keeps all of his accounts in a series of mahogany and brass desks and file cabinets that look totally out of place within the subdued yet ornate seventeenth-century decor. Next to this room and also opening to both the veranda and the patio comes the large dining room—sitting twenty-four—which is separated from the kitchen, located back of the house, by a large serving pantry.

The upper level houses the private rooms of the mansion and boasts of twelve magnificently appointed bedrooms, two of which were converted into inside bathrooms at the time of Dolores's birth.

And yet, despite the opulence of all the interiors, the house is primarily known for its entrance hall, which has a truly spectacular semicircular marble staircase with heavy balusters, each in the shape of a classic staff of wheat, each carved out of a solid piece of Cuban *ácana,* a wood hard as stone, and each adorned with mother-of-pearl insets.

Dolores rushes down this staircase, exuberantly happy because she no longer has to wear one of those ugly gray uniforms she had to wear at school. She is now reveling in her new daring *above*-the-ankle peach-color dress and her matching wide-brim hat, tilted just a bit too much.

Her aunt Ausencia—who violently disapproves of Dolores's too-modern outfit—is meanwhile slowly following her niece downstairs. She is barely able to avoid tripping over her long black skirt that goes all the way down to the floor, as a skirt should, because she is trying to put on her old-fashioned black lace gloves as she keeps telling Dolores, "Please, Dolores, please! Slow down! That's not the way a decent young lady behaves! Slow down! *Slow down!*"

But who can slow down a tropical hurricane?

Outside the main entrance door, which is wide open, horses are heard whinnying, ready to go.

Though La Habana of 1911 already boasts of hundreds of noisy Model T cars sputtering all over its crowded streets, not a single one has yet arrived permanently in Batabanó; and the two that have been seen on its scarcely populated main street have been looked at from far away and with a great amount of suspicion by all the *guajiros,* as Cuban country folk are called. Dolores, of course, strongly believes that her family should own a car, but so far she has not been able to convince either her father or anyone else in her family. So, since she cannot ride to town in a car, what other choice does she have? To town she rides, next to her aunt, in an elegant *volanta,* a fancy horse-drawn two-wheel open carriage—which to Dolores is a worthless relic from another century—driven by Pablo, one of the family hands.

Pablo, past seventy, is an old Negro who had been a slave at one time but who was freed when a group of criollo Cubans abolished slavery in 1868. Pablo decided to stay at the family house, doing the same work he had been doing before "The Emancipation," but he is a free man now, and that has made a huge difference in the way he carries himself. He has known Dolores since she was born and loves her as if of his own family, which in a way she is. But his love for Dolores verges on adoration. It had been Dolores who, while still a child, had spent a lot of time with him summer after summer, patiently teaching him to read and write, something Pablo will always be thankful for.

So to town they ride, the old maid, the Negro, and the young girl.

This trip is a real adventure for Dolores. This is the first time the young girl has been on her own, so to speak. She has spent most of her life up to now in a very exclusive boarding school for wealthy girls located in La Habana run by impossible-to-deal-with nuns, where she was sent when she was barely six years old. She spends time with her family in Batabanó only during summers, and her best friend there—her only friend—is Pablo. But she has finally completed her legally required education, and now she is back home for good.

She is just sixteen.

A few years after Columbus encountered the Americas on his way to India, the city of La Habana was founded on the south shore of Cuba, in a location very close to Batabanó, the little village where Dolores and Maximiliano first met. But in 1519, when a great bay was discovered on the north shore just a few miles away, the city moved, name and all. This was the same year Dolores's ancestors first arrived in Cuba.

The south shore of Cuba is more prone to hurricanes than the north shore, so it made sense to move La Habana from where it was to where it is now. Besides, the south shore tends to be swampy, and since mosquitoes love swamps and nobody loves mosquitoes, most people decided to move north.

However, some people, a very few, decided to stay behind, because in the sea near Batabanó lies one of the largest cradles of natural sponges in the whole world, and those sponges are considered the very best. For centuries they have been the main source of income for the area. That and the beautiful *caimán* skins, which are so highly valued. These two industries—plus sugar, of course—have made Batabanó a fairly successful little village. So much so that, in addition to the recently renovated Hotel Libertad, the old opera house—actually a small-time vaudeville theater—has just been altered to accommodate one of those new moving picture shows, which are all the rage.

The main street, which is well maintained and densely packed with dirt, is very dusty because it is the middle of the Cuban dry season, which lasts half a year, and it has not rained for many days. And yet, despite the dust and the heat—which is beginning to bother Ausencia, who has just opened her old-fashioned black lace parasol—there are a lot of men on the street, fully dressed in tight white-linen four-button suits and ties, wearing Panama hats, and carrying palmetto fans that they keep constantly in use. These men are for the most part tall blond American buyers who are looking at the sponges on display—some of which are truly gigantic—examining them carefully, and bargaining with the local sponge brokers, who answer their questions in bad pidgin English and outlandishly extravagant passionate gestures.

As Dolores and her aunt step out of the pharmacy, one of the oldest buildings in town, out of the corner of her eye Dolores senses she is being looked at. She turns around and notices a handsome young man staring at her from across the street.

He is tall and blond, just like one of those American buyers. But he is not one of them. He is not wearing a suit. He is wearing a white bib apron on top of a plain white shirt and pants. His face is deeply suntanned, and his piercing blue eyes sparkle as he looks at her intently.

She stares back at him, not really knowing what she is doing, and then her knees almost give way. She suddenly feels as if she has been taken ill. Her heart is beating so fast it seems it wants to jump out of her breast, her forehead is burning with fire, and yet her hands are cold as ice.

Her aunt Ausencia, who is supposed to be protecting the young girl from experiencing what she has just experienced, is busy trying to climb on top of the *volanta* without getting her fancy black leather high-top shoes dirty and fails to notice anything. But Pablo, who is sitting in the driver's seat, sees that the girl is about to faint.

"Something wrong, Miss Dolores?" he asks, deeply concerned.

Dolores looks at him as if she had just awakened from a dream. "Oh, no, Pablo, thank you, thank you. I'm all right. I'm all right."

"It's this sun," says the old aunt, already comfortably seated. "It's getting too hot, just too hot. Maybe we all should be getting home. Aren't you done with everything you came here for?"

Dolores first looks again at the handsome boy with the piercing blue eyes and then faces her aunt as she answers, "Yes, yes, I guess I am."

She starts to climb back into the *volanta,* but all the while she continues to look out of the corner of her eye at the smiling blond criollo who keeps staring at her, almost insolently.

From that day on, Dolores volunteers daily to go to town on errands, looking for this or that, always hoping to run again into the young man with the bold eyes. And invariably she manages to run into him.

Or is it him running into her?

It takes Dolores a long, long week after her eyes first met those of the blond young man to find out that his name is Maximiliano; that he comes from a family of Germans who arrived in Cuba in the late 1860s, when Mexico had an Austrian emperor; that he is named after his grandfather, who was named after that emperor; that he is the butcher's son; and that he works at his father's butcher shop.

No sooner does she find out all of this than she decides that she will go to the butcher shop the next day to buy some meat. But she also decides that she is going to go into the butcher shop all alone. Entirely and exclusively by herself. Minus the chaperone, that is.

The next morning, wearing a conservative dress and her hat at the proper angle—much to the surprise and approval of Ausencia—as they reach the butcher shop, Dolores tells her aunt that it is too hot, close to noon already, when the tropical sun is at its hottest; that it would just take a couple of minutes to buy the meat; that there are always flies inside a butcher shop; and besides, all those horrible smells! Why should her poor aunt suffer through that when right here on the shaded side of the street, just outside the butcher shop, there's a nice cool sea breeze blowing, which, by the way, doesn't it feel, Oh, so good?

All of this makes excellent sense to the tired old maid, who indeed decides to stay outside on the shaded side of the street enjoying the nice cool breeze from the sea, as her niece—who cares so much for her—volunteers to go into that horrid smelly butcher shop all by herself, the dear thing!

As she is about to enter the butcher shop, and after making sure she is not within sight of her aunt, Dolores bites her lips hard and pinches her cheeks even harder, to bring color to them, tilts her hat just a bit, smiles her best smile, and steps decisively into the shop. There she pretends to look at the different cuts of meat on display just as the young man in the white apron behind the counter pretends not to notice that she is in the store. After a short while she finally faces him and, smiling her most mischievous smile, places her order with him.

The young man takes his time to fill Dolores's order, and while he does that, smiling his most insolent smile, he surreptitiously manages to look at her, his eyes always finding hers looking back at him. Dolores watches him as he carefully wraps the meat she has ordered in brown paper. He ties the package with a thin jute string and then he turns around and looks at her. They are silently staring at each other, silently saying a lot to each other, when he hands her the neatly wrapped package.

It is then they touch.

It is accidental, a mere brushing of hands over the cold marble counter. Or so it seems.

But of course it isn't accidental at all.

Dolores leaves her hand on the cold marble surface for what seems to her the longest of times as her mischievous dark eyes meet the challenge in his insolent pale blue eyes, boldly smiling at her; and as they brush hands they both feel the warmth of that touch which makes them burn, Oh! Such a pleasurable burn!

Just then the butcher, the boy's father, asks Maximiliano to help with some other customers. The boy immediately stands up, straight as an arrow, and turns to face the other people in the shop.

But that first touch has taken place, and neither of them will ever be able to forget it.

★ ★ ★

2

Both Dolores's family and Maximiliano's family belong to the same town association, a culturally minded group called Liceo that organizes lectures, poetry readings, concerts, and, on rare occasions, dances—or "social events," as the townspeople call them—which take place under the stars in the central patio of the Liceo building to the accompaniment of a local band.

Somehow both Dolores and Maximiliano manage to go to the same social event at the Liceo, and while there they have the opportunity to dance a *danzón,* a daring dance new to the Cuba of 1911.

Cuban dance music is a mixture of lyrical white European melodies played against wild black African rhythms; and the bands that play it are typically as integrated as the music they play.

The Liceo band is no exception.

It is composed of several white and mulatto brass players—led by a black man who is a brilliant clarinet player—and of a large group of men who play African percussion instruments: the *timbales,* the bongo drums, a loud pair of drums that because they are played between the legs of a man have lent their name to the way Cuban men refer to their testicles; the *quijadas,* the jaws; the *güiro,* the scraping gourd; the *congas* and the *tumbadoras,* male and female African drums; the *cencerro,* the cow bell; and that pair of noisy female-breast-shaped gourds Cubans call *maracas.* All of these percussion players are black men except for the white man who plays the *claves,* the ebony sticks that give the danzón its magical beat.

The danzón is by far the most elegant and the most sensual of all Cuban dances: a perfect marriage of European prudishness and African voluptuousness. Technically speaking, the Cuban danzón is a very simple ballroom dance that can be learned in minutes. However, to be really good at it, the danzón has to be danced not with the feet but with the heart.

The man embraces the woman, as in most ballroom dances, except that in a danzón the woman holds a handkerchief in her right hand, the hand she places in his, so supposedly the flesh of their hands will not actually touch.

Cuban chaperones are well aware that whatever is going to happen between two people, it always begins with that first touch. That is why a chaperone who is worth her stuff always stands vigilant at every dance, her eagle-sharp eyes always making sure that first touch never takes place. Unless, of course, that is precisely what she is hoping for, in which case she just looks the other way.

Music begins.

The danzón opens with a loud introductory motif, almost a fanfare, that serves as a bridge into more lyrical passages during which the partners dance voluptuously yet prudishly since they make no eye contact with each other whatsoever. Every so often the opening motif is heard again, at which times the partners stop dancing, separate from each other, and do nothing but stare at each other until the next lyrical section begins.

According to the womenfolk, the breaks in the danzón were invented to allow the dancing girls to calm down and fan themselves since ladies are not supposed to perspire.

Not so, say the criollo men.

According to them the breaks were invented to allow the ever-present chaperone to take a good look at the innocent dancing men. If the chaperone notices some physical reaction on the man dancing with the girl she is taking care of—in other words, if she notices the man having an erection, which does tend to show easily enough through the thin linen pants all Cuban men wear—then the chaperone quietly and discreetly pulls the girl away, if the boy is not to her liking. Or else she pretends everything is just as it should be, ignores what she sees, does nothing, and lets nature continue its course.

Criollo men have several tricks that they teach each other on how *not* to get caught by the chaperone's ever-vigilant eye.

And needless to say, Maximiliano, the butcher's son, knows them all.

Maximiliano, cleanly shaven, smelling of cinnamon and bay rum, and wearing a white-linen suit that along with his blond hair makes his skin look that much darker, has been impatiently waiting for Dolores, who arrives late, wearing a brand-new ankle-length dress made of printed yellow voile, with silk roses at the waist, and a matching yellow ribbon holding her long black wavy hair.

Dolores pretends not to notice Maximiliano's eyes as she and her aunt enter the patio, but she knows he is there because she can feel those eyes of his as they burn her skin.

She sits quietly next to Ausencia at the end of the patio where all the women sit. And as her gray-haired aunt begins to tell her neighbor the kind of inconsequential things people tell each other on such occasions, Dolores looks across the patio to the other side, where all the men stand, just to find those burning blue eyes of his staring at her.

She bravely holds his stare, but somehow she fails to make herself smile. She feels ill at ease, self-conscious. As if she were in a beam of light. As if the magical tropical moon dangling in that beautiful dark-turquoise night sky has been placed there just to aim its beams of light at her. Or are those beams of light coming from his eyes? She looks away from him. She knows she has to, just to survive; her heart is beating so loudly.

The candles inside the perforated tin lanterns hanging all over the patio have been lit, creating innumerable miniature stars that flicker and scintillate over people's heads.

"Isn't this heavenly," says Ausencia to the older woman, who, sitting next to Ausencia, silently agrees with her as she first looks up at the beautiful night sky, then around the whole incandescent space, and then sighs. "And what a nice guava punch you girls have prepared for this festive occasion," Ausencia continues. "Exquisite! Simply exquisite!" she adds as she settles comfortably in her chair.

There's a brief silence as the musicians turn the music on their stands and face the black clarinet player who, after stomping his foot three times, nods his head as the band begins to play. But Dolores hears nothing. The world begins to swirl. But Dolores sees nothing. The patio is filled with the delicious aroma of black jasmine. But Dolores smells nothing. And then, all of a sudden, Dolores sees standing in front of her a broad smile of a face, which is his face; and hears a beautiful dark melody of a voice, which is his voice; and smells a sweet tempting smell, which is his smell. And before she realizes it, she feels him leading her to the center of the patio, where under the stars glittering above them, and lighted by the tropical moon that insists on focusing exclusively on the two of them, she finds herself seeing and hearing and smelling and feeling no one but him, who, close to her, is seeing and hearing and smelling and feeling no one but her, as they both wait for the opening fanfare of the danzón to end and for that magical moment in which he will have her in his arms for the very first time and she will find him in her arms for the very first time. Even though the flesh of their hands will not touch.

One danzón.

That is all Dolores and Maximiliano manage to dance. One danzón. That is all.

But what a danzón!

As they begin to dance, they carefully avoid each other's eyes, as they both know they must do. And yet, as they dance, each of them feels as if their eyes and their bodies were tied together—just as their souls are tied together—by an invisible ribbon, a ribbon that makes them move simultaneously and with the most elegant and precise accuracy, but each of them moving with such great freedom and sensual ease that the whole dance feels more like an intimate caress than like a dance at all. They dance, and they dance so well, and with such intensity of heart, that the entire room begins to melt with the heat they generate. Everybody's eyes are on the two of them, who have become one as they dance. But, as they dance, the eyes of the two of them have not yet met. No. Not yet.

The opening fanfare is heard again, far too soon, and Dolores and Maximiliano separate, as they know they must.

It is only then that they dare to look deep into each other's eyes.

And what has to happen happens.

And what happens is evidently impossible to disguise, even with Maximiliano's best tricks.

As soon as the danzón is finished, Dolores's aunt, Ausencia, claiming she has suddenly developed an unbearable headache, immediately takes her niece back home. She is so shocked at the audacity of that boy, as she calls the butcher's son, that she can barely speak. How dare that boy do a thing like that! How dare he!

Obviously the butcher's son is not considered a good match for Dolores. He does not come with land. Owning land is everything, especially if your father is a powerful landowner who dreams of being the largest landowner of the area, perhaps in all of Cuba. And Dolores's father is just that kind of a man. He is a Spaniard who is as land

hungry as the best of Spaniards were when they first arrived in Cuba.
So Dolores must be rushed home before the social event is over.

The third daughter in a family with no sons, Dolores never knew her mother, who died in childbirth. For years before Dolores was born her mother had unsuccessfully tried to provide her husband with a son. Three times she had miscarried prior to giving birth to Dolores. Years later Dolores's father married a young Cuban woman half his age, a woman who was only a few years older than Dolores herself, a woman Dolores never trusted. And both of Dolores's older sisters, much older than Dolores herself, had long ago married men of their father's choosing, and had long ago left the family home behind.

So Dolores has no one to confide in, except her old aunt Ausencia. And it is to this old maid Dolores turns for advice. But what advice can Ausencia offer this sixteen-year-old girl? What does an old maid like her know about these things?

As a young girl herself, Ausencia never had a boyfriend.

Once, when she was in her mid-thirties, a young man approached her, much younger than she at the time, and Dolores's father intervened and told Ausencia that the young man had come to her for her money and for her lands, but not for her. To prove it, Dolores's father had Ausencia transfer to his name the little bit of land she owned. When the young man was told about it, he quietly and discreetly disappeared from Ausencia's life. But the land was never transferred back to her.

There are those in town who believe that the whole thing was devised by Dolores's father to get hold of Ausencia's lands, which were immediately adjacent to his. Certainly Dolores's father always thought of those lands as his.

He, Dolores's father, was a Spaniard who came to Cuba a nobody, but a handsome nobody who married Dolores's mother, the only surviving child of a family of seven, a criollo girl with a huge dowry. He was not a bad man. He just did what many other men had done before him. He was land hungry all of his life, and land hungry he will die, after losing all of his lands at a cockfight, including the old maid's parcel.

When Dolores turns to her aunt for advice, she forces Ausencia to relive in a few seconds all that she had gone through, making the old woman remember things she thought long forgotten: the embarrassing pains she had experienced; the agonies of a doubt that grew bigger and bigger every time the young man came to call on her; the many times she looked in the mirror asking herself over and over again, Is it *me* he likes? Or is it *the money*? She remembers every word the young man told her, every promise that he made to her. And then she remembers that last meeting, that last time they saw each other, when he said, "It is best that we part, then," and when she answered, her heart breaking, "Yes, it is best. It is best." She doesn't want her niece to go through what she had to go through. She certainly doesn't want her niece to suffer as she did. She debates with herself. What can she tell Dolores?

One thing you do not ever say to a hot-blooded criollo girl is, Do not do this! But that is just what Aunt Ausencia tells her young niece.

She tells Dolores that the butcher's boy is nothing, and that he would never amount to anything. She tells Dolores that all the butcher's boy is after is the family's money, and the family's position, and the family's land. And she begs Dolores, for the benefit of the family, never *ever* to see that boy again.

Dolores is listening attentively to everything her old aunt is telling her, but her heart knows her aunt is wrong. Dolores has seen how Maximiliano's eyes look at her, and she knows he is not interested in the family's money, nor in the family's position, nor in the family's lands. She knows he is interested in *her,* the person she is, the woman she is and will be. No, her heart tells her what her aunt is saying might have been true for her, but it is not true for Dolores. How could it be?

She knows that she has felt elated every time Maximiliano stared at her. She knows that each time, she's felt her heart beat faster than the wings of a hummingbird. She knows that those times they've accidentally touched over the cold marble counter, they have felt, Oh, so good! And she also knows that just as she feels, so he feels too. Yes, she knows it. Beyond the slightest doubt.

Still, her aunt keeps talking and talking, desperately urging Dolores over and over again, "Promise me you won't see that boy again, Dolores, please, please! Promise me, and I won't tell your father a word of what you have told me. Promise me, Dolores, please, please! Promise me! Promise me!"

Dolores keeps looking at her aunt, pretending to listen, and suddenly she realizes that up to that moment she did not really know what was happening to her.

But that was then, a lifetime ago, when she did not know what she wanted.

Now, after The Night of the *Danzón,* life is different for her.

Now, now she knows exactly what *she* wants, which she knows is exactly what *he* wants. And placing obstacles in front of her is like throwing logs into a burning fire. They just fuel the flame inside her heart, a heart that keeps beating urgently, constantly reminding her of the creed all criollo Cubans live by: You desire something? Get it! Pay whatever the price. Suffer whatever the consequences. But just get it! As simple as that. And that criollo woman, Dolores, decides that she will follow her heart. Ausencia does not realize what she has done, but by telling Dolores "Don't you ever see that boy again," she has made up Dolores's mind for her. And once Dolores's mind is set, it is set.

Dolores looks at her aunt and smiles her broadest smile.

Ausencia, who hasn't stopped talking, looks at her, tilts her head to the side, and after a short silence, smiling back at her niece, she embraces Dolores tight to her as she whispers almost silently to herself, "Thank God! Thank God!"

The first thing Dolores does the next morning, as soon as she wakes up, is to ask her aunt to go shopping with her to La Habana, a trip that normally takes at least a couple of days.

Ausencia is delighted to see the high spirits of the young girl, and to herself she thinks that getting Dolores away from Batabanó for a few days is not such a bad idea at all. So she immediately consents to go with her to the capital, where they can stay with Fulgencia, Dolores's oldest married sister, who lives there.

No sooner do they get to La Habana than they go to Fin de Siècle, an exclusive French store that caters only to the very wealthy, where Dolores falls in love with a fine and delicate white linen, a fabric so exquisite and so expensive that the store just has samples of it and which has to be ordered directly from Paris.

Dolores decides to order the fabric nonetheless, and then waits. It takes forever for the fabric to get first to La Habana, then to Batabanó. When she finally gets it, Dolores draws on the thin gauzy material intricate patterns of hummingbirds and hibiscus flowers heavily intertwined. Then she begins to embroider it by hand, using the tiniest of stitches and the thinnest of white silk threads, a thread that makes her designs shimmer with a subtle elegant luster on the expensive white matte gauzy fabric.

Everybody in the household feels that the dress Dolores is making for herself is going to be very beautiful, what with all of that complicated embroidery. Her old aunt Ausencia is especially delighted to see her work so hard, keeping her mind occupied, with no time to think of the handsome butcher's son.

What nobody but Dolores knows is that the beautifully embroidered white-linen dress she is so intently working on is going to be her wedding dress, even if she has to wait almost two full years until she is eighteen before she can do as she wants.

And that is the dress she wears in the old sepia photograph Maximiliano keeps in his wallet, the one with the serious smile that has more than a touch of mischief.

★ ★ ★

3

The day Dolores turns eighteen she puts on her brand-new white-linen dress and asks Pablo to take her to town in the *volanta* before noon. It's her birthday today, and Dolores is happy.

"No," she tells Aunt Ausencia. "No need for you to come with me. I'm eighteen today. I can handle myself from now on."

She sees her aunt raise her eyebrows in alarm.

"Besides," she continues, "Pablo is with me. He can chaperone me."

She turns to Pablo and smiles at him with her famous mischievous eyes.

"Pablo," she says, "you will defend me if somebody tries to steal me away, won't you?"

"Child!" says her aunt as she crosses herself. "Don't you ever say a thing like that ever again!"

"Why, of course, Miss Dolores," answers Pablo. "Of course I'll defend you. With my life."

He is sitting on the *volanta,* in the driver's seat in front, waiting for the birthday girl to get in.

"See?" says Dolores as she climbs into the *volanta.* "No need for you to come."

"But—" begins the old maid, and then she realizes that there is nothing she can do. Dolores is her father's daughter, and, like her father, once she makes up her mind . . .

"Pablo," the aunt says, "don't you let your eyes off that girl, you promise?"

"Why sure, Miss Ausencia. I won't. I sure won't. You can rest assured of that!" And with that he slaps the horses with the loose reins and they begin to go on their own; they've been to town so many times they know their way blindfolded.

"Where to, Miss Dolores?" asks Pablo, as if he didn't know.

"You know."

"Excited?" asks Pablo, who turns around to face the birthday girl and adds, "Because I sure am!"

Dolores looks at Pablo and smiles. "Me too, Pablo. Me too."

The wedding is a plain civil ceremony that takes place at noon in the little office of the Hotel Libertad, the only hotel in Batabanó; a three-story building built not of brick, like most criollo buildings, but of wood studs and clapboards, in what Cubans call the American style.

Since the hotel caters almost exclusively to American businessmen, the owner had decided to build it and furnish it in a style those men were used to, but the local criollo carpenters managed to give it a criollo touch: Behind the elaborately carved central staircase, which is made of solid Cuban mahogany in a natural finish, there is a mural made of wood marquetry depicting Cuban farmers fighting for *libertad,* their machetes raised in defiance as they seem to be climbing a hill that follows closely the slant of the stairway.

The owner has kept the hotel as up to date as possible, and recently, during the last renovation, when electricity finally arrived in Batabanó, large white ceiling fans were installed in all the rooms, fans that make *guajiros* say "Aahhh . . ." as they look up at the really high ceilings of the hotel and see those fans move silently, as if by magic.

The criollo carpenters also provided the hotel with tall skinny windows, almost ceiling high, crowned with semicircular transoms in the shape of peacock tails made of multicolored stained glass, which cast a rainbow of sunshine on the handsome butcher's son and his young bride as they look into each other's eyes.

They are both dressed in immaculate white. He is holding a Panama hat in his callused hands; she, a bouquet of jasmine and hibiscus Pablo picked for her on their way to the village.

It had been Pablo who from the very first day after the night of the danzón had acted as a *correveidile* between Dolores and Maximiliano, constantly carrying secret love missives from the one to the other, and constantly covering for Dolores when she could not be found in her house, saying that she had been with him, teaching him.

For almost two whole years Pablo had been doing that, day and night, hoping never to be found out.

But now his labors are finally over. Now Pablo can look at the two of them with a smile so broad that it illuminates his wrinkled black face.

The ceremony is short and sweet.

The former slave who is now a free man gives the bride away. Later on, when he is asked to sign as a witness to the marriage, Pablo proudly does it, signing just the way he has been taught by the bride.

This is the first time Pablo would sign his name on an official document, something he could never have done before as a slave, but something he can do now that he is a free man.

And he signs in an elegant cursive style, "Pablo Fernán Fernán," just as white folk do, with two last names, his father's and his mother's, which are the same because they both had been slaves of the Fernán family. If only they had lived long enough to see him writing his name on such a fancy piece of paper, with such a beautiful border design. "Pablo Fernán Fernán," a free man. A Negro and a free man!

When the other witness, the butcher's son's best friend, Manolo González Pereira, signs his name on the same piece of paper, and the ceremony is officially over, Dolores turns to Pablo and kisses him on the cheek. And Pablo begins to cry.

Maximiliano shakes hands with him, and Pablo, wiping his tears so nobody will make fun of him, says to Maximiliano in a firmly stern voice, "Now, you better take good care of my child," and he looks at Maximiliano intently, because he means it.

Maximiliano embraces him, man to man, Cuban style. "You know I will, Pablo. You know I will," he says. And then he starts to walk Dolores upstairs, to the room he has rented to spend his first wedding afternoon with that beautiful woman, his wife, by his side.

The hotel lobby is crowded with people talking and gesturing and joking and laughing. But Dolores hears nothing.

As she goes up the stairs, the Cuban farmers on the mural by her side are fearlessly raising their machetes in frozen defiance as they climb up the hill. But Dolores sees nothing.

A door opens up to a large room that smells of sweet spices, of sugar and jasmine. But Dolores smells nothing.

And then, all of a sudden, Dolores sees, standing in front of her, that broad smile of a face, which is his face; and hears that beautiful dark melody of a voice, which is his voice; and smells that sweet tempting smell, which is his smell.

And before she realizes it, she feels him leading her to the four-poster bed, where under the sheer mosquito net enclosing them and under the white ceiling fan silently stirring over them, lighted by the bit of tropical sun that filtering through the closed shutters and the colored transoms above them insists on casting colorful rainbows of sunshine on the two of them, she finds herself seeing and hearing and smelling and feeling no one but him, who, close to her, is seeing and hearing and smelling and feeling no one but her, as they both wait for that magical moment in which, man and wife, he will have her in his arms for the very first time, and she will find him in her arms for the very first time. But this time the flesh of their hands will touch.

By the time Pablo drives Dolores back to her farmhouse later on that day, Dolores is already the butcher's son's wife, the marriage has been consummated, and now nothing, nobody, can pull them apart.

Maximiliano stayed at the hotel, as they had agreed, though he didn't want to. "No," she had firmly said to him. "This is something I have to do on my own."

As soon as they reach Dolores's rich country estate, she goes straight to her room on the second floor and begins packing her clothes, which she had not done before because she didn't want anyone to know of her plans and try to do something to thwart them. That is all she takes with her, her clothes. Her clothes and a photograph of her mother, the mother she never knew.

She kisses her mother's photograph, places it in one of her two straw suitcases, and, still wearing her beautiful white-linen dress, she begins to walk downstairs, carrying a suitcase in each hand.

Her father, the land-grabbing baron of Batabanó, has just arrived from his everyday ride around his vast properties. He is a handsome older man of fifty-two with dark-brown hair, barely touched by gray around the temples, a thick dark moustache, and dark piercing eyes. He is wearing his *polainas,* knee-high riding leggings made of leather, and still has his whip in his hand. He sees Dolores walking downstairs, a suitcase in each hand.

"What do you think you're doing?" he demands.

"Moving out," she says, her face defiant though her voice is quiet.

"Don't you talk to me in that tone of voice, young lady!"

"What tone of voice? You asked me a question; I answered it. Anything else you'd like to know?"

She is indeed his daughter. He cannot but admire her audacity, talking to him that way. But though he admires it, he cannot let her get away with it. He knows this is some game of power, and he—a gambler by nature—always likes to have the upper hand.

"You and Elmira had a fight?" Elmira was his young new wife.

"No. I have no reason to fight with her. Never had."

"So?"

The old aunt just comes in, rushing down the stairs, crying her eyes out. She has just talked to Pablo, who told her everything.

"Is somebody going to tell me what's happened here, in *my* own house, that I don't know of?"

"It's my fault," cries the old aunt. "It's all my fault. I never should have let her go to the village by herself. It's all my fault." Ausencia is weeping, her words barely intelligible. "It's all my fault. My fault."

Dolores places the suitcases on the floor, goes to her aunt, embraces and kisses her.

"It's not your fault, Aunt Ausencia. It's nobody's fault. There is no fault to talk about." She faces her father.

"I married Maximiliano, the butcher's son," she says quietly.

Her father stares at her, dumbfounded.

"This afternoon," Dolores adds, and shows him her wedding ring, a simple thin gold band she is wearing on her left hand. "For better or worse."

"You can't do that. Not without my permission," shouts her father, fire burning in his black piercing eyes. "You're not of age. I'll have him in prison, that upstart, that—"

"I'm eighteen today, Papá. Today is my birthday. Don't you remember?" She pauses, then adds, "Mamá died eighteen years ago . . . today."

For a second the baron of Batabanó, he who is always in control, does not know what to do or say. Then, suddenly, his rage bursts out, loud angry words spurting out of his mouth. "I'll have it annulled. No daughter of mine is ever going to marry a butcher's son!"

"This daughter has, Papá," Dolores answers calmly, gently, with no hurt and no resentment in her voice. She is kind and soothing as she tells her father, "I'm now his wife, Papá. In soul and in body. I spent the afternoon with him, in his bed. I am now his wife and nobody can ever alter that. Nobody can annul what he and I willingly and knowingly have done." She turns to her aunt. "Good-bye, Aunt Ausencia. I love you. You have always been like a second mother to me." Then she faces her father. "Tell Elmira and my sisters good-bye for me."

The gambler has not given up yet. He still has one last card to throw on the table, one he thinks is a trump.

"You realize, don't you, that when you walk out that door, when you leave this house, you realize that you will leave it for *ever*?"

But it doesn't work.

"I know that, Papá. Just like you did when you left Spain. Never to go back."

Her father whips the stair balustrade with such force that he breaks one of the old carved balusters. Never has he lost this way to anyone. Never!

"Goddamn you!" he screams at her. "You could have married the best around here! The very best!"

Dolores bravely holds her father's angry stare as she answers. "I did!"

Pablo, who has been standing at the door, quietly enters the house, picks up the two suitcases that are lying on the floor, places them inside the *volanta,* and then goes back into the house to escort Dolores.

"No!" screams the baron of Batabanó, now a bad loser. "Not in my volanta you are not! You may go to your husband if you wish, but not in *my* volanta!"

Dolores faces her father and quietly asks, "May I take the suitcases with me?"

Her father gives her an angry nod. "Yes! What do I want them for?"

Dolores goes to the *volanta,* takes out the suitcases Pablo had placed inside, and carrying one in each hand begins to walk. Pablo rushes to her and takes the suitcases from her hands.

"What do you think you're doing, Pablo?" screams the beaten gambler as Pablo pauses at the door.

"I am walking Miss Dolores to town, sir."

"You walk with her, you don't come back! You hear?"

"Yes, sir," Pablo says.

Dolores, upon hearing this, grabs the suitcases from Pablo's old hands, who determinedly grabs them back again.

"I am a free man, Miss Dolores. I can do as I please. And it is my pleasure to walk you to town, that is, if you let me."

The young girl looks at him for the longest time. Then she smiles at him, lets go of the suitcases, and begins to walk away from the house in which she was born.

Pablo, proudly, with his head high, begins to walk toward the gate, following the young girl, who does not look back.

It is only when they are both on the road leading to town that Pablo notices Dolores crying, and he begins to cry as well.

She looks at him.

"I love to cry at weddings," Pablo says. "Don't you, Miss Dolores?"

And she begins to laugh and cry at the same time.

"Me too, Pablo. Me too."

All of a sudden she realizes that this is after all her wedding day, and that from now on she is going to be spending the rest of her life with the handsome butcher's son, he with the insolent eyes and the golden hair.

And her heart begins to beat faster than the wings of the hummingbird, and she cannot wait to get to Batabanó, where her husband, *her husband!* awaits her. How can anyone be as happy as she is today!

And she laughs and cries out of sheer happiness, at the beauty of it all.

"Pablo," she says, "I'm so happy! So happy!"

And the old Negro, who used to be a slave but who is now finally a free man, finally free to do as he pleases, laughs and cries with her.

"Me too, Miss Dolores. Me too."

★ ★ ★

4

Life in Batabanó does not last long. The butcher's son has other dreams for himself and his young wife, and he begins to take steps to get both of them where he wants. Both of them and Pablo, of course. And of course, in addition to the three of them, a black woman cook who comes to their house early in the mornings to prepare all meals for them, as Maximiliano had promised Dolores.

Cooking is something Dolores has never done and never intended to do. That was part of the agreement she and Maximiliano made before they got married. Dolores said to him, when he followed her suggestion and proposed to her, "I'll marry you. I'll take care of the house and of the children to come, God willing. I'll sweep and dust and sew your clothes and serve your food at the table. But I am not cooking, period. So either you learn to cook for us, or else you have to promise me that you'll always have someone cook for us. That is all I ask. Say yes and I'll be yours forever."

What could Maximiliano say? He wanted this woman more than he had ever wanted anything in his entire life. So, of course, he said yes, and—criollo man that he is—he has kept his word of honor.

A criollo's word of honor is sacrosanct. Once it is given it is never, *never,* taken back. Such is the criollo's creed, no questions about it. So when Maximiliano said yes, he meant it. A cook he promised his wife and a cook he provided her. But a black woman cook, because as everybody knows, they are the best.

And now that they have a woman cook, plus Pablo and the two of them, all of a sudden the butcher's son has four mouths to feed, and he'd better do something about it.

And he does.

There is a small village named Surgidero, much smaller than Batabanó, located right by the shore itself, just a few miles closer to *caimán* country. The area of Surgidero is very humid and swampy, but lobsters have just been discovered there, and where there are lobsters there are men to catch them, and those men have to eat, and they have to eat well, and to eat well they need red meat, and somebody's got to butcher that meat, and if somebody's got to do it, why not Maximiliano?

So there, to the tiny village of Surgidero—a village so small it has only a single street with just a couple of stores and a few rapidly put together shacks—the butcher's son brings his new wife, and there he opens his own butcher shop.

Little by little, with the help of Pablo, business grows, just as Surgidero does; and the butcher's son, now the butcher of Surgidero, builds an inexpensive one-story American-style clapboard house with his own hands, where he lives with his new wife and their firstborn, a pretty girl they named Merced after Dolores's own mother.

Pablo is close to eighty now and his black curly hair has begun to show white, but he is still as strong as a bull. He helps Maximiliano at the butcher shop during the day, eats all of his meals with Maximiliano and Dolores at their new house, and each night, after dinner, he goes to sleep at a house he shares with some of his relatives and friends at the other end of town, which is not that far away.

This was Pablo's idea.

When Maximiliano told him he would be happy to have him live with them, Pablo answered using the old Cuban proverb *"Quien se casa, casa quiere,"* which to Pablo meant, "He who marries, wants to be left alone." And nothing, not even Dolores's persistent pleading, had made him budge.

To Dolores, Pablo *is* family and, deeply concerned about him, she takes excellent care of him. In fact, to Dolores, Pablo is the only member who remains of the family she once had, a family she lost on "The Day of *her* Emancipation," as Pablo calls it.

At first she would get letters from her aunt Ausencia and from her older married sisters, all of whom risked being thrown out of the family every time they dared send a letter to her. But soon even those letters failed to come. No doubt Dolores's father found out about the letters and demanded that everybody stop writing them. After all, one does not write to a dead person, does one?

Dolores was dead in her father's eyes, and that was that.

But she certainly is alive in the butcher's house, a tiny house that sees, first, the birth of Merced, and, then, of two other children, for as the butcher's business grows, so does his family.

MERCED, the oldest, who turned seven two days ago, is sound asleep in her bed clutching a pretty rag doll she just got from her parents as a birthday present. Merced has named her doll Esperanza, which means "Hope." She loves Esperanza so much that Merced will not let her go, not even for the tiniest moment. Suddenly Dolores rushes into the bedroom, in her nightgown, holding a bundle of blankets wrapped around Gustavo, the baby, in one of her arms. She kneels down by Merced's bed and with her free hand shakes Merced. A dog is barking and barking next door. "Merced! Merced! Honey, wake up! Wake up!" Dolores tries to sound gentle, though there's a strange urgency in her voice.

"What is it, Mommy?" Merced is rubbing her eyes as her mother keeps shaking her and urging her to wake up.

"Your pappy and I are playing a new game and we'd like all of you to play with us. Here, put on your slippers so you can play it too."

"Can Esperanza play too?"

"Of course, honey. We all are going to play it. You and Mani and"—she lifts the bundle in her arm up and shows Merced the little boy's face—"Look! Even your baby brother is going to be playing with us."

"How do you play it, Mommy?"

"It's easy. Let me show you."

The dog barking increases, becoming louder and louder. Maximiliano rushes in, holding the hand of a sleepy-looking five-year-old boy with black wavy hair.

"I have Mani with me. What else do we need?"

"I have a handkerchief with some money on the top drawer of the chiffonier," Dolores answers. "Can you get that? And see if"—the barking next door gets painfully loud—"Never mind that. Merced, honey, let's go. Come on, let's go." Dolores hurriedly throws a blanket around Merced and tells her, "I'll race you all to the butcher shop. Let's see who gets there first." Merced is looking for her slippers. "Never mind the slippers, honey. Just run!"

"Barefoot, Mommy?"

"Yes, honey, barefoot. It's more fun that way. Come on. Run! Run! I'll bet you I'll get there first if you don't run fast enough! Come on! Run, honey! Run! *Run!*"

They all begin running out of the house when Merced trips at the porch step and shouts, "Mommy, Mommy! I dropped Esperanza!"

"Don't worry, honey. We'll pick her up later on. Run! Run! Do you want to lose the race? Run! *Run!*"

The children race with their parents and they all reach the butcher shop, Maximiliano the first, who opens the shop. "You all stay here," says Maximiliano. "I'll get back to the house and see what I can get."

"Pappy," cries Merced, "bring me Esperanza. I lost her when I was running."

"Sure, honey." Maximiliano looks at Dolores. "There are cardboard boxes in back of the store. Mani, you help your mommy bring them in."

"What for?" asks Mani, who always sounds angry when he is sleepy.

Dolores signals Maximiliano to go while she answers Mani. "We're going to sleep here tonight, at the butcher shop. That's the game I was telling you all about."

"Mommy," asks Merced, "who won the race?"

Dolores embraces her and smiles her mischievous smile.

"We all did, honey. We all did, thank God!"

She looks out of the butcher shop and she sees dogs running wild, barking incessantly, women and children screaming, and half-dressed men rushing about as the homes they each left behind begin to get devoured by gigantic flames.

THE FIRE had started several houses down the line from Dolores and Maximiliano's home. One of the kerosene lanterns lighting the street had fallen and had struck some straw that ignited, and from there the fire took off, spreading wild and fast, because it was the dry season in Cuba and it had not rained in more than three weeks. Somebody who smelled the smoke ran out, saw the fire, and immediately began to ring the emergency bell, as half-dressed men ran into the streets and began harnessing the horses for the fire truck. Meanwhile some of the other men went around from house to house shouting "Fire! Fire!"

Dolores had not heard them. It had been the strained barking of Facundo, the little dog next door, that had waked her up. She looked out the window and saw flames a couple of houses away from theirs. She woke up Maximiliano, pointed to the fire, and all she had time to say was, "The children!" Maximiliano woke up Mani while Dolores wrapped Gustavo, the baby, and with him in her arms woke up Merced. Now they are all asleep on cardboard boxes that have been flattened and laid on the cold tile floor of the butcher shop. They are all asleep except for Dolores, who is holding tight to her baby.

It's been a long time since Maximiliano left the butcher shop. Dolores would like to go where the fire is being fought, but she does not want to leave the children alone. She hears the noises quieting down little by little, and almost no barking at all. She waits, sitting quietly by her children, as the tropical sun begins to rise, tingeing the sparkling white-tiled butcher shop with the color of embers.

Maximiliano comes in carrying a small bundle. He is sweaty and tired and covered with black soot, but he has not been burned.

"The house is gone," he says.

Because the house was built in the American style, with clapboards and wood studs, it burned to the ground. Merced, who has been sleeping with her head on her mother's lap, wakes up and sees her father. "At least we were able to stop the fire before it crossed the street. But our entire block is gone. Thank God it didn't get to the butcher shop!"

It was good it didn't because Maximiliano, who had never borrowed a penny in his entire life, had just borrowed a lot of money to put in the back of the shop a brand-new cooler—one of those expensive refrigerated ones that no longer required the daily delivery of tons of ice that had been needed to keep the meat hanging from the hooks in edible condition.

What if the fire had burned the new cooler? How would he have paid for it? A penny owed is sacred to a criollo man, as sacred as an agreement. Once a criollo man's word is given, it is given for good, and nothing, *nothing,* can make him break it. That is part of what makes a criollo man a criollo man. Spaniards are different. They break their agreements as easily as they break their word. That's why, as Cubans say, Spaniards are Spaniards, and criollo men are criollo men, and never shall the two of them mix. Just like *aceite y vinagre,* oil and vinegar.

"I couldn't get much out of the house, but I got you this," says Maximiliano as he goes through the contents of the bundle, finds what he is looking for, and shows Dolores the old cameo photograph of her mother that she kept in their bedroom, on top of the chiffonier.

Dolores looks at it.

She had totally forgotten about it. How could she? Her mother's photograph, the only token she has of the mother she never knew. How could she have forgotten it? She takes it in her hands and kisses it. And then, suddenly, she begins to weep.

Maximiliano kneels down next to Dolores and embraces her. "We got out all that mattered, didn't we?" There's a short pause during which all he hears is Dolores weeping as she keeps staring at her mother's photograph. "Well," he adds as he tightens his embrace, "didn't we?"

Dolores nods and buries her head in her husband's chest while he holds her close to him.

Merced is listening, but does not understand what is happening. She has never seen her father like that, so dirty and so tired.

Dolores erases her tears and becomes her practical self once again. "Did anybody get hurt?" she asks.

"Eusebio," says Maximiliano. "But not too bad," he quickly adds. "He just thought that one of his kids was still in the house and he ran in before anybody could stop him. Fernando saw him running in and he shouted to me because I was closer to Eusebio. I ran to him and I was able to stop him just in the nick of time. One of the big roof beams fell, I swear it, two inches away from his head. And then what do you think he did? He started beating me! Beating me and weeping at the same time, calling me all sorts of names, because I had not let him in the house. He thought he had lost one of his kids. And then Susana told him to calm down, that he was disgracing himself, and pointed to their children as she counted them, one, two, three, four, five, six, seven, eight, nine, and the last one, the baby in her hands, ten. 'You see,' she said, 'we are all here.' And then Eusebio began to laugh and laugh, even though it must have hurt a lot every time he did, because he had a couple of bad blisters around his mouth. I bet you can still hear him laughing! But he almost broke my jaw, that stubborn mule!"

Maximiliano caresses his sore jaw, and then looks at Dolores and smiles at her. "Come to think of it, how many kids do we have?" he asks jokingly, and then proceeds to count them. "Let's see: One, two, three, and . . . hey, who is this pretty girl with the teary eyes?" he says, grabbing Dolores's face in his soot-stained hands. "Is she one of mine?"

Dolores nods and smiles, and Maximiliano kisses the tip of her nose. "I think this girl is my favorite one," he says and then kisses her again, this time staining her face with the soot from his face.

NOW THAT THE FIRE is over, Dolores, wearing nothing but a nightgown and a shawl over her shoulders, and holding her sleeping baby in her arms, goes back with her two other children to the site where their house once stood, and finds Pablo there, staring in silence at the charred remains. Maximiliano is with the rest of the men at a town meeting where decisions are being made as to how they all can help each other until the burned houses are reconstructed.

The fire is over, but not before it devoured an entire block. All the houses on their side of the street have burned. The place looks gray, empty. Desolate.

Pablo moves close to Dolores, looks at her, and says nothing as he places his arm tight around the shoulders of Mani, who looks up at Pablo, adoringly.

Mani loves Pablo. Almost as much as Pablo loves Mani.

Mani knows that Pablo knows many many things, and the old man has been teaching every one of them to Mani.

Pablo has taught Mani how to grab frogs, approaching them slowly from behind, pretending you are not looking at them, because frogs are very smart, and if they see you looking at them, they jump away from you. "That is why you always whistle and look the other way until you're ready to grab them. And then . . . *Wham!* Grab'm quickly. But make sure you don't grab'm too hard, you don't want to hurt'm."

Pablo has taught Mani the difference between a frog that lives in water and a toad that lives on land. "Toads are much easier to grab. They're not as quick as frogs. Bigger, yes, but not quicker."

Pablo has taught Mani how to bait a hook and how to get the right kind of worms to catch catfish, those ugly-looking fish with the cat whiskers that are Pablo's favorite, and also Mani's. He has taught Mani how to run the line at the bottom of the pond, very slowly, very very slowly, because catfish are very very lazy, and if they see a worm going by too fast, they sure are not going to go for it. "You kind of have to let the worm fall in the catfish's mouth, that's how lazy those catfishes are."

And Pablo has taught Mani how to light a cigar, using a match and turning the cigar around ever so slowly so it burns uniformly all around the bottom edge first. It is only then you inhale it. Mani inhaled it once, just to see what it was like. He didn't like it. Pablo made Mani promise he'd not say anything about this inhaling to Miss Dolores, as Pablo calls Mani's mother, because Miss Dolores has a temper, and neither Pablo nor Mani wants to see her get angry.

Yes, Mani loves Pablo. Almost as much as Pablo loves Mani.

Pablo tousles Mani's black wavy hair, then folds up the long sleeves of his pale-blue cotton shirt, lifts up first a large partly burned wood beam, still warm to the touch, and then another, and carrying them to one end of the lot, places one a few feet from the other, as he says, "Hey, Mani, what about giving me a hand?" Mani immediately goes to where Pablo is and begins helping him, as they both start to make a pile of whatever wood is left that could be reused.

Dolores carefully hands the sleeping baby to Merced and, without saying a word, she folds the long sleeves of her white nightgown and, tying the shawl tight around her waist, bends down and begins to clear the mess, looking for anything that can be salvaged.

Merced, who is holding the baby in her arms, thinking that this is part of the game, starts to rake the ashes with her feet when suddenly she steps on something. She kneels down, picks it up with her free hand, and discovers it is Esperanza, her birthday rag doll, which has partly burned. Instantly Merced begins to cry. "Mommy, look!" she barely manages to say, her words almost unintelligible. "Esperanza!

She's all burned!" Her crying turns into weeping, and her weeping awakens the baby, who begins to cry as well.

Dolores rushes to her side, sees the doll, "Oh, look at Esperanza!" she says. Then, taking the baby back in her arms and cradling him, she points to Pablo with her head as she adds, "Go show her to Pablo."

Merced, still weeping, raises her teary eyes and looks up at her mother, not understanding why she should do a thing like that.

Dolores kneels down to her level and tells her, softly, gently, in that quiet way of hers, "She's now as wrinkled and as black as Pablo is. Isn't she beautiful?"

Merced looks at Esperanza and suddenly she sees in the partly burned doll a new kind of beauty that wasn't there before. She runs to Pablo, her tears almost gone, and shows it to him. "Look, Pablo," she says, "Esperanza is now as wrinkled and as black as you are!"

Pablo laughs loudly. "Child," he says, "no one can ever be as wrinkled and as black as I am!" He takes the doll in his big callused hands and looks at it. "But look," he adds, and taking a bandanna from his back pocket he wraps it around the partly burned doll, "now that she's like an old black woman, she's got to dress like old black women do!" Then he hands it to Merced, who smiles as she looks at Esperanza, now a black rag doll that is wearing a red bandanna for a dress.

Dolores, still cradling the baby in her arms, suddenly sees, covered by a pile of ashes and debris, the heavy chest she used to keep at the foot of the bed she and Maximiliano shared.

It is badly charred.

Without saying a word, she hands the baby back to Merced, who now cradles Esperanza in one arm and her baby brother in the other.

Dolores bends down, stares at the blackened chest, and after a short hesitation opens it.

Its contents are miraculously intact.

Dolores searches through it and finds at the bottom of it a white gown, neatly folded and carefully wrapped with lots and lots of tissue paper.

Her wedding dress!

She unfolds it, holds it in her arms, and, as she looks at the intricate patterns of white silk hummingbirds and hibiscus flowers intertwined, she realizes that this is like leaving her old house behind, with nothing but what she's wearing, and of all things, this old dress.

She did it once; she can do it again.

And though unaware that she has been crying, suddenly she begins to laugh.

Hearing her, Pablo, next to Mani at the other end of the lot, looks at her and seeing her holding up her old wedding dress in her arms, he also begins to laugh.

And their loud laughter makes Mani and Merced laugh loudly as well, though they do not understand why.

★ ★ ★

5

Merced and Mani are taken to their grandparents' home, the big old house of the butcher of Batabanó, Maximiliano's father, while Maximiliano, Dolores, and the baby stay in Surgidero, rebuilding their home with the help of Pablo.

Luckily, Maximiliano had kept all of his money locked safely in the butcher shop, money he had saved a penny at a time over the last eight years. And now this money is going to build their new house, and it is going to build it right. Criollo style. With thick brick walls that fire cannot devour.

The walls are going to be stuccoed on the outside, plastered on the inside, and painted a pale cream, Dolores's favorite color; the cement floors are going to be tiled with terra-cotta tiles, so easy to keep clean; and to top it all, the house is going to have a beautiful Spanish red-tile roof. It is going to be a small house, to be sure, but it is going to have everything. There will be three bedrooms and a bathroom, and the bathroom is even going to have a bidet! And the entire house is going to have electricity too! There's even going to be a central patio, which, though tiny, is going to be large enough to house plenty of plants and still leave room for a pet, a little white mutt of a dog for the children to play with, the son of Facundo, the neighboring dog whose loud barking awoke Dolores and saved the family the night of the *big* fire.

Once it is finished it is going to be a beautiful house, closer to the butcher shop, and closer to the ocean. And they will be able to hear the sound of the surf, luring them to sleep.

The day they break ground to build their new house, Maximiliano and Dolores give Pablo, as a present for his eighty-first birthday, the lot next door to theirs.

There, on Pablo's lot, while their new house is being built, Maximiliano builds Pablo a simple small house—a one-room shack actually—which is all Pablo needs to sleep in, since he has all of his meals with Dolores's family, which is his family too; meals they all share at the back of the butcher shop, where a small shed has been hastily erected to house Maximiliano, Dolores, and the baby while construction on their new house goes on.

Pablo is thrilled when he sees his name carefully spelled out on the written deed. Pablo Fernán Fernán is now not only a free man, but a landowner as well. His bed and the land on which it stands are his and only his.

But one morning Pablo does not wake up.

The wake is held in the Cuban Negro tradition, with plenty of black coffee and plenty of black rum, and plenty of black drumming and of black dancing all night long, to celebrate Pablo's life.

Many white people dance at Pablo's wake and laugh and cry at the same time at the beauty of it all, including Dolores and Maximiliano, who dance one danzón for Pablo.

Late the next afternoon, following the funeral, Dolores, needing to be alone, leaves the baby with Maximiliano and slowly walks the six miles to Maximiliano's parents' home in Batabanó, to tell the children about Pablo's death. It's almost dinnertime when she gets there.

When she tells Merced, the young girl hugs Esperanza tight in her arms and cries.

When Mani finds out, he goes outside the old house, sits at the foot of a large banana tree in the front yard, and does nothing.

Dolores looks at her son and after a long while goes to sit by his side, places her arm around his shoulders, pulls him close to her, and says nothing.

For a long long while they are both silent, Dolores and Mani, sitting side by side under the old banana tree.

Mani is the first to speak. "Mommy," he says as he looks up at her, "do they have black stars?"

Dolores tightens her grip on her son and looks up at the deep turquoise sky, now darkened by the approach of night.

Mani raises his eyes and looks up at the dark sky as if searching for something. "Pablo told me once that when people die they become stars," Mani says. "And then a few days later I asked him if they had black stars, and you know what he told me?"

Dolores looks at her son, still looking up at the dark sky.

"He said he didn't know."

Mani then turns to his mother and looks at her with a puzzled look on his face. "Isn't that strange, Mommy? I always thought Pablo knew *everything*. But he said he didn't know. That's what he said. He looked up at the sky hard, real hard, like I was doing right now, and then he said, 'Maybe there are and maybe there aren't, but if there are I sure cannot see them.' "

Mani gets close to his mother, who hugs him tight as he adds, "I guess that's about the only thing in the world Pablo didn't know."

Dolores looks at Mani and smiles her most gentle smile.

"Oh, Mani! Didn't you see that Pablo was just teasing you . . . ? You know how he was, always teasing you. Of course he knew. He knew that there are tons and tons of them. It's just that you cannot see them with your eyes. But with your heart you can see them. He once showed me how to do it. All you have to do is close your eyes first, but you have to close them really really tight, and then ask your heart. Can your heart see them?"

Mani closes his eyes really really tight, and after a little while he opens them as wide as they could be and says as if in shock, "Oh, Mommy! I saw them! I saw them! I could see them!"

Later on that night, when Maximiliano arrives with the baby to take Dolores back to Surgidero, Mani asks his father if he has ever seen black stars. And when his father says, "No, I haven't," Mani teaches him how to see them.

★ ★ ★

6

Merced and Mani love the big old house of Maximiliano's parents, where they have been living now for almost a whole year; a house that a generation ago had seen the birth of seven children, but a house that until Maximiliano's children arrived had not heard children's laughter for a long long time. There Maximiliano's parents took the children under their wings and grew used to them.

This house is old, really old. So old it does not even have an indoor bathroom. But it does have a huge central patio filled with tropical plants; and it does have a large orchard surrounding the house filled with lots of fruit-bearing trees: mangoes, papayas, bananas, and especially the sweet guavas Merced loves so much.

Of course boys will do as boys do, and Mani, now six, is no exception. He is always finding boylike things to do while his sister does whatever it is girls always do, stuff Mani makes great fun of.

Always the daring one, one afternoon after school, Mani picks up one of those huge bullfrogs that proliferate all over the island, the singing kind, and he takes it to Merced, who screams when she sees it, much to Mani's delight.

"You don't have to be afraid of it," says Mani, as he thrusts the bullfrog in her face. He is expecting Merced to run away, but Merced, who is a bull of a girl, does not.

"I'm not afraid of it," she lies. She is very much afraid of it, but she is not going to let Mani know that. Merced is not only older than Mani, but much bigger as well, and she certainly is not going to give this little brother of hers the pleasure of seeing her afraid of anything.

"Oh, no?" Mani asks. "We'll see."

He takes a salt shaker he had hidden in his pants, pulls it out, and begins to sprinkle salt on top of the bullfrog. "They explode if you put enough salt on them."

"They do not," stubbornly says Merced, fearing that perhaps they do.

"They do," says Mani. "Pablo told me they did, and Pablo knew *everything*. Watch."

Merced's eyes are glued to the bullfrog in Mani's hands.

Mani, keeping his eyes on Merced, keeps sprinkling more and more salt on the poor creature, which begins to inflate like a balloon until suddenly its skin bursts open, spewing its insides all over Merced, who screams and runs to the house calling her *abuela,* her grandmother, Maximiliano's mother, who, hearing the commotion, immediately runs to her aid.

Maximiliano's mother is a no-nonsense kind of a woman who carries herself straight as an arrow despite being almost fifty-seven years old. Tall and thin for a criollo woman, she is as stern looking as any woman can ever be. She has a habit of biting her lips when she is angry, and even today, whenever her grown-up children see that look on her face, they all shiver because they know what comes next.

The old lady has raised seven kids of her own, all of them married by now and all of them living far away, except for Maximiliano and his family. And now she has to deal with this boy Mani, who is as difficult as they come. But if she was able to break Maximiliano and tame the wildness out of him, surely she can tame Maximiliano's boy. And yet, though she knows she is not supposed to have any favorites among her grandchildren, she knows that this boy Mani holds a special place in her heart.

But she'll be damned before she lets him know that. No, sir. Not until the taming is done. So she rushes in, wiping her hands on the white apron, sees the frog, realizes what has happened, shakes her head, bites her lips, and using her strong bony knuckles, hits hard, really hard, on the head of Mani, who will not cry.

"That boy is evil," she tells Dolores. "You are just too easy on him."

The women are having dark Cuban coffee as they sit on cane rocking chairs, rocking gently on the outside porch of Maximiliano's parents' house. Dolores is listening patiently to what the old lady has to say.

"That boy needs a strong hand."

Dolores has come to pick up her children. She has been missing them, and so has Maximiliano, but they had to work hard to get their new house built as soon as they have. And now that their new house in Surgidero is finally completed, Dolores has come to gather her children and take them where they belong: Home.

The thank-yous are said, and the you're-welcomes, and the good-lucks, and the do-not-forget-the-way-back-heres. Then the good-byes are said, and the children are gone, and the big old house is suddenly empty and quiet. No noises. No playing. No screaming at dead frogs, or dead rats, or dead birds. No more children fighting. No more spanking. No more shouting. No more laughter. After months and months the old house is finally tranquil. And silent. And empty.

A WEEK LATER Maximiliano's father, the butcher of Batabanó, is at Maximiliano's butcher shop in Surgidero, and father and son are sharing a little rum as they talk at the end of the day.

Maximiliano has closed the shop. All the meat has been neatly stored, and Maximiliano's father has nothing but praise for the way his son has organized his shop. This is a professional man admiring the work of another professional man, which fills both men with pride. The father is proud because his son is turning out to be a truly great butcher, an artist of a butcher, if he may say so. The son is proud because he can see in his father's eyes that his admiration is honest and that his praise comes, not from someone who is just Maximiliano's own father, but from someone who is indeed a great artist of a butcher himself.

"And what a great thing that new refrigerated cooler is! So much more room! How easy it makes everything! There's nothing like progress, is there?"

Maximiliano opens a bottle of dark Cuban rum and offers it to his father, who raises a toast to the cooler and shoots some of the fiery liquid down his throat. He then passes the bottle back to his son, who answers his father's toast, as the old man speaks.

"Son," he says, "your mother misses the children a lot. So . . ."

He has come to Surgidero at the urging of his wife to talk to his son. He grabs the bottle from his son and shoots some more rum down his throat again. Then wipes his mouth as he continues.

"So what she wants me to tell you is this. Now remember it is her idea. You know how impossible women can be sometimes, and your mother is certainly no exception to the rule. She's been making my life miserable, what with all of this thing about missing the kids, and about how lonesome and sad our house is, and how she's getting old and how she wants her grandchildren around her, and—well, you know how she is. So . . ."

He takes another shot of that dark rum that burns—Oh, so good—down his throat, and then offers the bottle back to his son, who again shoots some down his throat.

It's getting late in the afternoon, and the mosquitoes have begun to appear, attracted by the drying blood. Maximiliano pulls out a pail of water and a clean rag, and begins to wipe clean the white marble counter, listening as his father goes on.

"So she asked me to ask you if you wouldn't mind sending one of your kids to live with us for a while, just so we can have some laughter back in the house."

He pauses. He didn't mean to say "we." He had meant to say "she." "So *she* can have some laughter back in the house," that's what he had meant to say, that's what he should have said. But that's not what he said. A mistake. He wonders if his son realizes what he just did.

He looks at Maximiliano, but Maximiliano is busy, scrubbing and scrubbing the same piece of countertop, as if he had just discovered a stain that will *not* come off, which of course it won't because there is no stain there, no stain at all. Maximiliano says nothing. He just remains silent as he keeps rubbing and polishing the same piece of marble.

"What about Mani?" the old man says and pauses. "Your mother tells me that boy needs a strong hand, and you know how Dolores is, she cannot harm a fly. So she lets the boy get away with everything."

Maximiliano does not like what he hears, but this is, after all, his father, and a criollo son must do as a criollo son must: When a father speaks, one looks down, one listens, one nods, and one says nothing. And though Maximiliano does not like what he hears, he keeps silent, nodding his head as he keeps on rubbing and rubbing, listening patiently to his father. This is the same man who has been a great influence—and a great help—all of Maximiliano's life. Particularly after the big fire, when the children moved into his father's old house for a long long while. And the old man has not accepted anything from Maximiliano in repayment, not even a single penny.

"What do you say, son?" asks Maximiliano's father.

Maximiliano stops his polishing for a while. He answers his father, but he doesn't look at him. "I'll tell Dolores," he says. Because he is not looking at his father, he fails to see the big smile on his father's face, a big smile that freezes when Maximiliano finishes his sentence. "Let me see what she has to say."

Blood suddenly rushes to the old man's head, and a thick vein on the side of his forehead begins to pulsate so rapidly it seems it is going to burst as the old man smacks his fist hard on the white marble counter. "You'll do *what*? *Ask* Dolores? Since when does a son of mine have to get a woman's permission to do anything? Is she the one with the balls in your family?"

The old man knows how to hurt a criollo man, and hurt he does. In truth, it is *he* who wants his grandson next to him. It was *his* idea, not his wife's. Sure, she had complained about missing the children, but it had been he who came up with the suggestion of bringing Mani to live with them, a suggestion he is now drilling into his son's head.

"If I had thought I needed her approval, I would have gone straight to her, not to you! I guess I was wrong!" he adds, with venom in his voice. "I thought my son was still a man!"

He steals the rag Maximiliano has been using to wipe the marble counter from his son's hands. "Boy," he says, "you better look at me when I'm talking to you!" and then he throws the rag so violently into the pail of water that it splashes all over the recently mopped floor. "I didn't raise you to be second to anyone, and certainly not to a woman, even if she is the daughter of the richest man in town, you hear me?"

Maximiliano hasn't said a word. He just keeps looking down at the marble counter, saying nothing. But his hands have become fists, their knuckles white with impotent rage.

The old man takes a deep breath, and just as suddenly as it got started, the storm subsides. The old man is gentle again. "I'm sorry, son," he says, lowering his voice. "It's your mother. She's driving me crazy." He looks at his son, who raises his eyes just long enough to meet those of the old man for the briefest of seconds. And the hurt in his son's eyes lets the old man know that the battle is over.

"It's just for a little while," he says, dismissing the whole thing as inconsequential. "Just until your mother grows out of that mood she's been in since the children left the house." Then he adds, lowering his voice confidentially, "She's getting old, you know. She thinks she's got nothing to do with her life, that she's not needed anymore. That's enough to drive anybody crazy, you know." He pauses. *"Anybody."*

Maximiliano has been trying to avoid his father's inquisitive eyes, but now he looks at him as his father smiles and offers Maximiliano his hand in a handshake.

"Just for a few days?" the old man says as he extends his hand to his son.

Maximiliano pauses. Then shakes his father's hand.

"Just for a few days," he says.

And another criollo agreement has been sealed.

THAT VERY same night, despite Dolores's protestations, Mani goes with his grandfather back to the house in Batabanó where the old lady with the bony knuckles is going to put some sense into his head.

Dolores doesn't like having her son taken away from her and begs and begs Maximiliano to let her talk to the old man. But Maximiliano will not let her. What for? Isn't he the man of his family?

So he tells Dolores, "We have other children. They have none."

And he tells Dolores, "We owe them a lot. It is just for a little while."

And he tells Dolores, "Don't you see they are doing it to help us? They know we have lost a lot and they don't want to give us money and make us feel like we need their help."

And he tells Dolores, "As soon as we have some money stashed away again, then we'll bring Mani home."

And he tells Dolores, "We'll get to see him once, twice a week, won't we? As often as we want, won't we?"

And he tells Dolores he's given his word of honor, and his word of honor is final. And that is it.

What he doesn't tell Dolores is that Maximiliano has never told the old man Dolores wants to talk with him.

Why should she? Isn't that a man's job, to make decisions about a man's own son? Isn't that the job of the man of his family? Isn't he the man of his family? Who is going to run this family? A woman?

No.

This is something for the two men to discuss alone, over a shot of rum, and then another. Maximiliano doesn't like to have his son away from him either, and pleads his case, over and over, but the old man always has reasons, strong convincing reasons, to keep Mani next to him.

"Oh, no! You can't take him home now! Do you want to break your mother's heart? Look at her, she's like a different woman since Mani is living with us, isn't she? Besides, he just started school! Let's wait till school is over, all right?"

And they shake hands again, and then . . .

"But, son, you know he's got to stay here and help us during the summer. I'm too old to do all the work by myself. Besides, you know he likes it here, don't you, Mani? As soon as the summer is over, all right?"

And they shake hands again, and then . . .

"Oh, but you can't do that now! He's going to miss all of his schoolmates, aren't you, Mani? As soon as the school year is over, all right?"

And they shake hands again. And once again the never-ending cycle starts all over. Again. And again. And again.

That is how "Just for a few days" becomes "Just for a few weeks," and then "Just for a few months," and then "Just for a few years."

And that is how Mani grows up and grows up in his grandparents' house year after year, away from a family he seldom gets to see; away from parents he seldom gets to be with; and away from a father he longs to be near, a father he longs to get to know.

After the first year, Mani begins to question if his parents care for him.

After the second year, Mani begins to question if his parents ever loved him.

And after the third, and fourth, and fifth years Mani begins to question and question if those people he has been calling father and mother, if those people are really his parents at all.

Maybe, he thinks, he is really an adopted child, as some of the other boys at school tell him he is: Someone somebody didn't want; someone somebody just wanted to get rid of; someone to be ashamed of.

Or maybe, he thinks, he did something really bad, something awful that he doesn't remember doing, maybe that's what it is. But what was it? What did he do that these people he calls parents are so ashamed of? Throwing salt on the bullfrog? Was that it?

Or maybe, he thinks, there's really something evil about him, as the old lady with the sharp knuckles is always telling him. Is that it? Is that what's wrong with him? Is he really evil? Is that why he was abandoned?

Every night he goes to bed hoping to find out the answers to his questions.

Every night he goes to bed yearning to wake up and find those people he calls parents at the foot of his bed saying, "Son, we just came to take you home. You are not evil. We love you. We are not ashamed of you. We are proud of you."

Every night he goes to bed praying for it to happen.

And every morning, when he wakes up and finds nobody there, he says to himself, *Maybe tomorrow.*

Maybe tomorrow.

★ ★ ★

7

Tropical hurricanes get started when least expected.

It doesn't take much to get them going. Just the right amount of humidity and the right atmospheric pressure at the right time of the year under the right phase of the moon and suddenly, there you are, in the middle of one without even realizing it.

Cubans are used to hurricanes. Every year they come, like clockwork. The problem with hurricanes is that you never know in advance how bad one is going to be. You don't even know how bad a hurricane is when you are living through it. You just hope you'll survive it without getting hurt too badly or without losing much of whatever little you own.

At the first warning sign of a hurricane, windows are closed, shutters are nailed down, doors are locked, people hide themselves inside the cocoon of their homes. And then the waiting begins.

The waiting is the worst part of it all.

You wait and wait and wait and then, all of a sudden, everything happens at the same time. The wind begins to howl around you, the electricity goes, running water stops running, candles are lit, and buckets—filled with water that has been stored in the bathtub—are taken to the kitchen where the water is boiled to make coffee for the adults who gather around the dining-room table, and cocoa for the children who hide under it. There, under that huge dining table that is able to accommodate the huge extended families all Cubans have, the children huddle tight against each other and ask if they are going to die. The womenfolk get their rosaries out and begin their litany of Our Fathers and Hail Marys while the menfolk, who cannot stand still, pace all over the house, making sure the shutters are properly nailed, propping furniture against the wavering doors, listening to the sound and fury of the howling wind, and wondering how much more they can take of the women's unending praying and praying.

Eventually the howling becomes first a hiss, then a song; the torrential downpour becomes first a rain, then a dance; the ominous, opaque shroud of black sky becomes first a thick veil of gray, then a limpid translucent white. And before you realize it, as if by magic, the ocean is emerald green again; the sky is turquoise blue again; the tropical sun is smiling again; the menfolk go to the windows, pull out the nails of the shutters, and open them wide; the children come out from under the large dining table where they have been hiding; and the womenfolk, still apprehensive, finally dare to look out the windows and sigh. "It was just a little scare," you hear them say. "Just that, a little scare." And most hurricanes are just that, a little scare. But sometimes they are not. Sometimes they come loud and strong.

And loud and strong this hurricane comes.

Alfonso, the owner of the liquor store, one of the few people in Surgidero who has a radio, hears that this hurricane is going to go straight across Surgidero and that it is bound to be quite bad, and he quickly spreads the word. All of the people of Surgidero move up the hill, to Batabanó, away from the shore; all except the very few who decide to brave the hurricane in their homes by the angry ocean.

Maximiliano takes Dolores and their other children to his parents' house in Batabanó, where he knows they will be safe. He has decided to leave them there and then come back to Surgidero, to face the hurricane alone in their criollo-style house by the sea.

"Dolores," he tells his wife for the hundredth time, "please, understand. I have to go back to Surgidero, just in case something goes wrong; just in case some of our neighbors need my help. If that happens, I don't want to be worrying about you or the children. I'll be safe there," he adds, jovially. "Don't you worry about me. I'm sure I'll be able to survive a couple of days without you. I promise you, I won't starve."

Despite Dolores's reasoning and pleading, Maximiliano is about to leave when the gusts of wind become so powerful that one of the large shutters of the big old house flies off and almost hits Dolores as she is kissing Maximiliano good-bye. Maximiliano runs after the shutter, grabs it, takes it back to the old house, and begins to nail it in place as another one flies off, and then another one.

By then the sky has grown completely black, and the children inside the house have begun to cry, all except Mani, who is at the door looking at this man he calls father nail another shutter safely in place; a man he has seen only once or twice a month for the last five years of his life; a man almost totally unknown to him.

"Mani!" Maximiliano has to shout to be heard above the noise of the howling wind. "Hold this end for me, will you?"

The boy moves to Maximiliano and holds the end of one shutter as his father hammers it in place, the rain falling heavy on the two of them.

Like his older sister Merced, Mani takes after his mother. His hair is dark, and so are his eyes, which remain fastened on Maximiliano as he begins to go around the house one last time to make sure it is as safe as he can make it. Mani follows him.

Suddenly a gigantic bolt of lightning zigzags out of the black sky.

Maximiliano's mother comes out to the porch and screams at her son and at Mani. "What do you all think you are doing? Didn't you all see that lightning! You all come back here this minute or I'll come out and get you all if it's the last thing I ever do on this Earth before I die and the worms devour my wrinkled old body!" She looks at them and she is biting hard at her lips, which as they all know is a dangerous sign.

"Hey, Mani," shouts Maximiliano as he smiles and winks at his son, "we better go in or she's likely to crack my skull with those hard knuckles of hers!"

But Mani does not smile back.

He looks intently at Maximiliano, the man he calls father, and he wonders, Is this man *really* my father? Am I *really* his son?

Simultaneously, he lifts his left hand—he is left-handed, just like his mother, Dolores, and his sister, Merced—and, unaware that he is doing it, scratches the top of his head as he looks at his father, a puzzling look on his face; a look that Maximiliano cannot understand. What is Mani trying to tell him with that look? he wonders.

"What?" shouts Maximiliano, misunderstanding his son's gesture. "She has never cracked *your* skull?" He smiles at his son. "She sure did it to *me*! I'd better have a talk with that old lady! Come on, Mani! Let's go in."

Maximiliano places his right arm around Mani's shoulders, and they start walking toward the old lady, who is still biting hard at her lips.

"Get in!" she orders as they reach the safety of the front porch. Maximiliano lets the boy in and is about to turn around and leave when his mother stops him. "Where do you think you're going? You too! In!"

Maximiliano looks at her and for the first time in his life he no longer sees the mother he knew but a different one, a woman much smaller and much older than the one he remembers: Her gray hair is thinning, her mouth has tiny wrinkles surrounding it, and despite the demanding tone of her voice, her eyes have an imploring look to them that Maximiliano does not remember ever seeing there before.

Maximiliano feels a sudden tenderness toward this woman, something he has never felt before. He feels he would like to embrace her and hug her tight to him and tell her with his hug how much he loves this old woman so new to him. He has never thought of his parents as old. But now that he is looking at his mother, he sees in her a new kind of beauty that wasn't there before.

"In! In!" repeats the old lady with the thinning gray hair gathered tightly in a bun and the back still straight as an arrow as she defiantly points to the dark cavernous space inside the house. "Don't you hear me? *In!*" Maximiliano smiles at her and enters obediently while she closes the door behind him.

The rest of the children, seeing their father inside with them, feel safe and stop their crying.

Maximiliano and Dolores have four of them by now: Merced, the oldest, a dark bull of a girl who never does as she is supposed to, now almost a teenager; followed by Mani, who is four months short of being twelve and who is being tamed by his grandmother; followed by Gustavo, a shy eight-year-old boy with light hair and blue eyes hiding behind tiny glasses, who is always lost and always found with his nose inside a book; followed by a four-year-old girl, Marguita, little Marga, the new baby with the long curly blond hair and the mischievous eyes, who always gets anything she wants.

The old lady hands clean well-worn towels to Maximiliano and Mani. Dolores notices how Maximiliano looks at his mother as he dries his bristly gold hair and sees in his face something she has never seen before, something different she cannot understand. Tonight she will ask him. Maximiliano, the towel around his neck, goes to his wife. "That coffee sure smells good," he says. "Is there any left?"

The room is dark. Only a tiny amount of light can be seen coming through the almost invisible cracks around windows and doors. The light casts a strange glow on the room as the dust, unsettled by the cold air rushing through those cracks, begins to swirl and dance. A candle is lit and placed inside a glass hurricane shade, and then another and then another.

Mani, still partly wet, sits silently on the floor far away from the other children, his towel around his neck. Merced and Gustavo, hiding under the dining table, try to play jacks, which is almost impossible, because Marguita, also under the table, keeps grabbing either the jacks or the bouncing rubber ball, making Merced angry. Dolores brings Maximiliano a demitasse of the good-smelling coffee, which he sips slowly as he looks first at his mother and then at his wife. Dolores notices his glance again and still is unable to understand what it means.

Maximiliano's father, who had been napping upstairs, comes down into the room and sits at the dining table. He seems tired. Maximiliano looks at his father and sees in him that same kind of beauty his mother now has, a new kind of beauty he had never seen before.

Mani, who had been sitting on the floor, stands up, moves close to his grandfather, and stands next to him, his left arm around the old man's shoulders, as he looks at Maximiliano with that same puzzling look in his eyes Maximiliano had seen a short while ago, a look that Maximiliano still cannot understand. What is Mani trying to tell him with that look?

And they all wait.

Sometimes hurricanes come loud and strong.

Sometimes they do—like this one, the hurricane of September 17, 1926, the worst hurricane ever to hit the little island of Cuba. Loud and strong this hurricane comes, with powerful surging waves that rage and pound thunderously at the shore of Surgidero.

After the hurricane is over, and after saying good-bye to Mani, who stays in Batabanó with his grandparents, Maximiliano and the rest of his family return to their home in Surgidero, to find that everything is gone.

Everything.

There is no longer a Surgidero.

Nothing is left of the entire village. Not a WELCOME-TO-SURGIDERO sign. Not an electrical pole. Not a church bell tower. Not a trace of the pharmacy, or of the liquor store, or of the new school. Not even a trace of its only street. And certainly not a trace of the butcher shop. Of the people who stayed in Surgidero none survived. Not a single one. Raging ocean water had flooded the town, had pounded furiously at it, and while masonry buildings made with bricks may withstand a fire, they cannot withstand the immense power of Ogún, the angry black god of the sea.

Surgidero is gone, totally gone. Consumed.

As the survivors arrive from the different places they hid during the hurricane, they find it almost impossible to tell where any of the houses once stood.

Dolores, embraced by Maximiliano, scans the whole area, looking all over, and as she does, she says a silent prayer thanking her Little Virgin for saving her husband. Then she sees something encased in the sand not too far from where she stands and, breaking the embrace, she moves toward it. The ocean water laps at her feet as she gets closer to it. With her feet she dislodges whatever that is that's encased in the sand and looks at it. And then she knows what it is. There, at her feet, she sees the cast-iron filigree treadle of her sewing machine, a brand-new Singer sewing machine Maximiliano had given her last year for her birthday, which is also their anniversary, so she could sew to her heart's content. That machine had been her pride and joy.

Dolores has not shed a tear all of this time. It is only when she sees that piece of her sewing machine encased in the sand as the ocean water laps at her feet that she realizes that there, where she is now standing, there, right there, there was once a house, and that house had been theirs. It is only then that she begins to sob.

"Sshhhh!" whispers her husband, who has moved to her and is holding her tightly to him. "Look," he reminds her. "We still have our children. And I still have you. What more can I ask for?"

She buries her head against her husband's strong chest while he embraces her, standing firm, staring at the ocean, which still sounds demanding.

A long while goes by.

"Maybe I should write to Papá," Dolores finally manages to say. "Maybe I should ask him for some—"

But Maximiliano is not listening.

The butcher's son, no longer a boy but a man now, is standing where his home once stood and he is staring past the ocean, past the horizon, past the sky. He is in a world of his own. He does not feel the rain on his face, nor does he see the water at his feet, nor does he hear his wife talking softly to him, nor his children silently crying in the background.

"You know what?" he says to Dolores as he is staring past it all. "It's as if God were telling us to move on. To leave all of this behind."

It has begun to rain again, but he doesn't realize it.

"Twice I've been warned," he continues. "Twice my home has been destroyed and twice my family has been miraculously saved. Dolores," he says, excitement growing in his speech as he looks at her, "this time we are going. This time we are getting away from all of this."

He is looking at her and smiles at her as he kisses the tip of her criollo nose, which is the perfect size in her beautiful criollo face, covered with raindrops.

And just as their criollo ancestors once moved the entire city of La Habana, name and all, from where it formerly stood, which is not too far from where Maximiliano is standing right now; just as they did, this criollo man decides that he too is moving his entire family, all of it, north, to the capital. To the great city of La Habana.

"I don't know why I didn't think of it before," he says to his wife. Then, lowering his voice, he whispers to her, "But if we are going to be poor, we might as well be poor in La Habana." And he holds her tight to him as he asks her, "What do you say?"

Gustavo and Merced are looking at both of them, not knowing

what to do, while Marguita, the baby, squats, and, after failing to lift the heavy cast-iron treadle of the Singer machine still deeply encased in the sand, begins to play with it, inserting her tiny fingers in its filigree holes and caressing it as water keeps lapping at her parents' feet.

Dolores, who has been looking at the children, tells her husband, "I could go to Papá and—"

"No," Maximiliano interrupts. "We don't need his help."

"It is not for us. It's for the children."

"The children will be all right. They are not going to starve."

Dolores is about to say something when her husband stops her.

"Listen," he says, "if I am going to open a brand-new butcher shop and start from scratch again, I can open it *anywhere*. Dolores, don't you see? God's been telling us something and we've got to listen to Him. There's a reason for all of this. There's got to be a reason for all of this, don't you see that?"

Dolores is looking at her handsome husband, with the wet shirt sticking to him and with rivulets of water running down his face, and she knows that as long as he is there, everything will be all right, just as he says it will be. Still, four children is a large burden. And this time they have lost everything. *Everything*. Butcher shop and all. She insists. She has to insist. Practical Dolores tries again. "Please, let me go to Papá and ask him for some—"

Maximiliano, the former butcher of Surgidero, looks sternly at his wife. "When you married me," he says, "you said for better or worse, didn't you?"

She nods in agreement.

"Well," he adds, "what has it been so far?" And he looks at her with those insolent eyes of his, still insolent after these many years.

Dolores looks up at this criollo man with the challenging eyes and the halo of gold hair. She meets his eyes and answers, smiling her mischievous smile.

"For better. Always. It has always been for better."

"Well, then," he smiles back at her, "why change it? Why go back to your father now? He doesn't need us. We don't need him. That makes us even."

And then he kisses her, in front of their children. He kisses her not the way married people kiss but the way lovers kiss.

And their daughter Merced, the one who never does as she is supposed to and who is almost a teenager, pretends to look down at the water lapping at their feet, but out of the corner of her eye she manages to look at her parents as they kiss. And though a little embarrassed, she cannot hide a smile.

★ ★ ★

8

There is only one problem with the move to La Habana: What to do with Mani.

"What do you mean he is not coming with us? Of course he is. You don't think I'm going to leave him here, do you?"

Dolores, the criollo woman who eloped with the butcher's son, is claiming her right. She is lying in bed, whispering to Maximiliano, for she doesn't want Maximiliano's parents to hear this conversation that is so important not only to Maximiliano and her, but to their child as well.

"He's my son," she goes on pleading her case. "My older son. He's almost a man already and I haven't seen him grow up. I am not going to leave him behind. I am not going to die without seeing him grow hair on his chest!"

They have nothing.

After the big fire they still had the butcher shop, and a little money stowed away.

But this time they have *nothing*.

They have been sleeping on borrowed beds, eating borrowed food, living in a borrowed house. The move to La Habana has to be financed by Maximiliano's father, in whose house they have been living and eating and sleeping.

They owe the old man a lot, Dolores acknowledges that much. But she is not about to trade her son for her keep. That boy is coming with her or she is not going anywhere. "Wherever I go, he goes," she says.

And she means it.

She is sorry she ever gave up her son the first time, when Maximiliano came to her and told her to get Mani's things ready, that he was going to live with his grandparents for "just a few days."

That had been a big enough mistake.

But at least while they were in Surgidero, not too far from her child, they still got to see each other every other week or so. True, it was never as often as she would have liked, but still often enough. No, she says to herself, shaking her head as she thinks. Even that much was not often enough. No. It certainly was not often enough. Not at all.

But now that they are moving to La Habana, well . . . That's another story. La Habana is a long, long way away. No. This time the boy goes with her. Period.

Dolores remains quiet and calm. She does not raise her voice, does not gesticulate, does not cry. There's no need for any of that. Her decision has been made and it is final. She is her father's daughter. She is the same woman who planned her wedding to the last exquisite detail and who carried it through to its successful conclusion. She waited almost two long years to get her way then. She knows she can wait for as long as she has to in order to get her way now. But she knows she won't have to wait. No. Not this time.

Maximiliano, lying in bed next to her, looks at her with admiring eyes. He with the insolent eyes loves to see the insolence in hers, the audacity. How can a woman so little talk to him like that? And yet he knows she is absolutely right. He himself has been missing his son, his older son, whom he has only seen grow up in bursts for he has only been able to see him once or twice a month.

He remembers that puzzling look in Mani's eyes the day of the hurricane. What did that look mean?

He hasn't told Dolores about that because he has not been able to describe it even to himself.

What was Mani telling him with that look?

Soon Mani will be a man, and Maximiliano knows how much a boy needs his father at a time like that for only a father can tell a boy about the ways of the world, about what it is like to be a man.

Yes, Dolores is right. The boy needs to be with them. Maximiliano looks at her and knows that he is going to give in to her. But not right away. He wants to see her angry. Not much, just a little bit, because he loves to see the fire in those dark sparkling eyes of hers.

"Are you going to tell me what to do?" he asks, pretending to be irate. But he is a bad actor, and Dolores can see through it.

"Of course not," she answers demurely. "You can do whatever you want." She pauses. "And so can I." And then she smiles and her defiant eyes take on the mischievous look of that eighteen-year-old girl in the old sepia photograph.

What else can Maximiliano do but kiss the tip of that beautiful criollo nose on that beautiful tiny criollo woman who has the will of a team of oxen? He kisses her and then adds, "I don't know why I give in to you as easily as I do. If you were a man, I swear I'd have to kill you, you know. Thank God you're a woman; otherwise I'd be doing time in jail for murder."

Dolores smiles as Maximiliano brings her closer to him, and then she whispers quietly in his ear, "You'll tell them, of course."

Maximiliano suddenly realizes that someone has to tell his parents about their decision. The thought had not entered his head until this very moment. This is something he does not want to do. Oh, no! This is something *she* will have to take care of. He has given in to her, so let her do her part, let her be the one to tell his parents. She's got to do it. He certainly couldn't do it. He wouldn't even know where or how to begin.

"You'll tell them, of course," she has said. And now, still in his arms, she looks at him, her mischievous eyes sparkling as she adds, "after all, you *are* the man in the family, aren't you?" And she begins to laugh softly so the rest of the family will not hear her.

"You! Devil!" says Maximiliano, and he too begins to laugh softly until she stifles his laughter with her hand.

"Sshhh! They are going to hear you!" she says, though she doesn't care, for now that they are looking at each other, each of them is finding in the other that which had been missing at one time but which has just been found again.

And each of them finds completion in the other.

THE NEXT MORNING, at the huge dining table where a hearty country breakfast of fried pork chops and bananas is being served by the women in the family to their children and husbands, Maximiliano announces that as soon as he can he is going to the big city of La Habana to see the lay of the land, and that he is taking Mani with him.

"Mani?" asks the boy's grandfather.

"Yes," answers Maximiliano. "I need to carry a lot of stuff with me and he is already almost as strong as I am. Aren't you, boy?"

The boy looks at that man he's been calling father and eagerly nods his agreement. Then, catching himself, he turns to his grandfather, Maximiliano's own father, and asks him, "May I go with him, *abuelo*? Please, please? May I? May I?"

Dolores, the boy's mother, is looking at the old man, who is looking at his own wife, the old lady with the bony hands and the strong knuckles.

"May I, *abuelo*? May I? May I?" Mani keeps asking.

What can the old man say? He looks at his wife first, who shakes her head from side to side. Then he looks at the boy, and he sees the eagerness in the boy's eyes. And the eagerness in his grandson's eyes is stronger than the *no* in his wife's eyes. The old man answers the boy, but he looks at his wife as he answers.

"Whatever your father wants, boy. Whatever your father wants."

Mani cannot believe his ears.

"Then I may go?"

His grandfather looks at him and nods gently. Then faces his own son. "How long do you think you'll be gone?"

"I don't know," Maximiliano answers. "It may take a couple of weeks, I guess. Maybe longer. I don't know. Until we find something we can afford."

"Will you come back?" asks Maximiliano's mother.

"I don't know, Mamá," answers Maximiliano. "There's going to be a lot of work just getting the whole move organized and—"

Dolores interrupts. "I can handle that. When you find something you like, just let us know. I can take care of things at this end. The children and I, we can handle everything. Just you go and don't you worry about any of us."

"But what about Mani?" asks Maximiliano's father.

"Yes, Maximiliano, what about his schooling?" adds Maximiliano's mother. "School will probably begin again in a couple of weeks, as soon as they clean up all of this hurricane mess, maybe even—"

"Mamá," answers Maximiliano, "I'm sure they also have schools in La Habana. Mani can go to school there. Besides"—Maximiliano goes to Mani, who is sitting at the table so excited he hasn't even drunk his milk yet, and places his arm around the boy's shoulders as he addresses the entire family—"I've been thinking . . ."

Maximiliano pulls Mani tight against him as he continues. "Mani is getting old enough to help me in the butcher shop, once we get a butcher shop." He faces his father. "Papá, you know I'll be needing a lot of help right at the very beginning, and I'm sure Mani will be able to help me after he comes back from school, just like I used to help you." He turns and faces his son. "What do you say to that, boy?"

What does he say to *that*?

To be near this man he calls father, this man he knows so little about, this man with the eyes of an emperor and the strength of a herd of bulls; to be with this woman he calls mother, with these children he calls brother and sisters; to be with these people he barely knows, these people he calls family, with whom he hasn't lived for the longest while. More than five years! Isn't that what he has been dreaming about for the longest while?

"What do you say to that, boy?" asks his father.

What does *he* say to that?

For the longest while he's been thinking that perhaps he is an adopted child, an abandoned child, a child nobody ever wanted. An evil child. Someone to be ashamed of. For the longest while.

And now this man he calls father is asking him to go with him to La Habana and help him in his butcher shop and stay with him there all the time. Isn't that what he's been praying for, yearning for, dreaming about, for the longest while?

"What do you say to that, boy?"

What *can* he say to that?

They are all looking at him, waiting for his answer.

The man he calls father is looking at him with a warm smile on his face, just as the woman he calls mother is looking at him with eyes filled with—is *that* love?

Maybe, just maybe these people are really his parents. Maybe, just maybe they do care for him. Maybe, just maybe he is not as bad as the lady with the bony knuckles says he is. And maybe, just maybe dreams can come true.

There is only one way to find out.

"Do you think I'll be able to do it?" the boy asks his father.

"Of course, son, of course," his father adds. "No child of mine cannot do *anything* once his mind is made up. All you have to do is decide what it is you want to do and then . . . do it! But I'm warning you, you've got to be real strong to be a good butcher. And I mean strong. Real strong. Are you real strong, Mani?"

Mani takes off his shirt, sucks his breath in, and bursting with pride shows his developing muscles to this man who has just called him son for the first time in his life.

Maximiliano looks at the boy, touches his bulging muscles, nods his head up and down admiringly, and calls his wife. "Dolores! Come here, Dolores! Come here! Feel these muscles! Dolores! You've just got to feel these muscles!"

Dolores rushes to her son and feels his strong arms.

"Aahhh . . ." she says, and then she adds, "all right. You can breathe now."

And Mani breathes.

And the whole family breathes as well, including the boy's *abuelo* and *abuela* who are looking at the boy as if for the first time in their lives and who realize how much he's grown since he first came to live with them, and how much the boy needs to be with those people he calls father and mother and brother and sisters.

And with their smiles, the boy's grandfather and grandmother let the boy Mani go, even though they know they may never see him again.

★ ★ ★

9

The good-byes were said early this morning, right as the deep orange tropical sun was beginning to lift its head above the horizon. Maximiliano and Mani are walking the long walk to the bus terminal, which is not a terminal at all but the house of Julio the driver at the other side of town, which is on the other side of the hill. They could have gone there by renting a horse carriage, but they had decided to save the money and walk. "Besides," Dolores had said, "the exercise is good for both of you."

Mani and Maximiliano, each carrying a straw suitcase, are impeccably dressed in white. Maximiliano is wearing a Cuban guayabera, a semitransparent cotton dress shirt with elaborate pleating down the front, worn like a jacket outside freshly ironed white-linen pants. Dolores herself had sewn the shirt and had done all the complicated pleating with meticulous care, using tiny, tiny blind hand stitches. Even if she still had the Singer sewing machine she lost in the hurricane, Dolores would still have sewn Maximiliano's guayabera by hand because that's the way it is done. Machines cannot sew shirts of that quality, and Dolores wanted her husband to look his very best on the way to La Habana. Her husband and her son. She had also sewn Mani's new white shirt and pants, which she has ironed starch stiff, making Mani feel very uncomfortable and ill at ease in his new clothes.

It has been a lot of work for Dolores, who stayed up all through two nights cutting and sewing and ironing and packing and unpacking and repacking again, but early this morning when she saw how handsome her two men looked, Dolores felt so proud of them and of her work that she cried and laughed at the beauty of it all.

It's a good thing the sun is not fully up yet. It is still cool and pleasant, and yet both Maximiliano and Mani are developing a little sweat as they walk because you first have to go all the way up the hill before you can get to the other side of it. Maximiliano gets out a red bandanna from one of the back pockets in his pants, wipes his forehead with it, and then ties it around his neck. Mani, walking side by side with his father, looks at Maximiliano and does just as he saw his father do, except that his handkerchief is white.

It's a long way to Julio's house.

On their way there, father and son see large uprooted trees that had been blocking the dirt road and which had to be pulled out of the way by teams of horses and oxen; houses whose roofs have flown away; dead animals lining the ditches; and confusion everywhere. The hurricane that had eradicated the tiny village of Surgidero had not been that much kinder with the larger village of Batabanó. Only the royal palm trees are still standing erect, vigilant sentinels against the pale-pink early morning sky, as if they had been totally untouched by the hurricane; tall and slender palm trees intelligent enough to bend to the powerful gusts of wind rather than to fight them.

"That's why they're still standing," says Maximiliano to his son. "Let that be a lesson to you, boy. When confronted with a hurricane, sometimes it is better to let it go by, even if it means you've got to bend a little. Look at the royal palms," he adds. "After the hurricane passes them by, they stand up again, just as they were, tall and handsome as if nothing had happened. In fact even stronger, because they found out that even though they had faced great danger they had been able to survive it."

The boy looks at them, lining the road, standing proud and tall, just as his father says.

"They produce no fruit we can eat, their bark cannot be used for tanning, they do not provide any shade. It's almost as if they had no use at all, isn't it? But"—he looks at them—"don't they look beautiful?"

The boy faces his father and nods.

"That's what they are for. For the beauty of it all. For you to admire them and to love them and to learn from them."

He stops walking, places his suitcase on the ground, goes through the change in his pockets, picks up a Cuban quarter, and shows it to his son.

"That's why we have them on our national shield and on our money. To remind us that we Cubans are just as they are, and that we have to stand tall and proud, just as they do, even if it means bending a little every now and then, because . . ."

He picks up a small branch out of one of those trees that did not bend to the hurricane and that is lying on the dry dirt road and shows it to his son. "Because if you don't bend, sometimes you break, just like this branch."

And he forces it until the branch cracks.

Julio's house is painted pastel pink and it has a large hand-painted sign in front reading TRANSPORTES, which is done in brilliant vermilion circus baroque lettering with a deep turquoise outline.

The bus is standing right outside the house. It is an old bus that has seen many coats of paint before and which now is painted the same chalky pastel pink as Julio's house.

At one time there was a commercial line of transportation between Batabanó and La Habana, but after the advent of synthetic sponges—when the natural sponge market dried up—the commercial line dried up as well. It was then that Julio the driver had decided to operate his single bus between those two places once a week. But now, after the hurricane, business was picking up since everyone seemed to want to move to La Habana at the same time, which was very good for business but very bad for Batabanó, and Julio had decided to travel to La Habana every other day, except for Sundays.

The bus is old and battered, but Julio the driver makes a point of keeping it in great running condition and immaculately clean. As Mani and Maximiliano board it, they can smell the fresh odor of castile soap on the cane seats, tight two-seat units placed every couple of feet behind each other at either side of the narrow center aisle. They place their straw suitcases on the overhead rack made of woven jute ropes and take their seats, Mani at the window, looking out.

It's not seven o'clock yet, and yet the bus is already almost totally full with men, women, and children, all of them wearing their very best, all of them talking and shouting and laughing at the same time. And then it's seven o'clock and Julio, who is always punctual, turns the ignition key and the bus starts.

Suddenly the loud talking and shouting and laughing stop and the crying starts as men and women and children in the bus say good-bye to a world they are leaving behind and look out the windows with anticipation in their eyes.

It is only forty miles between Batabanó and La Habana, but because of the hurricane, the connecting dirt road—that normally is in bad condition—is in an almost impassable condition. The ride is long and tiresome. Twice the bus has to stop because it gets stuck on muddy areas of the road, and twice the people in the bus have to get off, luggage and all, to lighten the load. Twice the men have taken off their fancy dress clothes and, bare chested and wearing only their underpants, twice they have pushed the bus out of the mud puddles while some of the women look the other way, but some do not.

A ride that normally takes no more than a couple of hours has lasted already more than five, and the end seems to be nowhere in sight. People in the bus are becoming anxious, hungry, and irritable. It's past noon and the October sun is unusually hot. Inside the overheated bus, a heated argument has started between two of the men who are shouting loud insults at each other, irate fighting cocks encouraged by their wives who are shouting equally obscene remarks at each other while some of the other women are trying to soothe the crying children who are annoying everybody.

But then, as the bus reaches the top of a hill, suddenly all arguments stop, and as if by magic everybody goes silent for a brief second, even the children, as soon as they hear the people in the front seats gasp an almost inaudible "Aahhh . . ."

There, in the distance, framed by royal palm trees and giant ferns, is the great city of La Habana, the city of a hundred churches, sparkling pale pink and pale yellow against a clear turquoise sky, surrounding a beautiful bay, the largest and safest bay in the whole Caribbean Sea. And past the city and past the churches and past the bay is the ocean, *el mar del norte,* glittering in the bright sunlight as if myriads of shimmering stars were hiding under its emerald surface.

Mani, wide eyed, stands up to get a better view, but the woman seated right behind him tells him to please sit down, that she also wants to see the incredible sight. And when she does see it, she also goes "Aahhh . . ." and then begins to cry.

Julio the driver loves to reach the top of this hill, and he always does it as slowly as he can because he knows at precisely what point those in the bus will sigh "Aahhh . . ." And even he, who has seen this sight many a time before, even he has to sigh today as well, because he is relieved. This long ride today has been particularly taxing. But now that he and his passengers have seen their destination so near, all the tiredness has gone and all that remains is excitement. If hope could be painted, the canvas would have to show the eyes of the people in the bus as they look through the tiny open windows of the tired bus at the great city of La Habana, their eyes filled with dreams and expectations.

MAXIMILIANO AND MANI have gotten off Julio's bus at the main terminal and from there they are walking west, facing the sun, as they have been told, along a long street called "Zanja," for "Ditch," because during colonial times that street was indeed a large ditch that served as a main sewer for the whole city.

As they walk, Mani tries to take it all in at one time, but it is impossible. His eyes simply cannot manage, there's so much to see! He looks up, and counts three, four, five, even six, imagine that! Six-story-high buildings! Crammed tight against each other; cantilevered balconies filled with huge tropical plants and brilliant flowers that spill over the street, making him feel he is walking beneath a garden; women of all colors and ages hanging freshly laundered white sheets in the drying sun on lines that stretch from one side of the street to the other, as they shout to each other or sing; and vendors, vendors everywhere, on bicycles, on foot, on horse-drawn carts, selling everything: hard brown sugar candy, *raspaduras;* and transparent candy, *pirulíes;* and crushed ice cones of all colors, *granizados;* and fruits of all kinds, *nísperos, mamoncillos, piñas,* even fruits he has never seen; and balloons; and flowers; and lottery tickets; and—and everything! And then the sidewalks are filled with so many people! Rushing men who bump into them, and look at them, and walk away from them, saying *Guajiros!;* and rushing women with tight short dresses that do not even cover their knees; and rushing nuns herding large disorganized bunches of neatly pressed, neatly starched uniformed children who look at him and make faces at him. And then, all of those cars! Running and pushing and rushing wild on the tight narrow cobblestone streets, their drivers moving as fast as they can; honking as often as they can; shouting insults to everybody as loud as they can; saying words he has never heard, but he can figure out what they mean.

Those cars rush by so close to him that he gets scared of being hit by them and begins to walk on the little space left of the skinny sidewalk between Maximiliano and the tall buildings. And as he walks he holds tight to Maximiliano's hand with his right hand, and carries with his left hand his straw suitcase that keeps bumping into everybody and that keeps getting heavier and heavier by the minute.

Maximiliano, who has been to La Habana before, looks straight in front as he walks, as if he knows exactly where he is, but every so often he stops at a corner and looks at the street sign, making sure he is not lost.

They keep on walking and walking, the torrid sun beating so hard on them and making them sweat so heavily that Maximiliano takes the red bandanna he has around his neck, wipes his forehead, and puts it back around his neck while Mani, who watches him carefully, does the same thing with his white linen handkerchief.

And then, when they reach a main avenue, a broad street with cars, and buses, and even tramways going in both directions, they turn left, walk a couple of blocks, turn again left, and look for number 675, which they finally find.

Number 675 is a small stucco house, only one story high, painted pastel yellow, with a pastel blue door that in the heat of the midafternoon sun seems particularly inviting. The house fits tight against other houses painted the same color and with very similar doors, all of them sharing a common Spanish red-tile roof. There lives Rubén, a cousin of Maximiliano, who, with his wife Aida, has been impatiently waiting for him and the boy.

Both Mani and Maximiliano sigh as they stand in front of the inviting door and knock at it. The door opens instantly, as if by magic.

"We've been so worried," says Rubén, a short stocky man with tawny skin and dark eyes. He welcomes them in. "Aida and I have been wondering if you got lost." He embraces Maximiliano in a deep man-to-man hug, Cuban style. "Aida was telling me for the hundredth time that I should have gone to the terminal to wait for you, and I was just going out right as you knocked at the door. Man, am I glad you found the way all right!" He looks at his wife, standing by his side, and adds jokingly, "Otherwise this woman would have killed me! But, come in! Come in!" He steps aside, lets Maximiliano and the boy in, and then he turns to Mani. "And now let me look at you!"

Rubén tries to lift Mani, but pretends to be unable to. "My! How much does he weigh?" he asks Maximiliano. And then he turns to Aida, a nice older woman with gray hair and an immense bust, barely contained by her tight dress. "He must be close to a hundred pounds already! Look at that boy, Aida! Why, he's almost a man! Doesn't time go fast?" He faces Mani again. "It seems to me it was just yesterday we all went to your baptism! Hey, Maximiliano, wasn't that a great party or what!"

Mani shies away from these people he has never met before who are somehow part of that family he calls his, but at the same time he is happy to hear what they are saying about him. Particularly the bit about his baptism. Inside his head he still believes he is an adopted child, a child nobody wanted. Or even worse, an illegitimate child, like one of those illegitimate children the other schoolchildren in Batabanó are always making fun of. But if Rubén and his family went to his baptism, maybe, just maybe, he is not an adopted child after all. Or could he still be one? Do they baptize adopted children?

"He's the spitting image of Dolores, isn't he?" says Aida, who is leading both of them, the boy and his father, to a small room in back of the house where a twin bed and a cot have been squeezed in. She looks carefully at Mani for a long time, and he doesn't know what to do with himself. "Except for the mouth," she adds, after a while. "That much he got from his father."

"And the muscles," Maximiliano adds emphatically, as he places the suitcases on the bed. "Show her, Mani." And Aida feels the muscles in the boy's arms, and she says, "Aahhh . . ." And everybody laughs.

"You sure can't deny you are your father's son," says Rubén as he and Maximiliano sit down on cane rocking chairs in the small central patio filled with tropical plants. The boy doesn't know what to do and stands awkwardly by his father.

"How about something to drink?" asks Rubén. "I've got the smoothest rum you've ever tasted. Havana Club." He pronounces it *Ahbahnah Kloob*. "Wait till you taste it. It's the best!"

Aida comes in bringing a small tray with several tiny demitasse cups, a pot of dark Cuban coffee that smells heavenly, a couple of shot glasses, a bottle of Ahbahnah Kloob, and a large glass of milk for the boy. She pours the coffee, gives it to the men, tells Mani to sit down in one of the empty rocking chairs, hands him the glass of milk, pours herself some coffee, and sits in the fourth rocking chair while the men shoot down some of the smoothest rum Maximiliano has ever tasted and follow it up with a sip of the dark coffee that smells, Oh, so good!

"And now," says Rubén, rocking gently, "tell us everything that happened in the last twelve years."

"Everything?" says Maximiliano jokingly.

"Everything!" answers Rubén with a broad smile as he winks an eye to the boy Mani, his dark eyes shining against his dark suntanned skin. "Every little thing!"

And the boy's father begins to tell them.

★ ★ ★

10

It takes Maximiliano and his son Mani a long two weeks and three days of walking and looking and looking and walking before they find a butcher shop Maximiliano likes.

It isn't perfect, but the location seems good, and the owner, Pancho, is willing to sell it for a good price, because he is getting on in years and he wants to retire to the country, away from the noises of the city, which he claims is growing too fast for him.

La Habana of 1926 is indeed moving at an accelerated pace. In fact, the whole island is. Cuba is growing extremely fast, because sugar is selling at a good price again, and as everybody knows, when sugar sells well, Cubans eat well. And when Cubans eat well . . . the island grows and grows.

To top it all off, for the last seven years, the island has become a gigantic tourist mecca. This has happened not only because of Cuba's beautiful beaches and beautiful skies and beautiful women and beautiful men, but primarily because of the passing in 1919 of the Eighteenth Amendment to the Constitution of the United States, the Prohibition Act, which did not allow people in that country to drink alcoholic beverages legally.

Since Cuba is just minutes away by ferry from the continent via Key West, and since in Cuba the drinking of alcohol has always been allowed—even encouraged—well, those in search of adventure and romance and a bit of liquor began to come to Cuba and drop their welcomed dollars on the island. And since most of those dollars have ended up in La Habana, people from all over the country, *guajiro* men and women like Maximiliano and his family, have been arriving here day after day, large daily herds being followed by even larger daily herds.

Maximiliano insists that before his deal with Pancho goes through, he and the boy must run the shop—in the presence of the owner, of course—to find out what business is like in the big city and to see if he and his son can get along with the city customers. Later on that night, before they go to sleep in their tiny room in Rubén's house, Maximiliano tells his son that he also wants to verify that the volume of sales is indeed what Pancho claims it to be.

Pancho is a criollo man, not a Spaniard, and so Maximiliano trusts him. But only to a certain degree.

"Some criollo men can be as bad as the worst of Spaniards," he tells Mani, who, lying in his cot, listens to him attentively. "Just as some Spaniards can be as good as the best of criollo men. Which means," he adds, as he sits on his bed and begins to remove his shoes, "that being a Spaniard or not doesn't make that much of a difference when dealing with people. Some people you can trust; some you can't. The problem," he continues, as he covers Mani with a sheet, "the problem is finding out which is which. And for that there's nothing better than time. Time lets you get to know a person fairly well." He smiles at his son. "Always remember that, Mani. Let time always be on your side."

Maximiliano, who is a very good businessman, very friendly and very cautious, shakes hands on this deal provided that he and his son run the shop for the next six months before the final payment is due, during which time Maximiliano and the owner will share the net profits half and half.

What he doesn't tell his son is that by doing this—basically working for the other man—he will be able to raise the money he needs to make that final payment, since he has only half of the total amount required at the moment.

Maximiliano doesn't like the idea of working for this other man. He has never known a boss other than his father, and that had been bad enough. But what choice does he have?

Pancho doesn't like the idea of having this *guajiro,* this country man run his shop, but the butcher shop has been on the market for a long while and he hasn't found any other takers. What other choice does he have?

They shake hands on the deal and each hopes for the best.

This butcher shop is located at the very corner of a very wide paved avenue called La Calzada and a very narrow unpaved side street people in the area call la Calle de los Toros, the Street of the Bulls, both of them at the edge of a working-class barrio that has a beautiful Cuban Indian name, Luyanó.

The corner shop opens to both La Calzada and the Street of the Bulls. It does not have doors. Instead it has two gates that meet at the pillar at the corner; heavy metal gates with heavy metal bars, which the boy Mani loves to lower and close at the end of his long working day at the shop.

Inside, the butcher shop is covered floor to ceiling with rectangular white tiles, laid in a brick pattern, kept resplendently shiny by Mani, who loves to see himself reflected in them as he wipes off the blood that occasionally spills on them.

Once a day, right before closing time, Mani climbs an old wood ladder to reach the upper tiles to wipe them clean. Mani loves that part of his job. The white glossy plaster ceiling is really high, and Mani loves to climb the tall ladder and look at the world from that height, because at times he feels he is flying and that the glittering reflections in the white tiles are stars in a magical world of his own.

There's a counter facing La Calzada and another one facing the Street of the Bulls. The two counters butt against each other, making an *L*. Each counter is made of a single slab of a marble so white, so grainless, and so shiny that it looks almost like white milky glass. Beneath them there are refrigeration cases with glass fronts where the different cuts and varieties of meat are displayed to tempt the potential buyers. At the end of each working day, whatever remains of that meat is taken out of the display cases and then Mani wipes perfectly clean the inside of the cases and the glass fronts.

At first Mani didn't like doing that part of his job, because he didn't like the smell inside those cases. Nonetheless, since he had to clean them, he decided that he would do so while holding his breath, and he started doing just that. Then, one day, while he was holding his breath, he heard Maximiliano shout at him, "*¡Respira, muchacho, respira!*" "Take a breath, boy, take a breath!" And Mani exhaled so loudly that even though his head was still inside the case, he heard Pancho and

Maximiliano laugh loud belly laughs, and the sound of their laughter made Mani laugh as well.

Since that time, every time he has to clean the cases, no sooner has he taken the meat out of them than he hears either Maximiliano or Pancho shout, "*¡Respira, muchacho, respira!*" and they all laugh together. This makes the cleaning of those cases less of a chore and more of a fun thing to do, even though he still does not like the smell inside them.

Then, after the cases are perfectly clean, Mani takes the unsold meat, wraps it carefully in wax paper so it won't dry out, and places it in the large cooler located at the back of the shop.

This cooler is not refrigerated, like the cooler Maximiliano had installed years ago in the state-of-the-art butcher shop he had in Surgidero, the one that Ogún, the angry black god of the sea claimed as his and destroyed with a single tidal wave. The cooler in this old shop is cooled by gigantic blocks of ice that are delivered to the butcher shop once a day, every day, very early in the morning, before the tropical sun rises, and *that* is *very* early.

Mani finds walking into this cooler a great experience, a real treat.

At first he was a little afraid of going inside, though he never showed it. But after a while he began to like it, because this place is like no other place in the world known to him.

If he is going to be in the cooler for a while, he puts on a thick sweater, much oversized for him. This sweater hangs from a large black-iron hook located by the thick insulated door leading into the cooler, which is normally closed. With the sweater on, Mani turns on the light inside the cooler, using a light switch located outside the door. He then opens the door, which is surprisingly lightweight for a door as thick as that one is, walks into the cooler, and carefully closes the door behind him so the heat of the butcher shop does not get inside.

Once inside, Mani is in a different world altogether.

It is cold, really cold. Huge blocks of ice are stacked one on top of the other, lining the walls, making Mani believe that he is inside an ice castle where the light, a single bare bulb hanging in the center of the cooler, reflects every which way, and where he doesn't really know what is real and what is not.

The ice is constantly melting and Mani has to keep constantly mopping the tiny hexagonal white-tile floor, constantly pushing the water on the floor in the direction of the central floor drain.

He loves doing that because it means he has to go around the skinned carcasses of bulls, which hang from large iron meat hooks all over the cooler, and he pretends he is in a magical forest, and that his mop is either a dog leading him, showing him the way; or a sword killing dragons; or when he straddles it, it even becomes a horse, like the one his grandfather had back in Batabanó and which he loved to ride.

That part of his job he really likes.

Just as he likes being close to this man he calls father and whom he has just begun to get to know.

He loves the way Maximiliano does everything. Mani is always watching him, imitating every single movement Maximiliano makes, and wondering if he himself is doing them right.

At the beginning of each working day, as soon as the blocks of ice are delivered to the shop and neatly stacked in the cooler and the meat has been properly rehung, Mani goes into the cooler with his father and between the two of them they select whatever chunk of meat he and his father are going to be working on that day. Half a carcass or a side of beef, let's say. Then they bring it into the shop.

There they place it on a huge wood cutting block smack in the center of the shop and made of a single piece of wood. And then, since business is always slow at that early time of day, Maximiliano begins to dress the meat, removing most of the excess fat, cleaning the meat, and placing it inside the glass-front cases.

Maximiliano is very careful about what goes where. He asks his son to step on the other side of the counter and help him place the different cuts of meat he's prepared on display exactly where he wants them, so they will look their very best. Then Mani helps him wrap the remaining cuts of meat in brown paper and returns them to the cooler, to one side, where there are lots of steel shelves.

Some butchers buy their meat precut, something that can be done for you at the slaughterhouse, for a price. But Maximiliano always buys it by the whole carcass; it is cheaper that way, and besides, since he is a *guajiro,* a country butcher, he doesn't mind doing the heavy work himself. In fact, he loves it because then he can cut the meat exactly the way he likes it. And he is very demanding about what he likes.

This shop is not exactly the way Maximiliano would like it to be, but then he didn't build it. So he has to make do the best he can, which is very difficult when someone else—Pancho, the current owner—is always telling him, "This is not the way we do things here in the city."

A week ago Pancho and Maximiliano had a huge fight, and Mani got very frightened.

Pancho, screaming at the top of his lungs, told Maximiliano that he was spending too much time preparing the meat, and that this was no way to run a shop in the city and make money. Maximiliano tried to make him understand, but Pancho, who would have none of it, shouted angrily, "Goddammit! This is still *my* shop, you hear! And in *my* shop you do as *I* tell you!"

Mani saw Maximiliano go white in the face, and for a moment he thought that Maximiliano, who had the large carving knife in his hand, was going to kill Pancho. He became so nervous that he quickly hid behind the huge butcher block in the center of the store. When Maximiliano heard him scurrying, he looked at Mani, his eyes focusing on him for a long while. Then, after taking a deep breath, he threw the knife on the counter and said nothing more to Pancho.

No one spoke for the rest of that afternoon. And when that night Mani and Maximiliano went to Rubén's house, Maximiliano went straight to bed and would not have anything to eat. And neither did Mani.

Maximiliano cannot help it. He is a good butcher, an artist of a butcher, and he takes his time to trim, prepare, and present the meat neatly to make it look its best. He is always telling Mani how one can tell the quality of a butcher just by looking at how the meat is trimmed, prepared, and presented.

And even though he does not do things the way they are done in the city, as soon as customers find out how good a butcher the new butcher is, customers begin telling other customers; and in no time at all customers from neighboring areas begin coming to Luyanó to buy the meat prepared by Maximiliano, the *guajiro* butcher.

The fact that almost all of his customers are women—most of them mulatto women—and that Maximiliano is as handsome and as nice a man as he is is not to be taken lightly.

Business begins to boom, much to Pancho's surprise. Though at first he couldn't believe it, now Pancho is used to seeing women customers waiting patiently in line to get their meat from the new butcher, "the nice *guajiro* who smiles at you as he waits on you."

Mani has seen how those women look at his father. And, of course, he has also seen how his father looks back at them. And Mani, who does everything just as his father does, looks at the women the same way his father does: up and down, slowly, admiringly, stopping on the way down at the women's large breasts—which the women love to sway gently from side to side when they notice him looking at them; and on the way up on their eyes—which sometimes look back at him with sparks so intense that it makes him tingle in a way that he finds intriguing and exciting at the same time.

Mani had been practicing this way of looking for a while and had not felt any of that tingling until Clotilde, a beautiful young mulatto woman with the darkest eyes, caught him looking at her. She waited until his eyes peered directly into hers, and then she looked back at Mani, and she did it in a very special way, a way totally unknown to him. And as she was looking at him, Mani felt an excitement he had never experienced before: a tantalizing tingling and swelling of that thing between his legs, which got hard and stiff and stood up in his pants.

He became so red in the face that he had to look away from Clotilde as he heard her tell Maximiliano, "Hey, *guajiro,* that kid of yours is going to be a hell of a good-looking man one of these days."

Maximiliano looked at him first, then back at Clotilde as he answered, "He's already a hell of a good-looking man." And then he added, a broad smile on his face, "Just like his father."

Clotilde looked back at Maximiliano, and staring straight into his eyes she said, a smirk on her face, "Enough talk, *guajiro,* and more action. I didn't come here to play no games."

"Oh, no?" asked Maximiliano.

"No," Clotilde answered, "I came here to ask you to give me the best you've got. And," she added, "I want it now."

"Right away," Maximiliano said, and he sliced for her a piece of *filete* fit for a queen. "Here, compliments of the house."

That night Mani went to bed and began thinking about that Clotilde woman and again that thing between his legs became hard and stiff. He wanted to ask his father what to do about it, but Maximiliano was already happily snoring away. Mani turned over in his cot and had a tough time falling asleep that night.

As business improves, Maximiliano feels better and better about the shop and about himself. And even before the store is finally his, he feels so confident in what he is doing that he decides that the time has come to bring his entire family to La Habana.

He's been missing Dolores a great deal: Five months is a long, long time when you're alone. Sure, he has found the time to give Clotilde the best he's got, and on more than one occasion. But that is not the same thing. What he's done with Clotilde is something he had to do because otherwise he would have gone crazy. If Clotilde knew that when he closes his eyes while he is with her he is really thinking of Dolores, she would probably have a fit, but he cannot help it. Sometimes Maximiliano wonders what kind of a love potion that criollo woman Dolores gave him, because he thinks of her all day long. And all night long.

That is why he's been working really hard, harder than he can ever remember, to get his entire family back with him, so that wife of his, with her temper and her sparks, can get back in his bed as soon as possible. Now. Today.

And that is why, as soon as he finds out that a place has become vacant across La Calzada, just a few steps from the Street of the Bulls—the lower level of a two-story two-family criollo-style house, one family to a floor—Maximiliano immediately rents it, even though he barely has the money to pay the two months in advance the landlord requires.

That night, after everybody is asleep in Rubén's house, Maximiliano goes to the dining room, turns on the bare bulb that hangs in its center, pulls out from his shirt pocket an old fountain pen with a thick nib that every so often splashes all over everything, and, ignoring the splashes, writes to Dolores:

> Dear wife Dolores:
>
> I hope that upon receipt of this letter you all are well.
>
> I just paid the deposit on a house in Luyanó, right across from the butcher shop, so now you all can come.
>
> It's a two-story house and the people on the second floor can look down into the patio, but they seem to be very nice and very clean. I told the owner to paint the walls your favorite color, pale cream. The floors are tiled with white and blue tiles. I think you'll like them.
>
> The house has three bedrooms and a bathroom. You and I can take the first bedroom, the one next to the living room. The girls can take the middle bedroom, by the bathroom, and the boys the one at the other end of the house.

Please give my regards to Papá and Mamá.

Tell Mamá there is a school nearby, and tell Papá that I already have all the money for the final payment of the butcher shop, but I am going to hold on to it until the very last minute. What I don't have is any money to buy furniture, because I had to pay two months' rent in advance, so that will have to wait, but I did buy a pair of cots, so Mani and I will be able to sleep in our house beginning tomorrow night, after the paint dries.

To celebrate our new house Pancho the butcher opened a new bottle of rum and we had a couple of drinks. Mani tasted it, but he didn't like it. He may think he is a man, and he may even look like one, but he is still a boy, smart as they come, though he doesn't talk much.

Oh, I almost forgot. Aida found us a cook! Tonight she cooked for all of us here, at Rubén's, and even Aida thought her black beans were out of this world! Her name is Zenaida. She is as black and as old as Pablo with not a single tooth in her mouth and she has twelve children!

And you thought four children was a large enough family! As soon as you get here we have to begin working on that! So, hurry up!

Dolores smiles as she folds the letter and then goes back to the borrowed bedroom with the borrowed bed where she has been sleeping by herself for what seems to be the longest time, places the letter on the bed, and begins packing her clothes, the few clothes she brought to the house of Batabanó before the powerful hurricane destroyed her own house.

If only she had known in advance what the hurricane was going to do to Surgidero, she could have brought so many other things she now misses. But no, none of that is important. Thank God she brought the old photograph of her mother with her. She doesn't know what she would have done if she had lost in the hurricane the only photograph she has of the mother she never knew. But after the incident with the big fire, that photograph goes wherever she goes, just like her children.

She kisses it, places it in the only remaining one of her two straw suitcases, an old battered suitcase that has traveled so much and which has survived the big fire and the hurricane, and as she places her mother's photograph inside, she remembers doing just that, many years ago, the day she walked out of her rich father's country estate.

She smiles her famous mischievous smile because she just imagined seeing a beautiful mermaid who deep inside the ocean is wearing her beautiful white wedding dress and admiring all of that intricate embroidery with the tiny blind stitches. But the practical side of her dismisses that thought. What would a mermaid be doing with a dress like that? she asks herself, as she closes the old suitcase. The other mermaids would probably make fun of her! That dress is so old-fashioned! I wonder what they wear in La Habana?

She sees herself reflected in the large oval mirror that stands to one side of her borrowed room. She stands up straight, her breasts out, and fixes her hair, still wavy and still black as ebony. Would anybody think she's the mother of four children already? She turned thirty-two just a month ago. The first time in her married life she spent her anniversary, which is also her birthday, sleeping on a bed alone.

What did Maximiliano do that night?

Did he miss her as she missed him? Did he think of her that night as she thought of him? Did he make love to her in his dreams as she made love to him in hers?

She gets closer to the mirror and looks at her eyes. No wrinkles. She laughs at herself, and stops, because suddenly she has seen wrinkles where there were none before.

But then the practical side of her tells her that she is not going to stop laughing just to avoid having wrinkles. Let them come when they will, she says to herself. I have earned them. And I shall wear them with pride.

Besides, older women can be very interesting too. But can they be interesting enough to hold a man like Maximiliano? That handsome man she's been married to for— She pauses. "My God," she says aloud, "it's already past fourteen years! Fourteen years and a few months!"

She unfolds his letter again, which was lying on the borrowed bed, and reads it again, pausing at the last sentences.

> And you thought four children was a large enough family! As soon as you get here we have to begin working on <u>that</u>! So, hurry up!

She kisses the letter and smiles, thinking of Maximiliano the butcher, that stubborn blond man with the insolent blue eyes she loves to look deep into, who is impatiently waiting for her. And she wonders what life is like in Luyanó, and why that street is called the Street of the Bulls.

11

The Street of the Bulls is not a very long street, maybe eleven or twelve short blocks total. It begins at a place where the cargo trains carrying the bulls stop, and it terminates at a place where the so-called Cuban slaughterhouse is located.

There is another slaughterhouse, the one people call the American slaughterhouse, located where it should be, where it makes sense, along the railroad tracks. This one used to be leased by a criollo man called Ferminio until the lease was taken over by The American Beef Company.

Since Cuban beef is excellent, and since Cuba is only ninety easy miles by sea to the United States, several American investors realized that Cuban beef could be produced, transported, marketed, and sold in the United States at a mere fraction of what Texas beef cost, which of course meant huge profits. So The American Beef Company was founded, which offered to pay more money for the lease of the slaughterhouse that Ferminio had been occupying up to that time.

Ferminio only had a criollo gentleman's agreement with the Spaniard who was the owner of the property, a mere handshake, with nothing in writing. So, no sooner had the American group made its sizable offer than Ferminio was quickly dispossessed and out of business.

The American slaughterhouse immediately began cutting beef the American way, to satisfy the needs of the American investors, who were providing their American market in the United States with beef American people bought as "American," which of course it was, since Cuba *is* in the Americas. But the "American" cut of beef—perpendicular to the grain—which produces porterhouse, Delmonico, T-bone steaks, and so on, has nothing in common with the criollo cut of meat—parallel to the grain—which produces *palomillas, faldas, boliches,* and so on. They are not the same cut with two different names, one in English, the other in Spanish. No. These cuts are so different they do not translate.

Since Cubans like their beef cut the criollo way, the way Ferminio had been doing for years, and since nobody else was doing it in that area of La Habana, Ferminio decided to build a slaughterhouse that would prepare beef the Cuban way and satisfy the needs of his Cuban market.

With the help of a couple of politician buddies of his who knew how to get things done, he did not lease but, instead, bought a huge tract of land, the only one that was available in the barrio of Luyanó, where most of his workers lived. Then, before he began the actual building of his new slaughterhouse, before he even broke ground, Ferminio secured with the help of his politician buddies—who were also his investors—the permission to use a narrow unpaved city street to take his bulls from the railroad tracks to his new place of business. Then, with this permission in his hands, Ferminio cajoled the railroad people to open a special stop, right at the foot of the Street of the Bulls, as people began referring to it. Then and only then did he build his new slaughterhouse, a model slaughterhouse with every modern convenience available and all the latest equipment, including specially built channels where the animal's blood is collected and saved, to make the famous blood sausages, which give that peculiar taste to the thick white bean soup Cubans so much love.

Ferminio had been in business again for just a few years when suddenly several people died in the United States after eating certain beef that was traced back to the American slaughterhouse in Cuba.

There was nothing wrong with Cuban beef. The American slaughterhouse was found to be improperly kept and improperly sanitized. The fault had been in the processing of the meat, not in the meat itself. The American investors had been trying to cut corners to make a quick buck. And a quick buck they made, until someone died, at which point the whole deceptive scheme came out in the open, and the American team stopped making bucks altogether. Nobody wanted to buy meat from the American slaughterhouse anymore. They spent a lot of money cleaning it, fixing it, and modernizing it. But to no avail. The American Beef Company finally went bankrupt, and the owner of the place found himself with a broken lease. True, it was written down. It was in fact a legal document of great beauty where everything was spelled out in great detail, except what to do with it now that it had become a worthless piece of paper.

It was then the owner thought of Ferminio.

The same Spaniard who owned the place and who had broken his gentleman's agreement with Ferminio, that very same man went to see Ferminio to offer him a good deal on the old lease.

And Ferminio, who was a criollo man who held to his agreements with the honor of a true gentleman and who didn't know about written law, did know exactly what to do with the worthless piece of paper the Spaniard had been left with in his hands. And he told the Spaniard exactly what to do with it.

Nobody knows if the Spaniard did what Ferminio told him to do with that piece of paper. It really didn't matter. The Spaniard ended up going bankrupt himself as well. And Ferminio, who didn't know about written law but who knew a good deal when he saw one, ended up buying the so-called American slaughterhouse, paying a penny on the Cuban peso for it. He figured business had grown so much the market could handle two slaughterhouses, and he was right. Cubans still call that slaughterhouse, the one by the tracks, the American one, even though now only criollo cuts are prepared there.

Ferminio no longer works the long hours he used to work at both his slaughterhouses. Eustaquio, his son, runs the American one, along the railroad tracks. Arsenio, a criollo man, runs the Cuban one, at the far end of the Street of the Bulls. But Ferminio keeps a close tab on everything that goes on in both his slaughterhouses, and he oversees all operations.

Though he is pushing sixty, Ferminio still is able to sacrifice a bull with ease. He does it with a single stroke of the hammer, driving the fatal spike deep into the bull's brain, as one of his assistants simultaneously slits the bull's throat and fills a tin cup with the bull's blood. Then he passes the cup to Ferminio, who drinks from it, and then Ferminio proceeds to pass the blood-filled cup around to all of his men, as is the custom. This is done to honor the bull in his death and to let the strength of the sacrificed animal go through the veins of the men and make them as strong as the bull was before his death. Life feeding on life.

This single-stroke killing is something Ferminio's men strive to achieve but few of them actually do. Arsenio can do it easily, but Eustaquio, Ferminio's own son, has never been able to. That is why the men at the slaughterhouses have the double ritual of the slitting of the bull's throat that is performed simultaneously with the hammering of the metal spike. This is done in order to kill the animal as fast and with as little pain as possible, to send the sacrificed bull as quickly as possible to whatever heaven bulls go.

Criollo men do care for the animals.

They certainly take good care of their bulls.

★ ★ ★

12

Watching the bulls stampede along the Street of the Bulls is something Mani has not gotten used to yet.

It may happen at any time of the day.

Or of the night.

First he hears a rumble, a distant rumble, like the soft distant rumble of a distant storm, the disturbing soft rumble of distant drums whose sudden and persistent beating and beating instantly awakens the sleepy tropical street; a narrow little street lined with tight little buildings crammed tight against each other.

Then he sees, at the far far end of the skinny little street, up the hill, where the little church is, a tiny cloud of reddish dust. And he sees that tiny cloud get larger and larger as it moves closer and closer and as the constant beating and beating of drums becomes faster and faster and louder and louder.

Then he begins to feel it, the trembling of the earth beneath his feet; a terrifying trembling that becomes more and more terrifying as the cloud of dust gets closer and closer and as the loud beating and beating of drums becomes louder and louder and madder and madder.

It is only then that he gets to see them: A river of beasts violently rushing down the hill. A torrent of sweating, panting, bellowing bulls, enveloped in a large cloud of the thickest red dust, thrusting down the narrow unpaved street; dislodging every single stone; causing the earsplitting noise of hundreds of raging bolting angered thunderstorms; and making the entire world shake as if the Earth is about to split open and swallow him whole while the turbulent herd, in a blind brutal frenzy, eyes bursting out of their orbits, furiously charges all the way to the distant slaughterhouse at the other far end of the shaken trembling street.

The people on the street shout and scream at the top of their lungs, "*¡Los toros! ¡Los toros!* The bulls!" and men as well as women suddenly scramble around, frenetically running in all directions, elbowing and shouldering and pushing and shoving, frantically trying to get out of the way of the bulls, hiding behind posts, flattening themselves against walls, locking themselves behind closed gates and closed shutters and closed windows and closed doors.

The men on horseback, the vaqueros, yell and scream and shout and swear and curse at the battering bulls and fire and shoot their guns in the air, daringly trying to steer the wildly deranged animals and give the whole nightmarish vision the semblance of order, while the bulls—trying to prove themselves—dash and leap and lunge and jump, each of them attempting to pass each other, each of them hoping to be the first one in that race, that desperate race whose final destination is nothing but death. They do not know it yet, but soon they will. But by then there is no turning back.

They are frightening.

They are frightening because they are frightened.

And they *are* frightening.

And yet Mani cannot keep himself from watching the unbridled animals rush by him, silently standing as if in a trance behind the heavy metal bars that make up the heavy metal gates that separate him, inside the butcher shop, from the riotous uncontrollable bulls; metal gates and metal bars that try to prevent those monstrous beasts with the smell of fear from entering his world.

But they fail to do so. The boy Mani lives in that world.

He lives in the shadows of those bulls.

He is too young to realize that those heavy metal bars meant to keep the bulls away from him are also destined to keep him away from the life of his dreams. He is too young to realize that those heavy metal gates meant to provide him with a sanctuary are also destined to become his prison. He is too young to realize that he, like the bulls, is also racing to his death, uncontrollably, unknowingly, along that very same street, following a narrow path dictated by others.

He just lives in that world where every so often he can watch in mournful silence the noble magnificent bulls rush and push and shove and jump and leap to their deaths along the unpaved narrow little street.

And sometimes he wonders what it would be like to run free and play on that street.

The first time Mani watched them, one of the bulls missed a step and fell right in front of the butcher shop. The other bulls tried to avoid him, but they couldn't, and the fallen bull's blood splattered all over the street, staining the stones as the dying animal bellowed one final time before he died.

Mani couldn't take his eyes off the fallen bull as the other bulls trampled all over him. The noise was deafening and the heavy gate facing the Street of the Bulls began shaking and clanking so violently that Mani thought it was going to give in. He was so frightened that he started to shiver and tremble, so much so that Maximiliano placed his strong arm around the boy's shoulders and held him close.

It was only then, when he felt the warmth of this man's touch, that Mani realized how cold he was, and how good it felt to have this godlike man embrace him.

Then, after the last of the bulls had rushed by and disappeared in the distance, Mani opened the gates again and waited for the truck from the slaughterhouse to come and pick up what was left of the dead bull.

He watched as the men carefully picked up all the pieces of the dismembered bull. And then, after they were done, Mani washed away the pools of blood still left all over the rocky street so mosquitoes wouldn't come.

But that was then.

Now he has seen the bulls rush by the butcher shop many times. He is still afraid of them, but he no longer shivers.

The minute he hears people screaming "*¡Los toros! ¡Los toros!*" he stops whatever it is he is doing, runs outside the butcher shop, quickly closes the heavy gate facing the Street of the Bulls, then runs inside the shop again, and from the inside he closes the other heavy metal gate, the one facing La Calzada. Then he runs back behind the display cases and stands there, waiting.

They all wait.

The three of them. Pancho and Maximiliano and Mani.

They all stop whatever it is they have been doing and they all stand, waiting and watching in mournful silence as the noble magnificent bulls rush unknowingly to their deaths along the narrow unpaved little street.

It is only after the torrential procession of the bulls ends, after the last of the bulls disappears down the road, that life goes back to what it was, as if nothing had happened.

★ ★ ★

13

Life at the butcher shop is not exactly what the boy Mani had in mind when he left behind his grandparents' home. There he used to play a lot. Here he has to work a lot. But he does get to spend a lot of time with Maximiliano, the man he calls father, and Mani truly likes that.

Several nights ago, the first night they both slept in the new, empty house Maximiliano had just rented, Mani was lying on his cot, pretending to be asleep while Maximiliano, sitting on the floor, again began counting the money he had saved, separating it into neat piles that he placed on the tile floor in front of him. Mani had seen him do this several times before, and each time he had noticed how the piles of paper money changed shape constantly as Maximiliano mumbled: rent, furniture, trip, food, Papá. He would take some money out of one pile and put it on another, just to move it back again, or to still another pile.

Mani didn't know what this all meant. At first he thought it was a game, but Maximiliano looked so serious as he was doing this that it didn't seem to Mani that this could be a game, because this man with the golden hair that has grown too long did not seem to be having a lot of fun doing it.

Then Mani saw Maximiliano raise his eyes, look around the room, stand up, go to his straw suitcase, open it, take out the old leather wallet Mani knows Maximiliano hides within one of the white shirts in the suitcase, open it, and take out an old photograph, the photograph of a young girl in an old-fashioned white long-skirt dress, that Mani knows Maximiliano keeps inside that wallet. Mani has been told that this is a photograph of Dolores the year she and Maximiliano got married, but Mani has never been able to see any similarity between the young girl in the photograph and that woman he calls mother.

Out of the corner of his eye Mani saw Maximiliano look at the photograph for the longest while and then, smiling, Mani saw how he put it back inside the wallet, stashed all the paper money back in the wallet, hid the wallet inside a white shirt inside the suitcase, and closed it. And then, on the way back to his cot, he stopped by Mani's cot for a brief second. It was then that Mani, who was keeping his eyes closed, felt this man's huge and callused hand brush his hair softly, so softly that Mani wondered if an angel had not done it.

That night he slept really well.

Today Mani is looking attentively at Maximiliano, the man with the huge callused hands whose touch is as gentle as the wings of an angel, who is showing him how to slice a cut of beef.

Mani learns by the minute. Though he knows that he is only a boy, Mani cannot fail to notice how his arms are growing bigger by the hour; how every single day it becomes easier and easier to lift the carcasses of the dead bulls in the cooler, the same bulls Mani sees rushing down the Street of the Bulls on their way to their deaths.

"The first thing you do," Maximiliano says, "is to make sure the knife is as sharp on both sides as you can make it."

Maximiliano pulls one of Mani's wavy black hairs, which makes Mani shout "Ouch!" and then Maximiliano, smiling, slides the hair along the blade of the knife in his hand, and the hair splits in half before Mani can see it happen.

"Then," Maximiliano continues, "you simply slide the knife on the meat. You've got to do it in one direction only, and with very little pressure, like this. When you get to the end of the knife you lift it up and start at the beginning of the cut again. You never go back and forth, like a saw. If you do that you'll break the meat fibers and it won't look as good and it won't taste as good. Now you do it. Remember, always in the same direction and with very little pressure."

Mani takes the sharp carving knife with his left hand and starts a new cut. It's not as easy as his father had made it look.

"Take your time," Maximiliano adds. "If it takes all day to do it well, well then that's what it takes. Just do it the best you can."

Mani does it just as Maximiliano has taught him, and he does it well, really well.

"Excellent, Mani," his father says. "Excellent. I couldn't have done it better myself!"

And Mani beams, smiling ear to ear, as he takes the slab of beef he has just cut and wraps it neatly in brown paper.

Sometimes, after Maximiliano and Mani have taken their noontime meal, which Zenaida prepares for them in their new house, and they are in their cots taking a siesta, Mani stands up and quietly tiptoes into the patio, which is almost totally empty except for a potted palm Aida gave them for good luck. There he lies down on the cold cement floor and looks up at the rectangular piece of brilliant turquoise sky that is framed by the pale cream stucco walls of this and the neighboring house.

Everything is quiet then.

He can hear only the sounds made by his father, happily snoring, and the distant noises made by the buses and trams on La Calzada as they go by.

Mani looks up and he sees huge cottony clouds gently gliding by, puffy clouds that seem to be shaped like huge stuffed animals. Puffy giraffes, and puffy lions, and puffy birds, and even puffy dragons—all the things he has learned about in school. He follows them with his eyes, as those huge puffy animals slide across that tiny rectangle of sky he calls his own, until they disappear from his sight.

Sometimes he falls asleep on the cold cement floor of the patio as he looks up at those magical puffy clouds with the infinite variety of shapes, and he dreams.

In his dreams he sees himself following them, the puffy friendly animals who are softly calling his name from far away, "Mani! Mani! Mani!" inviting him to join them, to come with them, to follow them, to find out where it is they all go. And just as he is about to find out their secret, he hears his father loudly calling his name, "Mani!" And he wakes up.

But before he stands up on his way back to work, he looks up once again at the deep turquoise rectangular piece of sky he loves so much and he sees more puffy animals, some of which he has not seen before: puffy seals, puffy elephants, puffy donkeys.

Even puffy bulls.

He sees cottonlike puffy bulls that do not rush anymore. They just slide by, floating gently and unafraid; cottonlike bulls that seem to be smiling at him as they glide ever so smoothly, dissolving ever so slowly and disappearing ever so quietly as they whisper ever so softly his name.

"Mani! Maaani! Maaaaani!"

The boy Mani stands up then and goes back to work. And on his way there he hopes that tomorrow he will find out the secret of the bulls: Where it is that they all go.

Because he knows that once he finds out where they all go, maybe then one day he will be able to follow them.

Part Two

Luyanó 1927–1933

14

Last time she saw La Habana she was a wealthy girl of seventeen with a dream.

With her dear aunt Ausencia by her side, she had left Batabanó, taken the railroad, and come to the capital. There she had stayed overnight with her sister Fulgencia, in their large house in El Cerro, at the top of the hill; and the following morning she had gone once again to her favorite store, Fin de Siècle, to look for a pair of shoes.

That was why she had come to La Habana that last time. Because she needed a pair of white shoes to go with her brand-new dress; that beautiful dress people said she had worked on for so long.

And she had.

But to her, all of that work had been nothing, because she knew that with every stitch she took, she was one stitch closer to him.

She had been welcomed at the fancy French store by the same old Cuban lady with the high-pitched voice whose French was so bad, and she had tried one pair of shoes after another, but none of them had been good enough to go with her dress.

And then the assistant to the old lady brought a pair, and without even trying them on she knew those were the right shoes, those were exactly the shoes she had been dreaming of.

"Strap slippers," the lady had called them. "The latest. Direct from Paris. The lightest shoes you'll ever put on your feet!"

She had taken them in her hands, each shoe as light as a feather, and had looked at them for the longest time before she had tried them on, closely studying them from every single angle, closely examining every single part, closely admiring every single detail: the fine white kid leather, so thin and so supple; the hand-sewn turned soles, so strong and so pliant; the fancy silk bow, so wide and so lustrous; the tiny pearl button, so small and so shiny; the white satin lining, so soft and so silky; the pretty French heels, so tall and so right.

She had not asked how much they were. She had never asked how much anything was. She had just tried them on, and the shoes had fit her as if they had been made for her, making her feet look more tiny and more delicate than they were. And the shoes were so light! And so comfortable! Beyond belief.

But that was back then, in 1913, more than fourteen years ago.

Today is 1927.

Today her shoes are heavy and sturdy, made of heavy black canvas with heavy rope soles and no heels.

Today her dress is made of heavy cheap cotton of dirt-hiding colors, not of light costly linen of the purest white.

Today she is not on the leather seat of a railroad car that smells of perfume but on the worn cane seat of a dilapidated old bus painted pastel pink that smells of castile soap and of sweat.

Today Ausencia is gone. And Fulgencia. And her sister Francisca. Lost to hearts that gave up on them. And gone is the old house in El Cerro, and the country estate in Batabanó, and the sugar plantation, and the sugar mill, all of it gone, lost to a cock with plumage quite fancy and talons quite sharp, but not quite sharp enough. And gone is her father, who could not bear the loss of so much. He's also gone, lost to a bullet.

Today she is thirty-two, and the wife of a butcher, and the mother of four.

And today she asks the price of everything.

And yet today she is the happiest woman in the world because she knows that at the end of the line that blond man with the piercing blue eyes, the head of an emperor, and the heart of a poet waits for her, as impatiently now as he did back then, fourteen years ago, when all dressed in white, his huge callused hands holding a Panama hat, he stood atop the steps of the Hotel Libertad.

CARRYING MARGUITA in her arms to save one fare, she is sitting on the aisle; Merced, to her right, at the window looking out; Gustavo, to her left, on the seat next to her immediately across the aisle.

Neither Merced nor Gustavo has said a word so far.

Maximiliano's mother gave each of them a small box filled with paper and pencils with which to entertain themselves, and a large net bag filled with fruits to eat during the trip. Before they left, the old lady took each child aside individually and told each of them to be quiet and to mind their mother during the trip, adding that if they did not behave like good grandchildren should, she herself was going to come to La Habana and break her knuckles on the misbehaving child's head. And though the children did not really believe her, they have been behaving like the angels they are. Merced, as usual, has been eating so many guavas she is on the verge of getting sick; Gustavo, as usual, has been reading some old books he knows already by heart; and Marguita, as usual, is asleep. She fell asleep the moment Julio turned the ignition key on and has yet to wake up, despite the *algarabía,* the high noise level inside the tired old bus.

Julio reaches the high hill, and the people in the front seat go "Aahhh . . ." and Merced and Gustavo stand up to look at La Habana, the city of a hundred churches, and Dolores does nothing but look at her children, hug her baby tight to her, and say a quick prayer thanking her Little Virgin for all the favors that have been granted to her.

It is only then she looks at La Habana—a sight she has not seen since she was seventeen—and this time, after she also gasps "Aahhh . . . " she laughs and she cries at the same time, like the rest of the people in the bus, at the beauty of it all.

And then, in no time at all, before she even realizes it, she sees, standing in front of her, a broad smile of a face, which is his face; and hears a beautiful dark melody of a voice, which is his voice; and smells a sweet tempting smell, which is his smell. And all of a sudden, she finds herself laughing and crying in his powerful arms inside *her* portal, the front porch of *her* house, the house Maximiliano has rented for *her* on La Calzada, just across from the butcher shop, a few steps from the Street of the Bulls, a house he had painted pale cream, which is *her* favorite color; a criollo-style house that she, as of this moment, has already made her own; an old small house, with no furniture, which to her seems like a miraculous palace.

* * *

15

No sooner has Dolores arrived in Luyanó than she catches Pilar, the fat woman with the glass eye who lives in the house next to Dolores's, peeking with her one good eye through her semiclosed window shutters into Dolores's patio.

Dolores, who has never seen this woman before, unfamiliar with the rules of this city game—totally new to her—and a little apprehensive about the way that strange woman is looking at her, dares to smile a polite "Hello."

Pilar, caught in the act, so to speak, has no choice but to pretend to be the friendly neighbor and answer back. She returns Dolores's warm hello with a dry one, and immediately warns Dolores about Eleuteria, whom Pilar calls the "evil tongue" of Luyanó.

"Eleuteria," Pilar says, speaking very softly and looking in all directions as she speaks, "is a skinny old lady who lives on the other side of La Calzada," in a house just across from Dolores's house, two doors away from the butcher shop. "She may be less than five feet tall," adds Pilar, "but she is as mean and as grumpy and as harsh as she is small. She is a real harpy, nasty, bitter, and cruel, because her husband abandoned her many years ago for a mulatto woman who knew how to smile. And ever since that time," Pilar continues, "all Eleuteria does is entertain herself by destroying the reputation of every nice person she has ever met. I'm just telling you this," concludes Pilar, "so you know."

Dolores, so warned, dreads meeting Eleuteria, the evil tongue of Luyanó.

But the next morning Dolores runs into her at the butcher shop, and the old lady, who is as short and as skinny as she was described by Pilar, introduces herself and welcomes Dolores to Luyanó with a warm smile.

Dolores finds her to be very nice, especially as she warns Dolores about Pilar, that mean, nasty harpy of a woman with one evil eye who lives next door to Dolores, who spends her entire day behind semiclosed shutters hoping to catch people doing anything wrong.

"I'm just telling you this," Eleuteria tells Dolores, "so you know."

Well, now Dolores knows.

A COUPLE OF weeks later, Dolores is coming back from the butcher shop, where she had brought Maximiliano his early morning coffee—a ritual she loves—and on the way back home, she decides to stop at the tiny fruit vendor's shop next to the butcher shop to buy some produce. It is there she meets Eleuteria again, who, upon seeing Dolores, moves really close to her, lowers her voice to a whisper, and with great sadness tells Dolores, "I'm so sorry about your case, my friend!"

Dolores looks at Eleuteria, a question on her face.

She has no idea what the skinny old lady with the beady eyes and the long vulturelike neck is talking about. What case of hers is this that is making Eleuteria feel so sorry for her?

Eleuteria, who enjoys seeing the puzzled look on Dolores's face, continues. "But you don't have to worry about it anymore." She pulls Dolores to one side, lowers her voice even more, and adds confidentially, "Whatever was going on between your husband and Clotilde, that mulatto woman your husband was having an affair with, is all over. I heard they had a big fight yesterday at the room he was keeping for her, and he ended up walking out on her. So you don't have to worry about it anymore. Your husband may leave you for a mulatto woman, like mine did, horns on him, the bastard! But he is not going to leave you for this one!"

Eleuteria says this to Dolores with relish, enjoying every word of it, hoping to see Dolores cry or scream or get mad or angry.

But Dolores is not of that kind.

She politely thanks Eleuteria for the information, and gently asks the old lady about Lucencia, Eleuteria's oldest daughter, whom rumor has it was found by Eleuteria with her breasts exposed, being fondled by one of the local policemen.

According to Pilar—who saw it all, or claims she did, watching from behind the shutters of her own house—*that* is the real reason why the girl has been jailed inside Eleuteria's house since last Sunday. And she's going to be jailed in there for a long while, Pilar told Dolores two days ago. At least until the policeman's wife gets back to La Habana from visiting her sister who had a baby out of wedlock in Guanabo, a nearby village. *That,* Pilar added, *that* is the real reason

Lucencia is jailed away; *that* and not the mysterious cold Eleuteria claims her daughter is suddenly afflicted with.

"I hope your daughter Lucencia recovers soon from the bad cold she caught the other night," Dolores tells Eleuteria. "It's so bad to stay out so late, and on a full moon night! It's easy to catch something really bad that way."

Eleuteria looks at Dolores with a puzzled look in her eyes. She wasn't expecting any comeback from this *guajiro* woman, this countrywoman, who is placing her, Eleuteria, slightly on the defensive. She is about to open her shriveled mouth again when Dolores says, before she leaves the fruit vendor's shop where they have been conversing, "Please, give my best regards to your other two daughters, Émora and Graciela. Isn't it nice," Dolores adds, her best smile on her face, "to have three daughters of marriageable age like you do? I hope they all get the kinds of husbands they deserve." And with that Dolores leaves the fruit vendor's shop and goes back to her house.

Eleuteria watches her go as she bites her lips and thinks, That countrywoman, she is not as dumb as I thought she was.

Dolores goes home and quietly closes the door behind her. Then she leans against the heavy door and closes her eyes.

She cannot deny to herself that she is hurt. Hurt and angry. Angry at herself for being so stupid, and angry at Eleuteria for being so vicious. No wonder they call her the evil tongue of Luyanó! And yet she knows that what Eleuteria just told her must be true. She knows it because she has often seen the way some of the women in Luyanó, the bad women, look at her husband. And of course, she has certainly seen the way her husband looks back at them. But, after all, he is a man, and he is certainly not blind. As long as he simply looked, what harm could there be in that? she had always thought. But this had obviously gone way beyond plain looking. And she, not knowing anything about it! Not even suspecting anything about it! How could she have been so blind?

Dolores is not dumb. She has often contemplated the possibility of something like this happening. Didn't her father keep several women in Batabanó?

Oh, yes, it was supposed to be a secret, but a secret everybody knew. Her own sisters told Dolores about it many years ago. So if her own father did it, why wouldn't Maximiliano? Criollo men always do that, her sisters told Dolores. Their own husbands, her sisters said, kept several women each. That's part of being a criollo man. Or so her sisters said. And there's nothing you can do about it, they told Dolores. When it happens to you, just pretend you don't know about it. That's what both Fulgencia and Francisca told her to do. Just pretend you don't know anything about it.

But could she?

Dolores has been preparing herself for this. She has often said to herself that when it happened to her she was not going to be hurt or get angry, because she knew that one gains nothing that way. Besides, she also knew that when it happened, whatever it was that happened, it would be just a passing thing, like one of those little hurricanes that make a lot of noise and turn out to be "just a little scare."

But what if this affair of Maximiliano's had not been "just a little scare"?

She's a woman with children. Four of them. A woman with children has to look the other way when something like this happens. A woman with children cannot break.

A woman with children has to bend.

Decisively, she goes to her bedroom and looks at herself in the mirror door of the chifforobe. She hasn't looked at herself in a long time. She sees her hair remains still black and wavy, her figure remains still pleasantly wrapped in a little meat, and her eyes remain still dark and sparkling.

Can that girl in the mirror hold that bull of a man she's married to? She sees the girl in the mirror nodding up and down, and Dolores agrees with her. Of course she can! How could she ever doubt that! Is that girl going to cry about this? Certainly not. Is that girl going to do something about this? Of course she is. The girl in the mirror smiles her most mischievous smile. Maybe what that man of hers needs is a good—

She hears a knock at the door. She fixes her hair and goes to see who it is.

Dolores opens the door and finds standing there, with an angry stare in her eyes, a voluptuous mulatto woman, one of those mulatto women who go to Maximiliano's butcher shop and ask him for the best he's got, something Dolores now knows Maximiliano gladly gives to them.

This woman has straightened shiny black hair, darting black eyes, sensual dark skin, and huge breasts, which she shows plenty of since she is wearing a very low-cut tight dress; in fact, the tightest dress Dolores has ever seen, a dress so tight that it seems it has been sewn onto her skin.

Dolores smiles at the mulatto woman and inquires, "May I help you?"

The mulatto woman is fuming.

"I just came to tell you," she says, the words spurting like venom out of her mouth, "that your husband and I have been sleeping together. And for a long while. I just came to tell you, so you know about it."

So this is Clotilde, Dolores says to herself as she looks at the mulatto woman. She probably would be really beautiful if she didn't wear all of that horrible makeup; and if she were to smile.

Dolores answers her with a kind smile. "Oh, thank you," she says, quietly and discreetly, without raising her voice or getting angry in the least, "but I already knew about it. That husband of mine! He sleeps around with a lot of women like you and then he gets rid of them as soon as they begin to bore him. That's the way that husband of mine is. What can I tell you?" Dolores shrugs her shoulders. "But you know what?" She pauses, looking at the mulatto woman who is now wearing a puzzled look on her face. "There are many, *many* churches in La Habana, I'm sure you know that," she says. And then, gently tapping her own breast with her left hand, she continues. "But there's only *one* cathedral!"

She smiles her famous mischievous smile as she adds, "I'm just telling you this so you know about it."

And then she stays at the door smiling her gentlest smile as she watches the frustrated mulatto woman walk away, her wooden sandals burning the sidewalk as they slap it, sending sparks with every step she takes.

After Dolores sees the raging mulatto woman turn the corner at Hermenegildo's bodega and disappear, walking up the Street of the Bulls, she closes the heavy front door slowly behind her and walks to her bedroom where again she looks at the girl in the mirror, who, looking back at her, begins to laugh.

Marguita, her baby girl of almost five, hearing her mother laugh, rushes to her and begins to laugh with her.

"Is this a new game, Mommy?" she asks.

Dolores gets down to Marguita's level, musses her pretty blond hair, so much like her father's, and then embraces her.

"Yes, *amorcito mío,* little love of mine, this is a new game."

TWO HOURS LATER, the beds now made, the house now dusted, the floors now mopped, the dirty clothes now laundered and drying in the sun, and the dried clothes now ironed, Dolores sits on the patio floor with Marguita by her side. It is almost noon, but in the shaded area of the patio, the cool cement floor of the patio feels refreshing and nice.

Dolores then begins to cut out the headlines of yesterday morning's newspaper and one by one she glues the individual letters on pieces of cardboard, making them look almost like cards in a deck.

Marguita, sitting on the floor by her mother's side, begins to align them in neat piles, the way she has been taught, identifying each letter as she goes. Marguita thinks she and her mother are playing, which of course they are. What Marguita does not realize is that she is learning to read.

Dolores has taught each and every one of her children how to read and write. Dolores herself has a beautiful cursive handwriting for which she won many awards while she was going to that private boarding school here in La Habana where she spent a long part of her life, a school run by impossible-to-deal-with nuns, but who nonetheless gave Dolores a great education. Dolores herself thought at one time that maybe she was destined to be a nun too. But then she ran into that blond, blue-eyed boy with the insolent eyes that made her melt the first time she dared to look into them and, at that moment, her life had taken a completely different course.

The minute she became the butcher's wife, Dolores realized that fancy private schools, like the one she and her sisters went to, were out of the question for her children. How could she and her husband ever be able to afford them? So she decided right then and there that she was going to school her children herself, the best she could. Hadn't she taught Pablo how to read and write? Well, if she had taught Pablo that much, that much she could teach her children as well.

And she has.

Not only do they know how to read and write, but they also know arithmetic, which she, the intelligent daughter of a land-grabbing father, teaches by using real money, money the children get to keep once they give the right answers.

She has also taught the children all they know about Cuban history. Dolores tells them about their great ancestor, the first viceroy of the Indies, who came to Batabanó, then called La Habana, in 1519, and who had fifteen children. And she also tells them how Cuban patriots like their father's grandfather had to leave behind the most important things in life, their wives and children, to fight a long and painful war so brave men like Pablo would not have to die being slaves.

The children also know geography, of which Dolores knows plenty;

and art, of which Dolores knows even more. All of her children know how to draw, which they all do well, especially Merced, her oldest, who has a natural ability for it.

Dolores is an artist herself. She makes her children's clothes as well as her own. And now that there's a little more money coming in, she is redoing whatever little dresses Merced has, making them conform to the fashions of La Habana, so she will not have to feel out of place when she goes to school, a public school on the Street of the Bulls within walking distance of their house where the rest of her children go, including Mani, who is not only back in school again but doing very well, despite helping his father for long hours at the butcher shop every day.

MANI, hard-working Mani, thinks that his kid brother, Gustavo, has it made.

New in the neighborhood, Gustavo is always running and playing on the Street of the Bulls, something Mani only dreams of doing, and Gustavo is no longer afraid of anything or of anybody.

Why should he be?

Every time he gets in a fight with one of the local bullies, one of those young little bulls of the area who claim the street as their own, Gustavo runs to his big brother, always working at the butcher shop, and big brother Mani—he with the bulging muscles and the frightening brow—quickly settles the score. Mani is more than happy to help Gustavo, a kid brother he barely knows, but who Mani knows it is his job to guide and protect.

That's what he told himself after one of those bullies threw one of the many loose rocks found on the Street of the Bulls at Gustavo and almost killed him. It hit him smack on the head, knocking his glasses off and knocking him out cold for what seemed to Mani a very, very long time.

The neighborhood women suddenly had begun screaming and shouting and crying, running around like chickens with their heads cut off, cackling and cackling and praying and praying as they carried the unconscious boy to his mother's house.

When Dolores saw Gustavo, his head totally covered with blood, she became so pale and weak that one of the women had to hold her so she would not fall. However, that lasted but a second. Dolores instantly became her practical self again. She had the boy brought into her bedroom, placed him on top of her bed, took a hand mirror from her dressing table and held it to Gustavo's mouth until the mirror clouded up with Gustavo's breath. It was only after she realized that her son was alive that she began to have heart palpitations and one of the women had to bring her a glass of water, which Dolores drank a little at a time while cleaning the blood off her son's head with her favorite handkerchief, one she had embroidered herself.

When Gustavo woke up, he found himself in his parents' bed, with Dolores sitting next to him, holding his hand and smiling as she cried tears of relief. They were surrounded by a whole lot of the neighboring women, many of whom Gustavo had never seen before, all of them staring at him and crossing themselves as they whispered to each other, "It's a miracle! Truly, truly! A miracle!"

When she heard what the neighboring women were whispering to each other, Dolores, who up to that point had been carefully inspecting every single inch of Gustavo's head to make sure it wasn't split, but who was now satisfied her son seemed to be all right, gently turned around and tenderly took the statue of her Little Virgin she always keeps by her side of the bed in her hands. She kissed it with immense devotion, once and again and again, talking to her Little Virgin as if the little statue were indeed alive, saying, "I knew you wouldn't let me down, my Little Virgin. I knew you wouldn't." And then she presented the statue to Gustavo and told him to kiss it because the Little Virgin had saved his life. Gustavo embarrassedly kissed the statue, much to the satisfaction of the neighboring women surrounding them, who, now that the boy was saved, began looking around the house and making a mental note of everything that was inside.

When Mani found out what had happened to his kid brother, he took to the streets, found the bully who had thrown the rock at Gustavo, knocked him cold in a clean fist fight, made him eat dirt, and let all the other kids in the barrio know that whoever fought Gustavo would have to fight him, Mani, as well. And ever since, Gustavo is no longer afraid of playing in the Street of the Bulls with the other kids. Now he even challenges them and is always looking for fights. He certainly is not going to allow them to call him names anymore, like they all did when he first arrived in Luyanó.

Gustavo knows those kids hate him, because he is so different from them all. Not only is he a country boy, a *guajiro,* an outsider, someone who does not belong in Luyanó, but, in addition to wearing glasses and knowing how to read, he happens to be white, blond, and blue-eyed just like Maximiliano the butcher, his father, while most of the other kids on the street are either mulattoes or Chinese or Negroes. And Gustavo feels they all resent him for that.

DOLORES LOOKS AT Marguita, blond, blue-eyed pretty little Marguita, who looks so much like her father, playing with her letter cards on the nice cool cement patio floor. And as she looks at her baby girl, she begins to think about that man of hers.

Dolores cannot deny how much she enjoys being with Maximiliano, that criollo man who probably keeps a woman behind every palm tree, as her own father did. She cannot deny it is a lot of fun being married to him, and though she still is a little hurt and a little angered by what happened with that Clotilde woman, she also realizes that, given the choice, she would much rather be married to a bull at stud than to a castrated ox, and she cannot deny she likes her bull at stud being just like he is. She cannot deny how much she loves that man. And how much she knows he loves her back. And as she looks at Marguita, neatly going through her play cards and spelling simple words, she cannot deny that he has given her four precious children.

Merced, the oldest, is bullheaded, like her father. And, yes, like Dolores herself, Dolores has to admit. But she has a nice heart, and now that she is becoming a young lady, she is helping a lot with the household chores, even assisting Zenaida in the kitchen in the evenings, after she gets back home from school.

Mani, now a teenager, is very bright, maybe too bright; and very quiet, maybe too quiet. He works hard at school all day, and when he comes home he goes to the butcher shop where he works even harder to help his father. He is strong, as strong as the young bullock he already is.

Gustavo, not yet eleven, is very shy, always hiding his nose in a book. After the incident of the rock, he and his brother, Mani, have become the best of friends: Gustavo always asking Mani to get him out of whatever trouble he finds himself in, and Mani always getting him out of it. Dolores is afraid that Gustavo takes advantage of his big brother, who has a heart the size of a mountain.

Sometimes Mani worries her. She catches him looking in the mid-distance, as if in a trance. She asks him what he is thinking about, and he says, "Nothing." But then she remembers she was a teenager once, and that she too used to look into the mid-distance and think of "nothing," just as her son does. It will go away, she says to herself, and hopes it will go away soon, whatever this "nothing" is Mani is always thinking of.

Marguita, of course, is Dolores's baby girl, the doll Dolores plays with all day long. She is surprising Dolores by how fast she is learning to read. Faster than the other kids. Or maybe Dolores has become a better teacher, maybe that's what it is.

Now, after Marguita's morning reading session is over, she and Dolores have begun to play hide and seek. Marguita loves this game, and she is hiding where she usually hides: behind the semiclosed shutter doors that separate the patio from the living room, a large empty room nobody ever uses that is located at the front of the house.

The primary function of this so-called living room, the fanciest of all of the rooms in Dolores's house, is to store overnight six old, large, and heavy high-back rocking chairs. Early each morning the six old bargain rockers are brought out to the front porch of the house—what Cubans call the *portal,* with the accent on the last syllable—and there they stay until it's time for all to go to bed. At that time Gustavo and Mani have to bring them back in, something they do reluctantly, as they say over and over again, "Why do we have to bring these things in? Why can't we leave them outside during the night? Who is going to steal these old rockers? They weigh a ton!" But as they complain and complain, they bring them in.

Maximiliano and Dolores still do not have much furniture: A few bargain beds, a few bargain chairs, a large bargain table, the old bargain rockers. Money does not come easy when you have to work twelve hours each day to break even, sometimes even more than that. But Maximiliano now owns his butcher shop free and clear. He does have to put in long hours there every single day. However, every single day, he closes the shop and comes home for his two-hour noontime break, which includes a feast of a meal and a well-deserved hour-long siesta, something he thoroughly enjoys, before he goes back to his bulls, his female customers, and his occasional mulatto women.

Marguita is hiding behind the semiclosed shutter doors when Maximiliano comes in for his afternoon meal and siesta. He finds Dolores in the empty living room alone, and thinking that nobody is watching, grabs her and kisses her not on the cheek, the way they kiss in front of their children, but on the mouth, passionately, the way they kiss when they are alone with each other.

Dolores kisses him back, that Clotilde woman already forgotten. And then, realizing all of a sudden that Marguita is hiding behind the shutter doors, she smiles at Maximiliano and points in Marguita's direction.

Maximiliano looks where Dolores is pointing, sees the little girl hiding behind the semiclosed shutter doors, smiles, and says to his wife, "Let her see us. She's got to learn sooner or later." Then he grabs Dolores and kisses her once more.

And then, out of the blue, he begins dancing with her while he sings to her a song he had written for her many years ago, soon after they first met.

> I am so close to being close to you.
> I am so near to being near to you.
> And yet, I know . . . I know I have miles to go.
> Is this my fate?
> To have you close,
> to have you near,
> and yet so far!

Marguita steps out from behind the shutters, looks at her parents as they dance, and, not saying a word, extends her pretty arms toward them. Dolores sees her and, without missing a single step, takes her in her arms, kisses her, and keeps on dancing with her husband, holding Marguita close to her.

> I'll find the way. I'll bring you close to me.
> I'll find the way. I'll have you here with me.
> Don't ask me how.
> Right now I can't tell you how, but . . .
> I'll find the way.
> I'll have you close,
> I'll have you near,
> I'll catch my star!

When Maximiliano stops his singing and thus his dancing with it, Marguita applauds with all her heart. Dolores kisses her baby girl once more and then she hands her to Maximiliano, who lifts Marguita high into the air and makes her feel like she's flying.

That afternoon, after they all had their noontime meal, while Merced is putting Marguita to bed to take her siesta, Marguita asks her sister, "Merced? Mommy and Pappy . . . are they *novios*? Sweethearts?"

Merced, not knowing how to answer, in turn asks Marguita, "Why do you ask? Do you think they are?"

Marguita nods her head up and down.

"Why do you think they are?" Merced asks Marguita.

"Because I saw them kiss on the mouth this afternoon," the little girl answers, innocently, making Merced become all red in the face.

LATER ON THAT NIGHT, after Dolores and Maximiliano have found completion in each other, they both lie in bed naked, sweaty, exhausted, embracing each other under a thin cotton sheet.

Maximiliano, facing up, has his left arm around his wife, whose head lies on his chest, her long black wavy hair brushing softly against him.

Dolores raises her head, looks at him, and notices he is not looking at her but at the high plaster ceiling. Then, placing her head in the same position it was before, she smiles to herself, and whispers. "I almost forgot to tell you. A friend of yours came to visit me today while you were at the shop."

Maximiliano keeps looking up at the high plaster ceiling, focusing on nothing. Paying little attention to her, he answers unconsciously, almost mechanically.

"Oh, yeah? Who?"

"Clotilde," Dolores says softly, as if the name meant nothing to her. But as she says it she rubs her hand against her husband's chest.

Maximiliano, half asleep, still looking at the ceiling, says, "Clotilde?" He honestly cannot place the name. He shakes his head. "Clotilde who?" he adds as he looks at Dolores.

Dolores raises her head and looks back at him, smiling her most mischievous smile.

"Oh!" Maximiliano says.

Dolores nods her head.

"Yes, that Clotilde," she says, still smiling.

There's a short pause, a short pause that is thoroughly enjoyed by Dolores, who smiles as she looks at her husband.

Maximiliano is at first puzzled by her look, but after a moment he smiles back at Dolores. "Twenty-three weeks and four days is a long long time without a woman," he says. Dolores is about to say something when he interrupts her by covering her lips with his index finger. "Particularly," he adds, "if that woman is you." And then he kisses the tip of her nose. "I see there's something else you'd like to know. I can read it in those impish eyes of yours. Isn't there?"

"Yes." She faces him, looking at him right in the eye, trying to be as serious as she can. "Is there anything that woman did to you that I have never done and that you would like me to do the next time we make love?"

There's a short pause, a short pause that this time is thoroughly enjoyed by Maximiliano, who smiles as he looks at his wife of fourteen years.

"No," he says, staring deep into her eyes. "You know how you and I look deep into each other's eyes as we make love?" Dolores nods. "I love the sparks your eyes send to me while I'm inside of you. I would not trade that look of yours for anything. That never happened when I was with Clotilde. When I was with her . . ." He pauses, and smiles at Dolores. "You may not believe it, but when I was with her, I just closed my eyes and pretended it was you in bed under me." He pauses again. Then adds, "But . . . it didn't work. It just wasn't the same."

Dolores tightens her embrace around her husband's chest.

"Tell me," she asks, teasingly, "would you have liked it better if it had worked?"

"Of course I would!" Maximiliano answers immediately as he laughs. And then it is his turn to face her with those insolent eyes of his. "Because that way I could get rid of you!" He bites her lips and adds jokingly, "How can anybody who almost became a nun be as knowledgeable as you are in bed? That is something I will never understand in my entire life!"

Dolores kisses his chest.

"I guess I just had it in me."

"Yeah, you probably did. But you still needed someone to bring it out, didn't you?"

She lifts her head and looks at him, already half asleep.

"I guess I did," she says. "I still do." She pauses and then adds, "And so do you."

And then, with her most mischievous smile on her lips, Dolores,

"The Cathedral," closes her eyes and falls asleep on her husband's chest, thanking her Little Virgin because she did not have to do what her older sisters did, what both her older sisters told her to do.

She thanked her Little Virgin because she did not have to pretend.

★ ★ ★

16

Merced, now almost fifteen, is becoming a young lady really fast. Already the neighborhood boys have begun to notice this criollo beauty, who, like her mother, is pleasantly wrapped in a little meat. She has beautiful wavy dark hair, which she keeps trimmed short to go with the times, and even more beautiful eyes, really dark, almost black, with long black silky eyelashes. She is still in school, and she has a great teacher, Señora González, who thinks Merced is very talented in art.

Merced is always drawing and sketching on any blank piece of paper she can get her hands on. She loves to use the plain brown butcher shop wrapping paper, which she transforms, by using a little bit of black charcoal and a little bit of white chalk, into beautiful drawings, where the color of the paper is made to represent the color of the skins of those people and animals Merced loves to sketch.

She works fast, with an intensity that is astonishing. Do you want to see her mad? Just interrupt her while she's in the middle of one of those drawings. Just do that and you'll see a female bull rush at you and let you have it.

Don't you let criollo women fool you. Don't you let their sweet frailness and quiet shyness take you for a ride.

Behind those weak, timid, sugary façades there lie strong, bold, sharp wills that roar through the impossible, capable of anything once they make up their mind. Criollo women are bull-like too, and don't you ever forget it.

Why do you think Spaniards don't use the female of the species in a bullfight? We are not talking cows here. We are talking female bulls, of the same wild species as the male bulls used in Spanish bullfights; a species still kept artificially wild to this day; a wild species that has never been tamed.

Those female bulls have horns, just as the male bulls have. Their horns are as sharp and as deadly as the male bull's horns. The female bulls can gore you as easily as the male bull. And yet they are not used in bullfights. Why? you ask. Because they are relentless in their pursuit of vengeance, that is why. Nature has endowed them with a strong will to protect their young, and when provoked they are murderous.

The bulls fight valiantly, with honorable nobility. As far as the bull is concerned, during the bullfight, he thinks that he is fighting a rival bull, just as they do in rutting season. And the bull thinks, just as he does in rutting season, that once one of the fighting bulls is declared the winner, the loser is let go, humiliated yes, but alive. The bull is not aware that a Spanish bullfight is to the death. He thinks that the worst that can happen to him is that he'll end up with his tail between his legs, no longer proud and arrogant, true. But alive.

Not the female. She fights to the death from the very start. She is not provoked as easily in the arena as the male is, but once provoked, beware! Because the bull closes his eyes when he rushes at you, but the female doesn't. She rushes at you with her eyes wide open.

You may jump out of the way of a bull coming at you with his eyes closed and evade his lethal horns. But you can never escape the rushing female's horns once her fiery eyes are set on you. Never. Her fight is to the death.

And it is not going to be hers.

Merced's astrological sign is Taurus, the bull. So if you add her astrological bullheadedness to her criollo woman bullheadedness, you end up with *some* bullheaded person! And since she is a female bull, when anybody gets in her way, she attacks with her eyes wide open. And to the death. Neither Gustavo nor Marguita ever attempt to do anything that may bring out that special bull-like quality Merced is becoming famous for. They have learned the hard way.

But not so Mani.

Mani loves to stir the bull in his older sister. He is a bull himself, and a male, and because he is a male he is not about to let Merced, a female, get the best of him. So he is always goading Merced, measuring how far he can go before Merced's bull comes out, which doesn't take much when Mani is the one doing the goading.

Merced has infinite patience with her brother Gustavo, who is always surprising her with little poems he writes to her and that he leaves under her pillow; and with Marguita, because Merced has adopted her as if she were her own daughter. But let Mani just move close to her and she immediately begins to look at him with the fiery eyes she reserves exclusively for Mani and which seem to be saying: "I'm looking at you. Beware. Beware." This, of course, only manages to excite Mani, who cannot wait to do something to disturb his dearest older sister, Merced.

Mani knows how much Merced hates being interrupted while she is drawing.

Even Dolores looks twice before she asks Merced to help her set the table, or sweep the floor, or what have you, just to make sure she is not interrupting her daughter while she is at work. She knows how extremely volatile Merced is for she has experienced quite a few of Merced's eruptions—never aimed at Dolores—eruptions that would make the mightiest volcano green with envy. So Dolores looks twice and makes sure Merced is done with whatever project or drawing she is working on before Dolores asks for her help.

Besides, there's enough of the artist in Dolores to understand Merced.

Dolores herself does not like being interrupted when she is cutting fabric to make a dress, because once fabric is cut, it is cut. You have to live with what you cut. And since fabric is expensive, Dolores just buys the minimum amount of yards required to make a dress, and every little bit counts. That is why Dolores waits until all of her children are in bed before she starts cutting a new dress. Dolores understands Merced's need to concentrate while she is drawing. Dressmaking is Dolores's art. Drawing is Merced's.

Interrupting Merced seems to be Mani's art.

Whenever Dolores hears violent screaming in her house, she shakes her head and calmly goes to the dining room, where Merced does her work on top of the large dining table. All Dolores has to do the minute she walks in the room is look at Mani, now a growing teenager. And Mani, who at heart is but a true angel, big and strong and powerful as he is, goes to one of the large armchairs at either side of the serving buffet, which occupies one wall of the dining room, and sits down.

"Five minutes," that's all Dolores has to say.

And Mani sits in his punishment chair for five long minutes, and while he sits he ponders what he can do next to make Merced's life miserable.

Dolores has a great technique to deal with her children. She never screams or shouts at them, or shows any sign of anger whatsoever. Long ago she learned, from the nuns who ran the private school where she and her sisters spent most of their childhood, that anger gets you nowhere. What the nuns did, which is what Dolores does, is to punish the misbehaving child by telling him or her to sit for a given period of time in what Dolores calls punishment chairs, two thronelike armchairs placed at either side of a large serving buffet in the dining room.

This dining-room set is a recent addition to Dolores's house. It replaced the old bargain table and chairs they first had when Dolores and her children arrived from Batabanó two and a half years ago. And it replaced it with style.

In contrast to the simple look of the rest of the sparse furnishings elsewhere in the house, this dining-room set is unbelievable. According to whoever looks at it, it is either the greatest criollo-baroque fantasy ever or the greatest of all frightening nightmares.

It is made of Cuban ebony, not ebonized wood, but *real* ebony that is black as coal. The entire set is heavily sculpted with gryphons and gargoyles staring at you. The large dining table normally seats ten but it is expandable to seat sixteen, something Dolores does at Christmas. With the table came eight regular dining chairs and two armchairs, the famous punishment chairs, thronelike in their massive scale. There is also a serving buffet, filled with drawers and drawers, and a huge china cabinet, glass fronted, where Dolores's never-to-be-used blue-and-white dishes are displayed. The real everyday dishes they all eat from are stored vertically in a dish rack located in the kitchen, where Zenaida is queen.

This new dining-room set was hand carved by a notorious cabinet-maker—a buddy of Maximiliano—with the same knife with which he killed his wife and her lover the day he found them in bed together.

He must have carved it while horrible doubts were going through his head about whether or not his wife really was placing horns on his head, because the entire set is filled with devillike faces staring at you, all of them with huge horns on their heads.

Obviously, this cabinetmaker friend of Maximiliano's did not want to be known as a *cabrón*.

There is no worse insult with which to hit a criollo man than to call him a *cabrón*. That's what Cubans call men whose wives sleep with men other than their husbands: *¡Cabrón!*

It is such a horrible insult that it is almost worse than being called queer, that's how bad a *cabrón* is to Cubans.

Criollo men want their women only to themselves, never to be shared with anybody else, under penalty of death. That's the way of the bulls. And that's the way of their women.

Cuban women do not ever lose their maiden names. After a Cuban woman marries, she signs her maiden name and then she adds, proudly, "of So-and-so." To a Cuban woman that little word "of" means: "I belong to a man. He is my rightful owner. He possesses me. He can do with me *whatever* he wants." That's the law of the land, where men are men, and women are men's possessions.

But every so often a woman challenges that law, sleeps with another man, and places horns on her husband's forehead. Once that happens, the man becomes a *cabrón*. And once a man becomes a *cabrón,* there is only one way and one way only that he can clear his name and become a man again: By killing both wife and lover. The biblical Jews tell you to stone the adulterous woman. Criollo men tell you to stone the both of them.

And what a life for the poor man who doesn't do it!

Family disowns him, friends laugh at him, the whole barrio scorns and shuns him. When people see the *cabrón* go by, they raise their hands at him with their index and pinky fingers extended out, holding the other fingers tight, making what they call the sign of the horns, and laugh derisively at the *cabrón* in his own face. They all do it, including his adulterous wife.

The *cabrón* will wear the stigma of the horns for life unless he does as he must: Two easy shots of a gun. Or two easy thrusts of a knife. That's all it takes. It is either that or an insufferable life, not only for the *cabrón,* but for all of his family as well because, how can a family like that be any good? A family that procreated that kind of a—

No. "Man" is no longer the word to apply to him, because he is not a man anymore.

You see, he is a *cabrón*.

But let the *cabrón* shoot those two easy gunshots. Let him stab those two easy hearts. Let him shed the cleansing blood. Let him do that, and suddenly the same people who laughed at him begin to applaud him as they look at him with admiration and pride.

"Now, there goes a real man," you will hear mothers tell their children as the former *cabrón*—who no longer is one—parades by, his chest bursting with pride, his head held high, and his gaze fixed on a criollo god who smiles down on him because justice—criollo justice—has been done; the same criollo god who smiles at the winning cock in Cuban cockfights, no matter how badly hurt and how badly wounded that cock may be.

Oh, sure, the killer goes to jail.

But do you think any Cuban man or woman would find him guilty of anything? Of course not.

A criollo man has got to do what he's got to do. This man in jail just did what anyone else would have done if he had been in his shoes.

Jail? Sure he goes to jail.

But just to walk out a free man, a proud man, a man women look at with respect and, yes, with desire, because that man is a real man, a bull of a man. A Cuban criollo cock.

Maximiliano's buddy, the cabinetmaker who carved that incredible dining set in Maximiliano's house with the same knife with which he killed his wife and her lover, needed money urgently to pay for his lawyers and for his wife's funeral. Maximiliano traded a few pounds of meat for it, and was able to get that incredible dining set for a song.

And now, when people first see it, after they all go "Aahhh . . ." Maximiliano enjoys retelling the story of the heavily sculpted set and of his now-famous buddy, the criollo man who carved it, a story that grows more and more wild and baroque every time he tells it.

★ ★ ★

17

The baby girl was born little and blue.

"Just like an iris," says her mother, Dolores, as she embraces her just-born daughter who has been placed next to her mother's heart, letting the baby girl listen to a heart that seems to be ticking "I love you. I love you. I love you."

Manuel, the doctor who delivered the baby girl, is talking to Maximiliano, giving him the bad news. "There is something wrong with the girl," he says. "I would have to conduct further testing, but just from looking at her, I believe there is something wrong with her heart."

Maximiliano sighs deeply. He knows how much Dolores wants this baby. She had a miscarriage not long after she first arrived in La Habana, which broke her heart. For a long while she would burst out crying for no reason at all. Maximiliano would embrace her, and Dolores would sink her beautiful criollo face in his chest, and say, "It's nothing. It's nothing." But Maximiliano knew. Maximiliano can stand anything, *anything,* but seeing Dolores cry. As far as he knows, she is always that girl who stole his heart with a single glance, even though to this day she says it was he who was staring at her. His love for her is and will always be the intense love a criollo man feels for his wife, a wife who is now in a hospital bed holding a baby as beautiful as an iris, with a wounded heart. "Is there anything we can do?" he asks Manuel.

"First we have to determine what, if anything, is wrong with the girl. I may be mistaken. I hope I am. But if I am not, then we will talk. Now you go inside and meet your new baby daughter. I'll set the wheels in motion on this side."

Maximiliano enters the hospital room Dolores is in, her baby girl by her side. He has never seen his baby daughter. He walks into the room and he sees her, silently lying next to her mother's heart. How long does it take to fall in love with a baby? That's how long it took Maximiliano to fall in love with his baby girl, a baby girl so little he is afraid to touch her. He extends his huge callused hands to her, then hesitates, and dares to touch the tip of the baby's hair with just one finger.

He says nothing. He doesn't have to. He looks at Dolores and sees in Dolores's eyes that she knows that this baby is special. Her baby girl Iris is not like her other babies, those who have grown up to become young men and young women. And yet do you love less simply because you love just for a little time? Love doesn't know about time. It sparks and then it lasts forever, a heaven-sent, everlasting fire that keeps your loved one alive for eternity, long after that loved one is gone.

Iris is gone.

The little blue baby girl was wrapped delicately by her mother's hands with the finest white linen that had been embroidered by Dolores as she stayed awake night after night watching her baby girl debate whether to stay or to go. But the baby girl chose to go, and her mother herself wrapped her the way you wrap the most precious object you ever held in your life. And then Dolores herself placed her baby girl inside a tiny box that had been lined with white silk. Dolores would not allow anyone else to do it. She herself closed the white lid, but not before she placed a blue iris next to her child inside.

When they took her baby girl away, Dolores felt that part of her own heart was leaving her, to accompany her daughter inside a white box, covered with a white shroud.

THEY ARE now back home, after the funeral.

It has been a long, long day, but now everybody is gone, and the children are all asleep. Merced has behaved like a grown woman. Last night, after she put Marguita to bed—little six-year-old Marguita who did not really understand what was happening—Merced took care of serving dark Cuban coffee to all the people who kept vigil, staying overnight with the family who was spending one last night with Iris, as the baby girl had been baptized before she went to sleep.

But that was last night, a long long time ago.

Tonight Maximiliano and Dolores are alone in their bedroom. They are still wearing their mourning clothes. He is all dressed in white, a white-linen suit that had been freshly ironed this morning but which is badly wrinkled by now. He has a black band around his left arm.

Dolores refused to wear black for her child. She too is all in white, like a bride. She is not even wearing a black band on her sleeve. Only around her heart, which nobody can see but her husband.

Maximiliano looks at her. She is not crying. She ran out of tears long ago. She is not saying anything. She also ran out of words long ago.

Maximiliano smiles at her. "Do you realize how lucky Iris was?" he says to his wife, who looks at him with a puzzled look on her face. "She knew life," Maximiliano adds. "She tasted her mother's milk." He pauses. "You never did."

Dolores is looking at him, but her thoughts are far away, on a pretty little girl blue, with a blue little heart, suckling at her mother's breasts. The thought is too much for her to bear. She leans heavily on Maximiliano, who embraces her, that woman he loves beyond eternity, that wife with the broken heart, sheltering her tight to him. He asks her, whispering in her ear, "Don't you think her life needs to be celebrated?"

They are standing, next to each other, Maximiliano gently embracing his wife who is sinking her head in his chest, each of them holding the other; each of them holding on to the other. The room is dark, lighted only by the moon, which is casting dark-blue shadows around them.

It is only now that Maximiliano the butcher can give himself permission to cry, now, alone like this, holding his wife, in the dark where he cannot be seen. And as he cries, he begins to hum softly in his wife's ears the song he had written for her many, many years ago.

Then, holding on to his wife, who is leaning heavily in his arms, while he whispers their song in her ears, they begin to move gently ever so gently to the music, as they dance a danzón for Iris, to celebrate the beauty of her life, to celebrate the beauty of it all.

★ ★ ★

18

Mani, who got home from school a few minutes ago, has just put on a freshly ironed clean white apron and is on his way out the door to the butcher shop across La Calzada when Merced arrives home jumping up and down with great excitement.

"Mommy! Mommy! Guess what! Mommy! *Mommy!*"

Merced, who is very late today, ignores Mani as she bypasses him. She rushes into the dining room where she finds Dolores working on a dress for Marguita, who will be seven in two weeks and wants a new dress for her upcoming birthday, a dress made up of *new* fabric, not a dress made over from one Merced had before. Merced kisses her mother and jumping up and down breathlessly tells Dolores that she has just been accepted to the Academia de San Alejandro, the fine arts academy.

Señora González, Merced's teacher, unbeknownst to Merced herself, had applied to the academy in Merced's name. She didn't tell the young girl in case she was rejected, but she sent to the faculty of the academy seven of Merced's drawings—with her name covered up since the competition is anonymous—and today the answer had come in the mail addressed to Señora González, at Merced's school.

Señora González asked Merced to stay in school for a few minutes after the last classroom session of the day, and it was then that she surprised Merced with the great news. She explained to Merced that at the academy all expenses are totally paid for, except for art supplies and transportation. And that out of two hundred seven applications, the academy had accepted only thirty, and that she, Merced, had been one of the few girls accepted. Since the drawings are always sent anonymously, the awards are given exclusively on the merits of the work submitted to the faculty panel that selects the most talented students for the incoming year, which means that the faculty must have really liked Merced's sepia drawings a lot.

Merced is listening to all of this and she feels that she is in a different world. Is this really happening to her? She sat down when Señora González told her about being accepted at the academy. She still feels this is all a dream, and Señora González, who knows her well, tells her, "It's true, Merced. Pinch yourself. It is all true. Here is the letter." And after Señora González gives Merced the letter that says that she, Merced, is to begin school at the academy next semester, Señora González pulls out something wrapped by herself in a beautiful shiny red paper with a bow made of a real red silk ribbon.

"Here," Señora González tells Merced, "this is a present for you."

"For me?" Merced looks at her teacher, who nods her head up and down as she looks at Merced with a mixture of love and pride in her eyes. "May I open it now?"

"Go ahead," the teacher says.

Merced undoes the bow very carefully, not to hurt the beautiful red ribbon and as carefully she unfolds the shiny red paper, hoping that she may be able to reuse it someday. And then her eyes light up. There, in her hands, is a beautifully bound book, with the name *Apollo* embossed in gold on its cover.

She opens it and sees that the book is profusely illustrated with beautiful drawings and photographs of Greek and Hellenic architecture, sculpture, bas-reliefs, frescoes, vases. Merced looks at Señora González not knowing what to say.

"Look at the front page," Señora González says.

Merced turns to the first page of the book and there, in Señora González's own beautiful handwriting, she finds something written in an alphabet she cannot understand, Εὐχαριστῶ, and underneath it, Señora González's own signature.

Señora González gets close to Merced, and pointing to the writing on the page she says, "It's a Greek word, written in Greek. It is pronounced Eh-far-is-*toh*, with the accent on the last syllable. It means 'thank you.' "

Merced looks at her teacher, bewildered.

Señora González adds, "A teacher always dreams of finding a student who will make years and years of training and dealing with thousands of misbehaving students and hundreds of ununderstanding colleagues seem worthwhile. And when a teacher finds such a student, all a teacher can say is: 'Thank you. *Efaristó.*' " She smiles at Merced and tells her, "This book is the required book for your history of art course next semester. I thought you could get a head start." Then Señora González moves closer to Merced and turns the pages of the book. "Isn't it beautiful?" she says.

"Oh, yes!" Merced answers.

"Use it in good health. And now, go! Your mother may be getting nervous that you are not home yet."

Merced is home, and she is jumping up and down and she is showing her mother, Dolores, the book *Apollo,* and the letter from San Alejandro, and the seven drawings that won her admission to the academy, and she is so excited she can hardly believe this is really happening, but she feels the book with caressing hands, and the book seems real.

Pilar, the glass-eyed lady next door who is always looking through the semiclosed shutters with her good eye, cannot stand the commotion any longer and daring to open the shutters in full asks, demands actually, "What is going on? What is happening?" And when she is told, she congratulates Merced and Dolores, and within five minutes the word spreads around the barrio like wildfire and soon everybody in the entire neighborhood knows about Merced and her being accepted at the academy, and neighbors are all coming to the house to look at Merced's drawings and when they see them they all go "Aahhh . . ."

Dolores makes pot after pot of coffee and everybody is telling her what a great daughter Merced is, and Dolores says, "All my children are great." Maximiliano, who has seen all of these women rush into his house, charges in, still in his bloody apron, and after he's told the great news, he embraces Merced and Dolores and he opens a bottle of expensive rum and shoots down a shot in Merced's name before he charges back to the butcher shop, where Mani has been left alone to take care of all of those women in line waiting for meat for their evening meal.

And soon it's evening meal time, and soon it is time to go to bed, and soon all the lights are out, and soon you can hear Maximiliano, who has been drinking more of that great smooth rum to celebrate his daughter's achievements, snore deep and soundly as the tropical moon casts dark-blue shadows all over the patio of the house.

Mani, stealthily, surreptitiously, goes into Merced's room and finds Merced sound asleep holding in her hands the book *Apollo.*

He tiptoes to where she is and little by little, with the utmost care, steals the book from his sister's hands and then goes back to the room he shares with his kid brother, Gustavo, the little brother who is always getting into fights he never intends to fight.

Mani means to hide the book.

He sits on his bed, wondering where he can hide it best so he won't be blamed for it but so Merced will *definitely* know that it was he who hid it. As he thinks about it, he opens the book and sees several drawings and photographs of naked men and women who make him laugh, but he stifles his laughter with his left hand, what he calls his *good* hand. Then he lies back on his bed, still holding the book *Apollo* in his hands, and begins to leaf through it back to front. As he does that, his eyes open up, suddenly, to a world he did not know existed. And just as he once longed to be close to the man with the bloodstained apron and the head of an emperor he calls father, Mani, no longer a boy but not yet a man, now begins to long to be part of this other world, this strange new world of beauty he has uncovered in his older sister's book.

He decides not to hide the book *Apollo*.

Stealthily again, tiptoeing again, Mani goes back to Merced's room and there, very carefully so as not to wake Merced up, he returns the book to his sister's hands. Then he moves back to his own room and falls asleep, dreaming.

Two days later his back bends under the heavy weight of dead bulls, and he sees his arms bulge with strong muscles that are growing stronger and stronger by the minute. The white-marble counter under his care shines bright from his constant wiping of it, reflecting the face of a young bullock, Mani himself, who stares back at him with a frightening brow, frightening because he is frightened. Mani is frightened of his own dreams. But since he knows that bullocks like him are not supposed to be frightened by anything, he quickly dismisses those dreams out of his eyes and goes back to the walk-in cooler, where it is nice and cold, grabs another one of the dead bulls hanging from the large meat hooks, brings it to the huge butcher-block table in the middle of the butcher shop, and begins to cut it the way he's been taught, with the sharpest of knives and the softest of pressure, always in the same direction, not to bruise the meat fibers, so it will taste its best.

Mani is alone in the store. Maximiliano left last night for a fishing trip with his buddy Manuel, the doctor, and Mani is in full charge of the butcher shop all day long today. Saturday. This Saturday is going to be a long, long day.

He begins to cut the bull in pieces, and he concentrates fiercely and exclusively on what he is doing, not daring to think of tomorrow, but living this today, this ever-present today that stains his hands red with blood as well as his brow, when he wipes the cold sweat from it.

He longs for the night to come.

Because in the middle of the night, in the silence of the room he shares with his kid brother, Gustavo, in the silence of that room, with his kid brother fast asleep, unknown to anyone else, he steals again Merced's book *Apollo,* opens it again to any page, and under the light of the tropical moon, he travels again into a world he longs to be in, to belong to. A world which to him is as important as an anchor is to a boat in a tropical hurricane.

And Mani, not yet fifteen, after returning the book *Apollo* to his sister's caressing hands, falls asleep holding on to this anchor while lulled by the singing breezes that seem to be whispering in his ears: "*Efaristó,* Apollo! *Efaristó*!"

★ ★ ★

19

No sooner has Merced begun going to the Academy of Fine Arts than the price of sugar, Cuba's only industry, collapses. The waves generated by the stock market earthquake that took place on Black Thursday in the New York City of 1929 finally reached the island two years later, and poverty is everywhere. As the Cuban saying goes, "When sugar is high, we all gorge. When sugar is low, we all starve." Nineteen thirty-one does not look too promising, even in La Habana. The time of starvation has just begun.

Business at the butcher shop slows down almost to a halt. Thank God for the mulatto women kept by the Chinese men in the opium business who keep the butcher shop going. They keep asking Maximiliano for the best he's got, and they keep getting it. But the rest of the people on the Street of the Bulls, how can they afford the luxury of meat on the table when they can barely afford rice and beans? If only a way could be found to bring down the price of a pound of meat! And such a way is found when the pound of meat in the butcher shop suddenly becomes fourteen ounces instead of sixteen, which instantly drops the price per "pound" and causes business to boom. Of course, this was done secretly, with the encouragement, consent, and approval of the city meat inspector, whose idea this was, and who collects a few extra pesos from Maximiliano once a month, every time he comes to seal the weighing scales.

While everybody in the little island is getting skinny, the city inspectors are getting fat; but not as fat as the mayors of cities, who collect from the inspectors; and not as fat as the senators, who collect from the mayors; and not as fat as the president himself, who collects from everybody. So those two little ounces of meat in every pound stolen from the people who cannot afford it to begin with end up in the fat bellies of the aging bulls who run the country. But since everybody knows about it and everybody does it, well, then, everything is all right, as it should be. In fact, it would have been foolish not to do it.

The night the city meat inspector made that suggestion, after everybody was in bed, Maximiliano told Mani, who was not so sure they were doing the right thing, "One thing you must never do, son, is to run against the bulls when they are rushing down the street. Only a crazy person would do that. When the bulls charge down the street, there are two choices you can make: Either you step out of the way, the way most people around here do, or else you run with them. All the other butchers in Cuba are running with them. If we don't do as they all do, we'd be out of business in seconds. So, I ask you, Mani, what else can we do?"

Mani, now a grown man, shook his head, not knowing what to say. "After all, son," Maximiliano added, "if that's what the city meat inspector suggests, who are we, just a pair of *guajiros,* to say no, eh?" He winked an eye at his son, who looked at him and, not saying a single word, had no choice but to smile. What is the sense of arguing with this man? He had seen that Maximiliano had already made up his mind. And once his mind is set . . . it is set. And Maximiliano had decided to run with the bulls.

The city meat inspector comes to the butcher shop once a month, seals the measuring scales, places his signature over the seal, gets a few pesos under the table, and leaves for the next butcher shop to do the very same thing. It all sounds great. But there's a catch. And the catch is that not all weighing scales had to be sealed.

Sure, the scales weighing food to be sold to the public, those have to be sealed. Maximiliano's scale is sealed. And so is Hermenegildo's, whose bodega, the dry-goods store located on the corner directly across La Calzada from the butcher shop, also sells by the pound.

Hermenegildo's scale is inspected and sealed by a different city inspector, but a city inspector whose pound happens to measure only fourteen ounces also.

Maximiliano knows it. When he agreed to do as the city meat inspector suggested, the first thing Maximiliano did was to ask Dolores to go to Hermenegildo's bodega and buy a pound of black beans. When Dolores brought it back to Maximiliano, he placed it on his scale and, lo and behold! Hermenegildo's pound of black beans read exactly one pound on Maximiliano's scale, the one that had just been sealed by the city meat inspector. That's how Maximiliano found out that the scale across La Calzada was as well sealed and as accurate as his was.

However, scales to dispatch drugs do not have to be sealed.

And it so happens that on the corner that is on the other side of the Street of the Bulls directly across from the butcher shop, the corner that is catty-corner from Hermenegildo's bodega, on that corner is located the pharmacy of Señor Pauli.

This is a neatly organized old-fashioned pharmacy, a small one-story shop that smells of camphor and alcohol, where prescriptions are filled the old-fashioned way by the hand of Señor Pauli himself, using two grams of this, one gram of that. To do this, Señor Pauli uses a very accurate and well-balanced scale where the pound still measures sixteen very accurate ounces on the dot.

Eleuteria, the evil tongue of Luyanó, normally a vociferous woman, is today screaming her lungs out and lashing venomous insults to Maximiliano because her pound of meat, the one she has just bought and the one she has just checked at Señor Pauli's pharmacy, that pound of expensive meat weighs only fourteen ounces!

Maximiliano, whose motto has always been "The customer is always right," lives by those words, and now, as cool as a cucumber, Maximiliano calmly answers the old lady, his voice as soft and as gentle as can be.

"Señora Eleuteria, I am so glad you have called my attention to this fact. But"—he adds as he points to the seal on his scale—"as you can see, this scale has been sealed by the city meat inspector and if you look real close . . ." With his hand he invites Eleuteria to get close to the scale and look at it, something Eleuteria the evil tongue of Luyanó manages to do, bringing her evil eye to within an inch of the seal. "If you look real close," Maximiliano continues, "you can well see that the original seal, dated and signed by the city meat inspector himself three weeks ago, is intact. That it has not been broken."

His voice is melodious and soothing as he adds, "Maybe the inspector made a mistake. Maybe his measuring tools were not properly calibrated. That I don't know. I would personally find that hard to believe, him being such a reputable city inspector. You know how the city must give him the best there is to inspect with. But, if you allow me, may I ask you something?"

He smiles his best smile at the skinny old lady with the beady eyes.

"Have you tried weighing the package of meat you bought here at Hermenegildo's scale across La Calzada?"

The old lady stares at him, sparks flying out of her evil eyes.

"Have you?"

The old lady has no choice but to nod her head up and down and admit she has.

"And what did it read?" asks Maximiliano, in his most angelic voice.

Eleuteria, who up to this moment has been shouting and gesticulating violently, aware that all of the other customers in the butcher shop are staring at her, now decides to lower her voice as she gives her answer to Maximiliano.

"One pound," she whispers.

"Excuse me, Señora Eleuteria," says the butcher of Luyanó, "with all of this noise I couldn't hear what you just said. Could you speak a little louder, please?"

He says this to Eleuteria, but as he speaks he is looking at all the other customers in the butcher shop who are carefully listening to what the old lady has to say. Maximiliano pauses and looks at the old lady. For a moment the street noises seem to disappear completely, as if to frame the old lady's answer.

"One pound," she shouts, angrily.

"Oh!" says Maximiliano, the image of candor. "Did you say . . . *one pound*?"

He pauses for a long while, smiles winningly at all of his other customers, and then lowers his voice as he addresses Eleuteria again.

"Señora Eleuteria, has it occurred to you that perhaps, just perhaps, the scale of Señor Pauli may not be correct?"

Maximiliano lets the thought sink into the thick skull of Eleuteria. The other customers are still listening silently to their conversation. Maximiliano continues.

"He is getting on in years, Señor Pauli, is he not? Have you seen the thick glasses he wears?"

Eleuteria is looking at him with a puzzled look on her face, a mixture of admiration and hatred, a look Maximiliano answers with his most soothing smile. Now that he has the old lady where he wants her, Maximiliano—great hunter that he is—goes for the kill.

"But, nonetheless," he says loud enough for the entire world of the Street of the Bulls to hear, "why don't you let me give your name to the city meat inspector next time he comes, and maybe you would like to file an *official complaint* with him."

This "official complaint" bit works really well.

No one on the Street of the Bulls wants to play around with the law and, least of all, challenge it.

Maximiliano sees the doubt in Eleuteria's old tired eyes, small and beady, which, when added to her long skinny neck and her balding head, make her look more like a vulture than like the cranky little old lady she is.

He quickly adds, "However, just in case you may be right, here, take this for your girls."

And with his fancy butcher knife, the one with the curved blade he uses only to carve the most expensive cuts of meat, so sharp it can split a hair in two, with that knife he slices a bit of a really good cut of meat, does not weigh it, wraps it himself in brown wax paper, and hands it to the old lady as he says, "The inspector is due here in a couple of days, next Thursday, in case you would like to talk to him."

Eleuteria does not come back the following Thursday, of course.

But given the fact that she is who she is—no wonder they call her the evil tongue of Luyanó; and given the fact that by complaining she got a good chunk of *filete,* the best possible cut of beef; the following Tuesday—the day she knows meat is freshly delivered to the butcher shop—she is back there again, complaining again about the so-called incorrect weight of her meat, as measured again on Señor Pauli's scale.

"Señora Eleuteria," Maximiliano states simply, "I told you last week that the meat inspector was due here last Thursday, and look at the date on the new seal."

Eleuteria looks at the seal.

It is true what the butcher says. It is dated and signed as of last Thursday.

"Probably Señor Pauli's scale is not right," Maximiliano says. "It does not have to be sealed by the law, like mine is. Or like Hermenegildo's scale across La Calzada is." And then he smiles at her with the most candid of eyes, but eyes that are filled with mischief, as he adds, "But I'm sure you know *that,* Señora Eleuteria, don't you?"

Eleuteria, who has run out of arguments, raises her indignant head and looks the butcher in the eye, the very image of insolence. And suddenly she is aware that something is not right. She looks deep into Maximiliano's eyes and seeing the smirk in his eyes, she suddenly knows she's defeated.

She is fuming.

Her? Eleuteria? Defeated?

And of all people, by this damn *guajiro? That* would be the day! She has never felt so humiliated. What can she do?

Eleuteria looks at him, fire burning in her eyes, and Maximiliano, always a gentleman, says to her, "But here," he pauses as he looks for something behind the counter.

Oh, good! the old lady says to herself. The trick works! She's getting a consolation prize, like she did last time. Her faith in herself has suddenly been restored. I'm going to do this every week from now on! she thinks. And she smiles for the first time, in eager anticipation. Maybe she is not defeated after all. Maybe she is not defeated at all.

"Here, Señora Eleuteria," Maximiliano says. "For your dog."

And he hands her a bone.

Eleuteria looks first at the bone and then at Maximiliano, her beady eyes made into the thinnest of slits. She snorts, *Hhh!* and then, uttering no further sounds, rejects Maximiliano's peace offering, turns around with a violence that belies her size, and in a raging huff, storms away.

Then a fast exit.

No witch on a broom has ever exited as fast.

She flies away in a black cloud of burning furor, and as she does, you can hear her mutter to herself, "You'll pay for this, butcher man! You'll pay for this!"

But when she reaches her home she is angry at herself because she acted like a fool. That bone, she thinks, could have made a good soup.

20

A butcher's life is never easy.

And it certainly is not easy now, during the worst depression Cuba—and the rest of the world—ever experienced. Nineteen thirty-two is even worse than the year preceding it. One out of four Cubans is out of a job. And those who are working can barely put food on the table. That goes for Maximiliano as well, who, in addition to feeding Dolores, Marguita, Zenaida and himself, has to feed three growing teenagers who it appears have bottomless stomachs.

True, you never hear any of those three complain. Whatever Zenaida places on the table, they all eat, and eat, and eat, leaving nothing on their plates, which pleases Zenaida tremendously. And then, after each meal, Mani and Gustavo just go back to the bedroom they share, where Gustavo—who was just thirteen last week—either reads or does his schoolwork while Mani, now sixteen, almost invariably falls asleep on the spot. The boys are no trouble, no trouble at all. But Merced, well, that's another story. She goes to the living room, sits in a rocker, grabs a newspaper, looks in the social pages, and then sighs.

A seventeen-year-old girl may survive with just cornmeal mush with sweetened condensed milk poured on top, a delicious meal. And if that is all there is, well, then, that is all there is; a seventeen-year-old girl can survive with that.

But a seventeen-year-old girl cannot survive without being dressed "à la mode." Fashionable dresses she dreams of, and fashionable dresses she must have, so fashionable dresses must somehow be provided for her, at whatever the cost.

Dolores knows she is good with a needle and thread. The problem is finding the fabrics. And for this she enlists the help of Maximiliano. It becomes his job to find and supply the fabrics needed to make suitable dresses not only for Merced, but also for the other two ladies in his household: Dolores, the one; and Marguita, the other, who, now that she is nearing eight, also has to be dressed fashionably, of course, as all girls must.

Since he has to work so hard to sell those fourteen-ounce pounds of meat to buy fabrics so the females in his family can dress properly, and since there are three of them, quantity, not necessarily quality, is what Maximiliano is after when he goes shopping and wheeling and dealing not only for fabrics but for everything else as well.

That is why every so often he comes into the house and he drops on the large dining-room table rolls of fabrics of God knows what colors and patterns: fabric remnants that nobody but nobody else in his right mind would ever think of buying. And Dolores has to cut them, and sew them, and make them into dresses she and her girls have to wear, like it or not.

And yet this is where Dolores shines.

It is true she does not cook, but she does know how to make a great-looking dress and embroider it by hand if she has to.

Dolores begins by looking at fashion magazines Merced brings from the school library. Then she looks at the fabrics on the table. Then she gives a big sigh. Then another one, even bigger. And only then does she begin to cut.

By mixing fabrics and by adding a little bit of criollo taste to the insipid European designs worn by the skinny elongated women in those fancy magazines, Dolores concocts original creations the likes of which would never have made it into any of those French fashion magazines, true, but that are creations nonetheless.

The dresses she makes for Merced, especially, are spectacular original designs that clothe her handsomely, bringing out her shapely criollo form and making the other girls in the barrio envy her.

You can always tell when Merced goes by because you hear each and every young man on the street whistle at her, calling her "*¡Sabrosona!*" "Very tasty!" and whisper to her as she passes by, "Mamacita, if you cook the way you walk, I'd even eat what you burn!" Merced, just as Dolores did, brings out the little bit of poet each man in the Luyanó barrio has within himself.

All of this whistling and shouting and whispering is something that may infuriate some of the other girls in the barrio who go out into the streets clad in layer upon layer of girdle upon girdle, hoping the street poetry aimed at them disappears. Not so Merced. This is something she truly enjoys, having men whistle at her. She has begun to cultivate a kind of walk that is almost mulatto woman style—no girdle, no nothing, a walk so hot that it makes men perspire.

"Mamacita"—one man says and fans himself with the palm of his hand as she flows by—"*¡qué calor!*" while another one whistles at her, and yet another one adds, "Mamacita, you're making the palm trees rage with envy with that walk of yours!"

Oh, sure, just like the other girls in the barrio, Merced pretends she does not hear the street poetry. She certainly never looks back at the poet because, as everybody knows, that is never done. True, on occasion she has taken out her compact from her purse and, pretending to be fixing a strand of her wavy hair or an earring, she has looked in the mirror to see what the impertinent poet looks like; Dolores herself taught her that trick. But if by any chance her eyes happen to catch the poet's eyes in the mirror, she immediately puts it down and, pretending to be angry, she pouts and starts to walk away fast, leaving the poet behind, feeling his eyes on her body, and enjoying his staring at her. However, that is something she's seldom done. Most of the time, she just keeps on walking by as if nothing has been said. But as she walks, she smiles.

She cannot deny she likes the idea of palm trees envious of her. It is not her fault she is built the way she is. She likes the way she is turning out to be. Now when she looks at herself in the mirror, she finally approves of herself, finally, after so long.

Once, when she was nearly ten, Dolores caught Merced naked, tiptoeing in front of the mirror in the bathroom, pinching her nipples, and trying to make them look as if they were fully grown breasts. Unnoticed by the young girl, Dolores saw the disappointment in her daughter's eyes, and though Dolores was tempted to laugh at it, she managed to control herself as she stepped into the bathroom with clean towels that smelled of water of violets.

"Mommy," Merced said when she saw Dolores come in, "do you think I will ever be beautiful?" And then she looked at herself in the mirror again, a mirror that reflected a maturing girl dreaming of being a woman, with a sad look on her face. Dolores looked at her daughter and smiled.

"Merced," she said, "do you think I am beautiful?"

Merced looked at her mother with a puzzled look on her face, as if she could not believe her mother's own question; her mother, who is the most beautiful woman Merced has ever known.

"Oh, Mommy," she said, "you are the most beautiful woman in the whole world!"

"Well," added Dolores, "would you believe that for a long long while I did not think of myself as beautiful?" She has been drying Merced's long hair, which is as dark and as wavy as hers. "I never thought of myself as beautiful until the day I met your pappy. When he looked at me the day we met, he—oh, I'm sorry, honey. Did that hurt?" She had accidentally pulled Merced's hair, but Merced didn't mind. She wanted to know the end of the story her mother was telling her.

"So, what happened, Mommy, when Pappy looked at you?"

"When he looked at me? When he looked at me, all of a sudden I just felt beautiful. Oh, so beautiful! Do you want to know what I did?"

"Oh, yes, Mommy, please, please!"

"Here, I'll help you get dressed while I tell you. But first let's brush this hair. You know, Merced, your hair is so much like mine. So wavy and so black. Just say 'Ouch' if I hurt you, all right, honey?"

The little girl on her way to womanhood nodded her head up and down, and waited for her mother to go on with her tale.

"Well," added Dolores as she began to brush Merced's hair, "this is what I did. I got to my house, and I went up to my bedroom on the second floor, and I closed the door, and, making sure nobody saw me, I took all my clothes off, and—"

"Ouch!"

"Oh, I'm sorry, honey." She looked at Merced in the mirror. "Did it hurt much?"

Merced waved her pretty hand in the air as she smiled at her mother in the mirror. "Just a little bit."

"Oh, then," said Dolores, "it wasn't so bad." She went back to brushing Merced's hair, and she saw in the mirror Merced's expectant look. "Oh, I forgot. Where was I?" said Dolores.

"You took all your clothes off," Merced said, prompting her mother.

"Oh, yes!" Dolores said. "I took all of my clothes off and I looked at myself in the mirror. I had a tall, skinny mirror in the shape of an oval. Do you know what an oval shape is like?"

"Yes," Merced said. "Like this," and she drew in the air an oval shape. "Like an egg."

"Yes," said Dolores. "Like an egg. Only that this mirror was tall and skinny. It had a frame of real Cuban mahogany, which is neither red nor orange, not too light, not too dark, like . . . like . . ."

"Like the color of rooftiles?"

"Yes," answered Dolores smiling at her daughter. "Very much like that. And the mirror had a beveled edge that reflected the lights every which way, and sometimes it made me think that there was a rainbow inside my room. Oh, Merced, it was *so* beautiful! It was really beautiful. It had a swivel base and—all right, this looks really good. What do you think?"

She had stopped brushing her daughter's hair and they were both looking at each other in the bathroom mirror, which was short and fat and did not have a frame made of mahogany and did not have a swivel base or a bevel edge and was not really beautiful at all, but a mirror that was reflecting two faces that looked a lot alike, each smiling at each other.

"Here, let's put these on," Dolores said as she helped Merced get into pink panties that had a tiny dove embroidered by Dolores herself on each leg. "And now on with your dress. I brought you these two. Which one do you want to put on? This one?" She showed Merced a light-green cotton dress, the color of fresh limes. "Or this one?" A cream dress with a thin red ribbon ornamenting the collar.

"That one, the cream one."

"All right, raise your arms. Now, where was I?"

Merced answered as she raised her arms in the air, "You were naked in front of the mirror. How old were you then, Mommy?"

"I was sixteen." And she paused.

She was remembering things she thought were long forgotten, and she was remembering them with so much clarity that it was almost as if she were reliving that moment.

"And then what happened, Mommy?"

Dolores woke up from her memory dream.

"Oh, I just looked in the mirror and I saw that the girl I was looking at in the mirror, I saw that she was beautiful, really beautiful."

What Dolores did not tell Merced is that as she was standing there, naked, looking at herself in front of the tall skinny oval mirror, she was thinking of the blond boy with the insolent eyes she had just met, and what he would be saying—and doing—if he ever saw her naked like that.

"Do you think that will ever happen to me?" asked Merced.

"Of course, honey," answered her mother. "One day soon, before you even realize it, a boy will look at you in such a special way that you will never forget it, and the look in that boy's eyes will make you realize that you are beautiful. Because . . ." Dolores added, looking deep into Merced's eyes and smiling that famous mischievous smile of hers, "because you are never beautiful until that happens to you. And then, after it happens to you . . . then you'll be beautiful for the rest of your life."

Merced looks at herself in the mirror. She is now seventeen going on eighteen and she likes what she sees in the mirror. She approves of herself. She is not ugly. That much she knows. The men on the Street of the Bulls tell her so. But she is not beautiful yet. That special boy has not looked at her yet and let her know that she is beautiful.

Her mother has told her that when that happens it is as if all of a sudden you get to bloom in one single moment, and you understand everything there is to understand and you stop asking questions.

Her mother has told her that a moment like that is so wonderful that it makes you feel as if you have been dead up to that time and suddenly you are born into a world so filled with joy that it makes you realize that anything else is meaningless. That *that* is what you were put on Earth for. For a moment like that.

Her mother has told her that when that moment happens, you have to hold it in your hands, clasp your fingers tight around it, and never let it go, because in that moment you are one with the universe and the universe is one with you.

And then, her mother has told her, then you get to laugh and cry at the same time at the beauty of it all.

Merced looks at herself in the mirror and prays silently.

"O God, please, make it happen for me. Make me feel beautiful, please, please. Make me feel beautiful."

★ ★ ★

21

As she goes to the Academia de San Alejandro, the fine arts school, Merced is not concerned with whether she is beautiful or not. She is only concerned with learning, getting good grades, and doing a good job.

She has been studying with Maestro Romanat, a cranky old devil of a teacher who makes all the students work ten times as hard as they can and whose comments on their work can bring anyone, not only

Merced, to tears. But he is a great painter, no question about that. His canvases have a luminosity that is hard to believe and a swiftness of brushwork, almost a madness of brushwork, which is impossible to imitate.

Merced looks at his canvases and she would swear the people portrayed in them are alive. She sees breath coming out of the mouths of the men and women who populate his paintings, and she sees life hiding behind their eyes. But then she gets close to the canvas and all she sees is a series of brush strokes that give the impression they have been done by a madman, because they appear to be brusque, and aimless, and formless, which they are until she steps back. Then, suddenly, each brush stroke falls in the right place, and what seemed aimless and formless becomes whatever it is supposed to become, and a lot more, because the painting is alive, with a life of its own Merced finds incomprehensible.

He is the only painter in the academy whose subject matter is strictly Cuban, not mythical like most of the other teachers' work is. Maestro Romanat paints criollo women walking, and you can see them dance as you look at them; he paints men at a cockfight, and you can hear them shouting and swearing and praying for their cock to win; he paints the sun rising over slender royal palm trees, and you'd swear you can see them sway in the gentle breeze. How does he do that?

Maestro Romanat, who is an excellent teacher, shares his secrets with his class.

"Don't paint the object. Paint its soul. Life without soul is meaningless. Life without soul is death. Open your eyes and look for the soul of your subject. Do not give up until you find it. And when you find it, look at it with your eyes closed, and then go ahead and put it on canvas."

He pauses and looks at his class. Twenty-seven boys and three girls, all of them wearing paint smocks that once were pure white, surround him as he stands next to an easel where he has placed one of his canvases.

The room, which smells of oils and turpentine, is large and airy, with a very high ceiling illuminated by a series of clerestory windows, all of them facing north, letting the cool light permeate the room with a delicate softness. It looks more like a factory than like a school. Except that in this factory the pale-cream walls and the terra-cotta tile floor are covered with myriads of small globs of paint in all possible shapes and colors, the result of many years of students shaking their brushes to get the right feel, the right point at the end of each brush stroke.

"You do that with your eyes closed?" a boy at the back of the class asks, his voice shaking.

"And how can an object have a soul?" asks another.

Maestro Romanat looks at each of the members of his class as he speaks.

"If you look at anything with love, you bring out its soul. But souls are very shy. You only get to see them for the briefest of seconds. So when you coerce a soul to come out and you get to see it, immediately close your eyes to engrave it in your mind. Once it is there, you can always recall it. To recall it, all you have to do is close your eyes again and call the soul with your love. And the soul comes. It is only then you can see it again. With your eyes closed. Then and only then can you see the beauty of it all. And it is only after you have seen that beauty that you can paint it. Otherwise you'll be doing nothing but dirtying the canvas with meaningless brush strokes and you may have the semblance of a painting. But a painting without a soul is not a painting. It is nothing. It is dead."

Romanat picks up a drawing Merced has done of an iris and places it on the easel, on top of his canvas.

"This drawing," the teacher says, "has soul. I may never have seen an iris before in my entire life, but if I were to look at this drawing, not knowing what an iris is, I would have to say 'What a beautiful flower!' Notice I did not say 'What a beautiful *drawing*!' No. I said, 'What a beautiful *flower*!' Notice I didn't say, 'Look at that line,' or 'Look at that shape,' or 'What a beautiful composition.' And yes, the line is beautiful, and the shape, and the composition. But artists, real artists do not talk that way. Artists know better than that. If one thousand years from today somebody were to look at this drawing, or at any drawing that you make, all you want them to see is how beautiful life was when you who drew that drawing were alive. I said 'beautiful,' not 'pretty.' There may be a lot of pain in the soul you are looking at, but if you look at all of that pain with honesty and with love, the pain transforms itself into a special kind of beauty, because souls do not know how to lie, and all souls are beautiful. And if you are honest in your work and you show the honesty of a soul, then by doing that, you will be helping that future viewer of your work cope with the problems of his or her life. That is what art is all about. Sharing love by sharing souls." He pauses as he looks at each and every one of his students. "Art," he adds, "does *not* imitate life. Art is much more powerful than that. Art brings life back. And it does it by exposing the soul of things, the secrets we all carry inside."

He looks at Merced, who is standing at the back of the class, and as he looks at her, all of the students in the class look at her as well. Merced is not aware of this. Her eyes are nailed to the eyes of the cranky old devil of a teacher who is talking about her work and, unbelievably, praising it.

"I don't know," continues Maestro Romanat, "what Merced's secret was when she drew this iris, but I can tell you one thing I know . . ."

He turns and faces first the rest of his class, then Merced's drawing. "Merced saw its soul. And she lets me see it every time I look at this drawing. And seeing that soul makes me content because it makes me a better man. All I can say to Merced for this drawing is not that it is beautiful or not. All I can say to her is 'thank you.' "

He looks at Merced again, as he adds, with a smile, "You have shown me the soul of an iris, and I thank you for that."

Merced blushes, and as she blushes she thinks she cannot wait to go home and tell her mother about what Maestro Romanat said about her work.

But when she gets home the reality of the times stares her starkly in the face.

Sugar is low, and when sugar is low, Cubans starve. And sugar is very low. At the lowest it has ever been in a long long while.

San Alejandro, the academy, is far from Luyanó. Going there is five cents and coming back another five cents, twice a day, and then there are art supplies to be bought and they are expensive. How can Merced and her family afford the luxury of having her go to art school?

True, there are scholarships available to pay for all of those extra expenses. But things being as bad as they are, and those Cuban fat mayors and senators and presidents dreaming of nothing but to get fatter, they decide to cut down the number of scholarships to the very minimum, and those that are available are to be given to boys with outstanding abilities. Boys, not girls. After all, who has ever heard of a woman painter, eh?

Money is tight, really tight. All Cubans are tightening their belts, including Maximiliano's family. Even Zenaida the cook has to go. Now it is up to Merced to cook. All extra expenses have to be pared down to the barest minimum. And that means art school also has to go.

Five students get a monthly scholarship to cover transportation and art supplies. Merced is not one of them. None of the girls is. Maestro Romanat fought valiantly to get a scholarship for her, but the rest of the members of the faculty, who do not like Maestro Romanat's choice of subject matter in his nonclassical paintings, voted against his recommendations as a way of voting against him.

He has offered to give Merced materials from his own studio, but he cannot afford to pay those daily twenty cents needed for Merced to come to the academy. Merced decides she would try walking to school every day, but now that Zenaida is gone she is needed at home to cook for the family, and she just cannot manage to walk that huge distance four times a day since she has to be home to help prepare the noontime meal as well. So Merced's dream has to be postponed, at least for a little while.

On the last day of classes Maestro Romanat asks Merced whether he can keep her drawing of the iris she made while in his class. Merced is flabbergasted. This is indeed an honor she never dreamed she could experience. "I don't have enough money to pay you what that drawing is worth," the old teacher adds. "But I can trade it for one of my canvases, so choose one."

"I can't accept that, Maestro," she says, shaking her head. "I would be honored to have you accept my drawing as a—"

The old man stops her. "Merced, the only thing an artist has to sell is his work. Never give it away or else people will think you do not value it. Instead, trade your very best for someone else's very best, whether that person is a plumber or a president." He pauses, then adds, "Or even an old cranky devil of a teacher." He smiles at her and says, winking an eye, "Now, if you think that none of my canvases is worth your drawing, that I will accept because perhaps they are not."

Merced smiles back at him. "Can I really choose one?"

"Of course you can."

Merced takes home a small canvas that shows a *guajira,* dressed in an old sweat-stained dress, who is sitting in a rocking chair as she sings her naked baby to sleep during a hot afternoon. The mother's face is wrinkled and tired. The child seems uncomfortable in his mother's arms. And yet mother and child are tenderly looking at each other, unaware that in the background a hatless *guajiro* is reclining on the portal's railing as he lovingly looks at his wife and child, his face heavily wrinkled and heavily suntanned except for a pale band across his forehead, where the hat he normally wears protects that area from the sun.

The image is painted with no apparent concern for perspective. It is as if the eye of the painter had first focused on the woman, then on the child, then on the man, and then superimposed all of those different views one on top of another, eliminating everything but what each person in the painting feels for each other.

The painting is entitled *Trinidad.* Trinity.

After showing the small frameless painting to her mother, Merced props it against the wall on top of the tall chest of drawers in the bedroom she shares with her little sister, Marguita, who, not yet nine, doesn't think much of the painting because it looks all wrong to her.

Dolores knows how painful all of this has been for her daughter.

"But it is not fair, Mamá," cries Merced. "Maestro Romanat told the whole class my drawings were good, that they have soul. Some of the boys got scholarships, but—"

Dolores embraces her daughter close to her. "Shhh . . . Don't you cry. You know you make me cry when I see you crying. Do you want to see me cry?"

Dolores gives Merced a handkerchief that has been hand embroidered by Dolores herself. "Here, let me see those beautiful eyes!"

Merced looks at her mother.

"If I had had those long eyelashes of yours . . ." Dolores begins to say, and then stops.

"What?" asks Merced.

"I was just thinking," says Dolores. "Did you know that at one time, when I was about your age, I wanted to have blue eyes? Did you know that? I would have given anything then to have blue eyes. I thought that blue eyes were so beautiful! But if I had had blue eyes, I don't know if your father would have looked at me the way he did. And then I would have missed all of you. So you know what?" she adds jovially. "By not having those blue eyes I so much wanted, I ended up here embracing you like this."

She embraces Merced, kisses gently the forehead of her child, and adds confidentially, looking deep into her daughter's dark eyes, "Merced, a lot of things happen in life, things that at first appear to be horrible. And at first you don't understand how things like that can happen to you. Or why. But then, after a while, you suddenly realize that what really mattered was not that they happened at all, but whether you took advantage of them when they happened and made the best of them. Do you know what I mean?"

Merced smiles and shakes her head, just as if she were a little girl again in her mommy's arms.

"I guess you have to be as old as I am to understand it," Dolores adds. She then places Merced at arm's length and looks at her.

"Do you remember Esperanza? What she used to look like when we first gave her to you, and what she looked like after the big fire?"

Merced nods.

"When you first looked at her after she survived the fire, an old wrinkled doll, partly burned, didn't you think she was ugly?"

"I certainly did not," Merced says, hurt. "I always loved Esperanza. I still do, I want you to—"

"Oh, I know you love her now as much as you did then but, nonetheless, you still thought she was ugly then, right after the big fire, because she was different. She wasn't the same Esperanza we had given to you."

"Well, maybe I did," Merced says, after a short pause. "But only at first," she quickly adds. "You know that. Now I think she is more beautiful than she ever was. She is so beautiful now that I would not have her any other way."

"So my little love," Dolores adds, "the same thing is going to happen to you as soon as you survive *your* big fire, the very same thing. You will also be more beautiful, just like Esperanza. You already are. Look at you now," she tells her. "So you have to stop schooling for a while—that may sound really bad. But you are starting cooking, and that may be really good. I always wanted to cook, but I never had anybody teach me how to do it, did you know that?"

Merced shakes her head again.

"I have secrets too, you know," her mother continues. "I never told your father, but I was told that Maximiliano's mother was a great cook and I didn't want him to be unhappy with me, so I asked him to promise me to always have somebody cook for us. That's why I did it. I was afraid of my mother-in-law, and now that you know your father's mother, tell me the truth, was I right in being afraid of her or was I right?"

And Dolores taps the head of Merced with her knuckles, making an imitation of the old lady with the bony hands and the straight back as she changes her voice, trying to sound like the old lady herself as she bites her lips and hits harder and harder on Merced's head saying, "Was I right or was I right?"

Merced begins to laugh, belly laughs, as she says to her mother, "If she ever gets to hear you!"

"God forbid!" says Dolores in her own voice, and begins to laugh. "She'd probably crack my head with those bony knuckles of hers!"

The two of them are now laughing really loud when Dolores hears Maximiliano open the entrance door.

"Sshhh!" she tells Merced. "Don't you let your father know!"

Maximiliano comes in, inquiring.

"You two sound like two hens cackling after they just laid a golden egg each. What is going on?"

"Here?" says Dolores, winking an eye at Merced. "Nothing," she adds. "Just girl talk, that was all. Just girl talk."

THAT NIGHT, after they all have gone to sleep, when Mani enters his sisters' room to steal once more the book *Apollo,* he stops in front of the painting and stares at it for the longest time.

The room is not too dark. A little bit of light comes through the tall window behind Merced's bed. This light is coming from Hermenegildo's bodega, whose storage room in the back is still lit.

Mani stares at the painting and the little bit of light in the room enveloping the painting makes it look as if the whole scene were taking place at night instead of at noon.

Someone turns the lights off in Hermenegildo's storage room, and Merced's room suddenly becomes almost totally dark. And yet despite the almost total darkness, for the briefest of seconds the painting acquires a peculiar luminosity in Mani's eyes and seems to glow in the dark. It is only when Mani sees the rocking chair move and hears the baby's hungry cry that he is startled. He rubs his eyes, and the room becomes again the room familiar to him.

Mani goes back to his room, lies in his bed, and as he tries to fall asleep he wonders, How did the painter do that?

After a long while, unable to go to sleep, Mani pulls the thin cotton sheet covering him to one side and steps out of his bed quietly, as quietly as he can, making sure he does not disturb his brother, Gustavo, who is sleeping soundly in the bed next to him.

He puts on the pair of white-cotton trousers he had carefully folded and placed across the tall footboard of his white-enamel metal bed, and after making sure nobody is up, he tiptoes barefoot to the girls' bedroom again where he stands in front of Maestro Romanat's painting.

It takes a long time for his eyes to grow used to the almost total darkness of the room and get to see the painting, because the room is lighted exclusively by a tiny night-light kept by the side of the bed of Marguita, who is afraid of the dark. But after his eyes finally get used to the dark, he stares at the painting intently for a long, long while.

Then, carefully, he grabs the canvas in his hands and stealthily leaves the girls' room.

Still barefoot, he tiptoes across the patio, goes through the living room, where all the rockers are quietly sleeping, and opens the front door, as carefully and as slowly as he can. Quietly, trying to make no noise at all, he steps out, and after making sure that the door latch is in the open-from-the-outside position, he closes the door silently behind him and crosses La Calzada, which is totally empty and silent at this time of night.

He goes to the butcher shop, raises the gate facing the Street of the Bulls just high enough for him to squeeze under it, places the painting flat on the white-marble countertop, and turns on the three-bare-bulb lighting fixture hanging in the center of the butcher shop. The suddenly bursting light instantly reflects from the hundreds of sparkling white tiles lining the walls, transforming the whole of the butcher shop into a brilliant white star, shining blindingly bright in the darkness of the moonless night enveloping the barrio.

Mani stares at the picture for a long, long while in this bright light.

The people in the painting are alive, no doubt about that. He sees the spark of life in their eyes.

Not only can he see the spark of life in the eyes of each of the three people in the painting, but he can also hear their thoughts. He hears what the man is thinking as he looks at the woman; what the woman is thinking as she looks at the baby in her arms. He can even hear what the baby is thinking.

Then, determinedly, he rips a piece of the plain brown wrapping paper Maximiliano keeps in a roll on the counter in back of the shop, places it on the white-marble counter next to where he placed the painting, takes the waxy black crayon he and his father use to write prices with, and while staring at the painting begins to draw on the wrapping paper his own version of what he sees. But the lights above him, shining powerfully on the highly varnished surface of the canvas, create reflected circles of intense white light that, blinding him, do not let him see the painting in all of its details.

He tries squinting first one eye, then the other. But it doesn't work. There are always those blinding circles of white light that mask whatever it is he wants to look at.

After a short while of frustration, he decides to try something different. Carefully, he places the painting standing up, leaning against the heavy scale on top of the white-marble counter. But the slick marble surface is too polished and too slippery for the painting to stand, and it begins to slide down.

He looks around the butcher shop for something heavy to hold the canvas in place, and finding the large wooden scrub brush with metal bristles he uses to clean the open wire shelves inside the cooler, places it at the foot of the painting, propping it against the scale.

It works.

The canvas now stands almost perfectly straight up, and he can now see the whole of the painting with no blinding reflections.

Then, with a swift quick bold stroke, he begins to draw on the surface of the paper.

He does not look at the paper.

He stares at the painting, and as he stares at it, his hand begins to move as of its own while his eyes move unhurriedly on the surface of the canvas, slowly and deliberately trailing the contour of the man, which becomes the contour of the railing against which the man is leaning, which becomes the contour of the rocker touching the railing, which becomes the contour of the woman in the rocker, which becomes the contour of the child in her arms.

It is only when his eyes, which have been moving steadily on the canvas, reach the eyes of the baby in the woman's arms that Mani looks at his drawing. But he started his sketching too close to the edge of the paper and his drawing has extended past it onto the white-marble surface.

He did not realize what he was doing.

He has to erase the marks the wax crayon has left on the white marble.

He doesn't want Maximiliano to know what he has done.

He doesn't want *anybody* to know what he has done. But *especially* Maximiliano.

He *certainly* does not want Maximiliano to know what he has done.

He gets a soiled rag from under the white-enamel sink in the back corner, turns on the faucet, wets the rag, squeezes it of excess water, and then, going to the counter covered with the black markings of the wax crayon, he is about to wipe clean the white-marble surface when he looks at the drawing in front of him.

He had not looked at it before.

He had been so upset by the black crayon marks on the white-marble counter that he had not looked at his drawing. Now he looks at it. And what he sees bewilders him. It doesn't look at all like the painting. No, not at all.

What he has in front of him is nothing but a continuous single line that starting with the man leaning on the railing has sinuously found its way into the eyes of the child in the woman's arms; a continuous single line that lies now on the plain brown paper, now on the white-marble surface; a thick continuous single line that, boldly outlining the people in his drawing, has somehow managed to pull them all together, tying them together the same way Maximiliano and Dolores are tied together when they dance; a strong continuous single line that envelops the three different people in his drawing making them into one single whole.

A family.

Mani stares at his drawing first. Then at Romanat's painting. Then at his own drawing again.

So that's what a family is, he thinks.

He looks at the family in his drawing for a long, long time, and then as he begins to wipe the part of the single line lying on the white-marble surface, he begins to wonder what it would feel like to be the child in the woman's arms, the one whose father is looking at him, his eyes filled with intense love. And with pride.

★ ★ ★

22

Bulls have dreams, you know. They are not that different from anybody else. We all have dreams, which we all hope to see come true, if not in our own lifetimes, well then in our children's, or in our children's children's. We all pass our dreams—just as we pass everything else—to our children, who inherit those dreams, and who sometimes make those inherited dreams, dreams of their own. And sometimes dreams do come true. It may take a little while, and a little cajoling here and there, but sometimes dreams do come true.

Maximiliano the butcher has dreams too.

Like his father before him, and his father's father before them, Maximiliano dreams of having his sons enter the family business and become butchers, like himself.

Being a butcher is a great thing. He has managed really well in raising a family as large as the one he has, especially during the conditions in his lifetime, which have been less than ideal. Twice he has started from scratch. And twice he has managed to come out all right. His family is good looking and healthy; food has never been lacking on his table; and his sons are the two strong bullocks they now are, almost fully grown men by now.

Mani, now almost twenty, has been helping him full time at the butcher shop on the Street of the Bulls in Luyanó for the last three and a half years already, since he finished his required schooling—which in Cuba is completed at about age sixteen—and he has developed a talent for dealing with his customers, taking his time to let them know exactly what it is they really want, which is the essential quality of a good businessman. He is still not a great butcher, but he sure is on his way to getting there.

Gustavo, who turned sixteen five months ago, has just finished his required schooling and is now old enough to help in the butcher shop and learn his trade. Maximiliano has brought him in to help as well, and he is in the process of teaching him the basics of how to be a good butcher.

Maximiliano needs all the help he can get. A lot of money has to be made just to make the butcher shop break even, and to provide enough food for all those growing kids, who it appears never ever stop eating. He cannot afford extra help outside of his family. Besides, even if he could, he has never thought of that possibility. He has two boys, hasn't he? And he is going to make butchers out of the two of them.

He never consulted the boys. Why should he? He knows that being a butcher is good for you. It keeps you healthy, and strong, and in excellent shape, and on top of that, you are your own boss. What else can anyone ask for? So why should he consult his boys about their future? Certainly nobody consulted him when he became a butcher. He just did as his father did, just as his father's father did before he left fourteen kids behind to go fight a war and liberate Cuba.

Maximiliano admires his grandfather, the Cuban hero, after whom he was named. Maximiliano knows that it took a lot of courage for the old man to do as he did. He himself doesn't know if he could have done what the old man did. Sure, when the old man left his family behind to fight a war, by that time his oldest boy, Maximiliano's father—who would grow up to be the butcher of Batabanó—was already a teenager, as strong as Mani is today, and he told his father not to worry about them. He promised his father he would provide food for his father's table by working in his father's butcher shop, which he did until the time came when the boy himself was old enough to join the Cuban Liberation Army, which he did two years later.

Those two men, Maximiliano's father and grandfather, knew that food is not all a family ever needs. A family, just like a person, needs pride, and a sense of being important, and a sense of doing the right thing. Food fuels the body, but dreams fuel the soul. Food without dreams is meaningless, as meaningless as a painting without a soul. And those two men, Maximiliano's father and grandfather, had had dreams. They could not feel proud as long as a single slave worked under the slashing whip of the cruel Spaniards; they could not feel important as long as a single black woman was forced against her own will to serve as a concubine to someone who claimed her as her master; they could not feel they were doing the right thing as long as their country was not free to fly her own flag. They could not have honor until they were able to stand, tall and proud, like the royal palm tree, under that beautiful flag with a lone star floating on a triangular sea of red blood, the spilled blood of the thousands of criollo men who made it possible for Pablo to die a free man and for Maximiliano to own his own butcher shop and raise his own family with dignity and pride. Those men had had dreams, and they had made them come true.

That is just what Maximiliano tells his children over and over again. "A life without dreams," he says, "is absurd. All you have to do," he adds, "is decide what it is that you want to do, and then do it. Never give up until you get it done. But I'm warning you," he always adds, "you've got to be real strong to make your dreams come true, real strong, like your grandfather and your grandfather's father. Real strong." Then he looks at his children and smiles at them. "Are you real strong?"

Every time Maximiliano asks this question of his teenage boys, Mani, dark-haired dark-eyed Mani, always answers by showing the strong muscles in his arms, just as he did when he was a child, back in Batabanó. Gustavo, blond-haired blue-eyed Gustavo, does not do that. He just listens to his father, hides behind his glasses, and ponders, the way he always does.

It's early Monday morning. Gustavo and Mani have just finished stacking the huge blocks of ice inside the walk-in cooler at the back of the shop and hanging all the meat in its proper place, each carcass hanging where it should, according to how long it has been in the cooler. They bring out a side of beef, which they place on the large butcher-block stump located right in the center of the shop as Maximiliano pulls out his large butcher knives and begins to sharpen them.

They are wearing white long bib aprons with the faintest ghosts of bloodstains, because it is difficult to remove bloodstains once they set in. Dolores washes and bleaches those aprons daily, and then she irons them herself, something Maximiliano has repeatedly told her not to do but that she does nonetheless. She loves to see her three men wearing bright and clean and freshly ironed white aprons, and she does it daily, just for the pleasure she gets in looking at them. "For the beauty of it all," she tells Maximiliano every time he asks her why she does that. "For the beauty of it all," she says. "No other reason. Just that."

She has just brought her three men freshly made coffee that smells, Oh, so good! And she stands there, inside the butcher shop, sipping her own tiny cup of dark Cuban coffee. Manuel the doctor has told her not to drink it, because it is bad for her heart, but she drinks just a little bit of it just once a day, early in the morning, because she likes to sip it while she looks at her three men all dressed in white inside the butcher shop, which is lined floor to ceiling with white tiles that shine like mirrors.

As they sip their delicious coffee, Dolores and Mani stand by the side of the butcher shop that is next to the Street of the Bulls. They are both looking out, enjoying the early morning cool air and the beautiful turquoise sky floating above that promises this to be a particularly beautiful day. Gustavo and his father are leaning on the counter facing La Calzada.

Gustavo finishes his coffee first, and while the rest of them are still enjoying their coffee, he bursts out.

"There's something I have to tell you, Dad."

His father looks at him, still holding his cup of coffee, a demitasse size, that holds just a few drops of that rich dark coffee Dolores loves so much to taste when it is hot, steaming hot, as this coffee is today.

"Shoot," says Maximiliano, answering Gustavo's opening.

There's a long pause.

Dolores and Mani turn around to face Gustavo, who is not facing anybody as he answers. He does not want to face anybody, and particularly not his father, because he knows that what he is going to say is going to hurt him a lot. And yet he's got to say it or else he's going to go crazy.

"I don't want to be a butcher," he says, and instinctively moves back as if he were afraid of his father's reaction.

Maximiliano has not once in his entire life raised a hand to any of his kids. A good belting now and then, perhaps. But only the boys and only aimed at their legs. Dolores with her punishment chair technique has achieved wonders and seldom if ever has Maximiliano had to use the belt; an old thick battered belt that, nonetheless, hangs prominently displayed on Maximiliano's bedroom door, which is always kept open.

The boys have never been hit by their father. And yet Gustavo moves back as if to put distance between Maximiliano and him.

Dolores and Mani are looking at Gustavo as Maximiliano, still sipping his coffee, says quietly, "And what *do* you want to be?" He blows on his coffee to cool it down. The coffee is still so hot steam is still coming out of it.

This time Gustavo faces his father. "I want to be a poet."

His father raises his eyes and looks at Gustavo. "A poet?" he asks, with a genuinely puzzled look on his face.

"A poet," Gustavo answers decisively. "A poet and a writer. Maybe work for a newspaper. Become a newspaperman, or a reporter. I'd like that." His face lights up as if by magic when he says that. The pondering boy who never tells anything to anybody is coming alive. He is smiling. A tentative smile, true, but a smile nonetheless.

Maximiliano looks at Gustavo and places the now-empty cup on the marble counter. Dolores carefully picks it up and places it on the little white tray she used to bring the coffee from their house across La Calzada. Mani is looking at both Gustavo and his father with puzzled eyes.

Up to that point Gustavo has always been Mani's baby brother, the one who gets into trouble all the time just to run to Mani who always manages to get Gustavo out of whatever trouble he's created for himself. Mani has gotten Gustavo out of many a trouble indeed. Gustavo has never fought a single one of the many fights he's always starting in the neighborhood. The rest of the bullocks on the street know about Mani and how protective he is of his baby brother. All Mani has to do is to frown and all the other bullocks instantly back away, because they have all seen that frown before and because they all know where that frown leads to: Eating dirt.

But this Gustavo whom Mani is looking at today, this Gustavo is a man, not a boy anymore. Not only that. He is a man Mani does not know. Gustavo, who has always confided in Mani, has not told Mani a word of what he was planning to do this morning, what he is doing right now. This Gustavo, this one who is bravely holding Maximiliano's eyes, is a Gustavo Mani does not know but a Gustavo Mani cannot help but admire. This Gustavo has guts. Guts enough to state his case, and maybe guts enough to defend it. Mani is puzzled and intrigued by this Gustavo, and so is Dolores, who is simply standing there, not saying a word. This is between Gustavo and his father.

Gustavo has not told her anything. He never tells anybody anything. He has always been such a shy boy. But this Gustavo she is looking at today is no longer shy. This Gustavo is daring, as daring as she herself was when she challenged her father's authority. This Gustavo she likes. She can see her own blood in her son, and though she has not said a word, she is proud of this boy who is looking at his father the way two men look at each other: eye to eye. And that is good. That is the kind of man she likes. That is the kind of man she always meant to raise, and that is the kind of man she has succeeded in raising. She is proud of herself. She has always been proud of her children and of her husband and of her life, but this is a different kind of pride. This is the pride of a teacher who sees one of her students graduate to a higher level of learning.

Silently, quietly, she places the three cups on the little white tray and she waits. She knows how strongly Maximiliano feels about his boys' helping with the family business, and she roots for her husband. But she also can see the courage that Gustavo is showing by stepping out and challenging his own father, and she roots for Gustavo as well. She wonders, Is this how her poor aunt Ausencia, her old maid of an aunt felt when she, Dolores, challenged the baron of Batabanó? Was she rooting for both of them then?

"A poet?" asks Maximiliano. "Or a reporter? Which?"

As he asks these questions he picks two of his large butcher knives and begins to sharpen them by rubbing one against the other, something he is always doing. He does this automatically, just as some people bite their fingernails, without realizing what they are doing. Maximiliano rubs one knife against the other and waits for Gustavo's answer.

"You can be both," says Gustavo, "can't you? At the same time?"

Gustavo is not sure. His answer was meant to be a statement, but somehow he made it sound like a question. Yet Maximiliano takes it to be a statement because he knows, as Mani and Dolores know as well, that that's how Gustavo meant it to sound. Maximiliano nods his head up and down, still sharpening his knives.

"Yes," he answers, "I guess you're right. A poet . . ." He pauses and thinks about it. Maximiliano, who has written poems to Dolores and lyrics to popular songs, thinks about what it is like to be a poet. And then he adds, "A poet is a reporter, of sorts." He goes on nodding his head as he automatically takes a different set of knives and goes on sharpening them. "I don't know of any reporter who is a poet," he continues with his thoughts, stating them as they come into his head. "But that doesn't mean that it is not possible. I guess it can be." He looks Gustavo in the eye and blurts, "Is that what you want to do? For the rest of your life?" He underlines "the rest of your life," making it sound like a very long time indeed.

Gustavo pauses for a brief second.

Then he looks his father in the eye as he answers. "It would be fun."

That must have been the magic word, the word Maximiliano was hoping to hear. Maximiliano loves his work. He loves cutting the meat, and trimming it, and fixing it the proper way, and talking to his customers, and being his own boss. He's never worked for anybody. Oh, sure, he worked for his father, but he was learning his trade back then. And then he worked *with* Pancho, not *for* Pancho, for half a year. True, he didn't quite like that, but he was buying his butcher shop by working with Pancho, so that really does not count. No. He has always been his own boss and he likes that. He loves his work and he has a lot of fun doing it. He enjoys, truly enjoys, every single day, one at a time. Even when his home was burned, even when everything he ever owned was claimed by Ogún, the angry black god of the sea, even then he enjoyed each day, because each day is like a challenge and Maximiliano loves challenges. They make him grow stronger and wiser, each challenge does. And he likes that.

"All right," Maximiliano tells Gustavo. He is looking at his son and smiling. For a second or so he has stopped sharpening his knives. "If that's what you want, do it," he adds. "The worst that can happen is that you'll die fighting to make your dream come true, and since we all have to die, what better way of dying is there?"

Mani is in a state of shock, still unable to believe his own ears.

Dolores finishes her coffee, which is now cold, but she doesn't mind that.

Gustavo removes his apron and he hangs it on the hook by the door to the cooler, which is closed.

Dolores has not said a word.

She picks up the little white tray, now with four empty little white cups, and starts for her house.

Gustavo begins to follow her when he turns and faces his father.

Maximiliano has begun to work on the side of beef on the butcher-block table in the middle of the butcher shop, assisted by Mani, when Gustavo asks him, "If I fail, can I come back here?"

Maximiliano stops in the middle of a cut, something Mani has never ever seen him do. He answers, "Of course, son. What kind of a question is that? What do you think fathers are for? Of course you can come back here at any time. But you won't fail." He smiles at Gustavo, who is now looking at his father with very different eyes, because his father is looking at him with pride, and Gustavo can see it in his father's eyes.

This is something Gustavo has never seen before. It has always been there, but Gustavo has never seen it before. And now that he sees it, Gustavo realizes how much this strong handsome bull of a man who looks like an emperor loves him, and that makes him feel good.

Maximiliano looks at Gustavo and gives his son one of those disarming smiles he is famous for as he says, "Now, go! Mani and I have a lot of work to do!" And he goes back to work, restarting the cut he was making before Gustavo interrupted him.

Gustavo goes home.

It is now midmorning.

Mani, who is assisting his father, goes to the cooler to bring out another piece of beef, and on his way there he notices Gustavo's apron hanging on the hook by the cooler's door, on top of the sweater that always hangs there.

He looks at it.

And he wonders if he would ever dare to hang his own apron on that hook.

Part Three

Weddings 1936–1938

23

Nineteen thirty-six is no different from the five years preceding it. Money is still tight, really tight. Worse than tight.

That is why, when Ferminio, the owner of the two slaughterhouses in Luyanó, invited Maximiliano and his entire family to the wedding of his only daughter, Fernanda, and to the reception following it, Dolores—not being able to afford a suitable gift—offered to embroider all the roses on the wedding gown by hand, as a wedding present. She just never suspected, when she made the offer, that there would be so many roses!

For days on end, weeks on end now, she has been embroidering rose after rose after rose! But the end is near. Ten skirt panels completed. Two more panels to go. Twelve roses to a panel. Twenty-four more roses.

She sighs.

When the time came for Ferminio's daughter, Fernanda, to marry Arsenio, the criollo man who has been running Ferminio's Cuban slaughterhouse for the last several years, the bride asked her parents for the simplest of weddings, something that pleased Ferminio exceedingly.

But neither bride nor Ferminio was taking into account the bride's mother.

Albertina, Ferminio's wife, always dreamed of a white-veil church wedding for herself, the kind she did not get when she got married; and now that her only daughter is going to get married, she has decided to give Fernanda the wedding that she, Albertina, never had. And when Albertina makes up her mind, Albertina has her way, whether the world likes it or not.

And she is having her way. She's plain gone crazy spending every penny Ferminio has ever saved on their daughter's wedding.

"Throwing the house out the window," as Cubans say.

For the wedding mass, Albertina is having the main altar of The Most Glorious Cathedral of La Habana completely covered with long-stem roses, and Fernanda, the bride, will arrive, accompanied by her father, in a fancy four-horse open *volanta,* driven by a tall black man in full livery.

The reception afterward will be at the largest private banquet hall of El Hotel Nacional, a spectacular building located in the north of La Habana, right by the shore, in the most exclusive of neighborhoods. It is going to be catered by El Siglo Veinte, the best restaurant in the hotel, with no limit as to what guests can drink; and it is going to be harmonized by Las Hermanas Albaracoa, an all-girl orchestra, and La Orquesta Sensación, which will entertain the public alternatively, so music will never stop.

When Ferminio, who has to approve the bills, tells her she's gone absolutely mad, Albertina answers, "Ferminio, dear, you know about bulls. I know about weddings."

And yet for all that spending and spending, the wedding gown, designed by the bride herself, is being lovingly and exquisitely hand sewn by Albertina herself with the help of her best friends, including Dolores, who is doing all of the embroidery.

Embroidering does not come easily to Dolores anymore. After all, she has no longer the eyesight nor the stamina of the sixteen-year-old girl she once was. She is the mother of four grown-up children, a mature woman of forty-two who has to wear reading glasses to embroider and who pulls gray hairs out of her beautiful head of black hair far too often. And though she has gained a few extra pounds and a few extra wrinkles, she is still handsome and mischievous. Or so claims Maximiliano, whose short bristly blond hair has also begun to turn gray, though it doesn't show as much.

She picks up the next to last skirt panel, places it on her knees, sets the embroidering hoop tight, and, as she begins to embroider again, her mind travels into that strange land the past is, where impossible-to-deal-with nuns coexist with flames of fire and with tidal waves and with an old pink bus and with mulatto women and with a girl born little and blue and with another girl in a white gauzy dress embroidered with hummingbirds and hibiscus climbing the steps to her wedding bed. What happened to those years in between? They have gone by so fast! Next year it will be her silver wedding anniversary already! Can that be possible? She shakes her head in disbelief. How could it be? She feels so young inside! But when she thinks of her children she has to nod yes, because her children are now women and men. Even Marguita, her youngest, not yet fourteen—who no longer likes to be called Marguita but insists on being called Marga, something nobody ever does—even she is already the kind of young woman the boys in Luyanó like to whistle at, something Marguita, blond blue-eyed puritanical Marguita, hates, because it embarrasses her.

Dolores cuts the silken thread with her teeth. Why did Fernanda have to design a wedding dress with a skirt made of twelve panels? Well, one more rose. The last rose on this panel. Only twelve more roses to go!

She sighs again.

And then she smiles her famous mischievous smile, because she has suddenly imagined herself embroidering the wedding dress of her own daughter Merced.

She pauses.

How long will it be before she will have grandchildren playing around her? She would love that. It's been such a long long time since a child has been around her! Ever since her baby girl Iris left her, years ago. A lifetime ago.

She raises her head and listens. The house seems extremely silent today.

She looks around the house and realizes that she is totally alone. Even Merced, who is in charge of cooking since Zenaida was let go, is out shopping. Dolores feels strange being so totally by herself. She cannot remember when was the last time she was totally alone in her house, like she is today. The house suddenly feels so quiet, so silent, so empty. So immense.

And suddenly Dolores is able to understand how Maximiliano's mother, that old lady with the bony knuckles, must have felt when she fought to keep Mani with her for . . . how long was it? Too long. An eternity.

She remembers thinking at the time that she could never forgive that old woman for what she did: Steal a child away from his own mother, bully her into giving away her own son.

What a cruel thing to do that was.

But now, today, as she sits in a rocking chair embroidering roses on someone else's wedding gown, she realizes that soon her children will all be gone and that soon this big old house is going to be silent all the time, as it is right now. Quiet. Silent. Empty.

Immense.

It is then she understands how that poor old woman must have felt.

And, for the first time in her life, Dolores is able to forgive that old woman for what she did.

★ ★ ★

24

The banquet hall of El Hotel Nacional is truly magnificent.

The walls are covered with Cuban mahogany panels framing large beveled mirrors reflecting mirrors reflecting the many arrangements of long-stem roses Albertina, Ferminio's wife, has ordered to decorate the hall for her daughter's wedding reception. From the elaborately coffered high ceiling hang three huge chandeliers made with Venetian glass, which scintillate as if made of stars, stars that reflect on the travertine marble floors, as sparkling as the beveled mirrors on the walls. And yet, despite its rigid formality and understated elegance, the room is bursting at the seams. Nothing can ever be formal or understated about any group of Cubans, period. And especially not when they are having a party.

And what a party this is!

Champagne is running freely for the ladies, and dark rum for the men while the famous Albaracoa band, a band made exclusively of great-looking mulatto women—who are great musicians as well—is playing a *son oriental,* a kind of dance music new to La Habana of 1936.

Fidelia, the trumpet player, is particularly good tonight—the champagne is bringing out the best in her, or so it appears. And so is Hortensia, the girl who plays the bongo drums, who is also inspired tonight. In fact, all of the girls are inspired tonight. These girls are real sisters. They come from Santiago, the second largest city in Cuba, located at the other end of the island, the east end, where the mountains are really high and where the music is really hot; and they have brought to

La Habana a fast new rhythm that makes the blood boil in your veins and brings wings to your feet, as Cubans are fond of saying.

Mani, now twenty-one, all dressed up in a white-linen suit and tie, his dark curly hair glistening with pomade, stands all by himself enjoying his dark rum. He has never been to a place like this, and he looks at it all, focusing on small details while the rest of the world recedes into an out-of-focus fog. It probably is the effect of the potent strong rum on the inexperienced young man, but little by little a series of visual images, something like paintings, begins to take shape in his mind.

He notices how the dimmed incandescent lights reflecting on the reddish-mahogany room tinge the dark-brown faces of the mulatto girls in the band, making them a pale-pink purple, almost lilac; their long-skirted white-ruffled dresses, split in front so their shapely legs show, become ivory, the color of aged piano keys; their manicured straightened black hair becomes dark navy with highlights of turquoise and emerald; and their lips, their tempting big lips become a deep red so dark and so glossy that they reflect the stars hidden in the crystal chandeliers.

Suddenly, looking at those girls on the raised stage, he realizes that his blood has rushed within his body, and his maleness, standing at attention, has begun to show through his thin white-linen pants. For a moment he feels self-conscious and doesn't know what to do. Should he put his hands in his pockets and try to disguise what is happening to him? But then he decides that after all this is a wedding, and wedding parties are held precisely to celebrate that kind of rushing of blood.

So he has his shot glass filled again with that smooth rum that feels so good, raises it in the air, shoots it down his throat, and looks, with the insolent eyes he inherited from Maximiliano, at each one of the girls, stripping them of their clothes with his dark piercing eyes and dreaming what it would be like to enter them, the whiteness of him against the darkness of them.

Hortensia, the girl playing the bongo drums, notices him. She looks first deeply into his eyes, and then Mani sees her slide her eyes downward until they pause between his legs and dwell on what seems to be aiming at her. She smiles ear to ear, nudges her sister, Fidelia, who is playing the trumpet next to her, and with a quick jerk of her eyes, points at Mani, who is now staring at the two of them. It doesn't take long for the whole band of girls to be looking at that handsome bullock who is looking at all of them with those dark piercing eyes filled with mischief. And yet none of the girls, not a single one of them, has missed a single note. They are inspired tonight, no question about it.

As the all-girl band takes a well-deserved break and right before the next band takes over for the second half of the hour, Gustavo—not yet twenty, but looking a lot older in his suit and tie—talks with Tonio, a young man he has just met, who has just told Gustavo he works at a book publishing house, the latest division of Athena, the largest bookstore in all of La Habana. Although they are really close to each other and no band is playing, the two of them have to yell to one another to be heard, because the noise in the banquet hall is still phenomenal, if not deafening.

Gustavo is big, tall, blond, and blue-eyed, like his father, but with Dolores's wavy hair and mischievous eyes, hidden behind glasses. Tonio, on the other hand, is slender, not as tall as Gustavo, with dark-brown hair that is beginning to recede and with dark-brown eyes, which he also hides behind glasses, thick glasses, because he is badly nearsighted. "The publishing company is not much of a thing yet," Tonio shouts, "but already our first book is coming out. *Geography of Cuba,* by Dr. Alfonso Madrero. Do you know him? He teaches at the university."

Tonio's excitement is contagious. Gustavo wants to know everything about the company, and the book, and the author, and how long it took him to write it, and how long it is, and who drew the maps, and then a million other questions that fascinate him and which Tonio is delighted to answer. Before the party is over Tonio asks Gustavo to come visit him at the bookstore tomorrow morning, Monday, that there may be a job there for him. Gustavo is so excited by this prospect that he can barely sleep that night, and yet he doesn't tell anybody about it.

For the last three years, since he hung his apron in the butcher shop, Gustavo has been working as a delivery boy for Hermenegildo, who gives him Sundays and Mondays off. And for the last three years every Monday he has worn his very best and he has gone from one newspaper office to the next asking for a job, any kind of a job: proofreader, errand boy, sweeper, anything. But to no avail. The situation in Cuba is so bad that no jobs are to be found anywhere, in any field, period. And yet Gustavo hasn't given up on his dreams. He has learned to make the most out of his job, and now he truly likes it and enjoys it. He has found out that while he delivers the groceries he has plenty of time to think and improvise poems, poems he gets to work on and polish as he recites them as loud as he can while fighting the heavy noisy traffic of La Habana with his battered old delivery bicycle. Then, when he is happy with any one of them, he gets to write it down during his noontime siesta break, or else late at night, in the room he shares with his big brother, Mani.

Gustavo has not been able to close his eyes all night long. He has been turning and turning on his bed and looking and looking at the clock on his night table every few seconds, it seems to him. He opens his eyes again and again checks the clock. *Ten to seven?* He must have dozed off. How could that have happened to him, and of all days, today! He jumps out of bed, rushes to the kitchen, opens the ice box, washes his face in the melted ice water, runs back to his room, dresses up, rushes out of the house, gets the number 10 bus that goes from Luyanó to Galiano, and by two minutes to eight he is at the Athena bookstore, waiting for Tonio, who gets there running, ten minutes later.

Tonio brings Gustavo into the store and takes him to meet Collazo, the owner of the store, who is Tonio's uncle. "Uncle Collazo," he says, "this is my friend Gustavo. He wants to be a poet."

No further introduction is needed. By the end of the week Gustavo is working at the bookstore, one step closer to the fulfillment of his dreams. And since he dreams of being a poet, Collazo has assigned to him the entire poetry section, which is vast. Collazo himself encourages Gustavo to take any book he wishes home, read it, and evaluate it for his customers.

Gustavo is in seventh heaven. He looks around the book stacks, picks up first one book, then another, and leafs through them, reading names he has never heard before, having the time of his life, and getting paid for doing it. He's got to thank Tonio, his guardian angel.

But how?

On his first day at work, Gustavo finds out that Tonio also lives in Luyanó. "Hey, Tonio," he says, "why don't you come spend some time with us next Sunday afternoon? I'd like you to meet my family. And especially," he adds, "I'd like my family to meet *you*."

Tonio says nothing.

"Maybe we can go to the movies, or something. What do you say?"

Tonio begins to shake his head from side to side, but Gustavo will not take no for an answer. "Come on, Tonio," he insists. "As a favor to me. What have you got to lose, eh?"

Tonio looks at his new friend, who is smiling warmly at him, and then, though he is still shaking his head, he has no choice but to smile back at Gustavo.

It's two fifteen in the afternoon and Tonio is at the door of Maximiliano's house on La Calzada. He takes a handkerchief out of his coat pocket and wipes the sweat from his forehead. Then places it back, polishes his shoes using the back of the leg of his pants, straightens out his tie, and takes a deep breath. It is only then he knocks at the entrance door.

After a short while his call is answered by a beautiful young criollo woman, who opens the door for him. She has dark wavy hair, dark sparkling eyes, and is pleasantly wrapped in a little meat. For a moment Tonio does not know what to say.

Gustavo rushes to him. "Hey, *compadre,* how are you doing!" he says, as he extends his hand to Tonio. "Merced, this is Tonio, the guy who got me my job at the—oh, but you must have met him at Fernanda's wedding, didn't you?"

Tonio shakes his head, the gentleman in him politely answering for her, "I don't think so. I would have remembered if I did."

Merced, taken slightly aback by his answer, pauses for a short second, and then, smiling broadly, offers her hand to him. "It's a pleasure meeting you," she says.

"The pleasure is mine," answers Tonio, as he takes her hand in his.

"Come in," says Gustavo. "I want you to meet the rest of my family. That is," he adds jokingly, "if the two of you can ever come unglued."

Tonio, disconcerted momentarily, immediately lets go of Merced's hand.

But he does not fail to notice how Merced's sparkling dark eyes keep looking at him as she welcomes him into her house.

25

Hortensia, the mulatto woman bongo drum player of the Albaracoa band, she with the magic hands, is lying on a bed, totally naked. Next to her is her sister, Fidelia, the trumpet player, she with the magic mouth, also lying on the same bed and also totally naked. They are both looking at Mani, he with the insolent eyes, who is standing by them, at the foot of the bed, looking at them. Mani is still dressed. He has taken off the jacket of his white-linen suit that smells of violet water and rum and has loosened his tie, the only suit and tie he owns. He is standing there, in his pants, shirt, and suspenders, just looking at the two beautiful mulatto women naked in front of him, his stiff rod still straining inside his pants.

Mani and the girls have met many a time before at this very *posada,* one of those small nameless innlike places that are very well hidden in all neighborhoods in La Habana, and which have been specially designed for people in search of a place to have sex.

Outside each room in a *posada* there is a red light placed on top of the exterior door. When this light is lit it means that this exterior door leading into the room is unlocked, and the room unoccupied.

Once people enter the room and close that door behind them, they turn off the light outside, at which point a light inside the main desk lights up. The clerk walks a long internal corridor until he reaches the room just occupied, and there he knocks at an interior door separating this hallway from the room. This interior door has a small door in it, almost a peephole, except that this small door is located below eye level.

The people inside open this tiny door and, unseen by the clerk, pay him for the use of the room, the rates varying in accordance with the number of hours people in the room are planning to spend there.

No words are exchanged. The clerk has not seen the people inside the room. They have not seen the clerk. Privacy is thus totally secured. Who is in the room doing what with whom is whose business, and no one needs to know anything about it.

The *posada* Mani and the girls are in is located in Marianao, a beach area of small-time dance clubs and whorehouses frequented primarily by working-class Cubans. It is there the Albaracoa band has been playing for the last six months, at El Club Lunazul, just a few blocks away from this *posada.* Since the girls are working and making plenty of money, on weekend nights, after their last show is over, they go to the *posada,* where they get and pay for a room. Then they telephone Mani, who has remained behind at the club waiting for this call, and they tell him which room they are in. Mani has no car. He has taken the bus from his house on La Calzada in Luyanó to El Club Lunazul, a long trip that takes over an hour. After he gets his phone call, he walks from the club to the *posada,* during which time the girls strip off their clothes, smoke a few reefers, shoot some hot rum down their throats, and throw themselves naked in bed, waiting for him, their eyes nailed to the door to their room, which is closed but not locked.

All the lights in the room are out except for the light in the bathroom, which is on. The girls have closed the door to the bathroom leaving just the tiniest sliver of light coming through, casting just a hint of an ice-blue fluorescent light into the room that seems to cool the room, blazing hot with anticipation.

Mani is staring at both naked girls and as he does that he enters a world of his own, where something like paintings begin to take shape in his mind. Tonight he looks at the naked girls and he sees a pair of Cleopatras, two desirous Egyptian goddesses whose glistening sweaty dark-honey skins and parted red lips are barely brushed by a trace of the cold blue light magically bathing the room; two sculptural dark bodies languidly interwoven as they lie on white sheets turned incandescent pale blue by the magical light.

He takes the bottle of rum the girls have brought with them and shoots some of that smooth rum that feels so good down his throat, and again he looks at each one of the girls, his eyes moving slowly; the eyes of a painter carefully scrutinizing inch by inch the body of each girl.

Each of the girls follows Mani's glance and feels how his eyes caress and burn whatever part of their bodies Mani is looking at. Their eyes, their ears, their mouths, their necks, the gentle rise of their breasts, the soft suave curve of their armpits, their arms, their hands, their bellies, their thighs. Mani's glance stops when he reaches with his eyes the black hairy crotch of his first Cleopatra, who lazily opens her legs, languidly displaying herself to Mani. Then his eyes look at the black hairy crotch of his other Cleopatra, who also opens her legs to his demanding eyes.

The girls are so much alike Mani doesn't know which one is which. He doesn't care either. Soon he'll find out. When she with the magic hands and she with the magic mouth begin to bring out of him whatever it is stud bulls like him are made out of. But that time has not come yet.

He may just be a young man in the girls' eyes, but he is a young man who knows that it is only the beauty of prolonged agony that brings out the beauty of prolonged ecstasy. He has agonized a whole week to be with his Cleopatras, just as they have agonized a whole week to be with him. So agonizing a little bit longer won't hurt that much more, and if it does, it is the kind of hurt the three of them welcome.

He takes the bottle of rum, shoots some down his throat, and pours some on the girls' crotches. Then, still in his pants and shirt, his stiff rod bursting out of the imprisoning pants, he bends down and begins to sip each of the drops of rum that, catching a hint of the magical blue light bathing the room, seem to glitter like cold blue stars on the black curly pubic hair of each of the girls that smell of sweat and of rum and of drums and of sex as she and her sister bite each other's lips.

The next morning, Mani, in his bloodstained apron, is slicing through an expensive cut of meat the way he has been taught. He is doing this slowly, methodically, unconsciously, the way one finds oneself at times driving along a road one does not remember ever taking. His way of slicing is rhythmic, caressing, sensual. Placing almost no pressure on the knife, and letting the hair-splitting sharp knife do the work on its own, Mani glides his knife across the piece of meat, raises it, places it again in the same starting location, then glides it again just to raise it again just to place it again in the same starting location until the piece of meat finally delivers itself into his waiting hands. He then places it on a sheet of honey-colored wax paper, weighs it, wraps it, and gives it to his customer, a young white woman with just a trace of black in her—or is it Indian?—who has been admiring Mani as he works. Mani's movements have the grace and the beauty of a wild animal in the forest, the less conscious he is of them, the more graceful and beautiful they are.

Mani does not look at his customers. Well, he does look at them, but he does not look at them the way he looks at his Cleopatras. When he looks at his Cleopatras, he *sees* them, *seeing* in them what Merced's former art teacher calls the soul of the subjects, Merced has told him that much. Mani saw the souls of his Cleopatras that very first night they met, and since then, the two mulatto girls, whose souls Mani can command at his wish, have been delivering themselves to him, no questions asked.

They do not even know his name. They call him "Blanquito," for "Young White Man." Hortensia tells Fidelia that at times she feels like she is his slave, that Blanquito can do anything he wants with her. Fidelia answers that if this is what slavery is all about, then, Thank God, thank God for it.

The girls cannot understand what is happening to them.

Fidelia, the younger one of the two of them, is easily ten years older than Mani; Hortensia, two years older than Fidelia. The two girls have had lovers before, many of them; they have known life. But this Blanquito is different. He is able to see through them, and when he does that, each of them feels a tingling in her spine, a sensation so frighteningly painful and so deliciously pleasurable at the same time, they cannot wait till they go through it again. Every time they meet each of the girls asks herself, Will it happen tonight? And it does. It always does.

It is not simply the orgasmic catharsis he brings out in each of them. Some of their other lovers were also able to do that. No, it's not that. It is the way he looks at them as they surrender to him. There's ownership in those eyes of his, ownership blessed with both insolence and mischief. He looks at them, and as he looks at them his ardent glance brands their skins with the fire burning inside his demanding eyes. The girls feel tied beyond their control to this young white man, this Blanquito, who asks nothing of them, but who knows everything that needs to be known about them. All he does is look at them, and he commands them with those dark piercing eyes of his filled with so much mystery and magic.

Hortensia is so puzzled by all of this that she and her sister decide to go and consult a *santero,* a black man all dressed in white who commands the black gods, and they ask him what all of this means.

The *santero,* after drinking rum and smoking a thick cigar, begins having convulsions in their presence and speaking in a voice not his own. His eyes turn all white as he speaks, most of his words making no sense at all to the girls. But intermittently the girls seem to catch a phrase the *santero* repeats over and over again. "Red's his father, his mother, his brother, his lover," he says. "Red."

And then he passes out.

When he wakes up, minutes later, and asks if anything happened, the girls tell him what he said, and the *santero* gives each of the girls a bracelet of tiny red beads they each should tie tightly around their Blanquito's manly parts next time they meet.

Mani must have felt something at the time the *santero* was talking to the girls. Changó, the African god of sex, must have spoken to Mani and told him something, because next time they meet, after the girls had each tied tightly their red-bead bracelet around his manly parts—a sign of their possessing him—he asks the naked girls to stand in front of him. And while they are standing in front of him, he kneels in front of each of them and places the thinnest gold chain around each of their bellies—a sign of his possessing them—as he licks the rum out of their darkly perfumed crotches; the thin gold chains glittering fiery gold and ice blue against the dark-brown skins of his standing goddesses.

★ ★ ★

26

Nobody knows if Gustavo really loves Graciela. What everybody knows is that Graciela is the most desirable girl in all of Luyanó, and that because of that, Gustavo decided to make her his wife, just as he decided that he was going to be a poet and a reporter.

Graciela is the youngest daughter of Eleuteria, the evil tongue of Luyanó; that nasty bitter mean woman people fear so much that they take long detours to avoid walking on that side of La Calzada where her house is located. But even cranky old women with narrow beady eyes and thin long necks can produce an outstanding child.

Graciela is just that child.

Her hair is golden with a touch of copper, which, when the light of the tropical sun smiles on her, crowns her head with shimmering beams of light, transforming her into a goddess that seems to have descended from heaven to bring joy to all who look at her. Her smile is sincere, warm, kind; and so are her eyes, which are limpid, the color of olives. Her breasts are round and full, with just the right amount of roundness and fullness to satisfy the most demanding of men; her waist, narrow, but not too narrow; and her hips, plentiful, but not too plentiful. As she walks she dances, like all criollo women do, but she dances an elegant *danzón,* not a rowdy *conga,* which is all the rage in La Habana of 1937.

Her soul is the soul of a child, not a naïve or a gullible one, but an innocent one, a child who is not guilty. She gives the impression she was born without original sin. Women look at her without envy, because she is not envious or conceited in the least; and men look at her without lust, because she seems to be saying with every move she makes, with every pause she takes, that sensual love is something innocent, as innocent as she is; that her frank voluptuousness carries no sin.

It is precisely that sensual innocence that sets Graciela apart not only from her sisters and mother, but from all other women in Luyanó, except for perhaps Dolores, who shares a lot of those qualities Graciela has. And it is this Graciela Gustavo has decided to make his wife.

Gustavo knows that Graciela is loved, admired, respected, and desired by all the young men in the barrio, who night after night pass by her home, which is also Eleuteria's home, hoping to get through to Graciela.

But Eleuteria sits on her porch, night after night, with her beady eyes alert and with her frightening grimace pasted on her face, rocking and rocking and scaring away each one of those good-for-nothing young bullocks that come sniffing around. Eleuteria is Graciela's watchdog; a watchdog with a poisonous bite, something everybody is afraid of. There is only one way to get to Graciela, and that is by bypassing Eleuteria. At least that's what all the bullocks in the area think. And that is why they fail, because there is no way of bypassing Eleuteria.

But that is not the only way to get to Graciela, Gustavo thinks. There must be another way, and Gustavo, who has just finished reading Homer's *La Ilíada,* begins to plan Graciela's siege as if he were a Greek hero planning the taking of Troy. Those Greek men used a very clever stratagem: A hollow wooden horse hiding warriors, which allowed them to take Troy from the inside. And just like them, Gustavo has thought of a stratagem that will allow him to take his Troy also from the inside. And the time has come for Gustavo to put his stratagem to the test. He has decided to begin his siege today.

Nobody knows if he really loves Graciela.

That is not why he decided to make her his wife. Sure, he likes her, respects her, admires her, even desires her. But what makes her a trophy in Gustavo's eyes is that he knows she is desired by every young bully in the barrio, the same bullies who made his life miserable while he was growing up, laughing and sneering at him because he was who he was, someone who was not born in Luyanó, who didn't belong there, and who didn't want to belong there. He's going to show those bullies who is the most powerful of them all by marrying the Helen of their world, Graciela, that Greek-like goddess they all dream of, the one with the golden hair with a tinge of copper and a diadem of glittering sunbeams around her head. So Gustavo, big tall blond Gustavo, he with the pale-blue eyes that, hiding behind glasses, are filled with mischief, decides not to court Graciela in the least.

Instead, he begins to court Eleuteria.

"Good morning, Señora Eleuteria. How are you today? Isn't this your newspaper? Somebody must have dropped it in this puddle." Somebody? Yes, himself! "But don't worry. I'll get you another one. Oh, it's no bother. Why, Señora Eleuteria! Do you think I'd take a penny from you?"

"A butcher? Who? Me? No. A writer, that's what I will be one day, as soon as I find something or somebody to write about. Someone with an interesting life, a life filled with tragedy, with deception, with—what? *Yours?* You don't say! What kind of tragedy, Señora Eleuteria?"

"That man should be hung by his thumbs, Señora Eleuteria. He is just the kind of villain every writer dreams of writing about. If I ever were to write a book, he would be the—come to think of it, Señora Eleuteria, would you let me, I mean, would you be so kind as to let me write about you and that—what, dinner? Oh, no, Señora Eleuteria, I couldn't do that. I could never—well, thank you, Señora Eleuteria. I'm honored."

"Of course they are for you! Who would I buy flowers for, if not for you? Oh, don't mention it. Please, Señora Eleuteria, it's not such a big deal. After all, how often does one get invited to the house of someone whose life is that of a living Christian martyr? How did I know gardenias were your favorite flowers? I don't know. I just guessed. They smell like heaven, so I figured they belonged with you."

"Señora Eleuteria, please! If I got you flowers again it is just because I thought of you while I was at work at the bookstore, glancing over a book. Which book? *The Lives of the Saints,* which is where you belong. You are a writer's dream, Señora Eleuteria. A writer's dream."

"Who? Graciela? Do *I* find her beautiful? I honestly haven't noticed. I guess she must be. In fact, I'm sure she is. She is, after all, your daughter. Certainly she must have inherited something from you. The smile, perhaps? Or the beautiful eyes?"

"Only because you insist, Señora Eleuteria. I know she's beautiful and all, but—what? Oh, no, please, not at all. Please, tell her I really like her. I really do. Just explain to her that I don't really ignore her; it's just that, well, you know, with you around how could anybody—oh, no! I do like her. Yes, I do. A lot. It's just that she's so aloof toward me."

"No, I will not take no for an answer. You yourself have told me once and again that you never go anywhere, so taking you to the movies is not such a—oh, sure, she may come along. Certainly I can afford it! I'm a working man, Señora Eleuteria. I make enough money already to have a wife, that is if I were thinking along those lines, which I am not, not for the time being. Not until our book is finished."

"She likes *who*? *Me*? Is that really what she—*Me*? Take her to Florinda's birthday party? I'd be delighted to, but—I'll tell you why if you promise not to laugh at me, you promise? I don't know how to dance. What? Graciela? Teach me? Oh, no, I couldn't let her go through—well, if you insist. But only because you asked me to, Señora Eleuteria. Oh no, I really like her, I do. She's very nice and—yes, I do."

Nobody knows if Graciela really loves Gustavo.

What everybody knows is that Eleuteria, the evil tongue of Luyanó, thought that this was a match made in heaven and she pushed one way and then she pushed the other way until she got exactly the wedding that she wanted, a real church wedding with white veil, organ music, bridesmaids, rice, and all, something Eleuteria happily paid for.

And since Eleuteria's house was large and empty, now that she had managed to get her two older daughters married to men of her choosing, she invited the newlyweds to move in with her, which they did, occupying a large bedroom all by themselves, at the back end of Eleuteria's house.

It is clear that Gustavo has brought sunshine into Eleuteria's life. The old lady has begun to smile real smiles every so often, even though she still spits on the floor every time somebody mentions her husband's name. She has not seen that man ever since he abandoned her for a mulatto woman. She has not let that man attend the wedding of Graciela, just as she has not let that man attend the previous weddings of either of her other two daughters, because she will not allow that man near her or near any of her girls.

Every time she even thinks of that evil man, Eleuteria, the evil tongue of Luyanó, makes the sign of the horns and prays that the mulatto woman her husband ran off with will crown that evil man with horns so big he will have to bend down his head in order to go through a doorway, and make him the biggest *cabrón* of all Luyanó. She cannot wait for the day that happens. Ever since that man abandoned her, she has been kneeling in front of every saint, begging each and every one of them to give her what she wants. Somewhere up in the clouds there must be a saint to revenge abandoned women. Divine justice demands that. She will never give up until she finds who that saint is. She will get what she asks for. And when it happens, oh, yes! When it happens! That will be, aahhh . . . happiness! Perfect happiness!

And as she thinks that, her hands still making the sign of the horns, she spits on the floor, mentions the man's name, steps on her spit as if the spit were her husband, and crushes that spit with her feet with such violent intensity that sparks of fury can be seen coming from beneath her soles.

"Horns on you, *cabrón*! Horns on you!"

★ ★ ★

27

No sooner had Merced met Tonio than she realized that Tonio was as shy as she was bold, and in no time at all Merced, *La Tora,* the female bull—as her loving kinfolk call her behind her back—took over and convinced Tonio that a wedding should take place. And it did. They got married just a few weeks ago, November 12, 1937, to be exact, not quite two years since they first met.

However, because of the difficult economic conditions all over Cuba at the time of their marriage, Merced and Tonio had no choice but to move in with Tonio's parents in their large old house in Luyanó, a dark cavernous criollo-style house with a lot of room but with very little light.

And yet, as extremely tight as money was, Tonio and Merced did manage to have a honeymoon.

The Athena Book Publishing Company started its life by publishing textbooks, which have a built-in market of students and are therefore always very profitable.

The minute Collazo, the owner of the Athena bookstore, found out that Tonio could understand and speak fluent German, French, English, and a little bit of Hebrew—as well as Spanish, of course—Tonio was immediately given the job of translating foreign textbooks into Spanish, something Tonio has done magnificently well, specializing in books dealing with medicine. It is actually with the help of Tonio that the Athena Book Publishing Company has gotten a foothold in the rest of Latin America, because the very expensive medical books Tonio has translated are very clear and easy to understand. This makes them highly valued and esteemed by doctors all over the Spanish-speaking countries, doctors who have bought Tonio's translations in great quantities and at a great profit to Athena. And to Tonio.

To show his appreciation for Tonio and for his work, Collazo gave him, when he got married, a really nice bonus as a wedding present. And because he had been getting payments for his translations, and because he could speak fluent English, Tonio and Merced decided to spend their wedding night in Miami, Florida, where they stayed for a whole week.

A photograph taken by an itinerant photographer on the streets of lower Miami Beach shows them standing in front of a Studebaker by the ocean, framed by coconut trees. It is a joke photograph: Merced, wearing an elegant turban and smiling broadly, holds Tonio by the lapels of his jacket as he is pretending to run away from her, his thick eyeglasses sliding down his nose, letting us see his frightened eyes staring at the camera with the look of a hopeless victim—a castrated bull held by his tyrannical turbaned mistress.

Tonight is Friday night. Tonio has only been back at work for a couple of weeks after his honeymoon when all the guys at the bookstore decide to accompany Berto, who also works at the bookstore, to a jai alai game where Berto is competing for the championship.

Berto descends from a family that comes from Biscay, a province of Spain that produces the handsomest men in all of Spain, and Berto, handsome as a Greek god, is no exception.

Basque men are known to be tall, much taller than the average Spaniard; their eyes are deeply set, clear and blue, which when contrasted to their dark skin, makes them seem that much more clear and bright; and they are also hairy for the most part, with a black curly mane of hair that makes their beautifully proportioned heads look as if they had been crowned by bunches of the blackest grapes.

Basque men are also as quarrelsome as they are handsome.

Their tempers can rise in seconds to a climax of strength and power that knows no limits, but which quickly subside, disappearing soon again into their habitual state of mind, which is peaceful and kind.

Berto is just like that, but even better for he is always ready with a joke and a smile. Few of the other guys in the store have ever seen him angry, but everybody seems to know about his passionate fits of temperament, because he uses them to his advantage while playing his favorite sport, jai alai, or *pelota vasca,* the Basque national ball game.

Jai alai is played with a small rubber ball, hard as a rock, in a *cancha,* an enclosed three-wall court, where spectators sit on bleachers facing the long side of the court. The game has to be played fearlessly, with the power of gods, and with the speed of lightning. The players wear white long-sleeved shirts rolled up to their elbows, white pants, and a cummerbund, either black or red, so they can be identified. They do not use a racket but a long wicker basket in the shape of a *J*, a *cesta,* with which they catch the ball, swirl it furiously within the basket, and then throw it with lashing intensity, as if they were using a whip.

The game requires great strength and even greater stamina. It also requires great cunning and skill. It is a bulls' game, and Berto is excellent at it. The other guys at the bookstore have been accompanying Berto to the tournament games he has been playing and as usual with criollo men, they bet what they have—and what they don't have—on him. Though he is not yet a champion, Berto is on his way to becoming one. He certainly is the champion player in the bookstore, where his fellow workers have begun calling him *El Campeón* when they refer to him.

Today Berto is scheduled to play against Rufo, a Basque man said to have the strength of Samson, but not necessarily Samson's brains. This is a deciding game in the tournament, and Berto is there surrounded by the rest of the bookstore gang: Gustavo, the poet; Tonio, the linguist; Palmo, the manager of the bookstore; and Sergio and Mauro, who just started to work for Athena last year. They all have come to cheer Berto on and bet on him. Until they see Rufo. Even Berto had to do a double-take when he is placed in the center of the court next to this mountain of a man. Berto has never played against Rufo, and the odds show it. They are very high against Berto, of course, given the fact that Rufo's bulk—a Goliath of a man—makes Berto, who is no small man, look like a little David. Rufo may have strength to boast, but the game is also a game of agility and speed. And though Berto may lack Rufo's strength, he feels he has both the speed and the ability necessary if not to win at least to do a good job and give the spectators a good show for their money.

For the first three quarters of the game, Berto plays defensively, trying to find the heel in this Achilles of a man he is challenging and who is scoring point after point after point. The odds, which were high enough against Berto at the beginning of the match, have grown to be enormous. They were 8 to 1 to begin with. Now they have gone up to 26 to 1! The boys cannot let Berto think that they are not backing him, and before the beginning of the last quarter, they raise one hundred pesos among themselves, twenty pesos a head, which they bet on Berto. Berto, on the court, has just finished drying his sweaty face with a white towel and is readying himself to tackle the final quarter of this grueling game when Gustavo yells, hoping to be heard over the tumultuous crowd, "Hey, Berto! We've got one hundred pesos riding on you! You better do something about it!" "Or it's your job!" shouts Palmo, the manager, jokingly. Though he may mean it. One hundred pesos was a lot of money those days.

When he sees what the boys have done, a heavyset American guy who has been watching the game decides that maybe this Berto is not so bad after all. Berto has speed, which Rufo lacks; and Berto seems to think as he throws the ball, which Rufo never does. Before the quarter begins, the American man—in a three-piece pale-blue seersucker suit with sweat-stained armpits—calls Berto, who moves close to him, and says something to Berto that Berto does not understand. Berto calls Tonio, who translates for him. The American man tells Berto he's placing one thousand dollars on him—which if Berto should win would mean twenty-six thousand dollars to the man—and that if he wins he will give Berto 10 percent of his winnings. All that Berto has to do now is to beat the shit out of Rufo. Berto is flabbergasted. He suddenly realizes that he could make twenty-six hundred dollars! Dollars, not pesos. *Dollars!* in these next few minutes, an amount that is twice as much as his entire yearly salary at the bookstore. "So, *go!*" says the American man as translated by Tonio. "Break the guy's balls!" And Berto decides that is just exactly what he is going to do.

By now he has seen how Rufo has been playing and how Rufo tends to lean heavily on his right leg, favoring his left. So Berto decides he is going to find out how good Rufo's left leg is. Berto begins to play offensively, using brief powerful assaults, making Rufo move all over the court. Rufo, who has begun to pant, begins to lean on his left leg, which bending a little too much makes him miss the ball once and once again. The spirits are growing by the minute as the difference in score between Berto and Rufo diminishes. Drinks are passed around by the men watching the game. Rum for the boys, frozen daiquiries for the heavyset American man with the sweat-stained seersucker suit. The room is becoming hotter and hotter as Berto goes on gaining points and bringing the score closer and closer to a win that seemed impossible a few minutes ago and which now seems possible if only the clock would stop ticking. The crowd is screaming their lungs out. There is not a single woman in the crowd. These are all male bulls excited by the smell of sweat asking for blood.

Berto keeps hitting the balls and dancing all over the court as Rufo keeps missing them, still panting and still favoring his left leg. The crowd suddenly bursts into what seems to be a gigantic scream with the next ball because this time Rufo almost got it in time, but he didn't and the score is now tied. This Goliath has met his David and he doesn't like it. Rufo's anger is beginning to show on his face, and in his playing. He looks at Berto, his face livid with rage.

There are only a few seconds left of this final quarter, and the American man is screaming Spanish four-letter words he does not know the meaning of, but words that make him feel great as he shouts them. And the boys shout them as well. Berto sends a great shot that ricochets on two of the walls and the crowd goes insane because this time Rufo answers it. Rufo has found out Berto's game and he is not going to let Berto get away with it. A ball rebounds on all three walls and Rufo grabs it and is about to serve it, one final whiplash of a throw, when suddenly his left leg bends under him and he misses the shot. Rufo shouts *"¡Coño!"* a slang Cuban word used to show extreme futility against fate, and he shouts it loud enough for the whole world to hear, just as the clock ticks again. And this time the game is over. Rufo hits one of the walls with his basket and smashes it into myriads of pieces just as the boys get onto the court, embrace Berto, and begin to jump up and down, hugging each other as they scream and laugh at the same time. They are doing this for Berto, to honor him. They have not yet realized that their one hundred pesos have become twenty-six *hundred* pesos and that the sweaty man in the seersucker suit has just made twenty-six *thousand* dollars and that Berto has made twenty-six hundred *dollars*! That is, if the American man sticks to his word. And the American man does, and suddenly everybody's laughing and shouting and drinking out of the same bottle that they are all passing around, a bottle of Añejo, the most expensive rum money can buy, aged at least eight years, dark and smooth as only Añejo can be, 151 proof, which makes it more than 75 percent alcohol and which burns down your entire throat, Oh, so good! So damn good!

Berto and the rest of the boys, and even the Americano, who is now a buddy of them all, are hitting the rum when Mauro, the new stock boy at the store, suddenly says, "Let's go to Yarina's House," and they all cheer. That is just what they all need. A good fuck! That's just what they all need and what they all deserve. So the boys decide to go to the house of the notorious Yarina and get themselves the best whores money can buy. All of them except for Tonio, who decides to go home to Merced, his wife. "To give her the good news," he says. His twenty pesos have become five hundred twenty pesos! A fortune in those days, enough to buy a good used car.

The gang is standing under the street light right outside the Jai Alai Palace, waiting for Berto and the Americano, who had to go inside the manager's office to collect their money. They are all laughing and shouting, still in disbelief of their good fortunes, as they all share a second bottle of Añejo. Of course the boys have been making fun of poor Tonio, calling him a henpecked husband, and telling him he is afraid of that female bull he is married to. And Gustavo, who knows his sister really well, improvises a couple of verses to insult Tonio, telling him that she's probably home, biting her lips and getting her knuckles ready to break his skull! The boys in the gang call Tonio "chicken" and "asshole" and many other equal terms of love and endearment as Tonio, looking at them through his thick eyeglasses, shrugs his shoulders and laughs with them at himself.

"What do you mean you're going back to your wife?" says Berto, who has just appeared, a wad of dollars in his hand, and who has overheard the boys making fun of Tonio. "Of course you're coming with us!" Berto sounds half drunk. "We're all of us in this together. I thought we all decided we would go together to—"

Tonio interrupts him. "Oh, c'mon, guys. It's been a long day, and I'm dead tired and—"

But he never finishes his argument. Gustavo picks it up for him, using his most satirical voice, that of a young child about to be scolded. "Oh, yeah, and I have to get home right away because if I don't do it my wife will cut my balls off." No sooner has he said it than Gustavo reaches for Tonio's balls. "Wow!" he shouts. "He's still got some!" As the rest of the gang bursts into huge belly laughs, Tonio tries to get away from Gustavo, but Gustavo won't let him go. "At least I feel one," he goes on.

"Oh, c'mon, man!" says Tonio. "Cut it out, Gustavo! *Cut it out!*"

"Who? Me?" laughs Gustavo. "Cut the only ball you still have left? I thought that's something my sister is an expert at!" he adds, still holding on to Tonio's balls.

All the guys are now laughing loudly, including the Americano, who is now standing next to them, even though he does not understand a word of what's being said. Suddenly Gustavo shouts, "Sshhh, you guys!" He has let Tonio's balls go and has raised his hands, moving them around like a windmill, as he demands, "Let me talk, let me talk!" He keeps shouting and gesturing until he finally manages to silence the boisterous gang surrounding Tonio, all of them now looking at him intently, a jury staring at a man on trial.

"Tonio, man, listen to me," Gustavo says, as he embraces Tonio, brother to brother, his right arm around Tonio's shoulders. "Listen, Tonio." Gustavo has lowered his voice. "You've been married for less than a month. You still have time to show that woman of yours who's in command."

Tonio, who has never been so drunk in his entire life, looks around the group and he sees all of the gang nodding their heads up and down, including the Americano, who is aping the rest of the boys.

"Merced's my sister, and I love her but, man, if you don't put your pants on now, you're never gonna wear'm in your entire life." He now stands face-to-face with Tonio, holding Tonio's shoulders with both his hands. "Look at me," Gustavo demands, forcing Tonio to look him in the eye. "Do I worry if I stay out late? The first weekend after I married Graciela, I told that woman of mine that Friday nights are for the boys. And I went out with you guys, you all remember, don't you?" He faces the rest of the gang, all of whom nod their heads up and down, agreeing with him. Then he faces Tonio again. "I didn't get back till the next morning. And what did I say when she wanted to find out where I had been all night? I told her that was none of her damn business. And guess what? She just said, I hope you had a good time. And I said I did, and that was that! So, c'mon, man. Break loose from that woman of yours and come with us. You still can make it. A man *is* as a man *does,* you know what I mean? You're either a man or a mouse. The choice is yours. What is it going to be, Tonio?"

Tonio looks down at the floor.

Gustavo insists. "Man?" He pauses. "Or mouse?"

There's a long silence as all the guys stare at Tonio, poor drunk out of his mind Tonio, who, raising his badly out-of-focus eyes, slowly turns around, looking intently at each and every one of his jury through his thick eyeglasses, until he finally scratches his receding dark-brown hair and answers with a big doubt on his face.

"Man?"

And all the gang jumps up cheering, "Man! Man! Man!" including the Americano, who is cheering as well.

* * *

28

A month after her wedding, Merced has yet to experience that moment Dolores had described to her years ago when Dolores told her that the day would come when a boy would look at her in such a special way that she would never forget it. "And that boy," Dolores had added, "will make you realize that you are beautiful."

Merced *is* beautiful. Her hair is dark and wavy, her eyes almost black, her figure voluptuous, and her walk sensual. But somehow she lacks Dolores's openness and kindness. When you look into Merced's eyes you see deep pools of darkness that surround a question mark, because though she *is* beautiful, she has never *felt* beautiful. Certainly Tonio has never made her feel that wonderful moment her mother spoke about, a moment of such great intensity that you feel you are one with the universe and the universe one with you, and then you understand everything there is to understand and you stop asking questions.

Merced still hides those questions deep within her eyes.

Before she made Tonio propose to her, Merced was a little reluctant about getting married. She didn't want to leave her home, because she had been doing all the cooking there, and if she were to leave, who would cook for the family?

When Dolores was confronted by this gargantuan dilemma of Merced's, she had no choice but to smile at her daughter and then tell her never ever to worry about them. Hadn't they survived the biggest of all fires and the worst of all hurricanes? If they had survived all of that, they would certainly survive her leaving the house and getting married. Besides, Dolores added, now that Merced was going to be living elsewhere, they would be saving money, enough to get a new cook. And then Dolores told Merced that, given the choice of either a grand meal or a grandchild, she would rather have the latter, which made Merced laugh loudly, though not without embarrassment.

So once that gargantuan dilemma was answered and solved—the only one holding Merced from tying the knot—she went ahead full speed, made Tonio propose to her, taught him to say "yes" and to bow to her every command, and now he's a married man, and she, a married lady.

The newlyweds don't have much in the way of possessions.

But they do have a spectacular bedroom set Tonio bought Merced as a wedding present with money from his translations.

The elegant furniture is done with matched English oak veneers and ebonized wood, creating fanlike patterns. The large beveled mirror that is part of the dressing table with cantilevered glass shelves reflects the double bed, with built-in night tables at either side. There is also an armoire with a large beveled mirror and a chiffonier loaded with hundreds of drawers. On the wall behind the bed is Maestro Romanat's painting, which Tonio had matted with gray linen and framed with a simple thin molding of ebonized wood.

That furniture is all the newlyweds have to their name. That, and several bookcases, painted glossy black, scattered around the rest of the house, fitting where there is room for them, filled with books in all languages and in all subject matters.

The largest of these bookcases, which almost fills an entire wall in the living room, is dedicated exclusively to medical books. One of these books, a German book Tonio is translating at the present, is filled with photographs of naked men and of naked women showing different stages of venereal diseases in such an explicitly graphic manner that after looking at them one would swear never to have sexual contact with anybody else ever again. Tonio keeps leaving this book open on their bed, where he does most of his work, and Merced, every time she sees it, closes it and places it back where it belongs, in the large bookcase in the living room. She doesn't like to look at those frightening photographs of people covered with what she calls "love bruises." Even when she picks up the book, she does it with the tips of her fingers, as if she were holding a badly contagious dead rat in her hand, her left hand, because she is left-handed just as her brother Mani and her mother Dolores are.

No sooner does Merced walk into the living room than she hears her name being called, "Merced, Merced!"

Merced smiles, goes to one corner of the dark living room, and there, inside a large metal cage is an old parrot that likes to call her name. This parrot, Pepe Loreto, is a large tricolor tropical one that many years ago must have been very beautiful. It had been owned originally by Tonio's maternal grandfather, who died when Tonio was nine and left the boy the bird for Tonio to take care of. But now that Tonio is married, he has left his wife to take care of the old bird.

Pepe Loreto is very very old, so old that people in the family do not really know how old he is. At least sixty if not older. But regardless of how old he is, one thing is unquestionable: Pepe Loreto is as grumpy and as nasty a bird as they come.

He never talks when asked to. But the moment he realizes he is no longer the center of attention, that is, when people in the room are talking—and not about him, something he uncannily knows exactly when it happens—right then and there he begins to say his name over and over again, until all conversation ceases and everybody looks at him.

Once he's sure he has captured everybody's attention, he turns his back to all the people in the room, faces the corner behind him, and repeats the same word over and over again as he stares at the wall. "*¡Comemierdas! ¡Comemierdas!*" he squawks. "Assholes! Assholes!"

He is some nasty bird.

As nasty as Tonio's grandfather—long ago gone, thank God—the grumpy old man who taught the bird.

At Tonio's house nobody likes Pepe Loreto anymore, and consequently Pepe Loreto likes nobody back. But apparently, because Merced is new in the household, and because Merced doesn't know that she is not supposed to like him, and because Merced brings him his food, changes his water, places the old tired cover on and off his large cage in the living room, and takes care of him, Pepe Loreto has taken a liking to her. "Merced, Merced!" he calls, and Merced comes to him. And then Pepe Loreto looks at her, and he is not a nasty old grumpy bird anymore. "Merced, Merced! Kiss? Kiss?" he says.

And from the other side of the large cage, Merced sends Pepe Loreto a noisy little kiss that thrills Pepe Loreto and makes him open and close his red, yellow, and green feathers that have seen better times, ruffling them as if he were still a young parrot courting Merced, that pretty girl outside the cage who doesn't know she is beautiful yet.

29

After the boys make up Tonio's mind for him and Tonio finally says, "All right, you guys, you win," and after all the cheering and laughing and shouting cease, one of them—who? Gustavo?—one of them hails a taxi, and the six of them get into the taxi, all six of them, and they all tell the driver at the same time, when the driver asks them, "Where to?" "To Yarina's House!" they all say at the same time, and laugh, and pass a second bottle of Añejo around.

They are on their way to Yarina's, the six of them: Berto, *el campeón;* Tonio, the linguist; Gustavo, the poet; Palmo, the manager; Sergio, the serious one; and Mauro, the new stock boy, who is barely nineteen and whom everybody calls the baby, because he's the youngest one in the group.

The Americano who had been partying with them at the Jai Alai Palace chickened out at the last minute and stayed behind. He bade the boys good-bye the moment he saw that the first bottle of Añejo had been done for and a second one had just started to be passed around. "I b'lieve I've had enough of that thing," he told Tonio. He was so drunk he was barely able to speak. "How the hell do you all call that?" he asked, pointing to the Añejo bottle.

"Aguardiente," Tonio answered. "Fire Water."

The Americano nodded in agreement, and making esses as he walked, he went back to the bar at the Jai Alai Palace, where he ordered frozen daiquiries to soothe his burning throat.

In the taxi, Tonio, who is sitting tight against Berto—four guys had to squeeze into the backseat of the cab—takes a sip and another and still a third one. Berto looks at him. "The way to go, buddy," he says, and patting Tonio's shoulders with his right arm lets it rest there as they all laugh at Tonio, shy Tonio, who is going to Yarina's so he can show Merced who wears the pants in his house.

Tonio is playing with fire, though he doesn't know it yet.

From the moment Yarina opened the doors to her house almost twenty years ago, in 1919, right after the big world war—when millions of American Prohibition dollars found their way to Cuba and bought drinks, smokes, and whores—from that very first moment Yarina's House was, unquestionably, the most fancy and the most famous bordello in all of Cuba. But after an American president visited the establishment and made use of its abundant facilities, Yarina's House became not only the most famous bordello in all of Cuba, but in the whole American continent as well. And deservedly so. Yarina's House is an extraordinarily well-appointed exclusive establishment that caters to all tastes, always with total security, and always with absolute privacy. For a price, of course.

The men—and more recently women—who visit Yarina's House enter it through a very elegant large receiving room, sort of a museum room, where erotic paintings and sculptures as well as antique tools of the trade—Chinese ticklers, dildoes, three-ball strings, cock rings—are artfully displayed inside elaborately carved glass-front dark-mahogany and brass cabinets lining the walls. There the customer is greeted by Yarina herself, a former Cuban beauty who has kept her dark hair dark and her manners immaculate. The customer is then escorted to a private two-room suite where, on top of a glass-top cocktail table in the front room of the suite, photograph albums of naked women and men are found for the customer to select from. Once a selection has been made, if the person or persons selected are available, they show up individually in the privacy of the customer's own suite. Then it is up to the customer to decide which one of them—or which several of them—he or she wants to spend the time with during this visit. Large rooms are available at the customer's request for communal parties and events. The process is simple, quiet, and, above all, private. Payments are made directly to Yarina, who charges for the use of the facilities; the charges increase by the number of people the customer invites into the suite and by the rates of the individual or individuals selected. These rates are determined by age, looks, and experience, and they are posted on the back of the photographs of the models so the customer always knows in advance how much this visit is going to cost, as soon as he or she determines who his or her guest or guests are. Yarina keeps her house impeccably clean, and the members of her staff have to meet strict health regulations. Tipping is allowed, of course.

Recently, with the increased number of American tourists arriving daily on the island—and the consequent growth of business—Yarina has opened a large new room, what she calls her "Cabaret." This room, immediately adjacent to Yarina's House, may be entered directly from it. But in addition to this entrance, this cabaret has a separate entrance located on the opposite side of the block. Yarina built this entrance on purpose, to attract the many single American women tourists who arrive daily in La Habana and draw them into her establishment. That way women can visit the cabaret, claiming not to know the bordello is next door. If after they are inside some of the women decide to visit the rest of the establishment, well, that is something Yarina welcomes them to do, if they want to, for she knows women can learn a lot by using the facilities of her establishment, just as men can too.

In this beautifully appointed new room, Yarina's cabaret, linen-covered tables are set on semicircular platforms at different levels, where customers can order drinks and smokes as they watch a nightly show that consists of a series of live sex acts culminating with the appearance of a man whom American customers—women as well as men who frequent the cabaret—call *Supermán.*

It's almost eleven o'clock by the time Berto and his gang arrive, and Yarina welcomes them with open arms. There is nothing Yarina likes more than a whole bunch of horny guys arriving at her house together with a lot of money to play with.

"You gentlemen in for the show?" Yarina asks, "or do you—"

"What show?" Berto interrupts, as he jumps to the front of the pack. He has figured that since he is *el campeón,* and this party's on him, he will be the official means of communication between the pack, *his* pack, and Yarina.

"Well, if you gentlemen don't know what we can show you, then you don't know what you all are missing. We sure can't let that happen. You all may get to learn a thing or two," she adds, jokingly. "Especially you," she says pointing at Mauro the baby as she winks an eye at Berto, who winks back at her and answers, "That's just what we came here for! I'd certainly like to see what ladies like you can teach guys like us!"

"Then"—Yarina smiles as she leads the pack through—"you all came to the right place," she says. "But I'm warning you," she adds. "It may get mighty hot back there. Maybe even too hot for some of you gentlemen to handle it!"

"That'd be the day," answers Berto for his pack, as they all follow Yarina. "That'd be the day."

The large smoke-filled room is crowded with men and women of all creeds, colors, races, and nationalities. Almost all the tables are already taken. Yarina takes them to a large table slightly to the side of the stage that can hold six people easily, all of them having a clear view of the stage, now concealed by a red traveling curtain.

"The show will start in a few minutes," she says, a broad genuine smile on her face as she removes a sign reading RESERVADO from the top of the table. She then leaves Berto and his gang there, but not before she signals a young waitress who, wearing a semitransparent Greek-like tunic that flows gently over her naked body, lets the guys see she has no pubic hair as they place their order.

A fresh bottle of Añejo is brought in, and reefers, both of which are passed around, as is the custom.

The curtain parts and the show begins.

The boys laugh and blush and yell and cheer as they watch the people onstage and learn possibilities that even Berto, *El Campeón* himself—who claims to be the most experienced one in the group—did not know were possible.

Another bottle of Añejo is being shared and more reefers are being passed around when suddenly the lights dim down and the traveling curtain parts again.

A very tall and very handsome broad-shouldered light-skinned mulatto man, with long black curly hair and a black thick beard and moustache, is discovered onstage, naked, wearing a crown of thorns, his arms and feet tied with ropes to a cross, in a reenactment of the scene of the crucifixion. The man's eyes are downcast, looking at the floor, while his enormous flaccid uncircumcised penis is in a tight pool of light.

The man raises his black piercing eyes, looks at his audience, and as he does that, the audience goes quiet and silent. And so do the boys, who look at the man on the cross and do not know what to expect.

Somehow the sight of this naked man tied to a cross has stopped their laughing and joking, and all of them are now as silent and as quiet as the rest of the people in the room, so silent and so quiet that Tonio can hear how fast the blood is rushing in his veins and how fast his heart is beating in his chest as he looks at the naked man on the cross.

As the room grows totally silent, the man on the cross looks at each and every person in the audience, making direct eye-to-eye contact with each and every one of them, and as he does that—and with no assistance of any kind whatsoever—his flaccid penis begins to grow and harden. A large coral head begins to emerge through the tawny foreskin that surrounds it until, fully exposed, it becomes the focal point of a huge thick dark branch of a penis that, thick with pulsating veins nearly bursting with rushing blood, stands erect, perpendicular to the man on the cross, surrounded by a halo of the thickest and blackest pubic hair.

It is as if the energy the man on the cross sends with his eyes to each person in his audience were being magnified by that person's own energy; and the total energy—the energy of the man on the cross plus the energy of each and every person in his audience—makes the large penis of the man on the cross become larger and larger as it hardens and stiffens.

The audience is very quiet and very silent, and so are the boys, who have never seen anything like this. All of them have their eyes glued to the huge penis of the man on the cross. Berto, Gustavo, Palmo, Sergio, Mauro. All of them except Tonio, whose eyes are looking into the eyes of the man on the cross. The man on the cross notices Tonio staring at him. And as they each stare at each other, the questioning eyes of the man on the cross suddenly smile and radiate beams of immense ecstasy while the huge coral head that tops his thick branch of a penis bursts and spurts, ejaculating torrentially, showering the stage floor with what appears to be an unending supply of seminal fluid.

The spectacle is so awesome that the people in the audience literally gasp and stop breathing while it is happening. Because of the intense eye-to-eye contact, each person in the audience has felt as if he or she had sex with the handsome man tied to the cross; each person in the audience has felt that it had been he or she who caused the man on the cross to suffer that moment of such immense pain and of such immense pleasure that has made the man on the cross spurt his life-giving fluid out of his body.

The lights have gone totally out, and then slowly they have come back, restoring the room back to normal again, the curtain—already closed—concealing the man on the cross behind it. The whole thing has taken only a few minutes, but each and every person in the audience feels as if an eternity has gone by. The experience is so emotional, so disturbing, and so deeply religious at the same time that after it all has happened, people just wipe their eyes in disbelief and cannot wait to sign up for the following evening's show.

"Wow!" says Palmo, shaking his head. "Did you guys see that?"

"How can he do that?" blurts Sergio, the serious one, still in a state of shock.

"After seeing that guy there ain't no way I'm going back there with them whores," says Mauro the baby, who is barely nineteen. "Did you all see the size of that guy's *mandingo*?"

And with Mauro's use of the slang word, all the guys in the gang get back into laughing and joking and teasing, making fun of Mauro's *mandingo,* and of the guy's *mandingo,* and of the weirdness of the whole thing.

"Guys, we gotta get back here again and watch the whole thing again from the very beginning," says Gustavo. And all the guys nod their heads in agreement. "I'd certainly like to see if he can do that again!" Gustavo adds.

"No wonder they call him *Supermán,*" Palmo says in awe.

"There's gotta be a trick," Mauro adds. "You all know there's gotta be a trick to it. Nobody can do what he does every single night, night after night after night! You all know there's gotta be a trick to it." And they all go back to laughing and joking and teasing and passing reefers around and shooting down more of that good-tasting water that burns, Oh, so good!

All of them except for Tonio, who hasn't moved, who doesn't even dare to move, because just as the man on the cross had ejaculated spurting his semen all over the stage floor, his eyes nailed to the eyes of Tonio, just as the man on the cross had ejaculated, Tonio had ejaculated as well. At exactly the identical time both he and the man on the cross had shared the same moment of immense pleasurable pain, and both of them had come together, doing absolutely nothing but staring at each other eye to eye.

So this is what it feels like, thinks Tonio. The pleasure. No, no. No! Not the pleasure! He tries to discard that thought, but he cannot. The pleasure, yes, yes! The pleasure. And the repulsion. And the fear. And the desire. He felt it all at the same time. Now everything is in the open. Now he can no longer deny what he always knew. Now he can no longer hide his secret, a secret he has lived his entire life fighting against, because now . . . now the man on the cross knows. That must be his trick, Tonio thinks. That knowledge. The man on the cross can see through you, deep inside of you, and he knows the truth. It is that truth that makes him come as he does. It is his discovery of hidden secrets that makes the man on the cross a superman, a god. And now the man on the cross knows Tonio's secret. As he realizes that, Tonio begins to vomit.

Yarina, who has been standing in the back of the house like a watchful dog, checking that everything is going as it should, rushes to Tonio's side, accompanied by two of her bouncers.

"It's all right," she tells the rest of the boys. "This happens all the time. At the end of the show there's always some guy who gets sick." She signals the bouncers to help Tonio out of the room. Yarina continues. "What this boy needs is a little bit of fresh air. Take him outside."

Berto, who feels responsible for his entire pack of boys, tells the other boys to stay where they are while he rushes to Tonio and stands by his side. They are now both of them in the private terrace outside Yarina's cabaret. Berto offers his help to Tonio, but Tonio refuses it.

"I'm all right," Tonio says as he tries to stand up by himself. Berto offers his help again. Tonio refuses it again.

"I'm all right, goddammit! Can't you see I'm all right?" But as he says that he becomes sick again.

Berto holds him by the armpits and steadies him. "You stay here, leaning against this wall," Berto says, "while I go get a taxi." He rushes back into Yarina's cabaret, tells the boys to stay and have a good time, finds Yarina, gives her enough money to pay everybody's bills, and asks her to call a taxi for them. Then he rushes back to Tonio, who has become sick again.

Tonio has lost his glasses, which have fallen into a pool of vomit. He is on all fours trying to locate them but cannot find them. Berto gets them for him, washes them in the fountain, wipes them clean, and hands them to Tonio, who puts them on.

Tonio looks at Berto through them, and in his drunken stupor he does not see Berto's face, but the face of the man on the cross, who is looking at him with desirous eyes as he holds him. Desperately Tonio tries to get away from this man who is looking at him with a knowing smile on his face; from this man who knows his secret; from this man who knows.

"Steady, buddy," Berto tells Tonio, who is shaking badly as Berto holds him. "As soon as the taxi gets here I'll take you home and soon you'll be all right. Listen to me, buddy. I've been through this before. As soon as you get home everything will be all right, you'll see."

Tonio looks at Berto again and shakes his head in disbelief. This man who sounds like Berto is not Berto, but the man on the cross. How could that be? Tonio takes his glasses off and wipes them once, and wipes them again, and keeps wiping them just as a taxi turns the corner and enters the circular drive that leads from the street into Yarina's House.

"Where to?" asks the taximan.

"To Luyanó," Berto answers.

And the two men get in the backseat of the taxi and head for Luyanó, where the working-class bulls live.

★ ★ ★

30

Tonio's mother, Leonora, looks at Merced, who is sitting all alone in the living room in the rocking chair next to Pepe Loreto's cage, still uncovered. It's almost midnight and Merced hasn't eaten yet. "You all go ahead and eat," Merced had said when she served the dinner on the table, a great meal she had cooked herself. "I'm not hungry." Everybody else had dinner a long time ago and has already gone to bed. But not her. "Merced, child," says the kind old lady. "You sure you don't want to have anything to eat?"

Merced looks at her, a question in her eyes. Should she confide in her? She decides to. "Where do you think he is?"

The old lady, who has been married to that husband of hers for close to forty years and who knows what it is like to live with criollo men, tells Merced, "Don't worry about him, Merced. I'm sure he'll get home later on tonight so drunk he won't be able to even call your name, and then he's going to fall into bed and sleep it off until he wakes up, sometime Sunday, and then he's going to be *so* nice to you! Believe me, child. I know."

"He's done this before we got married?"

"Well, no, not that I remember. But all men do this." The old lady sits by Merced, and smiles at her. "You see, Merced," she says, "they have to prove to themselves that, even though they are married, they can still do as they please. So to prove they're still free, they go out and get drunk and vomit and the next day they do not remember what it was they did or why they did it. It may sound stupid to you and me, and it probably is, but that's the way our men are. They all do it. So, child," adds the knowledgeable kind lady, "go have something to eat, then get to your bed and don't worry. You only worry if he doesn't show up by tomorrow. But he will. They all do." The old lady grabs Merced's chin and winks at her. "And then, when he is sober, let him have it! Throw a big fight and make a lot of noise! The bigger the fight, the better! There's nothing like a great reconciliation after a big fight, Merced. In fact, the bigger the fight, the more fun the reconciliation." The old lady pats Merced's hands and smiles at Merced, who smiles back at her. Leonora leaves the room and as she does, Merced hears Pepe Loreto calling her.

"Merced, Merced! Kiss? Kiss?"

Merced goes to the parrot's cage, gives a seed to the old bird, sends him a kiss, making the old bird ruffle his tired old feathers in delight, covers the cage with the old faded tapestrylike cover, and turns off the light by the rocking chair. Suddenly the room is totally dark, lighted exclusively by the moon, beaming full, and casting blue shadows on the tiled floor of the living room. It was just last full moon Tonio had made love to her for the first time. That night, less than a month ago, had been a night of confusion. She didn't know until then that just as she was a virgin so was he.

TONIO IS in the taxi. He is still wiping his glasses, which still smell of vomit. He puts them on again and suddenly he realizes that the man inside the taxi is not *Supermán,* but Berto, who is sitting next to him. "What are you doing here?" he asks. His speech is slurred. He can barely get the words out.

Berto leans over to Tonio's side and opens wide the side window of the taxi close to Tonio to let as much fresh air as possible into the taxi while he answers. "Going to Luyanó."

"You? What for?"

"I've got this friend of mine who lives in that neck of the woods, and he is not feeling so good tonight, and I'm gonna stop by his house and make sure he's all right when we get there."

"At this time of night?"

"Sure, at this time of night. What time do you think it is? It's not even midnight yet. And let me tell you something, buddy. It's Friday night and I've got a bundle of money in my pocket!" He pulls out a wad of paper money from his left-hand pocket in his pants and shows it to Tonio. "Twenty-six one-hundred big ones!" He riffles them. "Well, twenty-five now, because I gave one to Yarina and told her to take good care of the rest of the boys."

Berto is as drunk as Tonio is, but he seems to be able to handle it better. He sticks his head out the side window by his side, which he has also opened wide. "Do this," he tells Tonio. "It'll make you feel a lot better!" Tonio does it. "Isn't it fun?" adds Berto. Tonio does not answer. "You know what we should do tonight?" Berto is now shouting at Tonio, who, sticking his head out of his window, is enjoying the gusts of cold night air as they refresh his face. "We should do something we have never done ever before! After all, how often does anybody make this kind of money in just fifteen minutes, eh? So, what do you say? How about doing something really wild!"

"Like what?" shouts Tonio back, his head still out the window.

"I don't know. Something like . . ." Berto pauses.

The taxi driver is taking them to Luyanó via a wide avenue that follows the length of the entire bay of La Habana. There are large ships moored everywhere, and everywhere there are sailors, and hookers, and drunkards, singing songs and dancing in the streets at the sound of the distant drumming that is always accompanying the nights of La Habana.

"I got it!" shouts Berto as he looks at the bay out his side window. He sticks his head back inside the taxi and tugs and tugs at Tonio until he also sticks his head back inside the taxi. Berto places his left arm around Tonio's shoulders, gets really close to him, and asks him, "How about taking a boat and going across the bay to Regla? Eh? Have you ever been to Regla at night?" Tonio shakes his head. "Man," adds Berto, "let's do it!" Tonio shakes his head one more time. "C'mon, man, let's do it. Don't you ever do anything just for the fun of it?"

Tonio looks at Berto and smiles for the first time. "I always do everything just for the fun of it. It so happens," he adds, "that, as the saying goes, *'I haven't lost anything in Regla,'* and even if I had, going to Regla in the middle of the night is not top priority on my list of fun things to do. Besides, as you can see"—he points to the city in front of them—"we are way past the docks already. We are entering the—"

Berto interrupts him. "Hey, look!" he says, and points to a brand-new six-story-high building with a large neon sign on top that lights on and off. "Over there!"

"What? The Hotel Royale?" asks Tonio tentatively.

"Yeah! Have you ever been there?" No sooner has Tonio shaken his head than Berto tells the taxi driver, "Stop! Stop! *Stop!*"

The taxi driver stops in front of the hotel, and Berto, sitting on the side of the cab facing the hotel, sticks his head out the window and looks up at the brand-new building that is not too far from the bay.

"I bet you anything"— says Berto, putting his head back inside the car and talking to Tonio—"I bet you *any*thing that you can see the bay from the top floor! You wanna bet?" Tonio bends down inside the taxi and tries to look up at the top floor of the hotel through Berto's side window but cannot manage to do it. Berto opens his door and gets out. "I'm going in and finding out. Wanna come?" He holds the door open for Tonio, who steps out into the night air as Berto gets out a ten-peso bill, pays the taxi driver, and says, "Keep the change!"

Three men, two guitar players and a maracas player, are standing by the entrance door to the hotel, singing. Berto gives them a tip, which they acknowledge with a nod of the head and keep on singing, while Tonio, on the sidewalk, looks up at the hotel, which closely resembles the one in Miami Beach where he spent his honeymoon, less than a month ago.

The entire building is stuccoed, painted in a pale pink, and each floor has several horizontal bands of stucco in different shades of turquoise. There's a central tower with circular windows that probably houses the stairs and which splits the building into two wings. Berto looks up and sees somebody opening the windows on the uppermost floor. They are corner windows and as they are opened, the corner seems to disappear. "Hey, Tonio," Berto says, "have you ever been in a hotel before?" Tonio nods. "Yes, when I was in Miami. But that was—"

"Well, I haven't been to any," interrupts Berto. "So, c'mon, let's check this one out!"

Tonio hesitates. He is looking at Berto, who is beginning to look like the fun-loving Berto he knows, not the man on the cross he thought he had seen in Berto's eyes not too long ago.

"What are you waiting for? Let's go have a drink. That's probably what you need. You know what they say, you gotta use a nail to get out another nail!" He smiles and he begins to walk up the few steps leading to the hotel lobby. He reaches the top, turns around, looks down at Tonio and shouts. "It's now or never, buddy. So, c'mon, make up your mind."

Tonio looks up at Berto, who is standing at the top of the steps looking down at him, his dark mane of hair framed by the hot pink and turquoise reflections of the neon sign that is flashing above their heads. "All right," he says, shrugging his shoulders. "All right. But only one drink, you hear."

Tonio cannot manage the steps all by himself. Berto rushes down to him, holds him by the armpits, and helps him go up the steps.

"I hear. Just one!"

They are now sitting at the bar. The room is done, floor, walls, and ceiling, in an intense dark blue, the color of tropical nights. There seem to be hundreds of tiny recessed incandescent lights resembling constellations of stars in the dark-blue ceiling. The bar itself has a lot of horizontal chrome bars reflecting the glittering stars above and the two men as they talk. Berto asks for an Añejo shot for himself with a beer chaser. The barman looks at Tonio, who has managed to clean himself up in the hotel bathroom, where he had to tip a guy a dime so he would let him have a clean towel.

Noticing that the barman is looking at him, Tonio turns to Berto with a puzzled look on his face. Then, all of a sudden realizing he is supposed to order a drink, turns to the barman. "The same," he says, "whatever it is my friend here's having." The barman goes to fetch their drinks as Berto faces Tonio, a big smile on his face.

"Wasn't that guy great?"

"Who?" says Tonio. "The barman?"

"No, man. *Supermán.* The guy at Yarina's."

Tonio takes his glasses off and begins to clean them again, though he has just gotten them perfectly clean in the men's room in the hotel.

"I don't know how he did it," Berto goes on, "but you know what?"

Tonio has put on his glasses again and faces Berto.

"All the time he was looking straight at me. Isn't that something? Here's this guy who's looking straight at me and he's getting this huge hard-on! And you know what? I was getting one too! Now isn't that something?"

The barman comes in carrying two shot glasses and two beer glasses. He pours lager beer into each of the tall glasses, a beer so light that it sparkles in the midnight-blue darkness of the room; gets a bottle of Añejo, opens it, fills the shot glasses to the brim, and leaves the two men alone.

"That guy," says Berto, as he takes his Añejo and shoots it down his throat, "*Supermán,* I mean. That guy . . . he knows." Berto follows his shot with some beer, and then he adds, as he looks at Tonio straight into his eyes, "That guy, he sure knows a *lot* about *something*!"

Tonio shoots his Añejo down his throat and follows it up with the cold soothing lager beer, as he looks back straight into the eyes of *El Campeón*.

And what he sees are not the eyes of Berto, but the eyes of that other man, the man on the cross, *Supermán*, looking back at him.

BY THE TIME Tonio gets home it is past five o'clock in the morning. Merced is awakened as he enters their bedroom. Tonio is still in a drunken stupor. Merced looks at him, but Tonio says nothing.

He sits on the edge of the bed and proceeds methodically to take off first his jacket, then his tie. Merced smells the strong alcohol smell on his breath and the faint smell of vomit on his clothes.

"Where have you been?" she asks, addressing her question in a rasping whisper at the man she sees in the mirror opposite their bed. She didn't mean to ask, but the question just blurted out by itself. Tonio does not answer. "I've been so worried about you." Tonio is beginning to unbutton his shirt. He doesn't look at her as he answers.

"Out with the boys. Just having a couple of drinks, that's all. A guy needs to be with other guys every so often, you know. That's part of what we guys do. You had no reason to worry about—about anything."

"But Tonio," she says, "you could have called me. I've been—"

Tonio interrupts her, raising his eyes and looking at her in the mirror. "I told you there is nothing to worry about. I was just—"

It is then Merced sees them.

"Oh, my God!" she gasps, and then covers her mouth with her left hand.

"What? What?"

"You are disgusting!"

Tonio has been taking off his shirt and Merced has seen hickeys on Tonio's neck and on his entire upper torso.

Tonio follows Merced's eyes in the big mirror facing him, looks at himself, and he sees them too, hickeys, on his torso, his arms, his neck.

"You are *disgusting*! You and your"—she pauses, just to spit the words out—"your disgusting *love bruises*!"

She says that with such repulsion that it makes Tonio look closer at himself in the mirror. She runs out of the bedroom and into the living room, where she sits, enraged, trembling and sobbing at the same time, deeply hurt and deeply desiring to hurt back.

She wants to scream and let everybody know about what that man, that innocent-looking man who hides behind those thick glasses, what that man has done to her, but she doesn't want *his* family to see her cry. She is Maximiliano's daughter. A female bull. And female bulls do not cry. They strike back. But that will have to wait. Right now she does not want him to see how deeply hurt she is.

So that is why, she says to herself. That is why he has never looked at me the way my mother told me he would. That is why things have not been working out between the two of us. That is why our lovemaking has been uninspired, with no passion, no nothing. Because he's found somebody else who brands him with disgusting love bruises! It must be a mulatto woman, she tells herself. What does she have that I don't have? What is lacking in me? She torments herself with question after question. She has the passion. She knows she has the fire. Why hasn't he ignited her? Why hasn't she ignited him? What is wrong with her? What is wrong with her?

She hears Pepe Loreto call her from beneath his night cover.

"Merced, Merced!"

She moves silently to the cage, removes the cover, and erasing her tears looks at the old bird, who repeats his name.

"Pepe Loreto, Pepe Loreto."

She takes a seed and gives it to him. She uses her left hand, because she is left-handed, and as Pepe Loreto takes the seed from her hand, she sees her wedding ring reflecting the light of the early tropical morning, deep orange, the color of embers. Merced hushes the bird who is now saying, "Merced, Merced! Kiss? Kiss?" as she covers his cage again. And then, looking at the ring on her left hand, she collapses on the old cane rocking chair next to Pepe Loreto's cage; a rocking chair that creaks gently every time she rocks, as she tries to put herself to sleep repeating in her mind the same words over and over again and again. What is wrong with me? What is wrong with me?

In their bedroom, Tonio looks at himself in the large beveled mirror of the elegant dressing table he had selected for his wife. He is in his undershorts, and he is pressing the tips of his fingers against his chest, touching each of the love bruises, kisses of fire branded on his skin that are burning without hurting. While looking in the mirror he notices the gold wedding band on his left hand which has begun to reflect the emberlike light of the early sun, and silently, so the rest of his family will not hear him, he sits on the edge of the bed and weeps, asking himself, What is wrong with me? What is wrong with me?

A long while goes by.

In the quietness of the early morning the other people in the house can be heard happily snoring in their bedrooms.

Pepe Loreto, hiding under his cover, aware that Merced is still in the living room close to him, keeps repeating over and over again, "Merced, Merced! Kiss? Kiss? Merced, Merced! Kiss? Kiss?"

And since nobody answers, just as the large grandfather clock in the living room bongs six times, the bird angrily adds, "*¡Comemierdas! ¡Comemierdas!*"

★ ★ ★

31

As Gustavo's wife, Graciela, approaches the butcher shop, she sees in front of her a large group of women who are standing in line, impatiently waiting for their turn at the counter; and as they wait and wait, all of them are following intently with their eyes a man who, carrying a bull draped over his back, brings it into the shop, places it inside Maximiliano's cooler, goes back out to the Street of the Bulls where his truck is parked the wrong way, gets inside the truck, walks out with another bull draped over his back, goes back into the butcher shop, and back into the cooler, and back out again.

Meanwhile, Mani and Maximiliano are busy, really busy behind the counter, taking orders, cutting meat, wrapping it, and dispatching it as fast as they can while they keep listening and listening to the constant whining and whining of the women who keep cackling and cackling in front of them, complaining and complaining while they keep on sighing, and drumming their feet on the tile floor, and fanning themselves, and looking at their watches, and talking and talking to each other about the meat being late; about, How much longer do we have to wait?; about, Why is this taking so long?; about, Please, butcher man, hurry up!; and about, Don't you know that we have to get back home and fix the noontime meal for our children and our husbands? Don't you know that meal takes hours to prepare? For God's sake, butcher man, look at the time, *look at the time!*

Nothing would have happened if Ferminio's meat delivery truck had not had a flat tire, or if that other guy, Ferminio's assistant—who normally drives Ferminio's truck—had not called in sick this morning.

But he did call in sick this morning, and someone did drop a nail on the streets, and Ferminio's truck loaded with meat did roll over the damn nail, and a tire did go flat.

And that's how this whole thing got started.

Since today is Tuesday, Ferminio's meat-delivery truck was due at the butcher shop, like on every Tuesday, early in the morning, before tropical sunrise, which is really early.

Mani and Maximiliano were at the butcher shop waiting for the truck to arrive to help unload it, but the truck did not show up. This had never happened before. There is no telephone at the butcher shop, so Maximiliano sent Mani home and told him to call Ferminio to find out what was going on. After a while Mani came back to the shop and told Maximiliano about the flat tire. "Ferminio told me," said Mani, "that as soon as they take care of it they'll be here."

It took a lot longer than they had anticipated.

By the time the truck finally made it to the butcher shop, it was almost noon and the shop was filled with customers, irate women who have been waiting a long time for their meat and who have been driving both Mani and Maximiliano crazy with their whining and sighing and arguing and complaining and cackling and cackling.

How did these frantic women expect the two of them to handle their orders when the meat has just arrived!

Ferminio's son-in-law, Arsenio, the one who married Fernanda at the cathedral, who has given Ferminio his first grandchildren, and who, like Ferminio, can easily kill a bull with a single blow of the hammer, that man was driving the truck today.

He is not the regular driver of the truck—Ferminio's assistant is—but when that guy called in sick this morning and Ferminio asked, "Who can drive?" and when nobody volunteered, Arsenio said he'd do it. So there he was, Arsenio, driving the delivery truck for the first time, all by himself, with no one to assist him. And the damn truck had to roll over a damn nail on the damn streets!

It took what, to Arsenio, seemed like hours before he could get to Maximiliano's shop. He parked the truck on the wrong side of the

Street of the Bulls so that the back of the truck was as close as possible to where the door to the cooler in Maximiliano's butcher shop is located, and then, since he was late, and since Mani and Maximiliano were busy trying to handle a huge crowd of cackling women, all of whom managed to get there at the very same time, Arsenio offered to unload the meat all by himself, something that is normally done with the help of both Maximiliano and Mani.

Arsenio is one of those criollo men whom no one can ever call handsome, but then he does not need to be. He exudes an animal quality, something brutally masculine, which makes him seem totally out of place among these women who, complaining and complaining about their meat being late, keep looking and looking at him out of the corner of their eyes, eyes that are half frightened, half desirous.

But Arsenio does not look back at any of them. He just wants to get the hell out of this place and back to where he belongs, with the bulls, at the slaughterhouse.

He is late, and he is tired, and he hates all of this midmorning traffic, which is ten times as heavy as the early morning traffic, and he's had a flat tire, and he didn't know where the spare was, and he had to find a damn phone to call the damn slaughterhouse where Ferminio told him where the damn spare was, and, let's face it, this has not been his day. He just wants to get this job done. This is his last delivery, thank God! And after this he can head back to the slaughterhouse at the other end of the street where at least things are peaceful and quiet, even as the bulls are getting killed, but he doesn't mind that. That he is used to. It is these cackling women! Who can *cope* with them! He doesn't understand how Maximiliano and his son can handle all of these women who seem to be wiggling worse than worms! Lord! Does he love working at the slaughterhouse where you're surrounded only by bulls and bull-like men!

Arsenio is solidly built, just like Mani and Maximiliano. He wears a blue work shirt, but he does not wear an undershirt, something both Mani and Maximiliano do. Arsenio's shirt is partially open at the top, revealing a hairy chest covered with big drops of sweat as he unloads the heavy bull carcasses off Ferminio's truck. He is wearing high black-rubber boots, the kind they all wear at the slaughterhouse, and his baggy brown pants, heavily stained with blood, are pushed inside his boots, making him look as if he were wearing some kind of very dirty army camouflage uniform. He wipes the sweat off his forehead every so often with a red bandanna, which he finally ties around his hair as a head band. His hair is black, so black it is almost blue. And so are his eyes, which are penetrating and deeply set.

He has a broken nose, something that happened to him years ago when he got involved in a serious fistfight with another of the guys at the slaughterhouse who ended up with a broken jaw, four broken ribs, and bruises everywhere, including a badly bruised ego. This guy had accused Arsenio of marrying Ferminio's daughter, Fernanda, to inherit Ferminio's business. It is true that Fernanda was not and never will be the most beautiful girl to look at in the world. But she was very nice to Arsenio, and what was Arsenio to do, a grown man already almost thirty and not yet married? The time had come for him to go ahead and settle down, and he did it.

That Fernanda came with the business was an additional asset, not to be undervalued. But that had not been the main reason for him to marry her. No. It just happened that Fernanda was the only decent woman he had ever met up to that time, and one only marries decent women to raise one's children. And children Arsenio wanted, like all men do, which he and Fernanda have two of already in their three years of marriage, a pair of twins, two pretty girls with even prettier smiles.

In addition to the broken nose, Arsenio has a thick bushy moustache, totally out of fashion in 1938, and several days' growth of beard. Arsenio did not shave this morning. The guys at the slaughterhouse seldom if ever shave. Most of them have fully grown beards and thick moustaches, which make them look totally out of place under the tropical sun. Arsenio hasn't bothered to shave in a couple of days. Today is Tuesday, the day meat is delivered to Maximiliano's butcher shop, so the last time he shaved was probably last Sunday morning when he took a long well-deserved shower. He had come back home late Saturday night, dead tired after spending a long hot day with the bulls, and a short hot night with a woman, the kind he likes to play with, the kind who likes her men sweaty and unshaved, which is all right with him.

To Arsenio, Fernanda is the mother of his girls, that is all. He has given her what she wanted and she has given him what he wanted. Arsenio respects her, admires her, and even in his own way loves her. But he has never desired her. She has never fulfilled that part of him. Their lovemaking is and has always been functional and to the point. Which incidentally is perfectly all right with Fernanda, to whom that part of love is best ignored.

So, when Arsenio feels the blood begin to rush in his veins, he does as he must. And after it's all done, well, back to business again. Those women mean little if anything to him. He knows that, Fernanda knows that, even Ferminio knows that. That's how it is.

That's the way of the bulls.

Arsenio has just finished unloading the truck and now he is leaning against the side wall of the butcher shop, which is totally covered with shiny white tiles that look like mirrors, that's how sparkling they are. He is counting the money Maximiliano has given him to pay for the meat.

Maximiliano deals in cash, and so does Ferminio, and so does everybody else in the Cuba of the time. The time of checks and banks has not arrived in their world yet. In their world, money is earned in cash; it is spent in cash. It is counted once. And then it is counted a second time. Then a receipt is signed and given, and that's the way criollo men do business: a handshake, cash, and a receipt.

Arsenio is counting the money a second time when he stops for a second or so, because he just felt something disturbing: an electrical current that has gone up and down his spine. He has felt this before every time something important is about to happen in his life. He felt it right before he killed his first bull. He felt it right before his twins were born. And he has just felt it again. What triggers it? He doesn't know. What is it? A vibration?

He looks up and notices a beautiful young woman who is standing last in line.

She wears no makeup. She has on a plain blue skirt and a thin white blouse with short sleeves through which he can make out the brassiere. She has beautiful breasts, round and full, which move ever so slowly as she breathes. Her hair is golden with a tinge of copper. Her eyes he cannot tell, because she has not looked at him.

He is looking at her, and he sees her naked, under him, pulsating with infinite pleasure as he is entering her slow and long, riding her high, the way he knows drives a woman like that wild, while he is licking her neck, her earlobes, her armpits, and sending her into a world she would never want to return from.

It lasts but a second, the vision.

Then he goes back to counting the money, but he's lost count and he has to start all over again.

Graciela is standing in line when she looks at the man leaning against the white-tile wall; a man who smells of sweat and blood even at that distance; an unshaven man with a broken nose who is counting his money as if nothing else matters.

And then he feels he is being looked at.

He raises his dark penetrating eyes, finds her receptive olive eyes looking at him, and stops counting again.

This time it is she who sees herself naked, under him, he who is entering her slow and long, possessing her the way she has read about, the way she has heard it talked about, the way she has dreamed about, the way it should be, the way it's got to be. The way it has never been with Gustavo, the man she is married to.

She sees herself being his, totally his, completely his, every pore of her skin, every inch of her body, every thought of her head. She feels every atom in her body pulsating to the same insane rhythm and speed as every atom in his body pulsates. She sees those deeply set and penetrating black eyes nailed to hers and she sees and hears and smells and feels nothing else.

This is the feeling to have when one dies, she feels, or when one is reborn again. This enrapturing frightening feeling that makes her tremble with a passion she has never experienced before. She feels the wetness between her thighs and wonders if it shows.

She knows he knows what she wants, and he knows he's got what she wants, and that he is going to give it to her, just as she knows that there is nothing, nothing in the whole world that can stop her from following this man wherever he wants to go; from doing whatever he wants to do whenever he wants to do it; from surrendering to him at whatever time of day or night, alone or in front of a thousand people. Who cares? Nothing, nothing in the world can stop her from completing herself, from finding in him that missing piece that makes the whole puzzle of her life suddenly comprehensible and astonishingly beautiful and simple at the same time. All that is needed now is the When and the Where. The What and the How have already been taken care of.

Her heart is beating so loudly and so fast that she thinks everybody must be listening to it. But nobody is. The other women who had been looking at the man with the red bandanna headband have by now lost interest in him, because he is not looking back. He is just doing his job and counting his money, which Arsenio has begun to do a third time around. But he stops before he is through.

He tells Maximiliano the butcher, "I have to go to the truck to get you a receipt."

He says that to Maximiliano, but he is looking at her.

And suddenly she realizes that the When is Now. And the Where is Here.

Arsenio goes to the front of the truck, looks around, and satisfied that nobody can see him, enters the cab of the truck on the passenger side and unlocks the secret compartment, carefully hidden under the passenger seat, where he has stored all the money that he has been paid for the other deliveries he has already made this morning.

Because of the way Arsenio parked the truck, absolutely no one in the butcher shop can see what it is he is doing in the front of the truck. Besides, since it is past noon, most people are already home for their noon meal and afternoon siesta; most people except the irate women still inside the butcher shop. As Arsenio looks around a second time, the narrow Street of the Bulls is totally deserted.

He opens the secret compartment, places the money Maximiliano just gave him inside, finds the book of receipts, makes one out to Maximiliano the butcher, closes the compartment, looks around again, sees nobody has seen him, steps back into the butcher shop, hands Maximiliano his receipt, says, "Thank you for your business," and exits.

Maximiliano takes the receipt in his hands, listens to what Arsenio has said, but does not answer it.

He still has a crowd of women, all of whom are clamoring for their meat right now and how is he going to let them have it if he has just gotten the damn meat delivered to the shop? So he and Mani begin to cut, weigh, wrap; cut, weigh, wrap; and pay no attention to Arsenio, who has gone back to his truck.

Arsenio folds the metal ramp back into the truck, closes the heavy loading doors, goes to the front of the truck, opens the driver's door, enters the truck, sits behind the wheel, and starts the truck, which begins to move up the hill.

He is driving on the Street of the Bulls with its thousands of loose rocks, of every shape and size, which make the truck shake violently every inch of the way up. His eyes are nailed to the hill in front of him. He shoves the truck into first gear and goes up the steep hill, not looking to his right.

He doesn't have to.

He knows she is there, sitting by his side, watching him in silence and waiting, her thighs wet with the same desire that has filled his body with wildly rushing pulsating blood.

★ ★ ★

32

Dolores knows as all mothers know that something is not right with Merced.

She has heard rumors.

But Dolores never listens to rumors. She does listen to Leonora, Tonio's mother, who has just come to visit Dolores.

The old lady wastes no time. Practical women never do. She sits down, sips some of that great dark Cuban coffee that Paula, the new cook, has just brought in, and then, immediately after Paula leaves the room, she blurts out, "Of course you know why I am here."

Dolores sips some of the coffee.

Manuel the doctor has told her once and again that he does not want her to have any of it, because it is so bad for her ailing heart and for her high blood pressure. But she sips it nonetheless. Silently, she nods her head up and down several times.

"What are we going to do?" asks the old lady.

Leonora is easily twenty years older than Dolores. Tonio was her last child, and she had him when she was in her mid-forties. At first, when her period failed to show up on time, she thought she was going through menopause, what she called the change of life, but when she went to her doctor he laughed at her.

"I didn't know the old man still had it in him," he said grinning ear to ear.

Leonora was both delighted with this news and yet apprehensive about it at the same time. She loved the idea of still being fertile at her age. But she didn't know how she was going to be able to handle raising this child. After all she'd be almost sixty when this child reached puberty and her husband way past seventy! How can a pair of old people deal with a teenager! It had been difficult enough to raise their other five children. But it would certainly be taxing to raise this one. And yet, if that's the way God wanted it . . . what else could they do? She thanked her doctor and went back home.

When she told her husband the news, the old bull went out with all of his buddies and did not come back for two whole nights. And when he did come back he was still so drunk he stayed in bed for two solid days. It had been some celebration! How often does a man pushing sixty get his woman pregnant?

"You know it must be bed problems," the old lady adds. Dolores agrees silently.

Dolores has been having bed problems of her own lately, what with her heart in the condition it is in and with that handsome man she's married to who still thinks he's a young bullock at stud. Love is one thing and what people do in bed another.

After the last time Dolores had one of her oppressive chest pains, Manuel the doctor had come and checked her thoroughly. Her blood pressure was up in the clouds, he said. And then he called Maximiliano into the room and told both of them, not without embarrassment, to stop all carnal relations, as he put it, for a while.

"Dr. Manuel," Dolores asked, "does that mean I can no longer be a woman to my husband?"

Manuel glanced at Maximiliano as he answered her. "Dolores, I am sure you will always be a woman to this man," he told her, politely evading the question. "All I'm asking both of you is a little sacrifice just until your pressure gets back to normal again, which won't be long if you follow the plan I just gave you." Then he turned to Maximiliano, "Maximiliano," he said, "make sure she follows it to the letter."

"Don't you worry," Maximiliano answered, "I'll make sure she sticks to it. And when she's well again . . ." He paused and looked at Dolores with those insolent eyes of his, "You and I are going to have a hell of a good time!"

Dolores chuckled, and covered her mouth with her left hand, the way she always does when she is embarrassed.

Dolores knows she has the whole of Maximiliano's love, no question about that. All she has to do is look at him and she sees the answer in his eyes. She also knows that a man needs to prove himself to himself constantly, to show he still has it in him. That's the way with criollo men. You cannot stop a bull from behaving like one, especially when they are aging bulls. She had seen her own father do that. Didn't he marry a girl half his age?

Dolores smiles to herself. She'll follow the plan, and she'll wait. And in the meantime, as long as she is still the cathedral, what difference does it make how many churches her Maximiliano goes to pray in?

Dolores looks at Leonora who just asked her, "Have you spoken to Merced?"

"No," Dolores answers, shaking her head. "Have you spoken to Tonio?"

"No." The old lady shakes her head several times. "Not really," she adds. "I started to, yesterday morning, but—"

The old lady takes a deep breath and then spurts out, "He spent all of last weekend out of the house, the *entire* weekend. He didn't come back until early Monday morning. I was awake in my room and I heard him come in. I thought maybe he'd be drunk, but he wasn't. He just went to his bedroom, took a shower, changed his clothes, and then left for the office. I don't think he and Merced ever exchanged one single word. This had never happened before, and, Dolores, I don't know what to do. She hasn't said anything to you?"

Dolores shakes her head, saying nothing.

The old lady places her tiny cup of coffee on a little white tray as she says, "I tell you, Dolores, the only bed problems I ever had in my life was having too much of you-know-what, but these two children of ours . . . I don't know. They do not seem to be having any."

★ ★ ★

33

It's Tuesday afternoon, and like every other Tuesday afternoon for the last many Tuesdays, Graciela is again with Arsenio, sharing a few stolen minutes with each other in the same small room in the same *posada* she and he spent that first afternoon together, many Tuesdays ago, the day of the flat tire, when they shared a few stolen minutes with each other for the very first time.

The room is very small and musty, but they do not notice it. They are standing in front of each other, his deep penetrating dark eyes staring deep into her eyes, the color of olives.

The room has just been paid for, the little door within the door to the corridor has been closed, the clerk has walked away, and they have finally been left alone. The strong direct amber light of the hot afternoon sun coming through the clear transoms above the shuttered high windows bathes them, outlining Arsenio's dark suntanned face with a heavy band of gold and streaking Graciela's copperlike hair, which, catching the sun, makes it glitter and dance in the semidarkness of the enclosed small musty room.

Outside the room there are buses running, and people chasing them, and vendors singing, and children screaming, and yet the two of them inside the room hear no sounds but the rhythmic humming of the ceiling fan moving ever so slowly above their heads and the rhythmic beating of the rushing blood boiling ever so violently in their veins as they stare at each other.

They say nothing to each other.

They have seldom spoken to each other since that first afternoon, when they both discovered they belonged together in a world of their own, a world where everything else vanishes and where nothing else is important except the two of them. They have so little time, they cannot say anything to each other.

Besides, they don't need to. What needs to be said is best said by doing.

She grabs his face in her hands, brings it down to her, and hungrily, almost desperately, bites his lips, hard, until she can taste his blood.

He takes her hands in his, forces them behind her back, pulls her toward him until her body melts into his, and tastes her lips, her nose, her earlobes, her neck.

He likes this woman. Lord! How he likes this woman! He cannot wait from one Tuesday to the next until he takes her.

He thinks of her all day long.

He wakes up and his first thought is of her.

He goes to the slaughterhouse, and on his way there he thinks of nothing but her.

He kills his first bull and he breathes and he thinks of her; he kills the next bull and he sweats and he thinks of her; and he thrusts the killing spike deep into the brains of yet another bull and he pauses and he thinks of her, of nothing but her.

He thinks of her while he is sharing the bulls' blood with the rest of the guys; while he is scrubbing his bloody hands under the rushing water of the cold faucet; while he is washing his face and wiping his eyes and sharing a joke with the rest of the guys.

He thinks of her while he goes back to that place he calls home and sits next to that woman he calls wife and shares a meal with those people he calls family.

He thinks of her while he restlessly turns around in his sleep, and it hurts.

It hurts to think of her.

It hurts every time, just like *aguardiente* hurts every time you shoot it down your throat but no sooner does it hurt than you want to have more of it.

It hurts all the time.

But it hurts the worst whenever he dreams of her at night, which he does night after night after night.

That first night, the night after she had awakened in him for the first time that fire he had he didn't even know was there, that very same night, he woke up in the middle of the night and embraced that wife of his sleeping by his side, his eyes closed, pretending that this woman was his copper goddess again, in his arms again, next to his body again, pressing hard again against him.

But then he opened his eyes and he felt so repulsed by what he saw himself doing that he had to stand up, rush to the bathroom, and vomit.

It was then he realized he could not be unfaithful to her, that goddesslike woman with the glittering copper hair and the olive eyes.

Since that night he has not even tried to make love to that other woman, the one he calls wife, the one who sleeps every night next to him.

And since that very night he has been dreaming about what it would be like to sleep one entire night long with his real woman, the one he was meant to be with, the one who sleeps every night next to another man she calls husband but who does not own her.

Just *one* night. That is all he asks for. Just that. One *entire* night.

He is not jealous of that other man of hers, just as she is not jealous of that other woman of his, because that man she calls husband has not, cannot, and will never be able to own her; just as that woman he calls wife has not, cannot, and will never be able to own him the way she, with a copper diadem between her legs, does.

He has taken her hands in his, has forced them behind her back, has pulled her toward him until her body has melted into his, and has tasted her lips, her nose, her earlobes, her neck.

She likes this man. Lord! How she likes this man! She cannot wait from one Tuesday to the next until he takes her.

She thinks of him all day long.

She wakes up and her first thought is of him.

She goes to the kitchen and on her way there she thinks of nothing but him.

She places the ground coffee in the flannel filter and she breathes and she thinks of him; she pours the boiling water over the coffee and she sweats and she thinks of him; and she breaks one egg and pours the milk and toasts the bread and she pauses and she thinks of him, of nothing but him.

She thinks of him while she is breaking fast with that man she calls husband; while she is scrubbing her hands under the rushing water of the cold faucet; while she is washing her face and wiping her eyes and sharing some words with that man by her side.

She thinks of him while she waits in that place she calls home and sits next to that man she calls husband and shares a meal with those people she calls family.

She thinks of him while she restlessly turns around in her sleep, and it hurts.

It hurts to think of him.

It hurts every time, just like *aguardiente* hurts every time you shoot it down your throat but no sooner does it hurt than you want to have more of it.

It hurts all the time.

But it hurts the worst whenever she dreams of him at night, which she does night after night after night.

That first night, the night after he had awakened in her for the first time that fire she had she didn't even know was there, that very same night, she woke up in the middle of the night and embraced that husband of hers sleeping by her side, her eyes closed, pretending that this man was her dark god again, in her arms again, next to her body again, pressing hard again against her.

But then she opened her eyes and she felt so repulsed by what she saw herself doing that she had to stand up, rush to the bathroom, and vomit.

It was then she realized she could not be unfaithful to him, that godlike man with the shiny black mane of hair and the dark mysterious eyes.

Since that night she has not even tried to make love to that other man, the one who sleeps every night next to her.

And since that very night she has been dreaming about what it would be like to sleep one entire night long with her real man, the one she was meant to be with, the one who sleeps every night next to another woman he calls wife but who does not own him.

Just *one* night. That is all she asks for. Just that. One *entire* night.

She is not jealous of that other woman of his, just as he is not jealous of that other man of hers, because that woman he calls wife has not, cannot, and will never be able to own him; just as that man she calls husband has not, cannot, and will never be able to own her the way he, with a scepter of power between his legs, does.

★ ★ ★

34

The call comes at eight twenty-seven in the morning, urgently asking for Merced.

Leonora, who answers the phone, calls her.

Merced rushes to the telephone, says yes, and then she listens for what seems to Leonora the longest of times. Merced hangs up the phone and turns to Leonora.

"They've found him. He's at the Hotel Royale. They want me to go there right away."

"Is he all right?" asks the old lady.

"They didn't say. I guess so. He's probably drunk out of his mind. They just want me to go there right away."

"I'll go with you," says the old lady, determinedly.

"No, Leonora," Merced says. "I think it's better you stay here, just in case there are more phone calls."

Merced runs to her bedroom. Tonio's bedroom. Their bedroom.

"Leonora," she shouts from the bedroom, "could you call me a taxi, please?" She picks up her purse, throws a few things inside, and almost without realizing it she sees her reflection in the large beveled mirror looking back at her.

It is only then she begins to tremble.

Tonio has been missing almost for a whole week.

He left Friday morning to go to work; worked all day at the bookstore, reading the galleys of the translation of the German book about venereal diseases that he had been working on for a long while and that he had just completed; left work; and that was the last anybody had seen of him.

He spent the entire weekend out of the house, but by now everybody in the household was used to that. But when he did not come back Monday morning to change clothes and go back to work, Merced called her brother Gustavo at the bookstore and inquired about him.

Neither Gustavo nor anybody else had seen him since last Friday night, when he left work. He seemed to be in an excellent mood that night. He had finished editing the galleys of the new book and he had told Palmo, now the general manager of Athena, the publishing company, that the book could finally be printed, that it was totally finished. Palmo invited him for a drink, but Tonio did not accept it. He told Palmo he had other things to take care of. Last time Gustavo saw him, Tonio was singing as he was leaving the bookstore, something which surprised Gustavo. "Hey, Tonio," Gustavo had said, "I didn't know you could sing."

"Of course I can," Tonio answered. "All Cuban men sing when they are happy, and I am a Cuban man, am I not?" And then he recited the lyrics of the song he was singing, a song quite popular at the time.

> I am like a swan who's dying,
> and as he dies he is singing:
> Please love me deeply, that's how I love.
> Please love me deeply, that's how I love.

"Leave it to Cuban songwriters," he told Gustavo, "to take an ancient myth that believes that swans never sing until the moment of their death, and then make a song out of it! And then listen to the melody! Just like the real swan song, which is supposed to be the most beautiful song ever to be heard! Isn't it beautiful?" Tonio sang it this time.

> I am like a swan who's dying,
> and as he dies he is singing:
> Please love me deeply, that's how I love.
> Please love me deeply, that's how I love.

Then, facing Gustavo, he said, "You know, Gustavo, I love that song. The first time I heard it, a trio of guys was playing it. It was also the first night I ever made love. Isn't that a coincidence?"

Gustavo meant to ask Tonio what he had meant by "a coincidence," but by that time, Tonio had already dashed off across the park, going uptown as he was singing. Gustavo thought he was going to meet Merced somewhere to celebrate his completing his last book and did not make much of it. He was surprised and deeply concerned when Merced called him Monday morning.

"But didn't he go out with you or any of the rest of the boys last Friday night?" Merced asked.

"No," answered Gustavo. "He did not go out with any of us. He hasn't done that since the day Berto won that famous game against Rufo at the Jai Alai Palace. And that happened at least six months ago."

Merced hung up.

She didn't know what to think. Nothing made any sense to her. After that night six months ago, she and Tonio had barely spoken to each other. The Tonio she married was gone that night when he came home covered with love bruises, and a new man came into her life that very same night: This other Tonio she had been living with since. A man totally unknown to her. And perhaps even to himself.

Sometimes she finds him alone in their bedroom, all windows and doors closed, drinking straight from a bottle of Añejo, and weeping at the same time; the German book filled with photographs of naked people covered with horrible and disgusting love bruises open on the bed, his translation notebook by its side, filled with page after page of his beautiful handwriting.

She has noticed that at times he starts to work, translating, and then suddenly he starts to cry. And yet he goes on with his work as he cries. Many times she has sat by his side on their bed and tried to take hold of his hand, to apologize, to say something, but to no avail. Each time she tries to start a conversation with him, he walks out of the house, offering no explanations, making no demands.

No, Merced did not understand anything.

What did Tonio mean when he told Gustavo about the swan song being played by a trio of guys the first time they ever made love?

That did not make any sense. They had spent their honeymoon in Miami, and she did not remember hearing any music at all that night, the night Tonio confessed to her that he was, just as she was, a virgin. He wasn't lying then. Or was he?

After her phone call to Gustavo, Merced told Leonora everything Gustavo had just told her, and they began calling all the hospitals, but none of them had any news of anybody by that name.

Merced went then to the police, to report him missing, and a very kind gentle older man, Detective Rolando Fernández, with warm blue eyes and abundant dark hair tinged with white, began asking her all sorts of intimate questions.

At first Merced felt intimidated by him, but this man was able to put her immediately at ease with his warm smile.

He soon found out how long they had been married, what had happened a few weeks ago, how his behavior had altered since that time, and he ventured a guess.

He told Merced that in his opinion Tonio must have been having an affair with some other woman and that probably he had left with her, abandoning Merced.

"You didn't call any of the airline companies, did you?" he asked.

Merced shook her head. "I'm sorry, I didn't think about that."

"That's perfectly all right," the blue-eyed detective continued, "we'll do that. That's what we are for. Did you check with the bank?"

"We don't deal with a bank," Merced answered.

"Are you missing any money? I mean, did he take a lot of money with him?"

"I don't think so. Except that he had just completed a new translation. Maybe he got paid in full for that. That money is extra, you know. I can call the company and—"

"We'll do that," he told her as he was writing notes on a small pad. "We'll check with his employer." He smiled at her as he added, "Now, you go home, and we'll call you the minute we have any news about him."

Merced got up from her chair and was about to leave when he stopped her.

"It happens to a lot of us, Señora," he said. "But don't worry. It doesn't take long for us men to find out whom we really love. And when he does that he'll come back to you. I can guarantee that. I hope you'll forgive him then." He pointed to a photo on his desk. "That was my wife. She never forgave me and now I've lost her forever."

Detective Fernández was a real nice man. He had been very helpful and very kind toward her.

And this is the same man who called her this morning and told her to come right away to the Hotel Royale; the very same man who is waiting for her at the Hotel Royale when a taxi delivers her to the door.

He takes her to a small office located behind the main desk, where a very nervous man, obviously the manager, stands up and begins to blurt out one apology after another.

"We didn't know. It wasn't our fault, you understand. There was no way, absolutely no way, any of us could have foreseen—"

The detective with the kind smile stops him. "Leave us alone for a few minutes," he demands. The manager debates what to do. The detective speaks to him again. "Please. She doesn't know."

The manager leaves the room and the detective closes the door behind him.

There follows a long silence.

By then Merced has realized that her suspicions are true. "He's dead, isn't he?"

The detective nods in agreement as he begins to lead her to a chair.

"How?"

"Sleeping pills. More than a hundred."

Merced leans against him and begins to weep, her head on his shoulder. The detective gently embraces her, like a father offering support to a helpless child.

"I'm sorry," Merced says after a long while, as she raises her head and looks at him.

"It's all right. This is part of my job," he says smiling at her. And then he adds, "I'm afraid we'll have to go upstairs, to identify him. It's just a formality and I know it's not going to be easy for you but it has to be done. He's been dead for more than three days. He left a sign outside his door saying he was not to be disturbed, and this morning the people next door complained about—about the smell. Do you think you can make it?"

The room is on the sixth floor, the uppermost floor of the hotel.

When they get there, all the windows are open wide, corner windows from where the beautiful La Habana Bay glimmers in the distance as if myriads of diamonds were hidden under its turquoise surface barely rippling in the gentlest of breezes.

He is lying in bed, without shoes, wearing white-linen pants and a white shirt, sleeping on his side, the way he always sleeps, his eyes closed, a rigid smile on his lips.

"That's how he was found. Nothing in this room has been disturbed, except for the door, which had to be opened by the manager. Is that your husband?"

Merced begins to walk slowly toward the bed, all by herself. Detective Fernández offers to accompany her with a gesture, but she looks at him and shakes her head. This is something she must do on her own.

It is a beautiful room.

He must have liked it a lot, Merced thinks. It goes perfectly with the elegant bedroom set he had bought for her. For them. For himself, as a wedding present. How long had she been married? How many weeks? Merced looks at the man lying on the bed and, though his toxic death has made his skin so dark he looks almost like a black man, she recognizes not the man she once married but a man just like him who seems to be at peace with himself.

"Yes," Merced answers, "that is—was—" She cannot finish.

The gentle detective helps her out of the room and takes her to the empty room next door, where he makes her sit on a large overstuffed armchair.

"May I get you some water?" he asks.

"No," Merced looks at him, and pretends to smile. "I'm all right. I'm all right."

The detective pulls two envelopes out of his pocket.

"Is this your husband's handwriting?" he asks her.

She looks at the envelopes and nods silently. That beautiful handwriting again. She touches the envelopes with the tips of the fingers of her left hand, what she calls her *good* hand, as if reaching for the envelopes. One of them reads "To whom it may concern" on the outside. The other one simply says "Merced."

"This one," says the detective pointing to the envelope addressed to To whom it may concern, "was unsealed. We have read it."

He hands it to Merced. It reads:

> From the moment I found out that I am living with a horrible incurable disease I decided to terminate my life and save myself and a lot of the people I love from the immense pain of seeing me die a painfully slow death. I waited to complete my last book, so my wife would have some money to live on for a while. Everything I own is hers. No one is to be blamed for my death. I acquired the pills by going to several different doctors and asking each of them for something to help me go to sleep. I didn't lie to them. I needed these pills to go to sleep. Sincerely.

Merced sighs as she finishes reading this letter.

What horrible incurable disease is Tonio talking about? Why didn't he confide in her? Or in someone else in his family? Or in one of his close friends? Merced shakes her head. She does not understand anything. She takes her left hand to her forehead and gently rubs it. Why can't she understand anything? What is wrong with her?

"This one is for you," says the detective as he hands her the second envelope. He looks at her as she takes it in her hand, and then he adds, "I'll leave you alone for a few minutes. I'll be right outside the door should you need me. Let me know when you want to leave and I'll drive you home. It'll be no problem at all. My car is parked right outside the hotel and I've already finished my part of this business in here. I'll be waiting for you. Take all the time you need." He leaves the room, closing the door behind him.

Merced tears the envelope open.

Inside there is an official-looking document, a will, properly drawn, notarized, and signed by Tonio and by two witnesses. In it Tonio leaves everything he owned, including the rights to all of his translations, to her, and asks to be cremated, his ashes thrown in La Habana Bay.

Next to this will is a folded piece of paper. Merced unfolds it and reads.

After a few minutes Merced opens the door, steps outside the hotel room, and asks the kind detective for some matches. He hands her a book of matches. She asks him to accompany her back into the room. There she hands the detective Tonio's will and then she sets the other piece of paper, the note addressed to her, on fire, placing it in an ashtray and looking at it as it burns. "He asked me to do this," Merced volunteers. "He said this would set me free."

Detective Fernández asks no questions when Merced, in a thread of a voice, begins to sing softly as the burning letter is totally reduced to ashes.

> I am like a swan who's dying,
> and as he dies he is singing:
> Please, love me deeply, that's how I love.
> Please, love me deeply, that's how I love.

THE BOYS at the bookstore are in shock.

Tonio's death takes everybody by surprise. And since he requested that his body be cremated, there is no Cuban-style funeral where people keep vigil with the dead person an entire night and then accompany him to the cemetery. Instead, the boys arrange, with Merced's consent, for a memorial service to be held at the bookstore after working hours.

Tonio acted wisely when he requested that his body be cremated, because the Catholic cemetery where the rest of his family is buried does not allow the burial of a person who has taken his own life.

Just as he acted wisely when, in his unsealed last letter to the world, he covered up the real reason for his taking his own life by blaming an unspecified "horrible incurable disease."

Tonio knew he had caused enough harm to Merced just by marrying her. At the time he thought that perhaps his marriage would change his inner feelings and make him into the kind of a man he was not. But it did not. His lying to her, his lying to himself, had not made his life any easier. Instead, it had made his life—and hers—a living hell.

Tonio knew that he had caused Merced, innocent Merced, enough pain and suffering as it was. He didn't want to cause her any more. He certainly didn't want her to live through the public humiliation and embarrassment of having to acknowledge marrying a man like him, a kind of man who, to Cubans—and even to himself—was not a man at all, but a repulsive freak.

And Tonio knew that this was something Merced would have to go through, should the real truth—his dishonorable shameful secret—come out.

Anticipating that, Tonio handled it all elegantly; as elegantly as he handled everything else about his death; as elegantly as his beautiful handwriting.

He did not lie. He didn't have to. He just told his own truth.

To him, what he had was a "horrible incurable disease."

And that was that.

Nobody sees Tonio dead, except for Merced. Not even Leonora. Merced transfers his remains to a crematory as soon as the autopsy is completed, and immediately after that she takes his ashes and spreads them on La Habana Bay, as Tonio requested, somewhere between La Habana on one side of the bay and Regla on the opposite side.

As far as people know, Tonio has gone on a trip, never to come back.

At the memorial service the boys hold for him, everybody remembers him just as he walked out of the bookstore that Friday a week and a half ago, when he was singing happily as he dashed off across the park.

Merced does not wear black to the memorial service. Dolores urges her to, but Merced refuses to. She does not even wear a black band around her arm, like all of the boys at the bookstore attending the service do. When she is asked to say a few words, she declines. The day following the memorial service she moves back into her old family house, Maximiliano's house.

She does not take the beautiful elegant bedroom set back with her. She leaves it in Leonora's house. She does take Maestro Romanat's painting back with her, though she leaves the ebony frame and the gray mat behind. And she does take Pepe Loreto with her and places him in the large patio, shaded by the balcony above, which also protects him from the rain.

Pepe Loreto is so disconcerted by the move that he even forgets his own name. He refuses to talk. But little by little he begins to enjoy the morning sun and the fresh air, which brings new life into his old bones.

At first, Marguita, little Marga—who is no longer little but already a young lady now, almost fifteen—is a little afraid of him; just as he is a little afraid of her. But all of a sudden, one day Pepe Loreto remembers his name, and soon after that he is calling Merced again, "Merced, Merced! Kiss? Kiss?" which always makes Marguita laugh because Pepe Loreto lisps as he says it.

Every month Merced gives Leonora and her family the same amount of money Tonio used to, which comes from Tonio's royalties. She has little or no money for herself. She does have a lot of time on her hands, now that Dolores has a new cook.

She goes back to the Academia de San Alejandro, just to find out that Maestro Romanat died two months ago, of a stroke. She cannot see herself studying with anyone else but her old teacher. And certainly not with any of those other teachers who used to despise Maestro Romanat's works, and whose works she doesn't like because they do not speak to her because she fails to find any soul in them.

She then decides the time has come for her to look for a job, so, setting aside forever her dream of becoming an artist, which she knows pays little to nothing, she gives Mani her book *Apollo,* which she knows he loves, and joins a business school to learn skills that do pay: bookkeeping and typing. And though she doesn't like typing, which she finds exceedingly boring, she discovers she enjoys bookkeeping a lot because she is good at numbers; and, to her surprise, she finds herself liking it.

All of that time Dolores keeps looking at her daughter with anxious eyes, hoping that Merced will open up to her. But Merced, beautiful dark-haired Merced with the sensual cadenced walk, does not do it.

Nobody knows much about Merced, who always keeps things to herself.

Nobody even knows about Tonio's private last letter to Merced, other than Merced and Detective Fernández, who came to the memorial service.

And what that letter said remains unknown to all but Merced.

The boys at the bookstore talk about cancer, and about syphilis, and about leprosy, and about God knows what many other "horrible incurable diseases" they all can think about.

They all do, except for Berto, kind Berto, friendly Berto, handsome as a Greek god Berto, *El Campeón,* who shrugs his broad shoulders and then says nothing every time someone asks him, What do you think is the reason that Tonio killed himself?

Part Four

Hurricane 1938

35

Today is another hot Tuesday afternoon, except that today is a hot and humid Tuesday afternoon in late September under a full moon—perfect weather to ignite a tropical hurricane, which usually gets started when least expected.

This one gets started by Eleuteria, who, almost by accident, provides the inflaming spark.

She sees Graciela getting ready to leave the house again, the way she has been doing for several weeks every Tuesday afternoon. Eleuteria has noticed this before, and every single time she has wondered where her daughter went and what she did every Tuesday afternoon.

This time Eleuteria can no longer hold her tongue.

Eleuteria's curiosity, which has been itching badly beneath her skin, forces the old lady to inquire. So she asks her daughter where she goes and what she does, and Graciela answers her with the total honesty and the total simplicity of an innocent heart.

Graciela does not lie to her mother.

She had told herself that she would never lie about what was going on between her and that man. She could not lie about it, even if she wanted. That man has taken possession of her and that is all there is to it.

Yes, she knows she is married to Gustavo, she answers her mother, her inquisitive mother who now that she has broken the seal of silence between the both of them wants to know everything there is to know about Graciela and that other man.

Yes, that man can do with her whatever it is he wants.

Yes, she would follow him to hell if such a place existed on Earth, because hell with that man would be paradise.

Graciela, now that the seal of silence has been broken between the two of them, pours out her heart to her mother, but her mother is no longer listening to her. All Eleuteria keeps hearing is herself, repeating over and over: This is not true, this is not happening to me, this is not happening, this is simply not happening at all.

And yet Eleuteria can understand perfectly well what Graciela is talking about for as Graciela speaks, Eleuteria remembers what it was like to be owned as her daughter is owned—possessed—by a man, the way she was possessed by her man, that evil man who abandoned her for a mulatto woman who knew how to smile. And she remembers hearing that same litany of words which keep repeating themselves over and over now, as they kept repeating themselves over and over then: This is not true, this is not happening to me, this is not happening, this is simply not happening at all.

Since an early age Eleuteria knew she was not beautiful. The other kids at school did not need to tell her as they all did. An unlying mirror plainly showed it to her the first time she saw herself reflected in it, and ever since mirrors have been showing it to her. Except for that one time when that evil man with the handsome face and the damned virile grin had come to her and called her beautiful.

She had not believed him.

She knew why he was coming to her.

She knew she was not beautiful, just as she knew she was one of the wealthiest girls in Luyanó, now that her father had died and had left all of his properties to her. She didn't own much: just that large house of hers and several little places on the "wrong" side of the Street of the Bulls, places her father rented to Chinese men so they could keep their mulatto women in them. Her father knew what he was doing in renting those places to Chinese men. He asked a lot of money for those miserable rooms, which Chinese men paid willingly and religiously, on the dot, every first day of each month.

What Eleuteria owned, now that her father had passed away, might not have seemed much to some of the other landowners in La Habana, but it certainly seemed quite a lot to the people of Luyanó, where the working-class bulls of La Habana owned absolutely nothing at all.

Eleuteria knew, or thought she knew, that those few things she owned were the reason why that man had come to her and called her beautiful. Just as she knew, or thought she knew, that she was not beautiful. At all.

And yet, that night, before she went to bed, she looked at herself in the mirror, and to her amazement, for the first time in her life, the mirror showed her a petite girl of twenty-two with a trim waist and sparkling eyes not yet filled with hate. And that girl in the mirror had been beautiful.

The afternoon is very hot and very humid. The sky has been turning ominously dark and drops of rain have already begun to fall. Eleuteria is desperately pacing the room, fanning herself nervously with a large palmetto fan. She stops. Looks at Graciela, who is standing by the door on her way out. Begins pacing again.

Eleuteria doesn't know what to do.

Unable to stop her daughter from destroying her own life, all she is able to do is to repeat to herself over and over, This is not true, this is not happening to me, this is not happening, this is simply not happening at all; a litany of words that she keeps repeating and repeating insistently, like a desperate silent prayer, until it is suddenly broken by a possibility. There may be a way out.

Time.

Time, Eleuteria knows, is her best ally, perhaps her only ally. She has to make time, somehow she has to create time, enough time to allow for the hurricane that is beginning to rush through their lives to run its course. Time, time, she needs to make time. That may be the way out. That may be the only way out.

"You are not going to meet with that man of yours now, are you?" Eleuteria asks Graciela in a pleading voice.

Graciela turns around and answers her mother with such a smile that it transforms her face, her eyes beaming with excitement. "Oh, yes! Mamá," she says, without the slightest trace of guilt. "Oh, yes!"

"But what about your husband? What if he calls?" Gustavo has just left the house after his noontime meal and a ten-minute siesta and has gone back to the bookstore.

"He never calls," Graciela says, in a matter-of-fact way. "But if he does call you may tell him the whole truth." Then she immediately adds, sincerely concerned, "No, no. Do not tell him. That is something I have to tell him myself. And I will."

She pauses for the briefest of seconds, then she adds decisively, "I will tell him tomorrow, when I come back."

"Tomorrow? When you come back? What do you mean when you—?"

"I have always dreamed of spending *one night* with that man, Mamá, one *entire* night together with—"

"Oh, no, Graciela, please! Please!" She rushes to her daughter and stands facing her. "Listen to your mother. Don't do such a stupid thing! Please! Don't spend a night out with that man. It would bring everything out in the open. Please, you don't know what you are doing, but I do. You don't realize it, but this is just a passing thing. It goes away, it always—"

Graciela interrupts. "It has not gone away for you yet, Mamá, has it?" She pauses. "Has it?" She pauses again. "After these many years . . . Has it?"

Eleuteria shakes her head unconsciously.

"Mamá," Graciela adds, this time with urgency in her voice, "I have to do it, don't you see I have no other choice? Even if it's only once I have to spend a whole night with that man, and then let the cards fall where they may. After that I will not care." She moves closer to her mother and adds vehemently, "I cannot go on living the way I have been living for the last three months. I cannot go on pretending I love Gustavo when it is not true. I cannot go on trying to please everybody else but me. I never did love him. Maybe everybody else thought I did, certainly you told me I did, but I didn't. And he doesn't love me, either. I didn't know it then, but I know better now."

Eleuteria is praying for Time as she is thinking, What can I do, what can I do, what can I do?

Graciela continues with her pleading.

"Mamá, don't you see? This is the best way, the only way. If truth hurts, it hurts only once and then it stops hurting. The way Gustavo and I are living, we are hurting each other day after day, night after night. I lie in bed next to him and let him take me and I feel so repulsed by his touching me I feel like vomiting. I cannot stand it anymore, Mamá. I just can't. I cannot go on living a life of deception like this, Mamá, for the rest of my life. I just cannot do it." Graciela forces her mother to look at her as she adds, "Neither could you, Mamá, could you?"

No, Eleuteria thinks. She could not live a life of deception, either. When things happened, when she was told by her neighborly friend Pilar about her husband and that other woman, she wanted to know the truth right away and just as she was she went to see the mulatto woman. All Eleuteria wanted to know was why. And all that woman had to do was to open the door for Eleuteria to have her answer.

She expected that mulatto woman to be sensual and beautiful, and she was. But she was not only sensual and beautiful; she was kind at the same time. When Eleuteria looked at her, she saw nothing but innocence in that other woman's eyes, and Eleuteria could not cope with that. She had been prepared to call that woman names, insult her, spit in her face, strike her if she had to, but the innocent smile in the eyes of that mulatto woman had disarmed her.

All of a sudden Eleuteria realized that she had never given that man she called husband that innocent smile this other woman offered in her eyes, because in the eyes of Eleuteria she had always hidden a question, a barrier of a question that was always there as she and that man ate, drank, slept, and made love. Is it *me* he wants? Or is it *the money?*

It was only after that man had finally left her that she realized that perhaps it was she he wanted all the time, because if money was what he wanted he could have stayed with her, like many other bulls in Luyanó do, married to women they do not love while keeping mulatto mistresses on the side.

But that man of hers had not done that. He had left her, and all of her money, to go live with that other woman, that beautiful mulatto woman with the gentle innocent smile.

And now Graciela, her father's daughter, is on the brink of doing the same thing! Doesn't she know that things are very different with a woman? Eleuteria asks herself. Maybe Graciela does not know, but she, Eleuteria, does. She knows that what a man can do a thousand times a woman cannot do. No, not even once. Not on the Street of the Bulls.

Eleuteria can see what lies ahead and she doesn't like what she sees, for all she sees is the black shroud of shame and the black shroud of death. She cannot allow her daughter to do this to herself and to the rest of her family. Eleuteria knows that she's got to do something, but what?

Time, she knows, she has to buy time.

Time.

This is all she is thinking about as she sees Graciela leave her house, heading to meet that man at the other end of town where wanton women meet their secret lovers.

Time.

How can I buy time?

She rushes to the door and grabs her daughter as she is about to leave.

"Please, Graciela," Eleuteria begs, "please. Do it for me. Don't spend the night out with that man. Please, listen . . ."

Graciela looks at her with her beautiful olive eyes. Eleuteria continues.

"Come back today, the way you have been coming back every other Tuesday, and keep things going just as they are. Nobody needs to know. Nobody will know. I'll protect you. I'll cover up for you. I'll lie for you. I'll do whatever you ask me to do. Just don't—"

Graciela interrupts her by kissing her on the cheek.

"I love you, Mamá," she tells her mother, and then she rushes for the bus that is just turning the corner, so she won't get wet in the rain.

★ ★ ★

36

Albertina, the wife of Ferminio, the owner of the slaughterhouses, opens the door to her modern house—the one a young Cuban architect designed with low ceilings, broad horizontal bands of windows, and a large yard all around it that separates it from the inquiring eyes of the too-friendly neighbors—and lets her daughter, Fernanda, and the girls in.

Fernanda, who married Arsenio at the cathedral more than three years ago, enters with her two pretty twins, who immediately run to their grandmother and cover her with hugs and kisses.

"What a pleasant surprise," says Albertina as Fernanda kisses her on the cheek. "I wasn't expecting you till the day after tomorrow. Don't tell me it's Thursday already, is it?"

"No, it's only Tuesday," answers Fernanda.

"Oh, I'm glad. I thought I had lost two days of my life, and at my age one cannot afford such a luxury. Did you have anything to eat yet?"

Fernanda shakes her head. "The girls did, but I didn't. I wasn't hungry."

"It's this heat and this humidity," Albertina says as she closes the entrance door behind her daughter. "I couldn't eat anything myself. Let's go into the kitchen and I'll fix you some of your favorite lemonade. How's Arsenio?" she adds. There's a short pause. Albertina turns and looks at Fernanda, who looks away from her.

"All right, I guess," Fernanda answers after a while. Then, after another pause, she adds, "He didn't come home for his noon meal today." She then faces her mother. "He never does on Tuesdays."

There's something in the way Fernanda has looked at her that bothers Albertina.

"María . . . !" she calls her maid, who promptly comes in. "María, please," Albertina says, "could you take the girls out to the backyard and look after them for a little while?"

María nods her head as she wipes her hands on her apron and takes the twins with her. She had been doing the dishes in Albertina's kitchen, the only room in that modern house Ferminio likes because from the large window in that room he can see there in the distance his Cuban slaughterhouse, the one that Fernanda's husband, Arsenio, manages.

"Your father just left, after he ate like a bull," says Albertina as she leads her daughter into the kitchen. "I don't know how he could eat so much on a day like this, with all of this heat. You all just missed him. Didn't you—"

She cannot finish her sentence. Fernanda has abruptly begun to cry. Albertina rushes to her. "What is wrong, child?"

She helps her daughter to a chair at the small dining table in the kitchen. Fernanda, who is still crying, cannot answer. Albertina goes to the faucet and fills a glass with cold water, which she offers Fernanda as she repeats, deeply concerned, "What is wrong, child? What is wrong?"

Fernanda drinks a little bit of the water her mother has offered her, and then she barely manages to answer her mother. "It's . . . I don't know, Mamá. It's . . . maybe nothing's wrong. I just don't know. It's just that . . . Arsenio and I . . . He—" Fernanda faces away from her mother and starts to cry again.

Albertina sits by her side and takes Fernanda's hands in hers as she says, "Arsenio and you . . . what, honey?" Fernanda cannot answer. "Bed problems?" asks Albertina. Fernanda nods as she begins to weep. "Oh, honey, don't cry like that! No man is worth a single one of your tears. Here"—she hands Fernanda her own handkerchief—"blow." Fernanda obediently does as her mother tells her. "Now, tell me. What has that man done to you?"

Fernanda shakes her head. "Nothing," she answers, still crying, still facing away from her mother.

"Nothing?"

"Nothing. For the last few weeks . . . Oh, Mamá, I don't know how to tell you this, but I have to tell somebody or I'll go crazy. I don't know now for how many weeks, he and I, we—we have done nothing."

Fernanda, who has been facing away from her mother, turns to her and confesses to her, her words spurting out like an unconfined torrent. "Something must be very wrong, Mamá. He has never been like that. We have never gone this long without . . ." She pauses again and again faces away from her mother as she adds, "Well . . . you know."

Albertina stands up and moves to the stove. "I'll make us some coffee so we can talk."

LATE THAT AFTERNOON Ferminio comes home earlier than usual. He is tired. Despite the steaming heat and the horrid humidity, which has been making him sweat like a pig, he had gone from his Cuban slaughterhouse, the one Arsenio handles, which is running as smoothly as can be, to his American one, the one his only son runs more or less well, and there—as if the heat and the humidity were not enough punishment—there he had to deal with an inspector, sent supposedly by the government, supposedly to look over the slaughtering of the bulls. According to his son, the inspector, Señor Gonzalo, had observed several "infractions," that's what the inspector called them.

Ferminio led Inspector Gonzalo into his small office, a hole of an office he had managed to carve out of some leftover space on the second floor of the old American slaughterhouse, and after they both sat down, Ferminio fished out from under a ton of papers lying all over the top of his old battered desk a small humidor, from which he offered a cigar to the inspector, who gladly accepted.

"I'm sure," said the knowing Ferminio, "that we can correct all of those 'infractions,' as you call them. Let me just call Senator Armández, who is our lawyer, and he'll be happy to—"

"Senator Armández is your lawyer?" asked the inspector.

"Oh, he's been our lawyer for many years." Ferminio smiled. "Not only our lawyer but one of our main investors, as well as the president himself. Didn't you know that?" Ferminio paused as he looked at the inspector, who, ready to light his cigar, match in hand, was looking at Ferminio with eyes open wide. The inspector suddenly shook his match, extinguishing the flame that had begun to burn his fingers.

"Oh, I don't think you have to disturb Senator Armández. The infractions I found were so minor that—"

Ferminio interrupted him. He liked to play this game when he had the upper hand. "In my slaughterhouse, Inspector Gonzalo," he said as he flicked a silver lighter on top of his desk and offered a light to the inspector, "we have never had any infractions or violations of any kind. My men take pride in their job, just as I do, and in fact we have been praised many times by the Department of Health, because we have the latest equipment and we do everything way above board."

Then, knowing the inspector needed to save face, he added, mercifully, "Perhaps what you thought were infractions were in fact nothing more than my son's failure to make you understand our way of doing things. Why don't you let me show our—"

He couldn't finish. "It won't be necessary," said the inspector as he looked at his notebook and ripped a few pages out of it. "Apparently I was mistaken. Somebody must have made an error. They didn't even give me the right information." The inspector managed to smile at Ferminio as he stood up. "Thanks for the cigar, Señor Ferminio," he said.

Ferminio was used to dealing with men like the inspector, desperate men always waiting for someone to break one of those infinite number of meaningless regulations that they themselves write into law, so they can then offer their assistance and that way get some money under the table.

But Ferminio also knew what it was like not to make much money and to have to support a family in times like these, when a lot of people had to go hungry. He remembered when he had been left bankrupt and empty handed with not a penny to his name, not that many years ago. Things had been hard then. He looked at the tall thin inspector with the sallow ivory-color skin. Things are still hard now.

"Inspector Gonzalo," Ferminio added at the door, "since I think you are not that familiar with our procedures, let me ask my son to prepare you a package of some of our cuts of meat so you and your family can taste them." The inspector turned around surprised and looked thankfully into Ferminio's eyes. "Let me know which cuts you and the rest of your family like the best."

After the inspector thanked him and left, Ferminio had sighed and had decided to get back home a little earlier today.

"FERNANDA AND THE GIRLS just left," Albertina tells him as he comes into the kitchen and asks María for some coffee. "Not more than a few minutes ago."

"Oh, I'm sorry I missed them." Ferminio sits in his kitchen chair and looks at his Cuban slaughterhouse in the far distance.

"She came to talk to me."

"Oh, yeah? What about?"

María brings a tiny demitasse of that dark Cuban coffee Ferminio loves so much and that Manuel the doctor told him he is not supposed to taste.

"Oh, the usual," says Albertina. Then she faces María. "María, could you go see if the twins left any of their toys in the yard? They always do, you know. If you find any, put them in the closet by the entrance door, and then you may go home. I'll fix dinner for the two of us."

No sooner has María left the room than Albertina moves to Ferminio, sits in her chair, opposite him, and point-blank asks him, "What is wrong with Arsenio?"

"With Arsenio? What do you mean?"

"Fernanda says something is very wrong with him. The two of them are sharing one bed but they are not—well, you know—sleeping together anymore."

Ferminio looks at Albertina. "Are you sure?"

"Yes. Fernanda told me."

"Hmmm!"

"*Hmmm?* Is that all you have to say? *Hmmm?*"

"What do you want me to say?"

"How would I know? I thought maybe you would know."

"Me? How would *I* know? This is the first time I've heard anything about all of—"

"Let's not start a fight. What I mean is, has he been having any trouble at work? Have you been working him too much?"

Albertina pauses. Then adds, "Maybe he is keeping a woman somewhere. He hasn't been home for his noon meal for the last few Tuesdays. Did you know that?"

Ferminio looks at Albertina, who is staring at him, and then he looks at the distant slaughterhouse, its large sloping tin roofs with huge overhangs reflecting the setting orange sun and the purple sky.

Ferminio is a bull, and all bulls must protect each other, no matter what. He's got to protect Arsenio, that honest hard-working bull of a man he likes and admires so much who married his daughter. He doesn't want to say the wrong thing. He wouldn't want to say the wrong thing even if he knew what was going on, but he doesn't know yet. He will. But right now he must cover up for Arsenio as he knows Arsenio would cover up for him.

"Tuesdays?"

He pauses, searching for an answer. He knows it's got to make sense. Whatever he may think about Albertina, one thing he can be sure of, and that is that she is *not* dumb. Suddenly he remembers the inspector. "Oh, *Tuesdays!*" he says. "I remember now."

He faces Albertina as he explains.

"That stupid government of ours has been having a series of weekly meetings, you know, the usual crap. They want to create a new bunch of stupid regulations we all have to comply with, and the industry is fighting them. They asked me to attend those damn stupid meetings, but I couldn't deal with that. I don't have the patience for that shit. I hate all of that. Arsenio hates it too, but someone from our slaughterhouses had to go, and well, you know what a good boy he is. He volunteered to do it, and thank God, he's doing it. I couldn't handle those sons of bitches. In fact, today I had no choice but to meet with Inspector Gonzalo himself. He was such an asshole, ask your son. He was there with me. All those damn inspectors want is money, you know, but I'll be damned if I'm going to give it to them. Our slaughterhouses are the best in all of the Americas, including the ones up north! How dare that man come to me and ask me for money, that damn bastard! As if we didn't pay enough to all of those sons of whores we have to hire to serve as our lawyers and advisers! I tell you, Albertina, this country is going to pieces! Thank God I don't think I'll live to see it happen!"

He strikes the linoleum-covered table with his fist, making the demitasse spill the little bit of coffee on the table.

"Goddammit," he shouts. "Now see what I've done! And this coffee smelled so good! Is there any more coffee left?" He turns and watches Albertina go to the stove.

That was good, he says to himself, that was really good, spilling some of that coffee. That has bought him some time. That asshole of a son-in-law of his Arsenio is probably keeping a bitch somewhere. Doesn't he know better than that? Meeting with her *every* Tuesday! And at noontime! That's so stupid, so utterly stupid! That is obviously what is happening. What other possible explanation can there be? It's obvious that woman must be his first affair. Doesn't that asshole have any brain at all? For God's sakes if you're gonna fuck the bitch, at least do it during working hours, alternate the times, and keep your wife happy. Even he, Ferminio, knows better than that!

Albertina brings him the pot of coffee, still steaming, and still holding a few more drops of the delicious infusion. "Calm down, Ferminio," she says as she pours a little bit into a clean demitasse. "Calm down. You know what the doctor said."

"Damn the doctors, and damn the lawyers! It's those damn lawyers I hate, Albertina. They are the ones who are milking all of us dry!"

And as he says that, he is thinking, Tomorrow I'll ask Arsenio what the fuck he thinks he is doing. That boy! How can anyone be as stupid as that?

"So," Albertina continues, "you don't think he's seeing another woman?"

"Of course not!" Ferminio answers. "With what time? He puts in over twelve hours every day!" He faces his wife and adds vehemently, "Albertina, you know what it is like to deal with bulls all day long, how tired you are at the end of a long day. You remember how tired I used to be whenever—"

"Of course I remember all of that, but . . . but that never stopped you from . . . from you know . . . well, from being a man to me."

"Yes, but you can't compare me to that boy, can you?" He grabs her and places her on his lap.

"Young people nowadays are not built the same way you and I were," he adds as he kisses her neck. "Tomorrow I'll have a talk with that asshole of a son-in-law we've got and after that everything will be all right, I promise you. Call Fernanda and tell her Pappy is taking care of it all."

Albertina begins to stand up.

"Yeah, but you can call her later on, can't you?" he says, pulling her again toward him, forcing her onto his lap. And then adds, half maliciously, "Do you know the best part of being a grandfather?"

Albertina looks at him and joining in the game raises her eyebrows and shakes her head. "No, tell me. What?"

Ferminio answers as he fondles his wife's breasts. "It's getting to fuck the grandmother!"

"You dirty old man, you!" Albertina adds as she laughingly lets that old bull of a man she's married to do whatever it is he wants to with her.

37

Despite the ominous dark sky and the little bit of rain that has just begun to fall, Merced is on the little boat that crosses the bay of La Habana going from the area known as La Habana Vieja, Old Havana, to Regla.

Ever since she spilled Tonio's ashes on those waters, Merced has taken a certain liking to this little boat, the *lanchita,* as they call it, and she has enjoyed this ride since that first day many a time, every time she goes near the bay for a job interview.

The *lanchero,* the man running the boat, has begun to recognize this beautiful young woman with the black wavy hair and the dark moody eyes who sits in the boat all the way to Regla and who doesn't get off there but who patiently waits in her seat under the canvas roof for the little boat to return one hour later to La Habana Vieja across the bay.

The first time it happened, he thought the woman did not speak Spanish, that she was perhaps a *gringa,* an American tourist, even though her beautifully shaped body, nicely wrapped in a little meat, belied that. He told her in his broken English that the trip had finished, that Regla was the end of the line, so to speak.

Merced did not understand a word of what the man was trying to tell her. She asked him in Spanish what he meant and the old man sighed, laughed at himself, and told her this time in Spanish that this was Regla, the end of the ride.

Merced answered that yes, she knew that was Regla, and would he mind if she waited there until they went back?

The *lanchero* didn't mind, though he said, "But I still have to charge you for the return. Is that all right?"

"That is all right," Merced said.

Since that first time Merced has taken that *lanchita* many a time, always enjoying the cool breezes blowing across the bay and always waiting for the return trip to carry her back home. It's only on her way back, when she reaches the center of the bay where she once dispersed Tonio's ashes on the ocean water, that she closes her eyes and says a silent prayer. The *lanchero* thinks that once he saw her cry.

MANI IS AT the butcher shop, sweating heavily in the humid heat of the steamy afternoon, working side by side with Maximiliano.

It's incredible how indelibly things are engraved into a child's soul.

After these many years working side by side with him, Mani still does not understand his own feelings toward this man whose age is beginning to show. Sometimes he loves him and admires him beyond comprehension; sometimes he is so immensely frightened by him that, unable to stand the sight of him, he recoils into himself, hating and despising him, that man he calls father, beyond understanding. For how long has he thought that this man is not his real father? That his family is not his real family? For how long has he thought that he is nothing but an adopted son, a child somebody abandoned, a child nobody wanted? An illegitimate child. Someone to be ashamed of. For how long? Inside of him, hidden deep inside of him, he still is not sure what he is. He has never been able to understand what happened to him. Why wasn't he allowed to spend his childhood with the rest of those people he calls family? Oh, sure, it has been explained to him many a time. But was that the truth, the real truth? He doesn't even trust his own birth certificate. Why should he, when he knows Maximiliano can work around the law and lie through his teeth if he has to? Isn't his pound of meat still fourteen ounces only?

He would have loved to believe all of that about his grandmother and his grandfather wanting him and all of that. But he has never been able to believe that story. Would he have been able to abandon a child of his like these people he calls parents did? He doesn't believe the answers he has been given. He doesn't trust those answers. He still doubts them. For many years he has been carrying those doubts inside of him, hiding them deep inside of him. Those horrible doubts that burden him, that he fears will burden him for the rest of his life, because how will he ever be able to know the truth, the real truth about himself, if he cannot trust any of the answers these people he calls family keep giving him?

The boy Mani, the same one who shivered at the first sight of the rushing bulls on the street, still lies hiding deep inside the man Mani, he with the bulging arms and the strength of a bull, and that boy will always be raising the same painful question over and over again.

Why?

That is why Mani has always done as he is told. To prove to these people he calls parents that even if he is an adopted child he is worthy of being their real child. That is why he has always been the obedient child, the one who is following his so-called father's footsteps, the one to carry on the family tradition. That is why he is what he is, the next generation butcher. That is what he is. That is all he is: a butcher. At least that is what he seems to be to all around him. But not to himself, nor to his two black goddesses, Hortensia and Fidelia. The three of them know who the real Mani is, a Mani unknown to everyone else: Mani, the dreamer, the conjurer, the magician, the maker of myths. Mani, the man with the mystical eyes who is able to command souls at his will.

It doesn't happen all the time, but when it happens Mani feels he is suddenly transported into a magical world, where he looks at things and he sees them as they really are, not as they pretend to be. He sees the souls of people and things. Those souls reveal themselves to him. When that happens, Mani closes his eyes and he engraves those souls into his memory, so he can recall them at any time after that.

He can recall the way he saw the souls of Hortensia and Fidelia that first time at the wedding reception with such fidelity that whenever he does it he feels that he is experiencing that moment again, reliving it as of new, as if it had never happened before, and yet knowing perfectly well that he has already lived through that experience.

He can recall the time he and his black goddesses first became entwined in the mutual possession ritual they have been practicing since that first time, and he can recall each time it happened after that.

He can recall the way the single bare bulb in the butcher shop walk-in cooler illuminates the carcass of many a bull, bringing them alive in a magical forest of their own, as he can recall the exact shade and hue and intensity and color of the sky the day Gustavo hung his apron on the black iron hook outside the cooler door.

He can recall what Dolores wore that day, and how the light of that early morning sky shaded her face, and how she smiled at Gustavo when she thought nobody was looking but Mani was.

He can recall the pride Mani saw in her eyes, a kind of pride he had never seen before and he has never seen since; a pride aimed at Gustavo; a pride he would have loved to have been aimed at him.

GUSTAVO IS AT work at the bookstore. A brand-new shipment of poetry books has just arrived, and he is in the process of cataloguing them. He picks one of the books, a thick anthology of Latin American poetry, which is beautifully bound in leather and printed on that thinnest of all papers, Bible paper as Berto, el campeón, told him it was called: a paper so thin it seems it should be transparent and yet a paper so dense it is totally opaque. Gustavo knows how expensive this book is. He smells the leather cover and admires the gold embossing on it.

He opens it at random and reads the first poem that catches his eye, a poem about Paris, the prince of Troy who, as he dies alone on the bloody fields of his plundered city, wonders if his Helen was worth that price. He closes the book and smiles as he carefully places it inside a glass-fronted display case reserved for high quality books.

Of course Helen was worth that price, he says to himself. Otherwise, who would have heard of Paris?

And then he wonders if Helen of Troy was as bad in bed as Graciela is. Thank God for Friday nights at Yarina's House. He smiles to himself as he remembers those nights. Now, *that* is poetry, he says to himself. *That* is *real* poetry.

MANI'S TWO BLACK goddesses, with the rest of their sisters that form the Albaracoa band, are rehearsing a new piece of music, a *susurro oriental,* a very different new kind of song that is filled with a slow almost painful sensuality, written by Hortensia with music by Fidelia. They are at the Casino Nacional, where the all-girl band has been playing now for more than three months.

Last Tuesday night, a week ago, a tall freckled blond man who spoke pidgin Spanish with a very thick foreign accent approached Alicina, the oldest of the girls and the leader of the band, and asked her to ask the rest of the girls if they were interested in going to Germany. Alicina had noticed this man who came night after night to the casino. He seemed to be very interested in their music, and Alicina thought that perhaps the man was also very interested in her as well. The man told Alicina that if they agreed to go to Germany he would act as their manager and get them a contract not only to play all the big cities there, but to record all of their music as well.

When Alicina told the rest of the girls, they all jumped up and down with excitement and broke open a bottle of Añejo to celebrate in advance this big break in their careers.

By Friday afternoon, when all of them were completely sober, the girls and the German man sat around a large unoccupied table on the second floor of the casino discussing the terms of a proposed agreement where the girls consented to go to Germany in six weeks, a week after their casino engagement ended.

Alicina and all of the girls thought this was an excellent opportunity. All of them thought so, including Hortensia and Fidelia, who agreed to their proposed trip, which would last half a year, even though they both felt very ill at ease about leaving Blanquito, as they call Mani, behind.

They didn't need to.

Late that Friday night, when the three of them met at their small *posada* room for their weekly rite of mutual possession, Mani, unaware of what was going on, had brought them a gift that he presented to them after they had completely exhausted every one of their wants, telling them, "As long as you keep this by your side, you'll always have a piece of me."

The gift was a framed small drawing of two voluptuous naked black goddesses encircling a naked godlike white man who, lying on white rumpled sheets between the two women, is embracing each of them as they all invitingly stare straight into the eye of the viewer, making the viewer partake in that instant of ecstasy the people in the drawing are experiencing after their wild night of orgiastic lovemaking.

The drawing was done with powerful thick fast madlike strokes of black chalk over dark-brown paper, accented with bold highlights done in a fluorescent pale blue. In the faint cold blue fluorescent light of the small *posada* room, the drawing seemed to shimmer with life.

Both Hortensia and Fidelia gasped when they looked at the drawing in this light, because as they each looked into the mirror directly above the bed where the three of them were lying, each saw herself in the identical position as that of the drawing, with Mani's eyes in the mirror staring at each of them with the identical look of ecstasy in his eyes as the white godlike man in Mani's drawing had. The girls were in awe. Some time in the past Blanquito had caught in a drawing a moment he knew was going to happen some time in the future. His drawing was the drawing of a clairvoyant, a visionary, a psychic, someone who is capable of knowing and anticipating the future. Because when the future moment came, it was identical to the moment he had caught in his drawing.

The girls realized that Blanquito was not only able to command souls to reveal themselves to him, but that in addition he had the capability to anticipate how souls would act, something the girls found immensely frightening, immensely pleasurable, and immensely disconcerting at the same time.

That happened last Friday, three days ago.

Last night, after the girls finally signed the contract with the German man, under the influence of the Añejo they all shared to celebrate their German tour, the girls went home and looked at the drawing again.

Blanquito was right.

When they looked at the drawing, they each felt that electrical current they loved and feared so much traveling up and down their spines.

It was then the girls wrote the song the band is now rehearsing, a very different new kind of song that is filled with a slow almost painful sensuality, written by Hortensia with music by Fidelia.

They have called their new song "A Piece of Me."

DETECTIVE FERNÁNDEZ IS sitting at his desk in the small office he shares with three other guys when the mail arrives. It's hot and it's humid, and the ceiling fan is not even working, and on top of everything the mail is late.

The guy who used to work the mail room at the police station quit last week for a similar job with a private company that pays a lot better, and a new man just started yesterday, Monday morning, doing that other guy's job, which so far he is not doing very well.

"Hey, Rolando," shouts one of the guys at the other end of the room as he throws a letter at Fernández, "this is for you."

Fernández grabs it, looks at the pale-blue envelope, and notices the beautiful handwriting on it, a handwriting he does not recognize. He turns the envelope around, to see who sent it, but the address written on the back is totally unfamiliar to him. He rips open one end of the envelope and finds inside a folded thank-you note. He looks at the signature first to see who sent it. A woman. He doesn't remember who this woman is. He reads the note.

Dear Detective Fernández:

I want to thank you for the kindness you showed me during one of the worst moments of my life. I am sorry I asked you to witness my burning of my late husband's last letter to me. I had no right to impose on you like that, and I apologize for doing it. And yet having you there gave me the courage to go ahead and do what my late husband asked me to do. He said it would set me free and he was right. I don't know if I would have been able to go through all I had to go through without your help.

Thank you again and may God bless you.

He reads the signature again and remembers the beautiful young widow with the dark moody eyes and the sad smile who signed that letter. He realizes that she must be using her maiden name again, that's why he didn't recognize the last name on the signature.

He smiles as he remembers her and is about to throw the letter in his wastebasket when he looks at it again, places it back into the torn envelope, and then leaves it on his desk, by the photograph of the wife he's lost forever. As soon as he finds the time he'll write her a note, asking her how she is doing. It is only then he remembers he still has something of that lovely young widow.

He turns around, looks in the pockets of his jacket, which is hanging on his chair, and finds an earring, a small silver-and-black earring with geometric designs on it.

When he drove the young widow back to her home from the Hotel Royale, she must have accidentally lost that earring in his car. He had not found it until two days ago when he decided the time had come, finally, to wash the car and clean it thoroughly. That's how he had found it. For a little while he thought it might have been his wife's, but he had lost her before he bought this car. And then he remembered the girl from the Hotel Royale.

Now he is glad she has written him that beautiful thank-you note and that he has kept the envelope. He picks it up again, writes her name and address down on a small clean envelope, places the earring inside, seals the envelope, and calls the mail boy.

Then realizing that this mail boy does not know right from left yet, puts the envelope in one of the pockets of his jacket, which is hanging on the back of his chair. I better mail it myself, he thinks.

MERCED ARRIVES back home right about noon.

Dolores, with her weak heart and her high blood pressure, has not been feeling very well and is lying in bed half asleep when Merced arrives. Her mere arrival brightens up Dolores's day, a sad day that needs brightening up indeed. It has been a hot and humid morning so far, and the sky of La Habana, normally a limpid turquoise, has turned really dark and ominous. It is just beginning to rain hard when Merced arrives.

Merced kisses her mother and, after finding out how Dolores feels, she immediately starts for the kitchen, at the far end of the house, to fetch a glass of water and the drops of medicine Dolores takes at noon. Normally, Marguita is the one who gives those drops to her mother, but she just called and told Dolores that she was going to be delayed at school because of the rain.

No sooner has Merced started for the kitchen than the heavenly smells coming from that direction stop her in her tracks. Paula, the new cook, is inspired today, Merced says to herself as she inhales the wonderful aroma.

Paula is preparing the noontime meal, a meal that to Cubans is the most important meal of the day, a succulent daily feast that takes hours to prepare, to be followed by a well-deserved siesta.

Merced, who by now knows something about cooking, nods her head in agreement as she acknowledges that whatever it is Paula is doing today, it works, because the food smells truly out of this world.

Divine.

Paula may not be as old or as skinny or as ugly or even as experienced as Zenaida, the former cook, but, *wow*! Can that black woman cook!

Because it has begun to rain hard, Merced does not go across the patio on her way to the kitchen. Instead, she walks from one room to the next until she reaches the last room leading directly into the dining room. She begins to enter the dining room on her way to the kitchen when she hears noises coming from the kitchen which do not sound like the kind of noises one normally makes when one is cooking.

Intrigued, not really knowing what is going on, and wanting to find out what it is that Paula is doing, Merced begins to walk quietly, silently, almost on her tiptoes, until she reaches the open doorway to the kitchen. Then she peeks inside, and what she sees paralyzes her.

Right there, in front of her very own eyes, with his wife lying sick in bed with a bad heart in his own house not two rooms away, is her own father, big blond blue-eyed Maximiliano, standing behind Paula. He has unbuttoned his pants, raised Paula's skirt, and with his eyes closed in ecstasy, he is entering her from the back, bull style. He is riding her hard and fast, as Paula, bent over the pots on the coal stove and with her eyes equally closed in intense pleasure, is squirming with delight as she automatically keeps stirring and stirring the thick bean soup she has been preparing all morning long so it will not stick and burn.

Because of the heavy rain neither Maximiliano nor Paula has heard Merced come in, and because their eyes are closed they haven't seen her either. But Merced certainly has seen them and heard them all right, and those disgusting sounds and that disgusting vision become deeply engraved in her mind.

How could her father do this to his own wife in his own house? What if it had been her mother entering the kitchen instead of her? What if Dolores had seen what she has just seen?

Dolores, with a weak heart?

Merced is so repulsed by what she has just seen that she feels like vomiting and begins to gag. But she does not want to be noticed. She certainly does not want her sick mother in bed to know what is going on. So, quietly, without making the slightest noise, she backs away into the dining room to get a hold of herself.

She suddenly realizes that all the stories she has heard about her father, he with his huge coterie of mulatto women, are true, absolutely true. She does know about Cuban criollo men and their craving for black women. Dolores herself had told Merced many a time about Dolores's own father and his many mulatto women. But somehow Merced never expected to find her own father doing such a thing anywhere, and least of all in his own house, with his own wife sick in bed with a heart condition just a couple of rooms away, and with, of all people, Paula, the new cook.

Merced is so shocked she feels outraged beyond description. Affronted. Violated. As if she herself had been raped. The image she had of a godlike emperor of a father suddenly collapses, and with it all the love she used to feel for that man collapses as well, being replaced by an immense rage that knows no limits. But as enraged as she may be, there's one thing she is sure of: She certainly is not going to give her father the pleasure of seeing her in that condition. No, not Merced.

Still in the dining room, she leans against the large serving buffet made of Cuban black ebony that is heavily carved, criollo style, with horned gargoyles and gryphons and which has a lot of drawers. She catches her breath, sighs deeply, and then begins to open and close those drawers, making a lot of noise, as if looking for something inside of them. Then she shouts loud, real loud, for all to hear. "Mamá! Mamá! Do you know where your drops are? I can't find them! Don't you always keep them here, in the buffet? Who gave you your drops last time?"

Her mother shouts back from her bedroom at the other end of the house. "They should be right there, with the other medicines, in the second drawer, to the right. Look under the napkins."

Merced opens and closes the same drawer several times. "I can't find them," she shouts.

"Maybe Marguita left them in the kitchen this morning," her mother answers. "Ask Paula. She must know where they are."

By that time Maximiliano has come into the dining room, carrying a tiny cup of black Cuban coffee in his left hand and nervously stirring it with his right. He looks flushed and a little out of breath, but his fly is buttoned closed and his shirt is neatly tucked inside his pants.

"Oh, I found them!" shouts Merced, opening the right drawer the minute she sees her father. "They were all the way in the back."

Maximiliano offers his cheek to Merced, which she obediently kisses, as she says, "*Stirring* your coffee? I thought criollo men *never* stirred their coffee!"

Maximiliano looks at her and smiles. "Sometimes they do," he says, brushing her away from him, "when they need the energy." He gulps down the coffee, places the empty cup on the dining table, and adds, "Where are those drops? I'll take them to your mother."

Merced hands him the tiny bottle of drops and a tiny silver spoon to pour them in, watches him go, and then, after taking a deep breath, somehow she manages to go into the kitchen, her eyes nailed on Paula who, stirring and stirring her famous bean soup, is beaming ear to ear as Merced gets a glass of cold water out of the ice box.

Maximiliano goes to his bedroom where he sits on the bed next to his sick wife.

Dolores has been sweating heavily in the hot and humid rainy afternoon and Maximiliano is looking at her tenderly, wiping her forehead delicately, when Merced enters the room, a glass of water in her hand.

Maximiliano takes the drops in his hands, carefully measures five of them into the tiny silver spoon, gives them to Dolores, who patiently opens her mouth, and then hands her the glass of water Merced has just given him.

Merced, standing at the foot of the bed, looks first at her mother, lying sick in bed, and her eyes cannot conceal the intense love now tinged with pity Merced feels for Dolores.

Then she looks at her father, and her eyes cannot disguise the intense hate and contempt she now feels for this man; a hate that is as immense as her former love for this man was; an unrelenting hate that burns like hot coals in her fiery eyes, because she, who loves her mother beyond belief, suddenly has found out why her mother is lying in bed with a broken heart.

And then, startled, she wonders, Oh, my God! Is this what would have happened to me if Tonio had not been . . . what he was?

★ ★ ★

38

The small *posada* room is totally dark as Gustavo's wife, Graciela, beautiful Graciela, opens the door, which had been ajar, waiting for her.

She stands at the door, a dark silhouette against a tempestuous sky. Her backlit copper hair, covered with a few drops of rain, seems to be crowned by the broad trail of delicate wispy clouds in the sky behind her; wispy clouds that usually herald a tropical hurricane. Soon they will depart in all directions, and then a thin watery veil will pervade the air, and in two more days cloudiness will become overwhelming and the wind will begin to swirl and then—But who cares what will happen in two more days?

She rushes to the man inside the room, Arsenio, the man who owns her, as he rushes to her; and he searches for her mouth avidly, with the same desperate hunger she searches for his.

ELEUTERIA, HER DISHEVELED gray hair covered with a small black veil, is at the little church of Our Lady of Perpetual Help at the top of the hill, right on the Street of the Bulls.

She has not been in that church for years. What for? None of those saints has ever answered her prayers. That evil man of hers has yet to be crowned with a set of horns. What kinds of saints are these who will not listen to the tortured prayer of an abandoned woman?

But desperate situations call for desperate remedies. Perhaps one of these saints will be able to show her the way.

Perhaps.

"Father Francisco, please, it's urgent, please. I need to confess to you something immediately. Please."

Eleuteria has gone to Father Francisco for help.

Never has she been as desperate as she is today. Graciela, her baby daughter, the one who's closest to her heart, has just left her house to be with the man who owns her, and before she left, she told Eleuteria she will spend the night out with that man and then tell the whole truth to her husband, which Eleuteria knows she will unless she can think of something.

Eleuteria knows that nothing but death can come out of that truth. She knows. She has seen it happen before; she will see it happen again. But not with her own daughter, she desperately pleads to each and every saint under the sun. No, not with Graciela, please, not with Graciela.

The truth must be concealed, hidden. Somehow that truth can never come out. No one must ever know. She told Graciela she would protect her, that she would cover up for her, that she would lie for her. But Graciela, who has never lied, would have none of that. She is following her father's footsteps, regardless of what happens next.

Eleuteria is desperate. She has to think of something. But because she has not been able to think of anything she has decided to consult with the saints, all of them, beginning with the white ones at the little church atop the hill.

She has approached Father Francisco pretending she wanted to confess something because she knows that anything she tells the old priest during confession will be a secret that will go to the tomb with him. She does not want anybody to know Graciela's secret, which is also Eleuteria's secret, soon to be Father Francisco's secret as well.

Father Francisco listens to Eleuteria in total silence. They are both inside a small wooden confessional, the only one in the little church, which is badly in need of a coat of paint.

After Eleuteria finishes her story, Father Francisco says nothing.

Eleuteria does not know what to do. She thinks the priest must have gone to sleep. She clears her throat and says, "I've finished, Father."

"But, my child," Father Francisco answers, "you have not confessed your sins. I can only help you with your sins. I can forgive only the sins you have committed. I cannot forgive other people's sins unless they themselves come to me for forgiveness. Until that happens, there is nothing I can do for them except pray for their repentance."

"But, Father," asks Eleuteria, "what can I do?"

"Pray for them, my child," answers the old priest, who has heard many a similar confession during his long life on the Street of the Bulls. "Pray that they may get to see the light of our Savior before they sin again against His holy sacrament of matrimony." And after saying this, he blesses Eleuteria, who leaves the church shaking her head, swearing she'll never return again to such a place. What for? To waste her time?

She turns around once more before she exits the little church and looks at the little white saints aligning the whitewashed walls, sitting on their little altars, lighted by little flickering candles encased inside little red glasses. What kind of help was that? she asks of each of them. What kind of guidance did she get?

Certainly none from these saints.

Removing the small black veil covering her gray hair, she walks precipitously toward the other side of the street, the wrong side, where the mulatto women live, and their black saints with them.

Perhaps one of them will be able to help her. Perhaps one of them will listen to her. Perhaps one of them will answer her questions. Perhaps one of them will tell her what to do.

Perhaps.

What has she got to lose?

She has heard about the *santeros,* those black priests and priestesses who command the black saints who are right now her last hope. Maybe one of those saints will make her see the way out of this dead-ending maze she finds herself in, and her feet lead her almost on their own to where a famous *santero* woman lives.

She does this with great trepidation.

She has heard lots and lots of stories about chickens being sacrificed, and blood being smeared, and cigars being smoked backward, and of rum being drunk and spat on the floor by the *santero* possessed by the god as the god tries to find a voice to speak. But she has never come directly in contact with one of these people, the black *santeros.* And yet, afraid as she is, what other choice does she have?

She knocks on the glossy turquoise door of one of the wooden shacks on the wrong side of the Street of the Bulls and waits for it to open; and while she waits she realizes she owns this little shack she is about to enter.

A black woman, dressed totally in white, her head covered with a white turban, opens it and welcomes her with a broad smile.

"Come in, sister. We were expecting you."

Eleuteria is shocked by this salutation and hesitates to come inside this tiny room she owns but that she has never seen. The black woman moves out of the way, lets Eleuteria in, and closes the door.

The room is entirely painted a deep glossy turquoise blue: walls, windows, shutters, doors, ceiling. Even the badly splintered wood floor is also painted the same deep glossy turquoise color.

In one corner of the room there is an elevated altar, and on the altar there's an almost lifesize plaster figure of a young white woman, a medieval Christian princess with the golden halo of sainthood around her head, wearing a semitransparent white nightgown, made of real fabric, partly ripped, which is overlaid with a brilliant red-velvet robe. This woman saint is holding a heavy steel sword in her left hand and a golden chalice in her right hand.

The statue has been beautifully polychromed and carefully made up. Her face is pink, her lips glossy red, her hair—which is real hair—golden, falling in long curls, and her blue eyes, made of glass, are looking up, staring at something above her, as if she were looking at a divine presence that is felt by all in the room but seen only by the red-robed princess.

The statue is placed on top of a series of platforms that look like a series of steps. On top of each of these steps different items are displayed: a bottle of rum, a couple of shot glasses, a few cigars, a transparent glass vase filled with paper money of all denominations, a small ivory knife with its blade of shiny steel, a bottle of Florida water, sticks of incense, and numerous votive candles flickering inside little red glasses.

In the dim light of the glossy turquoise room the lady on top of the steps seems to be too real. Eleuteria looks at her and she thinks she sees the statue's white nightgown move ever so slightly as the lady breathes.

"A hurricane has been building up in your life and our Father Changó told us about it," says the black woman all dressed in white as she points to the statue on the altar.

Eleuteria looks up at the statue the woman called Father Changó and what she sees is the statue of a female. The black woman follows her gaze and answers her unasked question.

"Father Changó is half man, half woman," she says. "He shows Himself as a woman with the fiery sword of a man. That's why Father Changó knows about sex from the two sides."

Changó, the Yoruba god of sex, was all male before he reached Cuba. When the black African slaves were forced to reject their gods and become Christians, they noticed that one of the white Christian saints dressed in red and carried a sword—just as Changó did in Africa—so they assumed that white saint was their old black god, but in a different costume. They did not know that the Christian saint they had adopted as Changó was a woman—Santa Bárbara—a medieval virgin who had defended her honor with a sword. After they realized their mistake, they had no choice but to rethink their myth. That is how Changó, the black male god of sex, ended up inhabiting the body of a white medieval virgin. And that is how the Cuban Changó now knows about sex from the two sides.

The black woman points to a table and chairs nearby and invites Eleuteria to sit in one of them.

"You came to ask Him about sex," the black woman says. "Ask."

Eleuteria sits, and the black woman corrects her, asking Eleuteria to sit facing Father Changó.

"Ask Him what you will. Only *He* can answer you. And He will."

The black woman's voice is gentle and soft. Eleuteria looks at her nervously. She has seen this woman only a few times in her lifetime. She has always looked the other way when any of the *santero* priests or priestesses walk on the Street of the Bulls. She has always thought that all of this *santero* business was a silly game. She never expected to see herself sitting inside this deep glossy turquoise room that seems to be shimmering, waiting to hear an oracle from Father Changó, a black man inside a white woman's body. But once she is there, she has got to try. She's gone this far; no sense in going back.

The black woman sits, patiently waiting. Eleuteria does not know how to begin. The black woman smiles at her, a kind gentle smile. Eleuteria looks up at Father Changó and suddenly Eleuteria, the evil tongue of Luyanó, begins to cry.

She has not cried as far back as she can remember.

She did not cry when her mother died, when she was nine; nor when her father died, when she was twenty-two; nor when that evil man abandoned her, when she was thirty-one. She did not cry when any of her three daughters were born. She did not cry since that day when she was seven and a girl at school had called her ugly, and then all the kids at school began to make fun of her, and she had run to her mother, still alive, and had asked her if she was ugly, and her mother had answered, "No child is ever ugly to God."

Little seven-year-old Eleuteria knew exactly what her own mother meant, and at that moment she swore she was never again going to cry, never again.

And yet here she is, crying her eyes out to Changó, the powerful black male god of sex who wears the robes of a delicate white Christian virgin.

GRACIELA IS NAKED, lying in bed, her legs spread apart. Arsenio is kneeling on the floor in front of her, his face buried in that copper diadem she keeps between her legs.

She looks up, and in the mirror above their heads, she sees his beautiful head of black hair lying between her legs as if it were an extension of her own body. She extends her hands, still looking in the mirror, and with them she first caresses his black mane of hair and then pushes it wildly against her body as an incredible sound begins to escape from her lips.

He answers that sound with an equally incredible sound of his own that begins to escape from his lips, and then he climbs on top of her, violently pressing down against her, frantically trying to crush his body into hers, as their desperate mouths in a deliriously frenetic frenzy search furiously for each other with brutal savagery.

THE BLACK WOMAN in the turquoise room has been sitting quietly in her chair when suddenly she begins to moan violently, and then two voices are heard coming from her mouth at the same time, both exploding with a bestial scream, the violent bestial scream of ultimate pain and of ultimate pleasure.

Eleuteria sits stunned in her chair, unable to say anything.

The oracle has spoken.

The black woman in the white dress has told her the god has spoken.

"Red's his father, his mother, his brother, his lover," the woman says. "Red."

And as she says it, she exposes her hands to Eleuteria, who, horrified, sees blood on them.

39

Not knowing whom to turn to, Gustavo does as he has always done whenever he is in a panic.

It's early Wednesday morning.

It's so early that the early tropical sun has not come up yet. The Street of the Bulls is still silent and quiet, and so is the whole of the barrio of Luyanó, which is still bathed in a sensual blue, the color of a tropical night languidly awakening.

Gustavo, who has not been able to sleep a drop all night long, unable to wait any longer, runs across La Calzada and rushes to his parents' house. Using his old set of keys, which he still has, he comes in, tiptoeing, trying not to wake anybody in the house. He certainly does not want to disturb Dolores, who has been ill now for almost a whole week.

Dolores has been complaining of lack of air to breathe, and unable to sleep lying down in her own bed she has been sleeping sitting up in a rocking chair in the living room for the last three or four nights. But last night she felt a lot better, and thanks to a sedative Manuel the doctor had given her, she had been able to fall asleep in her own bed, next to her husband, whose happy snores Gustavo can hear as he stealthily enters the house and goes to the room of his big brother, Mani.

He enters it and begins to shake Mani violently, trying to wake him up, as he urgently calls him, in a whispered voice that tries to sound gentle but which is filled with fear.

"Mani! Mani! Wake up! Please, wake up!"

Mani still sleeps in the same small room he and Gustavo used to share before Gustavo got married. Gustavo's bed is still there, perfectly made. Nobody knew what to do with it when Gustavo left the house, and since Gustavo had no use for it in Eleuteria's house across La Calzada, the bed has stayed right where it used to be all of this time.

However, that bed has been put to a great new use by Mani.

On top of that bed there is a bunch of drawings and sketches on papers of all sizes and colors that look like the work of a madman because they are done with strokes so violently wild and powerful that the chalk has often gone through the paper, leaving gaping holes in them.

These drawings have been done by Mani in the deep of the night, after everyone else has gone to sleep. Nobody has ever seen these drawings. Every morning, when Mani wakes up, he hides them, carefully placing them flat between two thick cardboards and storing them under the mattress of Gustavo's old bed.

Since Mani is always the first one to wake up, nobody has ever seen these drawings, except for Hortensia and Fidelia, Mani's black goddesses.

This morning, because Gustavo entered Mani's room so unexpectedly before Mani was awake, the drawings are still there, on top of Gustavo's old bed. On top of the drawings, weighing them down, is Merced's book *Apollo,* which Merced gave Mani as a gift.

Gustavo keeps stirring Mani, shaking him violently, his voice sounding each time more urgent and more demanding as he keeps repeating and repeating, "Mani! Wake up! Mani! Mani! Wake up! Wake up! Wake up!" until Mani finally begins to stir.

Mani is dead tired. He had begun work on a drawing in the middle of the night but something was wrong with it and he didn't know what. He passed out without completing it. Then he woke up again later, in the middle of the night, knowing exactly what to do, and with a few bold strokes was able to finish it. Then he passed out again, not that long ago, just to be awakened now by Gustavo who, grabbing him by the shoulders, is shaking him hard.

"Let go, man!" Mani snarls, still under the covering white-cotton sheet. "Let go! You're hurting me!"

Gustavo lets Mani go.

Mani rubs his eyes, still filled with sleep. "What the fuck do you think you're doing!" He sounds angry. Mani always sounds angry when he is sleepy. He looks around the room and sees it's still dark outside the windows. "It's still dark outside. What time is it?"

Gustavo bends down and whispers to him. "Sshhh! Don't wake them up!"

Mani lowers his voice as he begins to sit on his bed. "What the fuck is wrong with you, man? Don't you see what—"

Gustavo interrupts him. "Mani, I don't know what to do. I don't know what to do!" he whispers, and then begins to shake, as if he were still the little child who scared and afraid used to run to his big brother, Mani, each time he would get into trouble with the other boys on the Street of the Bulls, so Mani would fight Gustavo's fights for him.

It doesn't matter that Gustavo is taller than Mani by a whole head; it doesn't matter that Gustavo outweighs his brother by quite a few pounds; it doesn't matter that Gustavo hung his apron in the butcher shop while Mani only dreams of doing it.

To Gustavo, Mani is still his big brother, someone to run to when in need; just like to Mani, Gustavo is his kid brother, someone to protect and defend.

Seeing his brother in the state he is in has awakened Mani instantly, who now sits in bed, his eyes wide open.

"What's the matter?" Mani demands.

"It's Graciela," Gustavo says in a thread of a voice. Then he lowers his voice even more as he looks at the floor. "She didn't come home last night."

Merced, who always sleeps light, is standing by the door to Mani's room. She had come unnoticed by the two brothers and has heard Gustavo.

"She didn't come home last night?" she asks as she steps into the room.

Gustavo, who was sitting on Mani's bed facing Mani, his back to the door, jumps up as he hears Merced's voice behind him. He didn't want her, of all people, to know. He turns around, surprised by his sister, faces her, and says nothing. Then, under her inquisitive eyes, he has no choice but to shake his head.

"Eleuteria knows?" asks Merced.

"She's been crying all night long. All night long."

"Eleuteria?" asks Mani. "The evil tongue of—"

Merced silences Mani with a quick stare, then asks Gustavo, "Did the two of you have a fight?"

There's a long pause. Then Gustavo answers, tentatively, "Well, no . . . not a fight, not really . . ."

He still doesn't want her to know. He faces Mani and gives him a look new to Mani, a piercing look Mani is unable to decipher.

"That's exactly what happened," says Merced, who always knows everything. "You two had a fight and she didn't know what to do, so she ran to one of her sisters' houses. That's exactly what happened, isn't it? Gustavo, you know you can keep no secrets from me. I can see it in your eyes. Have you called them?"

Gustavo looks at Merced and shakes his head.

"Well, don't you think you should?" says Merced as she begins to leave Mani's room.

"Where are you going?" asks Gustavo.

"To call her sisters, stupid," says Merced, getting angry. "She's got to be with either the one or the other. And when I get Graciela on the phone you'd better talk to her and apologize for whatever it was you did."

She rushes out of the room, just to be stopped by Gustavo, who holds her by the arm. Merced turns to him, her eyes burning with fire.

"No, don't. She's not there."

"Oh, now you know where she is?"

"No, I don't. But I know she's not with her sisters. She—" Gustavo pauses. Then he begins to cry, like a baby.

Mani, who always sleeps naked, jumps out of bed and, naked as he is, embraces his frightened kid brother, a big frightened young bullock of twenty-three who is trembling.

Merced, noticing her brother is naked, looks the other way, but she does not fail to see the two bracelets of tiny red beads encircling Mani's manly parts.

"Hush, man!" Mani says to Gustavo. "You want Pappy to hear you?"

Gustavo is shaking badly.

Merced is standing at the door not knowing what to do.

Mani turns to Merced. "Merced, could you leave us alone for a while?" Merced debates what to do. "Please," adds Mani. "Why don't you make us some coffee?" His voice is soothing, but the look in his eyes is demanding, clearly telling her to go. Merced snorts, angrily bites her lips, and exits, leaving her brothers alone in their room.

Mani hugs his brother tight to him and lets him cry on his shoulder for a while, until Gustavo shakes his head, pulls away from Mani, and takes his glasses off.

"That's not what happened," he says as he wipes his glasses clean with Mani's cover sheet. "We didn't have a fight." He puts them on again and faces Mani.

"She's with another guy."

"What?"

"I got it out of Eleuteria. When Graciela did not show up by midnight I was about to dial the police and Eleuteria stopped me. She begged me not to do it. She said that the scandal would bring shame to all. I asked her what she meant, and she wouldn't say. But when I told her I'd call the police if she didn't tell me, then she told me." He pauses, takes a deep breath, and then adds, "Graciela's had a lover for the last few months."

"The fucking whore!" whispers Mani with rage in his voice.

"They've been seeing each other every Tuesday afternoon. For the last . . . I don't know for how many months, every Tuesday afternoon, while I was working at the bookstore, she was letting that man—" Again he begins to shake so badly he cannot complete his sentence.

"I'll kill her. I swear I'll kill her, the fucking whore," says Mani through his teeth, trying to control the anger in his voice, but failing to do so. "I'll kill them both, I swear it to God! Leave that to me!"

"Please, Mani, please," begs Gustavo. "Don't say a word of this to anybody. Please. Not even to Merced. Please, Mani, please. Swear it to me. Please, please, swear it to me."

Mani stares at Gustavo, puzzled.

"I don't want anybody to know about this. If the other guys in the barrio were to find out, what wouldn't they think of me? They'd laugh at me, all of them, they'd just laugh at me! They'd think I wasn't enough of a man for her. Please, Mani, I needed to tell someone. I needed to get it off my chest. But please, don't say a word of this to anybody. Please, my brother. I'm begging you, please." He stares at Mani through his glasses, and waits and waits.

Mani faces away from Gustavo and is silent for the longest while. He doesn't like to see his brother pleading like that. This is not the Gustavo who hung his apron at the butcher shop never to come back. That Gustavo he liked. That Gustavo was a man Mani could admire and respect, a man who had taught Mani a lesson in courage. That Gustavo would have never said a thing like what this other Gustavo just said. This Gustavo in front of him is the other Gustavo, the one afraid of the smallest bully on the Street of the Bulls. How can the two of them be so different? How can one Gustavo be afraid of the little bulls on the street and the other Gustavo defy the biggest bull of them all, the Champion Bull in a street that has known many a bull; the man Mani calls father, Maximiliano the butcher. Mani does not understand it. He simply cannot understand it. Without realizing it he has made fists of both his hands and he is pressing his hands closed so tight they have become almost white, livid with rage.

He looks at his kid brother again with an angry frown on his face and is about to say something when he sees the pain in Gustavo's eyes, and the pain in Gustavo's eyes disarms him. He opens his hands, shakes his head, and sighs.

Whoever this Gustavo is in front of him, this Gustavo is his kid brother, and if he's come to him for help . . . what else can a brother do? And yet he still feels that he has to make his brother understand that what must be done must be done.

"Gustavo," he says in as quiet and as soothing a way as he can manage, "don't you realize that whether you like it or not, sooner or later all of this is going to come out in the open? It would be a lot better if you were to strike now while the—"

"Oh, no, Mani. No." Gustavo interrupts. "You don't understand. Graciela told Eleuteria she'd be back tomorrow, and I'm sure she will. Then, when she comes back, things will be different, very different, because I will then walk out on her. Don't you see? I cannot let her walk out on me. I just cannot let her do that to me." Sensing some apprehension coming from Mani, Gustavo adds, "Please, Mani, please. Promise me you won't say a word of this to anybody. Please. Let me handle it my own way, please. I'd do it for you, my brother, if you were to ask me."

There's a long pause.

Mani looks at Gustavo for a long while, and then, reluctantly, Mani nods in agreement. "I won't say a word," he says.

He then holds his kid brother at arm's length and crosses his heart. "This is between you and me. If this is what you want, you can trust me. My lips are sealed. I won't say a word of this to anybody." He pauses, then shakes hands with his kid brother, who then hugs Mani in a tight brotherly embrace.

Mani has given Gustavo his word he will never say a word about what Gustavo has told him, and a criollo agreement has been sealed between the two brothers, never to be broken.

What Mani is perfectly aware of, but Gustavo isn't, is that Mani never agreed with Gustavo that he would *do* nothing about it.

Merced, who was in the kitchen making coffee, comes in bringing a little white tray with three tiny demitasse cups filled to the brim with coffee so hot that steam is coming out of them.

When Mani sees her come in, he quickly puts on his white baggy undershorts and begins to clear the top of Gustavo's old bed, cluttered with his drawings and sketches, but neither Gustavo nor Merced notices what he is doing.

Gustavo is now sitting on Mani's bed, atop the rumpled sheets, his shoulders slumped, his eyes fixed on the blue-and-white tile floor at his bare feet as Merced, at the doorway, is looking at him, the little white tray with the three tiny cups of steaming coffee still in her hands.

She says nothing.

She just stands there, leaning against the frame of the door, and waits, saying nothing.

Mani, who has just placed the cardboard-protected drawings beneath the mattress of Gustavo's old bed, turns around and reaches for one of the tiny coffee cups on the little white tray Merced is still holding in her hands. He takes it and brings it close to his lips. The coffee is so hot he has to blow on it to cool it before he can take a sip of it.

As he does that, he catches Merced looking at Gustavo, and suddenly that picture becomes engraved in his head.

Merced, naked under her semitransparent white nightgown, her bare breasts hanging free beneath it, leaning against the pale-cream door frame, holding a tiny white tray in her hands with two tiny white demitasse cups of steaming coffee, looking at Gustavo, lying on a bed covered with white rumpled sheets, in his badly wrinkled white pants and white sweat-stained sleeveless undershirt.

She, thinking of a husband, now gone; he, thinking of a wife, also gone; and both of them wondering why as the light of the rising sun begins to bathe the pale-cream room, which seemed blue in the night, with just a tinge of fire.

★ ★ ★

40

Detective Fernández answers the early morning phone call in the businesslike manner he always uses when he is at work, listens for a few seconds, and then smiles warmly.

"Of course I remember you!"

He turns around and, as he continues to talk into the telephone's mouthpiece, still holding the earpiece in his left hand, he begins to search with his right hand for something in the pockets of his jacket, which is hanging on the back of his chair, until he finds what he is looking for.

"As a matter of fact," he adds, looking at a small envelope in his hand, "I have something of yours. Have you been missing an earring?"

MERCED HAD BEEN DEBATING what to do.

The explanation Gustavo gave her this morning about Graciela did not make much sense, so the minute Gustavo went to work, as if nothing had happened, Merced went to see Eleuteria.

The evasive answers the old lady gave to Merced—something about Graciela's going to see her estranged father—did not quite agree with what Gustavo had told her, and Merced, inquisitive Merced, smelled that something was wrong. She knew it was none of her business, but after she had lived through what she had lived through, she did not wish any of that pain on her worst enemy, and certainly not on Gustavo, her favorite brother. Maybe if someone had started locating Tonio the minute he was missing, maybe he would still be alive.

Merced asked Mani if he thought they should call the police, but Mani just snarled at Merced, telling her that whatever happened between Graciela and Gustavo was none of her damn business and then walked away from her in a furious rage.

Merced has never been able to understand Mani; rude brusque angry Mani who wears red beaded bracelets around his manly parts. No one ever has. Mani lived away from the rest of the family for so long that nobody has ever been able to know what is going through his head at any time. Merced is sure that not even Dolores, his own mother, knows. Dark-haired, dark-eyed Mani has always been a mystery to all of them.

Not so blond blue-eyed Gustavo.

Gustavo is different, always easy to understand, transparent, especially to Merced. He has always been a good boy, loved by all, unable to kill a fly. Gustavo never threw a bullfrog in Merced's face or placed a dead rat under her bedspread, like Mani did many a time. Instead, Gustavo was always delighting her and Dolores and Marguita with pleasant little surprises: chocolate kisses, valentines, little poems, hidden under their pillows.

Dolores still keeps on top of her chiffonier, next to the old sepia photograph of her own mother, a crudely hand-cut heart Gustavo made for her. He had fashioned this heart out of some glossy red paper Merced had saved, which she kept in the bottommost drawer of her chest of drawers, where she keeps all sorts of odd things she has no longer use for but which were meaningful to her at some time in her past: old wrapping paper, a red-silk ribbon, an old rag doll partly burned, things like that.

The heart Gustavo made for his mother opens up and inside there is a poem, Gustavo's first, written for Dolores by Gustavo when he was just a child of five or six. Dolores had taught him how to read and write, and little Gustavo, without the help of anybody, had printed the five-word poem with big childlike letters going every which way.

"Para Mamá. Linda. Amorsito Mío." "For Mamá. Pretty. Little love of mine."

Gustavo misspelled the word *Amorcito* with an *s* instead of a *c,* but Dolores never corrected it. She loved the poem so much, misspelled word and all, that ever since that time she has kept on calling Gustavo *"Amorsito Mío,"* little love of mine, purposely mispronouncing the word. To this day she still calls him that, even though her little baby boy is now a big married man, but a big married man who is as full of surprises now as he was back then.

It was Gustavo who—when Merced moved back home after Tonio's death—surprised her with a tiny puppy, a limping black-and-white mutt of a dog he had rescued from the pound, with one droopy ear and a lot of charm, who seems to be as stupid as he is cute, and who has made Merced's life after Tonio's death a little more bearable. Merced fell in love with the puppy at once, and named him "Tontín," a diminutive term of endearment derived from the word *tonto,* which means *dumb.*

But even though the puppy may be dumb, Merced loves him dearly for Merced knows that one can love someone who is dumb as much as one can love someone who is smart. Pepe Loreto is smart. He may be as grumpy and as unbearable as he is old, yes, that is quite true, but he is also very smart, as smart as Tontín is dumb, and Merced loves them both with a love that is tinged with a drop of sadness for she sees a little of herself in each of them.

When Merced moved back home and brought Pepe Loreto to Dolores's beautiful sunny patio, the old parrot lived through a long period of adjustment when he felt totally out of place and miserable, just as Merced felt when she first moved into Tonio's parents' dark and cavernous house.

After the move, Pepe Loreto kept staring constantly at the pale-cream wall in front of him, constantly muttering his favorite insults to himself, and doing little else. He looked so sad and so lonely facing that pale-cream wall that on many occasions Merced thought that perhaps she had made a big mistake bringing him to her house. But she knew that back in Tonio's house no one would have taken care of the tired old bird, whom everybody disliked. So good faithful Merced kept patiently feeding the old parrot and talking to him even though he would no longer answer her back. He would not even face Merced when she spoke to him, that's how angry and hurt and sad and lonely and out of place the old decrepit parrot felt.

Early one morning Merced was rushing out of her house on her way to a job interview, when accidentally she left the door to Pepe Loreto's cage open after she fed him and changed his water. Pepe Loreto, who had been sulking as usual facing the wall in front of him, totally ignoring Merced, turned around after Merced left him. Then, realizing that the door to his cage was open, he stuck his head out the door, looked in all directions, carefully let himself fall to the floor, and once there he began walking around from one end of the patio to the other, slowly shuffling his tired old feet, to the amazement of all in the house.

When Merced returned that day, the old parrot, still on the patio floor, was talking again, saying his name, ruffling his tired old feathers, calling, "Merced, Merced!" and making a lisp as he squawked, a lisp that made Marguita laugh every time Pepe Loreto said, "Kissssss? Kissssss?"

Someone else had gotten the job ahead of her, and Merced was very depressed when she returned, but when she heard Pepe Loreto calling her, a weight lifted off her soul and she felt happy, truly happy, happy inside, where it counts. This had been the first time she had felt truly happy since she had come back from her honeymoon in Miami. She had been truly happy the whole of that week.

Or had she?

She never liked to think about any of that.

Those last few months of her life were like a dark parenthesis, something she knew had happened but something she had refused to accept. Thinking about them made her feel resentful, a resentment verging on anger, which she always directed at herself. How could she have been so dumb? Even Tontín was not as dumb as she had been. How could she have misunderstood everything so badly?

Now when she looks at it all in retrospect, everything seems so clear: Every word Tonio said, every action he took, every look in his eye. How could she have misunderstood it all so badly?

It all seemed to her that whatever had happened had happened to someone who looked like her, and dressed like her, and walked and smelled and even felt like her, but someone who was not her. No. It had not happened to her, the real her, the one who looks in the mirror every morning and still dreams of feeling beautiful, as Dolores told her she would feel one day, when the man destined by life to be hers looked at her. That had not happened to her. Tonio had never made her feel beautiful. Now she knew why, and she understood at last that whatever happened, it had not been her fault. It had not been his fault either. It had been no one's fault.

In his last letter to her he had told her that burning that letter of his would make her free. She burned the letter, and yet, though she claims to feel totally free, there she still is, answering the demands of Tonio's old parrot and sending Pepe Loreto the kisses he is asking for in that old ugly squawking voice of his. Pepe Loreto who, just like Tonio, makes her feel needed and perhaps even loved. But not yet beautiful.

Since that day, The Day of *his* Emancipation, Pepe Loreto is a different bird. Now that he is finally free, now he is finally happy. True, he cannot fly away, he is that old. But even if he could, why would he? He is the master of *his* patio, a bull of a parrot who commands not only a pretty girl, blond blue-eyed Marguita, who laughs at all his punch lines, but also a pretty servant, moody dark-eyed Merced, who gives him food and water when he wants it, and sends him kisses when he demands it. Pepe Loreto is a happy old bird. So happy, in fact, that it has been a long time since he has said his favorite insult, "*comemierdas.*" That's how happy Pepe Loreto feels in his new abode on La Calzada just a few steps from the Street of the Bulls.

At least, that's how happy Pepe Loreto *was* feeling, until the day Merced's little black-and-white mutt of a puppy arrived.

Pepe Loreto was pleasantly shuffling his tired old feet, walking on the patio—his patio—as slow as Napoleon on his way to the coronation, when he first saw that black-and-white little thing of a mutt with a funny limp rush, kind of sideways, toward him. Instantly he ruffled his feathers, put fire in his eyes, and using his least pleasant voice—a voice that is unpleasant enough when it tries to be pleasant—began shouting and squawking, calling the little dog "*¡Cuadrúpedo! ¡Cuadrúpedo!*" a word which to Pepe Loreto is, next to "*comemier-*

da," the epitome of an insult, he being a biped, like the rest of us. But unfortunately for Pepe Loreto, the more the old parrot spat it out, the more he insulted the poor mutt, the more fire he put in his angry words and the more he ruffled his feathers, the more the poor little mutt thought Pepe Loreto was playing and the more he seemed to love it—something that drove Pepe Loreto literally to the wall.

Exacerbated by the stupidity of the puppy, which failed to understand that Pepe Loreto, the master of *this* patio, didn't want that other ugly little thing there *at all,* the old bird went to where his cage was, stood under it, faced the wall, and shouted one insult after another.

"*¡Comemierda! ¡Cuadrúpedo! ¡Comemierda! ¡Cuadrúpedo! ¡Comemierda!*"

Maximiliano, who was looking at the puppy, shook his head and said to Merced, "Lord! That dog is so stupid! Doesn't he see that parrot wants to have nothing to do with him?"

Merced, who was looking at her new puppy with loving eyes, immediately came to his defense, saying that one is not stupid just because one happens to love somebody who doesn't love you back.

"All right, Tonto," Maximiliano said. "Dumb."

To which Merced answered, looking again at the puppy with her kind moody eyes, "He's too little for you to call him Tonto."

"Then," added Maximiliano, "call him Tontín."

And Tontín he has been called since: a little dumb quadruped of a puppy that loves and adores a smart obnoxious biped of a parrot who hates, loathes, and despises the black-and-white tiny mutt that loves him so much. And though Pepe Loreto hates Tontín, Merced loves the little mutt as much as she loves the old parrot, because they both make her happy.

Tontín sees her come in, and though he still limps, he rushes to her kind of sideways at the speed of lightning and begins to lick her all over, his tiny tail wagging so rapidly that it looks like a smudge of a tiny white cloud in the air.

Merced caresses him behind the ears and looks him in the eye and tells him he is a good dog, and Tontín returns her look adoringly, making Merced feel that she is needed.

She then hears Pepe Loreto at the other end of the patio muttering "*¡Cuadrúpedo! ¡Comemierda!*" and from where she is she sends the old parrot a noisy kiss that makes Pepe Loreto ruffle his wings and lisp, "Merced, Merced! Kissss! Kissss . . . !"

As Merced takes care of her feuding animals, Dolores watches and smiles as she silently thanks God for the smart old parrot and the dumb puppy dog, because Merced talks to each of them and tells them things Merced has never told anybody, not even Dolores, her own mother; things Dolores knows Merced needs to tell.

And though Dolores does not enjoy the constant barking, and the constant squawking, and the constant muttering of insults, and the constant commotion, she accepts all of that happily because she knows Merced needs it: Pepe Loreto is somehow Merced's last tie to a past she hesitates to break completely away from. And Tontín is somehow a measure of hope.

MERCED AND DETECTIVE FERNÁNDEZ are sharing a few drops of the blackest Cuban coffee served in the tiniest paper cup ever, as they both stand in front of a *timbiriche,* one of those little vending carts with a canvas roof one finds in Old Havana near office buildings.

Despite the ominous heat and the unbearable humidity, Detective Fernández is wearing his jacket and tie while Merced is wearing a bias-cut silver-gray dress made by Dolores, which accentuates her beautiful criollo-woman shape, and a hat to match, which manages to bring out the beauty of her dark wavy hair, so black and so glossy that, reflecting the tropical dark-turquoise sky, becomes almost dark blue.

"I didn't want to make this a formal request, you understand," Merced tells Detective Fernández. "I didn't want my family to know about this, just in case I'm totally wrong, and I hope I am. That's why I thought it would be better if we met here instead of—"

"I understand. How long has she actually been missing?"

"Only since last night, I believe." Merced pauses. "You don't think she—?" Merced does not finish her sentence. She thinks, Would Graciela do what Tonio did, for whatever the reasons? Merced shakes her head.

Detective Fernández is able to read her thoughts. "There's no reason to worry. After you called me I checked all the hospitals and had one of my men start calling the hotels. So far no one has been found meeting her description."

He pauses and looks at Merced. The young widow is such a beautiful woman with such dark moody eyes. If only she were to smile. He has never seen her smile.

"I'll go on checking," he adds, "but I'm sure everything will be all right. Didn't you tell me this was the first fight your brother ever had with his wife?"

Merced nods.

He continues, "Married people fight over stupid things all the time, making a mountain out of a molehill. I remember the first fight I ever had with my late wife." He smiles at Merced. "Sometimes good fights are very good—they make the reconciliations that much better."

Merced smiles. "That's exactly what my mother-in-law, I mean, my *former* mother-in-law used to say."

She looks at Detective Fernández, and by sheer accident their eyes meet as she catches him looking at her.

There is a short pause.

She has never realized that blue eyes could be so warm and so deep. She has never been looked at that way, with such intensity.

Then, simultaneously, they both say at exactly the identical time, "This coffee's so hot!"

When they notice what they have just done, they both begin to laugh at exactly the identical time again, loud belly laughs, and Merced, embarrassed, covers her mouth with her left hand, which is no longer wearing a wedding ring.

Two days ago Merced had taken off her wedding ring to wash her hands, as she had always done; and when she was about to put it back on, she asked herself, Why? Hadn't Tonio told her that he wanted her to be free? She didn't put it back on.

No one in the house noticed it. But Dolores did.

Late that night, when everyone else was asleep and Maximiliano's happy snores could be heard echoing all over the house, Dolores sat down with Merced and soothingly, in that quiet way of hers, asked her daughter about the ring. It was then Merced finally opened up to her mother and told her everything.

An unbridled torrent of words—words of guilt, and words of anger, and words of pain, and words of agony—spurted, apparently, out of Merced's mouth, but Dolores knew they were anguishingly pouring out of Merced's heart. And once water begins to gush out, who can contain a dam that breaks?

While Merced emptied her heart, Dolores listened to her daughter and did not say a thing.

When Merced finished, Dolores embraced Merced tight to her, erased her daughter's tears, walked her back to her bedroom, put her to sleep, and still did not say a thing.

But as she was leaving Merced's room, she saw the ring on top of Merced's chest of drawers and, opening the bottommost drawer, she sighed a deep sigh as she placed it there.

★ ★ ★

41

It is not even five o'clock in the morning when the phone by Ferminio's side of the bed rings. Ferminio is in the bathroom. He has just finished taking a shower and is getting ready to go to his Cuban slaughterhouse, the one he can see from the kitchen of his modern house; a house he dislikes so much, but a house Albertina, his wife of thirty-seven years, adores.

The phone rings again, and Albertina, who is already awake, rolls over the bed and answers it. She listens to it for a while, and then, placing her hand over the mouthpiece so she cannot be heard by the calling party, and using her sweetest tone of voice, she calls Ferminio, who is now in front of the bathroom sink attempting to shave.

"Ferminio, dear . . ."

Ferminio, still shaving, looks at her.

Albertina goes on, her voice as gentle as it can be. "Your son-in-law did not come home last night, did you know that?"

And then she shouts, her voice now loud and sharp, heavily loaded with anger. "Are you going to tell me now that you forgot to tell me there was a meeting last night between him and your government buddies?"

She waits for no answer. She uncovers the mouthpiece and tells her daughter in a soothing motherly voice, "Fernanda, don't worry, honey. I'll call you right back, after I have a good talk with that monster of a father you have."

She hangs up just as Ferminio enters the bedroom, totally naked, still partly wet from his morning shower, his manly parts heavily sprinkled with white talcum powder, his face partly covered with shaving soap, pointing the razor at his wife, and shaking it as he shouts back at her, "This is not the first time he has spent the night out, and you know it. So don't make a mountain out of a molehill. And yes! If he and those government buddies of his ever reached an agreement yesterday, I am sure there was a celebration of some kind. And if *I* had been there," he adds, angry words spurting out of his mouth, "I *too* would have gone out with them and done exactly what they probably did, which is to get fucking drunk and throw a good fuck with a fucking expensive whore paid by the goddamned fucking government!"

He says that and quickly rushes back into the bathroom, slamming the door behind him just in time to prevent the expensive porcelain figurine he just saw Albertina hurl at him from hitting him. He hears a loud crash on the other side of the door, and then cuts himself as he attempts to finish shaving.

"Goddamn that Arsenio! I'll skin him alive when I get my hands on him! That stupid porcelain figurine cost me an arm and a leg! Fucking son of a bitch! What the fuck does he think he's doing?"

It's only when Arsenio does not show up for work that Ferminio begins to wonder what is going on. This has never happened before. Arsenio has always been the first one to arrive at the slaughterhouse and the last one to leave. It is now way past noon and he has not shown up yet.

Ferminio, who has refused to answer any of Albertina's thousands of phone calls this morning, without saying a word to her, has one of his guys call all the hospitals and wonders whether he should dial the police.

THE MISTAKE ARSENIO MADE, if one can call that a mistake, was that he had paid in advance only the amount required to use the *posada* room for just a few hours, the way he always did every Tuesday. But this time they had stayed there already for God knows how many hours.

Graciela had been very late yesterday afternoon, almost two hours late. He had waited for her and waited for her and was wondering what had happened to her and whether he should stay any longer or call her or leave when the door to their small musty *posada* room finally opened up.

She did not say a word when she arrived. She did not have to. Arsenio knew right then, the minute he looked into her eyes and saw them aglow, that this was going to be the night the two of them had been dreaming about for many a painful night.

Arsenio buzzed the clerk, who came to the little door within the inner door, and delicately knocked at it. Arsenio, who was waiting for him, unlocked the little door, gave the man a twenty-peso bill, ordered a bottle of the best Añejo, and told the invisible clerk to keep the change.

Within minutes a tiny small tray holding two shot glasses was passed through the little door, accompanied by a bottle of the smoothest rum money can buy.

Arsenio broke the seal of the expensive rum bottle and was about to pour some into a shot glass when she took the bottle from his hands, drank from it staring at him, and passed it back to him, who drank from it staring back at her.

Nothing had been said. Nothing needed to be said. No explanations, no demands, no questions. That may happen later on, after the storm running through their veins has subsided.

But now, as the rum begins to flow, the wind begins to whirl, and the storm begins to roar, and the coastal waters begin to surge, and the level of the sea begins to rise and rise, until a sudden violent tide begins to invade the coast and powerful pounding waves begin to hammer at it, exploding with the apotheosic magnificence of a god with a scepter of power between his legs possessing and being possessed by a goddess with a diadem of copper between hers.

One night together. That was all each of them wanted. Just that. One entire night entirely to themselves.

And then came the slumber of the eye of the storm.

ELEUTERIA DOESN'T KNOW what to think or whom to thank. She doesn't know how, but somehow she has managed to buy time. One of her saints must be working for her, but which one of them? Maybe they all are. She says a quick prayer to each of them, including Father Changó, he with the shape of a woman.

After Gustavo forced an answer out of her and ran across La Calzada to his parents' house, she thought everything was over and prepared herself for the worst. But then he came back, much calmer, almost too serene, took a shower, got dressed, and went to work as if nothing had happened. He asked no further questions, made no further demands, offered no explanations. He just left, not tasting any of the breakfast Eleuteria had prepared for him.

Eleuteria loves Gustavo. She always did. From the very moment he got her a fresh newspaper after her own newspaper had fallen in a puddle of mud and Gustavo had refused to accept a penny for it, from that very first moment until today, when she saw him leave the house in total silence, without even a good-bye whistle.

Eleuteria loves to hear Gustavo whistle in the mornings. His happy sounds wake her up, as if awakened by the happy singing of birds. Gustavo has brought so much happiness into her life. And now this . . . !

She wanted to go to him and embrace him and tell him that it had not been her fault, that she knew nothing about it, that she loved him as the son she never had, that she was as hurt by all of this as he was. But then she thought of Graciela, her own flesh, her baby. And she knew that if she had to choose sides, as she knew she would, she would unquestionably choose the side of her own daughter, whether she deserved it or not. That was why, though she wanted to run to Gustavo and hug and caress him and mother him, she just stood there, on her porch, looking at him as he got on the bus that would take him to Athena, the bookstore named after the Greek goddess of wisdom. Maybe that goddess would enlighten him as to what to do next, Eleuteria prayed, because she, Eleuteria, certainly did not know.

ARSENIO WAS AWAKENED by a gentle tap that kept knocking on and on. He sat up in bed. The knocking was coming from the tiny door within the larger inner door of the small musty *posada* room where he and Graciela had spent the night, a room that smelled of expensive rum and of opulent sex.

Somehow he managed to make it to the door, sidestepping the two other bottles of Añejo, one of them still partly filled. He heard the gentle knocking again and a voice of an invisible woman on the other side of the door. He opened the little door, stepping out of the way, so the woman on the other side would not see him, naked as he was. The invisible woman asked him if they were planning to stay another day. At first Arsenio did not understand what she was talking about. His head was still swimming in the rum, as Cubans are fond of saying. Then he realized this must be another day.

"What time is it?" he asked.

"Two thirty."

"Two thirty? In the morning?"

"No, señor. In the afternoon."

"Two thirty in the *afternoon*? What day is it?"

"Wednesday, señor. I didn't mean to bother you, señor. I didn't know if the room was empty. Would you like me to come in and change the sheets for you? Or get you more towels?"

Arsenio did not know what to say. This was Wednesday afternoon already? Wednesday *afternoon?* He always made it to the slaughterhouse by four thirty in the morning!

The voice of a man was heard behind the interior door.

"Señor, this is the main desk clerk. I'm sorry to bother you, señor, but I have to charge you for the use of the room for a full day. You paid to use the room for six hours only. The balance you owe is four pesos and twenty-five cents. Could I trouble you to pay it now? My shift is up and I have to balance my books."

Arsenio nodded. It took him a long while to realize the man behind the door could not see him. "Sure," he added. "Just wait a moment." He walked to where he thought his pants were but could not find them. He looked under the bed, behind the bathroom door, inside the bathtub. He found them neatly folded, hanging in a tiny closet that was hidden behind the open bathroom door. Graciela must have done that, because he sure hadn't. He never hangs up any of his clothes. He got the wallet out of his back pocket and walked back to the door. There he opened his wallet and the first thing he saw when he opened it was the photograph of his two pretty girls, smiling at him. He smiled back at them as he got a five-peso bill from his wallet and handed it to the invisible clerk on the other side of the closed door with the tiny door built in it.

"Would you care for a receipt, señor?" the clerk asked.

"No, no, thank you. I don't need it."

"I'll be right back."

"Right back?"

"With the change."

"Oh, keep the change."

"Thank you, señor. Oh, I almost forgot. Will you be staying another day? Management requires payment in advance, you understand. It's nine pesos for a whole day."

Arsenio looked at Graciela asleep on the bed, and then at the two girls smiling at him in his wallet as he opened it, got a ten-peso bill out, and handed it to the clerk, telling him to keep the change.

The problem with hurricanes is that you never know in advance how bad a hurricane is going to be. You don't even know how bad a hurricane is as you are living through it. You just hope you'll survive it without getting hurt.

By the time Graciela woke up, three hours later, Arsenio had already been gone for several hours, back to where he belongs. Back to work. Back to his bulls.

WHEN SHE DID NOT find him in bed next to her, Graciela thought that maybe he was in the bathroom and went back to sleep.

After a while, she woke up again, and this time she thought he must have gone out to buy something to eat. She went into the bathroom and took a long sensual hot shower, caressing with her hands every part of her body he had caressed, and reliving in the shower every instant she had lived last night next to him. She couldn't wait for him to be back.

She turned off the water, slid open the shower curtain, and began drying herself with the rough *posada* towel, her eyes closed, in the tiny bathroom filled with the steam of her hot shower.

In the stupor of the dark rum still running through her veins, she felt it was he who, with his callused hands now roughly now delicately, was caressing every part of her body, burning her as he ran those big hands she worshiped so badly now slowly now fast over her entire body, filling her with ecstasy and anguish at the same time.

She went back to the tiny bedroom, picked up one of the rumpled sheets lying on top of the bed, and, burying her face in it, searched for his scent until she found it. She licked the sheet at that place, hoping to transfer his taste into her body, and as she was doing it, she thought of what it had been like to lick that magnificent scepter of power that man of hers keeps between his legs, and how enraptured she was when, kneeling in front of him, she had worshiped him.

She then shrouded herself with the sheet bearing his smell and lay in bed, carefully wrapped, looking at the entrance door, waiting for him to unwrap her.

After the first hour, she began to wonder if that man was coming back for her.

After the second hour, she began to wonder if that man ever meant to come back for her.

And after the third hour, she began to wonder if that man she had been calling hers, if that man had ever been hers at all.

42

It's late Wednesday afternoon and the sun has miraculously come out. It rains no longer. Even the wind has calmed down. Only a few light breezes are felt.

At the center of the most powerful hurricane there are always light breezes, even calm. There is even a place where there is no wind at all, the stagnation point, where a few small cottony clouds gently gliding by will soon build up to ominous thick dark towering clouds that, pressing tightly against each other, will make the angry hurricane roar and rage at its most violent.

Albertina is in Fernanda's house when Ferminio calls. Albertina rushes to the phone.

"It's your father," she tells Fernanda, standing by her side. "Can't you tell? Shouting as usual!" She speaks into the mouthpiece. "Lower your voice, Ferminio. I can hear you fine."

"What did I tell you this morning?" Ferminio is laughing at the same time that he is shouting over the phone to his wife. "That son of a bitch of a son-in-law of yours just came in, drunk out of his mind. It happened exactly as I told you. He and the other guys had the time of their lives! I just wish I had been there myself doing what they were doing instead of listening to all their dirty stories. I told the son of a bitch to go back home and sleep it off. I myself put him in a taxi. He should be there any minute now, so get out of there and let the two of them alone. As the saying goes, '*Entre marido y mujer,* nadie *se debe meter.*' *Nobody* should get in between man and wife. And that nobody means *you*! I'll be home in ten minutes and you'd better be there when I get there or there's going to be blood all over the Street of the Bulls! Good-bye." And waiting for no answer, Ferminio hangs up.

Fernanda is standing next to her mother, expectantly. Albertina looks at her, says between her teeth, "Men!" and then hangs up with such strength she alarms her daughter. "He hung up on me! Wait till I get a hold of him!"

She lowers her voice, grabs one of Fernanda's hands in hers, and pats it as she says, "He's all right, he's all right. Here we are, worrying sick about that man of yours and what was he doing? Getting drunk out of his mind!" She smiles at Fernanda, who has begun to cry. "He's on his way here. Your father just put him in a cab. Let him sleep it off, that's the best you can do, probably the only thing you'll be able to do." She stands up and begins to get ready to leave when she faces Fernanda one more time. "And then"—Albertina adds as she gathers her purse and gets a white-linen handkerchief out of it—"when he is sober, send the girls over to me, get rid of your maid, and let him have it! Here, blow!" She hands the handkerchief to Fernanda who obediently does as her mother tells her.

"I mean it," Albertina adds with vehemence. "Throw the biggest fit you have ever thrown in your life. Break a few dishes. No, don't break any dishes. Break something expensive. *That* really hurts them, if they had to pay a lot for it. Don't worry about it. He'll feel so guilty he'll get you another one even more expensive. So go, break something really expensive, throw it at him, scream at him, call him names, strike him, hit him, spit at him, and then get in bed with him and make me a grandson."

She smiles at Fernanda as she begins to walk to her house, just a few blocks away. Now on the sidewalk she turns one last time and tells her daughter, "Fernanda, honey, men are rough, and they like rough handling. So for your own good, stop being so sweet and so nice to him. Give him a little bit of hell. You'll be surprised what a little bit of hell can do for a woman."

Fernanda, dutiful Fernanda, watches Albertina go, still holding her mother's handkerchief in her hand as she waves good-bye to her. Then she rushes to her bedroom, closes the door behind her, kneels in front of a statue of the Little Virgin of Perpetual Help she keeps by her side of the bed, and thanks her Little Virgin for returning her lost husband back to her unharmed.

ELEUTERIA IS SITTING alone at the large dining table, a spread of food in front of her. Gustavo has refused to eat anything. He did not come home for his noon meal today. He told her he went for a walk around La Habana and grabbed something to eat, somewhere. He doesn't remember what or where. He is now in his bedroom, the marital bedroom he has shared with Graciela for more than a year, and he is lying on their marital bed, fully dressed, stretched out, his hands cradling his head on the pillow as he stares at the ceiling above him.

This room is painted pale turquoise, ceiling and all, the color of an early morning tropical sky. He remembers how beautiful Graciela's copper hair looks against the color of the tropical sky.

Now that she's done as she's done, Gustavo has begun to look at Graciela with different eyes. Who would have told him there was such a passion hidden inside that wife of his? He sure has never experienced it. Maybe it was his own fault. He never did anything to get that passion out of her. Now, in retrospect, was there anything he could have done to prevent what had happened? What *had* actually happened? What had that other man actually done to his wife?

Over at Yarina's house he's been to bed with a lot of whores who have taught him a lot. But he has never treated that wife of his as the whore she is underneath. He couldn't do that before. She always reminded Gustavo of his own mother, Dolores. Nice and calm and beautiful. And saintly. But now . . .

Now it may not be that bad, to have a *whore* for a wife. A *beautiful* whore for a wife. The *most* beautiful whore of a wife ever in Luyanó. No, it may not be that bad at all.

It is then the phone rings in the living room. He hears Eleuteria run to the phone and answer it. "Graciela!" the old lady says, on the verge of tears. "Thank God! Where are you?"

There's a long pause. A really long pause.

He hears nothing for a while but the sounds of tramways running on La Calzada and drumming, faint drumming, far in the distance.

Then he hears Eleuteria say, "Grab a taxi. I'll pay for it when you get here. Yes, yes, I have money." The old lady hangs up and then he hears silent sobbing.

He wants to go to the old lady and embrace her and tell her that he knows it has not been her fault, that he knows she knew nothing about it, that he knows she loves him as the son she never had, that he knows she was as hurt by all of this as he was. But then he thinks of Graciela, the old lady's own flesh, his wife. And he knows that if Eleuteria had to choose sides, as he knows she will, she would unquestionably choose the side of her own daughter, whether she deserved it or not. That was why, though he wants to run to Eleuteria and hug and caress her and kiss her like the mother she has always been to him, he just lies there, on his marital bed, looking up at the ceiling and remembering how beautiful Graciela's copper hair looks against the color of the tropical sky.

MERCED DID NOT come home for the noontime meal either.

She called Dolores and told her the most wonderful thing had happened to her. Dolores smiled at the phone as if she were smiling at her own child, who was jumping up and down with excitement at the other end of the line.

"Don't you want to know what it is?" she asked her mother.

"Of course, my little love," Dolores answered.

"Detective Fernández . . ." Merced starts to say. "Do you remember Detective Fernández? He was the one who helped me so much when Tonio died. You have to remember him. He came to the memorial service and stood way in the back. He's kind of tall and good-looking. Not too young. He must be forty, maybe. With a lot of dark hair and a little bit of gray around the sides of the head. He's very interesting looking. You have to remember him, Mamá, he was so nice to me. Well, he found out I was looking for a job and he wants me to meet a judge! Did you hear that, Mamá? A *judge!* He is a friend of Detective Fernández, and he told him he was looking for an assistant, and Detective Fernández thinks he might get me a job in his office. Wouldn't that be great? The three of us are going to eat at that new restaurant opposite Gustavo's bookstore, Floridita. Isn't that wonderful!"

Somehow, in between a sip of coffee shared while standing up in front of a *timbiriche* on the streets of Old Havana and this phone call, Merced has totally forgotten about Graciela and Gustavo. Things can change that quickly as soon as the tropical sun shows up and begins to smile. The ominous gray of the dark sky had disappeared, and with it all the gloomy thoughts that had been going through Merced's mind.

It was probably true what Detective Fernández said. Graciela and Gustavo just had a fight, and she was making a huge mountain out of a molehill. He had told her that by the time she'd get home later on today, Graciela would be back home with her husband, and they would have made up as if nothing had ever happened. In fact, he said, if she were to meet him at closing time, after her appointment with Judge Escolapio, he himself would drive her home and make sure everything was as it should be, over at her brother's house.

Detective Fernández had sounded so sure of himself and so optimistic he had made her feel instantly better and she had begun to laugh again, something she hadn't done in a long while.

Later on, in the fancy ladies' room at Floridita, Merced sits at the dressing table, begins to put on a drop of lipstick, and when she looks at herself in the mirror, she pauses.

There in the mirror is this lovely criollo woman, pleasantly wrapped in a little meat, with a trim waist and a spark in her eyes, wearing a pearl-gray dress, a matching hat, and a pair of earrings, black and white with geometric designs, that matches the pin on her dress.

And that woman is beautiful.

MANI IS SLICING through a piece of meat when he sees a taxi stop at the corner of La Calzada and the Street of the Bulls.

It's almost closing time and there are no customers in the butcher shop. Maximiliano told him to close up as he took off his bloodstained apron and threw it in a pail hidden under one of the counters.

Maximiliano is nearing an age when his energy is not what it used to be. Though he does not want to acknowledge it, he has started to leave the store earlier and earlier and has let Mani handle most of the heavy work by himself, which is precisely what Mani has been doing.

Mani did not want to go back home and face those people he calls family whom he figured by this time would all be asking what happened to Graciela and Gustavo. He's promised to keep silent, and the best way to keep silent is to be away from it all. So he is at the butcher shop preparing some cuts of meat when he sees Graciela get out of the taxi and enter Eleuteria's house, just to see her come immediately out again, money in her hand, and pay the driver, who leaves.

The bitch is back, just as Gustavo said she would be. Now it is up to Gustavo to do something about it.

He is looking at her and he's slicing the meat at the same time, the way he was taught, gently sliding the knife over it, always in the same direction with a knife so sharp it can split a hair in half, and without realizing it, he cuts himself, something he has never done before in his entire life.

"Goddamn that fucking bitch!" he utters. "See what she made me do! Goddammit!"

It's not a bad cut.

Because he was slicing so gently it didn't reach the bone. It may require a couple of stitches, but that is all. He is not going to lose that finger. He wraps a clean towel around it, manages to close the shop with his good hand, his left hand, and hails a cab cruising down La Calzada to take him to the clinic of Manuel the doctor.

Once inside the car, he turns around and through the back window he looks at Eleuteria's house.

Evening has begun to fall and the porch light is already on, as it is supposed to be; the old lady is rocking herself on her porch, as she is supposed to; people keep walking on the opposite side of the street, avoiding going by her house, as they are supposed to. Everything is exactly as it is supposed to be, exactly as if nothing out of the ordinary had happened.

And then it hits him like a painful vision.

The painful realization that Gustavo is not going to do anything about it.

The embarrassing realization that Gustavo, his kid brother, is absolutely not going to do anything about it.

The unbelievable realization that Gustavo, his kid brother, has become a *cabrón*.

★ ★ ★

43

It doesn't take long for a tranquil tropical paradise of a sky to become a violent tropical hell of a hurricane. Four or five days, at the most. The spiraling effect that begins so gently that it is barely noticeable begins to gather power and strength little by little, and as it grows and surges and billows and swells, it forces the gentle breezes to dance in a Dionysian frenzy, always faster and faster: a swirling whirling dance that gathering speed inebriates the lusty air with madness.

As the dance quickens and quickens, the maddened delicate breezes become hearty vigorous gusts of hungry winds, hungry howling winds that at first are satisfied with the stripping of leaves and small branches off trees. But as their hunger increases, they demand the toppling of shallow-rooted trees and the outright snapping of weaker trees. And when that is not enough to placate their insatiable appetite, roofs are lifted and large trees that do not bend to join in the dance are snapped, leveled, and devoured.

Then, suddenly, loose objects lifted and hurled by the powerful starving winds become missiles in the hands of the irate Ogún, black god of the storm, missiles that shatter glass, batter walls, and destroy lives as they dance.

The dance is at its wildest and most savage immediately after the transit of the tranquil eye.

It is then that the strongest gusts occur, new unwavering gusts that blow in a direction that is the total opposite to every one of all the preceding gusts; an unexpected turn of the hungry winds that is so immensely distressful because it is so immensely powerful and so immensely surprising; an unexpected turn of the hungry winds that carries with it the painful sounds of howling souls.

As Eleuteria, the evil tongue of Luyanó, remains sitting in her rocking chair on the porch of her house, pretending that everything is as it should be, as it has always been, Graciela enters the bedroom she and Gustavo have shared for more than a year and there she finds Gustavo lying on their marital bed, his head cradled by his hands, staring at the ceiling. She closes the open door behind her and moves closer to the foot of the bed, invading his field of vision, which is still concentrated on the pale-turquoise ceiling above them.

He sees the copper hair framing her beautiful head against the blue turquoise of the ceiling and smiles. Then he realizes this is not part of his dream. This woman in front of him is the *real* Graciela, the one he has never known, *the whore,* standing right there in front of him at the foot of the bed. He looks at her and Graciela fails to recognize him.

This man, this big tall blond man, lying on that bed who is smiling while he stares at her is not a man Graciela knows. This is not the man she married. This is not the Gustavo she has known so far. She never thought she could ever be afraid of the Gustavo she knew, but this man is not *that* Gustavo. She could be afraid of *this* Gustavo, but she is not. She is just startled by him; startled and intrigued by this man new to her who is lying on her marital bed: a man who hasn't moved; a big tall blond man totally unknown to her who just keeps staring at her. And smiling.

There's a long silence.

She notices how this man who has been staring at her has begun to slide his eyes slowly all over her, following the contour of her body, staring at her mouth, her neck, her breasts, her arms, her hands, her thighs, and she feels a strange coldness invading her as he looks at her, as he scrutinizes her with his icy blue eyes.

Then, slower than before, the eyes of this man slide up over her body again, and this time she feels them burning her hands, her arms, her breasts, her neck, her mouth, her eyes. His eyes stop moving and stare into Graciela's eyes. Graciela cannot understand what is hidden behind those intense pale-blue eyes that turn now icy cold now fiery hot as they stare deeply into her olive eyes.

Far away, the creaking of a rocking chair moving ever so gently can be heard, and farther away the noises of the street, and even farther away the distant drumming, the ever-present distant drumming that makes the nights of La Habana dance incessantly until dawn.

He hasn't moved. His hands are still cradling his head on his pillow while his eyes are still staring at her.

"What did he do to you?"

There's a long pause. They haven't stopped staring at each other.

"You really want to know?"

"Yes," he says, his eyes nailed to hers.

"He possessed me."

There's a long pause. They are still staring at each other, his pale-blue eyes piercing through her.

"How?"

No lights are on in the room. The moon is still full, but it has not yet made its appearance in the dark-blue sky. The turquoise and hot pink neon sign advertising Hermenegildo's bar next to his bodega across La Calzada has just been turned on, flashing on and off every few seconds, as it always does; and the room, in the increasing darkness of the early night, begins to pulsate with color to the same rhythm as the neon sign.

"He first made me stand in front of him as he lay in bed, just as you are, and told me to lift my skirt very slowly and display myself to him."

"Do it."

She begins to lift her skirt very slowly, with innocent sensuality, displaying herself to him, as her eyes are nailed to his.

"He told me never to wear underwear when I was with him."

She keeps on lifting her skirt very slowly until that copper diadem she keeps between her legs is uncovered, turning now ice blue now hot pink under the flashing neon lights.

"And then he told me to place my mound of Venus on his mouth."

"Do it."

With her skirt lifted above her waist, she kneels on the bed, straddling that man with the icy fiery eyes staring at her. Little by little she slides herself on top of his body until her body is almost, but not quite, touching the mouth of that man on the marital bed.

His eyes have never left her eyes.

She has been little by little filling his field of vision, invading it with her presence as she moved closer and closer to him.

Still with his eyes nailed to hers, she slowly lowers herself onto him, until she places her mound of Venus on the mouth of that man lying in their marital bed who, hungrily, begins to lick it, eating it as if he were eating the most deliciously soft tender moist and fleshy of all tropical fruits, letting the juices run all over his face.

And yet his eyes keep staring up at the eyes of that woman, so new to him, the one who kneeling on top of him is pressing her mound of Venus hard against his hungry mouth as she stares back at him, a stare that soon becomes a smile when she sees the smile in his eyes.

OLD HABITS die hard.

Eleuteria sees a car stop in front of Maximiliano's house across La Calzada and, sharpening her eyes, she focuses them in that direction, determined to find out what is going on. She sees an older man get out of the car, go around it, open the passenger door, and help Merced out of the car; Merced, the pretty young widow who has never once worn black.

"Ha!" Eleuteria says to herself. "With her husband still warm in his grave!"

Merced goes onto the porch of her house, but not before she waves at Eleuteria good evening. The old lady answers with her usual vulturelike smile.

"How is Graciela's father?" Merced asks, from across the street. She had been told by Eleuteria that Graciela, despite her mother's forbidding it, had gone to see that miserable man who fathered her, who was not feeling very well, and had stayed overnight with him.

"Bad weeds never die!" Eleuteria answers, spitting on the floor, stomping on her spit, and simultaneously making the sign of the horns with her right hand as she adds, "But Graciela is back, so that evil man can't be feeling that bad!"

"She's back already?" says Merced. "Give her my regards."

Detective Fernández, by Merced's side, gently elbows Merced as he whispers to her, "Didn't I tell you? It's a good thing we didn't bet on it, otherwise you'd have lost."

Merced opens the gate to the porch of her house, enters it, followed by Detective Fernández, and opens the entrance door just to be met by a rushing Tontín who jumps at her, licking her and wagging his pretty little bit of a tail.

"Tontín," Merced says, "I want you to meet my good friend Rolando."

Eleuteria, from across the street, hasn't missed a thing. And neither has Pilar, whose house is adjacent to Merced's, and who has been looking through the semiclosed shutters. For a split second the eyes of Eleuteria and Pilar meet. They each immediately look in the opposite direction.

Eleuteria wonders if Pilar heard her talk about that evil man of hers. She wishes she had not used him as an excuse to cover up for Graciela's disappearance, but that was the first thing that had come to her mind.

That man is always on her mind, that evil man with the handsome face and the virile grin. Eleuteria makes the sign of the horns again as she spits on the floor again, and again steps on her spit so hard sparks of fire can be seen coming from under her feet. "Horns on you, *cabrón*!" she mutters with venom in her mouth. "Horns on you!"

And then she realizes that under her roof, not too far away from her, there lies a *cabrón,* a real *cabrón,* a man with no balls whose wife has been entered and possessed by another man; a REAL *cabrón* with horns so big he will have to bend down in order to go through a doorway.

Suddenly a shiver runs through her spine, and she crosses herself. She walks into her house, looks toward the back, in the direction of the back bedroom, and sees the door to that bedroom closed. From where she is she can hear nothing. She has hidden all the knives in the house. And all the scissors. She is sure of that. But still . . .

Cautiously, she begins to tiptoe to the back bedroom. And still hears nothing. She crosses herself again, even though she does not believe in any of that, and silently prays to all her saints for her Graciela to be still alive. She gets close to the door to their bedroom, bends down a little bit, presses her ear against the door, and listens.

Then she stands up erect again, muttering to herself as she moves away from the door, Thank you, Father Changó! Thank you, thank you! She keeps repeating that, like a prayer, once and again and again as she goes back to her porch and sits again in her rocking chair where she begins to rock gently, adding with the even creaking of her chair as it rocks to the music of the distant drumming in the night.

As she rocks, Eleuteria, the evil tongue of Luyanó, keeps repeating to herself, Thank you, Father Changó! Thank you, thank you! over and over again, because all Eleuteria heard through the door was nothing but bed noises.

Thank you, Father Changó! Her daughter is safe! Thank you, thank you! The *cabrón*, her husband, has accepted her back, Thank you, Father Changó! as if nothing had happened.

She is disgusted by it, but disgusted as she is she keeps repeating over and over, Thank you, Father Changó! because her Graciela is alive. Thank you, thank you! because her daughter has placed horns on her husband's forehead and no one in the barrio knows about it. Thank you, Father Changó! she keeps repeating and repeating. Thank you, thank you! as she rocks and rocks. And the litany of thank-yous and the gentle rocking have begun to put her to sleep. Thank you, Father Changó! She can use the sleep. Thank you, thank you! She rocks and rocks. Thank you, Father Changó! She has not slept in such a long time. Thank you, thank you! Not since the middle of last night when she saw Gustavo cross the street and—

It is only then she stops rocking abruptly and shudders, her eyes filled with panic terror again, because it is only then she remembers word by word what that *cabrón* Gustavo told her last night when he came back.

And it is only then she realizes that there's someone else who knows. She crosses herself once again and cringes as her lips utter that someone's name.

Mani!

MANI'S FINGER has been stitched tight. Just as he thought, two stitches. He's seen worse. He has taken the tramway back home and gets out at the corner of La Calzada and the Street of the Bulls, right in front of his house. He goes in, and in the living room nobody ever uses, he finds Merced and Dolores, sitting in rocking chairs, talking to a man he thinks he has met before but cannot quite place. The man, who is also sitting in a rocking chair, stands up as he sees Mani come in.

"Oh, Mani," says Merced, also standing up, "you remember Rolando, don't you? He is the detective who helped me when Tonio—when Tonio passed away."

Mani extends his right hand to Rolando, who is extending his to Mani, when Dolores notices the bandages around one of Mani's fingers.

"Oh, my God! What happened?" she says, alarmed. "What happened to your finger?"

"Oh, it's nothing," Mani says. "I wasn't paying attention to what I was doing and I cut myself. But it's nothing. I went to Dr. Manuel and he took care of it. Mamá, it's nothing. Please, don't be alarmed. See"—he moves the bandaged finger in all directions—"nothing." Then he faces Rolando. "Maximiliano the butcher, my father, has told me I don't know how many times to pay attention to what I am doing when I am cutting through meat, because you can lose a finger, just like that!"

He snaps the fingers of his good hand, his left hand, as he continues. "*His* father lost the upper part of one of his fingers, without even realizing it. He even cut through the bone. We keep our knives so sharp in the butcher shop that they can split a hair in half. I should have listened to Dad, but, you know, one never learns through someone else's mistakes." Then he waves his bandaged finger again barely a couple of inches in front of his mother's eyes as he adds, jokingly, "It was almost dangling, but Dr. Manuel fixed it. You know he can fix anything with his eyes closed."

Merced shakes her head. "Don't joke like that," she says. "Don't you know Mamá is always worrying about each of us?"

Mani smiles at his mother and then looks around the house. Across the patio he sees Marguita, who is busy sitting at the large dining table doing her homework while on the patio floor Pepe Loreto is walking about as slowly as always, under the watchful eye of Tontín, who has become the old parrot's guardian. Maximiliano comes in, bringing a box with cigars in it.

"Isn't Gustavo here?" Mani asks, casually, hiding his right hand behind him so Maximiliano the butcher will not be able to see it.

"Gustavo?" says Maximiliano. "Why would he be here? Here, Rolando, have one of these. Montecristo. The best." Rolando takes one and smells it, closing his eyes as he does it, the way all criollo men do when evaluating a good cigar.

"Oh, I don't know," adds Mani. "I thought he might be here. I don't know why."

"Would you be here," adds Maximiliano as he offers a light to Rolando, "if you were married to Graciela?" Maximiliano inhales some of his cigar smoke and closing his eyes enjoys it as he tells Rolando, "Gustavo is my second son. He's been married now for . . . is it a year?"

"A year and two months. This coming Friday," says Merced, who is excellent with dates.

"I stand corrected," continues Maximiliano as he enjoys his cigar. "As I was saying, he's been married now for a year and two months. To the most beautiful girl in Luyanó." He looks at Dolores and adds, lovingly, "Except for this beautiful girl here."

To which Rolando adds, looking at Merced, a broad smile on his face, "And this other one here, don't forget."

Maximiliano looks at Merced, who is blushing. "Hey, I didn't realize it before but, Dolores, look at your daughter. She has her beauty up tonight, doesn't she?"

Dolores looks at her daughter and then, shaking her head, she looks back at her husband as she disagrees with him. "She *always* has her beauty up," she says. Then she looks again at Merced and adds, "But maybe today she's seen it."

There's a short embarrassing pause, broken by Maximiliano, who asks Rolando, "Well?"

Rolando answers, looking at Merced as he gently deposits the ashes of his Montecristo cigar into the standing ashtray. "The best!"

Merced looks away from Rolando and notices Mani looking nervously out the front windows in the direction of Eleuteria's house.

"Oh, Mani," she says, "I forgot to tell you. Graciela's father is much better. She's back already."

"She's back?" Mani asks, pretending he doesn't know.

"She's back," Merced answers, giving Mani a meaningful look.

Mani again looks out one of the two tall front windows with the semicircular transoms on top that face La Calzada. He knows Graciela has already been back for a long while. He saw her come in, almost a couple of hours ago. And yet Gustavo is still in her house and still with her, and still he hasn't done a thing about the bitch.

Only one word comes to his head.

He shakes his head, unconsciously, trying to shake that word out of his brain, but the word refuses to go.

Unwillingly, he clenches his two hands, making them into fists behind his back, just to feel the pain in his right hand, where he feels the blood powerfully pulsating in his partly cut finger covered with the bandage. And still the word will not leave him until he utters it to himself, speaking it through his teeth.

"*¡Cabrón!*"

★ ★ ★

44

It had been that photograph of his two girls that had made Arsenio abandon Graciela, leaving her alone still asleep in the small musty *posada* room. He had not even had the strength to kiss her one last time before he left the room. He had gotten dressed the best he could, and still in the stupor of almost three bottles of Añejo, he had hailed a taxi and given the driver the address of Ferminio's Cuban slaughterhouse, where he was due early Wednesday morning.

Now he has just awakened, and in his own bedroom, not really knowing how he got there. He looks at the clock next to his side of the bed, and the clock tells him it is twenty to nine. At night? Slowly he goes to the shuttered window and looks through it. At night.

He goes to the bathroom, looks in the mirror, and finds himself wearing pajamas. His head is still swimming. The last he remembers is seeing Graciela lying naked on the *posada* room bed, her body covered with sweat in the hot musty room, as he closed the door behind him.

He hears steps outside the bathroom door, looks out, and sees Fernanda come in, bringing a tray with food that smells, Oh, so good.

"Oh, good, you're awake," she says as she places the tray on the bed. "Here," she adds, "I brought you something to eat. You must be hungry." Arsenio goes to the bed, sits on it, then collapses on it. "How are you feeling?"

"All right, I guess." Does Fernanda know? How much does she know? What does she know? "What happened?" he manages to say.

"You don't remember?"

He shakes his head. "Not a thing," he says. He is going to play it safe. "All I remember is getting drunk."

"Papá should have never sent you to meet with those guys," says Fernanda. "They are used to drinking but you are not."

Arsenio begins to stir a thick bean soup rich with garlic and bacon fat which he loves. He says nothing. What does Ferminio know? The soup bowl is steaming. He blows on the soup to cool it before he tastes it.

"When you did not show up for work, Papá got very upset and he began calling his buddies, the ones you had been hanging out with. One of them, I forget who, told Papá that the last he saw you, you were lying asleep on the floor of—you should be ashamed of yourself! Going to a house of bad women!" She frowns at him, smiling at him at the same time. "I know nothing happened. Otherwise I would be killing you instead of feeding you. Here, have some of this bread. It's delicious." She had been buttering a thick slab of bread, which she has just offered her husband. "He told Papá you were so tired you had a couple of drinks and then all you did was to talk about bulls this and bulls that, boring them out of their minds, and then you passed out. This morning you must have managed somehow to get into a cab that took you to Papá's slaughterhouse. And Papá told the cabdriver to bring you home. And here you are. You don't remember any of it?"

Arsenio shakes his head, bites into the sourdough bread, and looks at Fernanda, the mother of his girls. He has never noticed it before, but Fernanda does look like his two girls. The way she is looking at him right now, she could be another one of them. He loves his girls. He remembers them looking at him in the photograph in his wallet. He also remembers Graciela, beautiful Graciela, who is now like a distant vision that has begun to fade. What does Graciela really look like? He tries hard to remember her face, but he cannot do it. And yet he remembers clearly the faces of his two girls in that photograph in his wallet, looking at him and smiling broadly at him as they were saying to him, Pappy? Where are you? We're missing you.

"Where are the girls?" he asks.

"They're already in bed. I told them you were not feeling very well and I sent them to bed early so they wouldn't disturb you."

"They would never disturb me. They're my girls."

"Do you want to see them? I can call them in, if you feel like it."

Arsenio shakes his head. He has just finished his soup and is eating a thin panfried palomilla steak with fried chopped onions on top. "No, let them be. I'll see them later on. When I'm totally sober." He looks at Fernanda and smiles. This is his first smile. "I don't know how you can put up with someone like me."

"I don't know how, either. Mamá told me I should break an expensive dish on your head and give you some hell, and I may still do that. But I'll do it tomorrow."

"She said that? The old bitch!" Arsenio laughs, and with his laughter he makes Fernanda laugh as well.

"Don't call her an old bitch! She is still my mother!"

"Well, all I can say is, Thank God you don't look like her!"

Fernanda looks at the two of them reflected in the large mirror that is part of the dressing table by her side of the bed. "I don't?" she says, looking at herself, straightening her back, and fixing her hair the way her mother does. "I thought I did. She is a very beautiful woman, even at her age."

"Who? Your mother?" says Arsenio, biting into his heavenly steak. "How can you say that? She's not beautiful."

He hasn't looked at Fernanda. But then he does. He looks in the mirror at Fernanda who is looking back at him. Fernanda, who looks so much like his girls.

"Your mother . . . she's all right"—he says, and then he adds, pointing at Fernanda with his fork, from where a thick chunk of meat is dangling—"now you . . . *you* are beautiful!"

He places the chunk of steak in his mouth and chews it with great satisfaction as Fernanda looks at her bull of a man in the mirror and smiles.

MANI IS TOSSING in his bed. He has not been able to sleep. He has not even been able to draw. His mind is blank. Blank except for the one word that keeps coming back to him, a word that has been haunting him all night long, repeating itself like a litany, an unbearable litany he can no longer stand.

¡Cabrón! ¡Cabrón! ¡Cabrón! ¡Cabrón! ¡Cabrón!

The idea that there is a *cabrón* in his family is inconceivable to him. It is making him crazy. No. His kid brother cannot be a *cabrón*. Gustavo will not be a *cabrón*. Mani will not allow it to happen. Gustavo must be planning something. Yes, that's what it is. That's why he hasn't walked out on that bitch yet. He is probably waiting to find out who the other man is, that's what he is doing, so he can get at the two of them at the same time. Wouldn't that be great? Graciela and her lover, both of them lying naked on the same bed, in a pool of blood.

He closes his eyes and tries to see that picture in his mind: the bitch and her lover dead in a pool of blood; but his mind will not let him see it. Something is wrong. Has he lost his powers? He grabs a chalk and begins to sketch on a piece of red paper, drawing with such an intensity he tears the paper with the chalk. Then he violently throws the chalk on the floor, smashing it into a million pieces. Goddammit, he says to himself. What is wrong with me? Why can't I see it happen?

He's got to talk to Gustavo, that's what he's got to do. Yes. Today. Now. No, not now. He cannot go into Eleuteria's house now at this time of night. That would be stupid. That would give their plans away. No, not now. Later on. Tomorrow morning. As soon as Gustavo is awake. Tomorrow morning as soon as Gustavo is awake Mani will meet with him and discuss everything with him, work out a plan, and then carry it through, settling everything the way everything should be settled, the only way out, the manly way. The way of the bulls. Yes! Everything will be settled, tomorrow morning. *Everything*.

Only then will he be able to rest.

"FERMINIO," SAYS ALBERTINA, "you don't really think I'm dumb, do you?" They are lying in bed next to each other in their large modern bedroom inside their large modern house that looks like a white cube sitting very ill at ease atop a hill somewhere near the Street of the Bulls.

Ferminio does not answer.

"You don't really think I swallowed all of that about new government regulations and inspectors and meetings every Tuesday and all of that, do you?" She is lying on her side, facing away from Ferminio and smiling. "All I had to do was ask your son, and he said, 'What meetings? What new rules? How come I don't know anything about it?' "

She has turned around and she is now looking at Ferminio, who is pretending to read the sports section of the newspaper in his hands. She takes the paper away from him and forces him to look at her.

"Ferminio, dear. You have never been able to lie to me. Oh, I know you have tried. And I know I have made you think you have succeeded, but you have not. I have forgiven you many lies before, and I know I'll have to forgive you many lies again. But this time you did not lie exclusively to me, but to Fernanda as well. So first thing tomorrow morning, you are going to call every one of your buddies, and you are going to tell them exactly what you say happened, just as you told Fernanda, and then you are going to make sure they all remember it perfectly well, exactly as you tell them. Because if they don't, if Fernanda ever gets an inkling that what really happened is not what you told her happened, I am going to make your life so miserable that you will wish you had not been born. Is that clear?"

Ferminio looks at her. "What makes you think I'd tell Eustaquio everything Arsenio and I do? He handles one part of the business, Arsenio and I the other part. And never the twain shall meet."

Albertina looks at him, shakes her head, and says as she turns away from him and puts out the light on her side of their bed, "Ferminio, dear, you know about bulls. I know about lying."

MANI CAN STAND it no longer. He's got to do something. He is so testy and so itchy and so angry that he's got to do something. He just has to. He jumps out of bed, puts on his white pants and shirt, and goes outside.

It is still very dark outside. The moon, still full, can just be seen above the tops of the cramped little buildings on the far side of the Street of the Bulls, casting its cold blue light all over the narrow little street.

Not knowing what to do, Mani crosses La Calzada and goes to the butcher shop. There's always something to do at the butcher shop.

He unlocks the heavy gate facing the Street of the Bulls, lifts it open, goes inside, turns the lights on, puts on the thick sweater by the door to the cooler, enters the cooler, looks through the dead carcasses, picks up the largest one of them, puts it on his broad shoulders, takes it outside the cooler, places it on the large solid chunk of wood that's in the center of the butcher shop, closes the cooler door, takes off his sweater, and hangs it on the hook by the cooler door where no aprons are hanging.

Goddammit! He forgot to get a clean apron!

He shakes his head. There's nothing he can do. One always starts the day with a clean apron.

Goddammit! Now he has to go back home to get one!

Leaving the large carcass of a dead bull on the sacrificial butcher-block table, he turns the lights off, goes outside the butcher shop, and begins to lower the gate behind him.

It is only then that he becomes aware of the distant rumbling and pounding and thundering, and of the trembling of the earth beneath his feet.

He hears the two or three people walking in the street at this time of night scream at each other way in the distance, *"¡Los toros! ¡Los toros!"* And he sees them scrambling out of the way of the rushing bulls, hiding wherever they can, praying that the bulls stay within the narrow path of the narrow street.

Mani barely has enough time to lift the heavy gate up again, get back inside the butcher shop, lower the gate, lock it from the inside, and stand behind the display cases, when the stampeding bulls charge by the butcher shop.

In the light of the moon the torrent of sweating panting bellowing bulls becomes a frightening nightmarish vision, a vision that becomes startling when the heavy drops of sweat on their dark strained muscular bodies begin to reflect the cold blue light of the moon and become flashing blue sparks that—glittering like stars all over the glistening bodies of the frightened animals—make them look like glittering shadows rushing by: the rushing glittering shadows of all the dead bulls that have ever roared their way through that narrow unpaved street.

Mani is watching the glistening animals roar as they thunder and bolt by him in front of the butcher shop when all of a sudden the deafening noise disappears, in a flash, to be followed by a long eerie silence.

Mani keeps seeing the glistening shadows go by and yet he hears nothing.

The roaring beasts have suddenly become enchanted animals silently stampeding in a magical forest of their own with stars on their backs reflecting the cold blue light of the tropical moon.

He shakes his head and puts his hands to his ears. He hears the sounds his hands make when he touches his ears. He has not gone deaf. He can hear the sounds of his hands touching his ears but he cannot hear the sounds of the rushing glistening shadows charging in total silence.

And then, out of that silence, as the glittering beasts keep rushing by, Mani hears the shadows of the bulls call his name ever so softly, as from far far away.

Mani! Maaani! Maaaaani!

Startled, unable to understand what is happening to him, he rubs his eyes in disbelief, looks out between the heavy metal bars that make the heavy metal gates meant to protect him, to provide him with a sanctuary, to keep the bulls away from him, and now he sees nothing.

The bulls are gone. Were they ever there?

He rubs his eyes again, and all of a sudden Mani, the man, he who can recall a moment with such fidelity that, whenever he does it, he feels that he is experiencing that moment again; that man, Mani, looks at himself and he sees not the man he is now but the boy he was many years ago: the boy Mani, who had stayed working late at the butcher shop and, on a dark October night like tonight, had seen for the first time the desperate bulls rush by him in the dark.

The boy Mani stands silently as if in a trance behind the heavy metal bars that make up the heavy metal gates that separate him from the turbulent herd of wild uncontrollable bulls; metal gates and metal bars that try to prevent those monstrous beasts with the smell of fear from entering his world. But they fail to do so. The boy Mani lives in that world. He lives in the shadows of those bulls.

He is too young to realize that those heavy metal bars meant to keep the bulls away from him are also destined to keep him away from the life of his dreams. He is too young to realize that those heavy metal bars meant to provide him with a sanctuary are also destined to become his jail. He is too young to realize that he, like the bulls, is also racing to his death, uncontrollably, unknowingly, along the same street, following a narrow path dictated by others.

The boy Mani is too young to realize all of that, but not too young to wonder what it is like to run free and play on that street.

But the boy Mani is long gone.

Or is he?

The man Mani rubs his eyes in disbelief, shakes his head, opens his eyes, raises them, looks around him, and what he sees frightens him.

The man Mani is suddenly old enough to realize that the heavy iron bars that encircle him are forcing him to live in the shadows of those bulls, making the smell of their fear enter the world he lives in. The man Mani is suddenly old enough to realize that the world he lives in is nothing but a jail that keeps him away from the life of his dreams. And the man Mani is suddenly old enough to realize that, as strong and as powerful as he knows he is, he still cannot muster up the courage to break through that prison of his.

Again he rubs his eyes in disbelief and shakes his head again, as if to eradicate the nightmarish vision. What is happening to him? He opens his eyes again and all of a sudden he realizes where he is. He had forgotten where he was.

He had totally forgotten that he is in the butcher shop. That he is standing behind the large chunk of wood smack in the center of the butcher shop. That he is looking down at the carcass of one of those bulls that rushed to his death on that street. That he is staring at a sacrificial beast lying lifeless on a bloodstained altar. That he is holding in his strong left hand a knife so sharp it can split a hair in two. That this sharpest of knives is the same knife that a few hours ago had cut through his finger almost to the bone and he had not even felt it. And that it was precisely with this sharpest of knives he was planning to cut into the dead bull in front of him.

He looks at the knife in his hand and almost unconsciously opens his hand. The knife falls to his feet, hits the tile floor, and the loud clanking it makes instantly awakens Mani, who suddenly remembers why he is there.

Gustavo. His kid brother. Needs him.

And then, remembering why he is there, the man Mani bends down, picks up the sharpest of knives, places it on the milky-white marble counter, and then looks at it, its blade glittering cold ice blue in the darkness of the tropical night.

★ ★ ★

45

Still in the dark, lit only by the moon, Mani lifts the carcass of the dead bull lying on the butcher shop altar and places it back in the cooler, feeling the way a pallbearer feels as he places the body of a loved one inside a frozen crypt, as brokenhearted as if he were entombing a part of himself. He has never felt like this before.

Silently he closes the cooler door behind him. Then he steps outside the butcher shop and slowly lowers the heavy metal gate facing the Street of the Bulls. He locks it, looks once more at the butcher shop, and then begins to walk silently along the Street of the Bulls, now totally empty. He cannot get out of his mind the startling vision of the glittering bulls roaring past him in total silence, a vision that, engraved in his brain, keeps repeating over and over in his mind.

He walks along the narrow street and purposefully dislodges with his feet a few stones as he goes by, to hear the sounds they make as they settle in a brand-new position in a brand-new location. And as he listens to the sounds of the settling stones, he hears again the shadows of the bulls calling his name ever so softly from very far away.

Mani! Maaani! Maaaaani!

He looks up at the sky, hoping to see cottonlike puffy bulls gently gliding by, but there are none. There are no clouds tonight. The night sky is dark, so dark it is almost pitch black. There is not a single hint of a cloud. Yet behind him there's the moon, the cold white moon that lights his world and casts a shadow at his feet, a long shadow that leads him, moving slowly along the street, gliding gently and silently in front of him, now over one stone and then another, until it reaches the other side of La Calzada, which seems to Mani to be, Oh, so wide! So interminably wide!

He enters the porch of Maximiliano's house, where he lives, and silently closes its gate, which he had left open behind him. Then, slowly, almost dragging his feet, he walks to the front door, turns the key in the lock, and forces himself to enter the place he calls home.

Suddenly his face is lit, as if struck by lightning.

There, in the living room, sitting in one of the rocking chairs, desperately gasping for air, is Dolores, the woman he calls mother.

Mani rushes to her, in panic fear. She was not there a few minutes ago, when he left the house. He was sure she was feeling all right then. He had seen her go to bed. And now she can hardly breathe.

"Mamá, Mamá! Are you all right?"

Dolores barely manages to nod.

"I'll call Dr. Manuel."

Dolores shakes her head. "No, no, no. No!" She says it so softly it can barely be heard. Mani moves close to her, kneels by her side, and takes one of her hands in his; her hand is icy cold. "Don't call him." She lets her head rest on the high-back rocking chair and closes her eyes as she whispers, "I'll be all right, my son, little love of mine. I'll be all right."

Minutes go by. The longest minutes in Mani's life. He had never realized how long a minute can be. His mouth is dry, so dry, he can barely swallow. He would go to the kitchen and get a glass of water, but he does not want to leave this woman he calls mother alone, this woman who has just called him son, who has just called him little love of mine.

Still kneeling by her side, Mani looks up at her, and for the first time in his life Mani no longer sees the woman he knows but a different one, a frail tiny woman much smaller and much older than the one he remembers. Her black and wavy hair is beginning to go gray, even white in places; her mouth has tiny wrinkles surrounding it; and her face has an imploring look to it that Mani does not remember ever seeing there before. He feels a sudden tenderness toward this woman, something he has never felt before. He feels he would like to embrace her and hug her tight to him and tell her with his hug how much he loves this older woman so beautiful and so new to him. He has never thought of either Maximiliano or Dolores as old before. But now that he is looking closely at this woman he calls mother, he sees in her a new kind of beauty that wasn't there before, and he loves her for it.

The living room is still dark. Only the barest hint of light can be seen starting to come through the tiny almost invisible cracks around the closed windows and doors, and through the colored transoms above them, which, backlighted by whatever little light there is, become dark ruby, and dark sapphire, and dark emerald. The dim-colored light coming through them casts a strange eerie glow to the room as the dust, unsettled by the cold early morning breezes, begins to swirl and dance.

After a long long while—an interminable time—Dolores looks down at Mani who, kneeling by her side, has been holding one of her cold wrinkled hands in his, warming it with his touch. She smiles at him. The cold morning air is good for her. She has begun to feel a lot better. She is breathing more easily now. The panic fear in Mani's eyes has begun to disappear. How much time has gone by? Minutes? Hours? A lifetime? Mani, who has been looking up at her, sees her smile, and her smile makes him smile as well.

"Mani . . ." She speaks in a soft and gentle voice, her everyday voice, a voice that is now totally free of the despair Mani thought he had heard in that voice just minutes before. "Do you remember Pablo?"

Mani nods his head up and down. How could he ever not remember Pablo, his best friend Pablo? He smiles as he thinks of him and wonders why Dolores should be thinking of Pablo right now.

Dolores sighs. "Pablo was like a father to me," she says, looking up, remembering. Then she looks at her son again and adds, "You know, Mani, I never knew my mother. I never felt I had one. I grew up not knowing what a mother is." She rests her head on the high back of the cane rocker, closes her eyes, and sighs again. "I never felt I had a father, either."

Mani nods, tightening the grip on her hand.

He knows what it feels like not to have a mother. Or a father. For how long has he been thinking that he does not have either? For how long has he been thinking that he is just an adopted son, an abandoned child, a child nobody ever really wanted? For how long has he been carrying these doubts inside of him, hiding them deep inside of him? Those horrible doubts that burden him, that he fears will burden him for the rest of his life, because how would he ever be able to know the truth—the real truth—about himself, if he cannot trust any of the answers these people he calls family keep giving him?

Dolores continues, her eyes still closed. "I never felt I had a father either, except for Pablo." She opens her eyes and looks at her son again. "Did you know, Mani, that he went hungry so we could eat? When your father and I got married, we had nothing. And Pablo went hungry so we could eat. He was a good man. And he loved you, Mani. Of all my children he loved you the most, because you were his best friend. And because you were as strong and as bullheaded as he was. You still are, aren't you?"

Mani, still kneeling by her side, nods as he smiles at her. "A little bit."

Dolores caresses his black wavy hair. "Mani," she says, "Eleuteria came to see me last night. She was desperate. I have never seen anybody as desperate as she was. She told me everything. She is very much afraid, Mani. She is very much afraid of you. She is more afraid of you than of anybody else."

Mani is startled. "What do you mean?"

"Mani, a mother knows. And she is a mother, just like I am." Dolores pauses. "You have always fought your brother's fights, Mani. And that is why she's so—" She pauses again. "My throat is so dry." She coughs.

Mani looks at her. "Mine too," he says. "Let me go get some water."

He lets her hand go, stands up, and rushes across the patio to the kitchen, bypassing Tontín, the tiny black-and-white puppy that has been sleeping on his bed on the patio floor, right under Pepe Loreto's cage, which is draped with the new canvas cover Dolores just made for it. Tontín opens up one eye, sees Mani go by, looks around, realizes it is still very dark, and then decides to go back to sleep.

Mani comes back with two glasses of water. He gives one to Dolores, who begins to sip it while Mani sits on the floor next to her and drinks his in one gulp—and still his throat feels dry.

"Mani, did you know I've seen some of your drawings?"

Mani looks up at this frail tiny beautiful woman he'd be proud to call mother.

"They are very beautiful."

Mani smiles at Dolores.

"I also saw the way you looked at Gustavo the day he hung up his apron at the butcher shop. I saw the look in your eyes then, Mani." She pauses as she looks into his eyes. "I know."

Mani tries to look away from her, but Dolores will not allow it. She grabs his face tenderly, with her free hand, and looks at him deep into his eyes.

"I have known it since that day. And Mani, I have spoken to your father about you. He also knows."

Mani is flabbergasted by this. "He does?" This time it is he who is looking deep into her eyes.

"We all have known for a long while, Mani. Every one of us. All anybody has to do is look at you in the eye and—" She begins to cough and takes another sip of water. Then she faces Mani again.

"Mani, tell me, is it because of us that you haven't left us? That you haven't married?" She pauses.

"Or is it because of you?"

Mani does not answer. He shakes his head, says nothing, and, facing away from her, looks down at the floor. For the longest time he remains silent, as if frozen in time and space, just looking down at the intricate pattern of the Cuban tiles and how Dolores's comfortably worn pale-pink slippers seem to intrude upon the design. For the longest time he just keeps looking down at the floor and at the intruding slippers, saying nothing. For the longest time.

Dolores has been looking at Mani all of this time, silently smiling at him, on the floor by her side, keeping her stronger hand, her left hand—which hasn't moved—on her son's wavy hair. Then, still keeping her hand on her son's hair, she leans back against the high-back rocker, looks up, and, unconsciously, her hand begins to caress Mani's hair again as she speaks.

"You know, Mani, when Pablo left with me, the day your father and I got married, he had nothing. I had a few clothes with me, but he had nothing. I was young and on my way to my husband; he was old and on his way to nothing. And despite all of that he left a warm house behind, and warm food and warm friends, just to be with me, just to walk me to my husband. He didn't know what was going to happen to him next. He didn't know if he was ever going to eat again, or where he was going to sleep, or what he was going to wear. But he did it nonetheless."

She looks down at her son, sitting on the floor at her feet, still staring at her worn pink slippers and the shiny tile floor.

"Pablo was a very brave man, Mani. Just like your father's grandfather, who left behind the only thing that matters in life, his wife and his children, to fight a war so men like Pablo would go free. I'm proud to say Pablo was a real father to me, much more so than the selfish father I had, the one who sent me to a fancy school and paid all the bills but who never loved me. Mamá loved him, I know that, and she wanted to give him the son he always wanted. But when *I* was born . . . And then Mamá died . . . I think he hated me from that day on. He never loved me."

Then, tenderly grabbing Mani's face in her hands, she makes her son look at her as she adds, "I'm afraid your father and I have been very selfish with you, Mani. We know we have. We shouldn't have been, but we have."

Mani looks at her, a question in his eyes.

"We missed you so much for those incredibly long long years you were not with us that when we finally were able to bring you back with us, we foolishly thought that we had to hold you tight, to keep you tight to us. We needed to fill the gap we had in our hearts for all those painful years when you were taken away from us. I know we have been very selfish with you, my little love. We know we shouldn't have been, but we have."

She is looking at him with eyes filled with love as she adds, "But, my son, little love of mine, we didn't know it then—we were too young to know it then—but we do now. Our hearts are filled with you. You will be with us forever wherever you are, just as we will be with you forever wherever we are. So, Mani, be brave like Pablo. Go free, my son. Follow your own path and go free."

She pauses for the barest of pauses.

"And let your brother go free too, Mani. Let him follow his own path too. You cannot live his life for him, my son. You don't have to."

Mani suddenly stands up as he shakes his head. For a little while he had forgotten completely about Gustavo. But now it all comes back to him. The rage, the fear. Everything. The embarrassment. The anger. Especially the anger. It is his anger that responds to Dolores.

"Mamá, you're talking like a woman. A woman does not understand a man. A woman cannot understand the way of men. I cannot let Gustavo become a—" He almost said it, that word that has been haunting him all night long, that horrible word. But he cannot say it. Not to this woman he calls mother he cannot say it. Not even to himself. "A—a whatever it is he has become. Does Papá know?"

Dolores shakes her head, looking up at him. "What Eleuteria told me was meant for my ears only, Mani. She made me promise I wouldn't tell anyone. But she knows you know. Gustavo told her."

"Don't tell Papá then. I can manage by myself. I'll take care of everything. I'll do what has to be done. If Gustavo doesn't do it, I will, you can be sure about that! Mamá, don't shake your head. You know I'm right. You know that one of us must do what has to be done. You know it has to be done. How could any of us stand tall and proud ever again unless—"

Dolores grabs Mani's left hand and tenderly kisses it, interrupting him with her gentle kiss. Mani looks down at her. Then he kneels by her side again. This time it is he who kisses her tired old hands. Dolores smiles at him.

"Mani, the royal palm trees stand tall and proud, don't they? And yet they bend down whenever a hurricane rushes through their lives, don't they?"

Her quiet speech silences Mani.

"Do you know why?"

Mani the man becomes a boy again as he listens to this frail tiny woman he calls mother.

"Because if they didn't, tall and proud and beautiful as they are, they would all break and die. And that would be everybody's loss. It takes courage to bend, Mani. It takes a lot of courage to bend. Sometimes it takes a lot more courage to bend and survive than to stand upright and die."

Mani stands up and begins to pace the living room frantically, like an enraged wild animal captured inside an imprisoning cage, his tight fists livid with rage. Without looking at her, angry words spurt out of his mouth.

"Mamá, you don't understand. You're just too good. You have always been too good. Please, understand. There are things a man must—"

"Mani," Dolores interrupts him, "for many years I have known about your father and his mulatto women."

Mani suddenly stops pacing around the room and faces her.

"What would have happened to all of us if I had not bent a little bit then?"

Mani faces away from her. He doesn't want her to see the painful embarrassment on his face. He didn't know she knew.

"Even yesterday, when Merced told me we had to let Paula go, I knew what had happened. She told me something about catching Paula stealing something or something like that. But, Mani, none of my children can lie to me. She was trying to cover up for another one of your father's things. She didn't have to. The minute she came to me with her tale I knew what had happened. I knew it. I have always known it."

Dolores takes another sip of water, keeping her eyes on Mani, who, still standing, is still facing away from her.

"The first time it happened, when I found out about it, I was deeply hurt and angry, just as Merced was yesterday, just as you are right now. But by then I had four children. I had to bend. And I did. And now that I am much older I know that I was right. None of those women has ever meant a thing to your father, Mani. None of them. Ever. I told your sister yesterday, and I'm telling you now. Your father is just like my own father was: an aging champion bull whose blond hair is turning gray and who's just afraid of getting old, so he has to prove to himself all the time that he is still a champion." She chuckles. "What he doesn't realize is that as long as he has to prove it, he is not the champion bull anymore, because champion bulls do not have to prove anything. They are not afraid."

Her mischievous eyes sparkle in the dark as she adds, "But your father is a champion bull nonetheless. He always was, always will be. He may not believe it, but I know he is. And, Mani, I also know that his love for me remains unchanged. I didn't know it then, the first time it happened. But now—now I know that love is a divine fire that once it is lit lasts forever. Your father and I love each other as much now as when we first met." She takes another sip of water, and still looking at her son—who will not look at her—she adds, "Mani, I bent. I bent and I survived that hurricane. And that hurricane brought me a priceless gift, little Iris. Don't you think that beautiful girl was worth the bending?"

Mani looks down at the floor again as he hesitantly has to nod in agreement. He knows Dolores's heart broke when she wrapped her little Iris in the white shroud of angels.

"So bend, my son, and let the hurricane rushing through our lives go by."

She takes a sip of water as she continues to look at the back of her son, who still refuses to look at her; who, still facing away from her, has yet to say a word.

There's a long pause.

She knows what Mani is thinking. She knows the horrible fight that is taking place inside that handsome head of her bullheaded son. She knows it because she had to struggle with those very same thoughts that are now fighting inside Mani's head.

Last night, when she first heard what Eleuteria told her, her head had ignited with a raging fire she thought sacred at the time. But then, after the old lady left her, she had time to think.

Graciela had come back to Gustavo, and Gustavo had accepted her back and decided to ignore the whole thing, just as she herself had done after that Clotilde woman incident. She didn't know if that would have been the decision she, Dolores, would have made had she been a man. But then it had not been her decision, but Gustavo's. And Gustavo had made his decision, defying his whole world, just as she had made her own decision many years ago, when she defied her whole world and eloped with the man she loved. Was she going to do to Gustavo, her son, what her own father did to her? Was she going to pretend that Gustavo, her son, was no longer her son? Was she going to pretend that Gustavo, *her own son,* who acted just as she had done, was dead in her eyes? She had shaken her head then.

No. She would not.

Gustavo had made his decision and she would respect it, learn to live with it, and defend it against their whole world if she had to. She knew that Gustavo was no less of a man when he accepted Graciela back, just as she knew she was no less of a woman when she accepted Maximiliano back. She knew *that* with an absolute certainty. And so did Gustavo, her son, the Gustavo who years ago, running against the bull of his father, challenged him so he could follow his own path; the same Gustavo who today, running against all the bulls of Luyanó, challenges them so he can follow his own path. *That* Gustavo. The Gustavo she loves and admires. But what about Mani?

Did Mani know . . . would Mani ever know what it is like to defy and challenge the entire world if it needs to be? Mani? Who has always been the good boy, the obedient boy, the boy who's always done as he's supposed to? Would Mani ever dare to run against the bulls? Mani? Or would he be scared to face them, as Merced's Tonio had been? Poor Tonio, who, not following his heart, had tried to do what was expected of him. Poor scared Tonio, who, not being able to do it, ended up hurting not only himself but many others as well with his fear?

She looks at Mani, who is still facing away from her, and she smiles, her eyes filled with the tenderness of a mother who sees the pain her child is going through.

Yes, she knows what Mani is thinking. She has always known. Just as she has always known what each one of her other children thinks. Mani may hold secrets for everyone else, but he has never been able to hold anything secret from her. And she also knows she must help him. Isn't that what mothers are for?

"You don't have to fight Gustavo's fights for him, Mani," she says, her voice kind and soft, filled with love. "You never did."

She pauses. Mani is still looking away from her.

"I know why you did it, but Mani, you don't have to prove anything anymore, do you, Mani?"

She pauses again.

"Mani, look at me, child."

Mani turns around slowly and sighs deeply as he faces her, his eyes downcast.

"Mani," she asks, "what are you afraid of?"

Mani suddenly lifts his head and stares at Dolores.

What is *he* afraid of?

He feels like screaming that question back at her. He has felt like screaming all night long, ever since he found out what Gustavo had become, and now he wants to scream at her.

What am *I* afraid of?

There is so much he wants to say, so much he needs to know, so much he needs to be sure of.

What am *I* afraid of?

He wants to scream at her, I'll tell you if you tell me, Why was I abandoned? Why was I given away like a broken toy or a worthless piece of nothing? Why didn't you care for me? Why didn't you fight for me if you are my mother as you say you are? Was it because you didn't want me? Was it because you didn't love me? Was it because I was not really your son? Or was it because you were ashamed of me? What had I done for you to be so ashamed of me?

What is *wrong* with me?

There's so much anger and so much pain inside of him that it is just waiting to burst out. So much rage. So much hurt. So much goddamn hurt! What is so goddamn wrong with *me* that you didn't want me?

Dolores, seeing all of that anger and rage on his face, involuntarily recoils from him. "Mani!" she gasps. "You look as frightening as one of those bulls that rush on the street on the way to the slaughterhouse!"

Mani rushes to his mother, his rage now hiding again behind the shield of his control, the cold controlling shield he has used all his life to hide behind. "Oh, Mamá, I'm sorry," he says as he kneels again by her side. "I didn't mean to frighten you."

She caresses his beautiful wavy dark hair so much like hers used to be, and looks deep into his dark eyes, still so much like hers. "Do you know why those bulls are so frightening, Mani?"

Mani looks at her.

"Because they are so frightened. It's their fear that makes them so frightening, Mani. That's all. Only their fear. And you know why?"

Mani shakes his head.

"Because we see our own fears reflected in theirs."

She pauses as she caresses his hair once again.

"But, Mani, we are not like those bulls. They are afraid because they have no choice. They *have* to follow someone else's path. They don't know where they are going. But we know they are rushing to their deaths, just as we know we are rushing to ours. And that is why we don't have to be afraid, Mani. Because we know with absolute certainty that no matter what path each of us takes, that path will eventually lead us to our own final destination, Mani. To our own death. So, Mani, my son, even if the rest of the world does not like it, we might as well choose a path of our own liking and move on it at our own speed, don't you think?"

Mani looks at her, a child again; a child who, just awakened from a horrible nightmare, finds this frail tiny woman with the soothing voice next to him.

"You don't have to follow anyone else's path, Mani. It just doesn't make any sense, does it? So just follow your own, my son, just follow your own."

Mani is enraptured by her voice. The soothing voice of a mother putting a child to sleep.

"Pablo did it. So did I. So did your father's father and grandfather. So does your father, in his own way. And so must you, Mani. So must you, my son, little love of mine. So must you."

She takes the strong left hand of her boy in her stronger left hand. His hand is cold, icy cold. She places it between both her hands and rubs it warm as she adds, "I have never asked you for anything, Mani. Now I'm going to ask you for something."

Mani tries to evade his mother's eyes.

He knows he must do as he must, as a man must. He knows he cannot let the world laugh at them, his family, him, just because Gustavo is what he is. He knows that he will have to say no to whatever this something is this woman he calls mother is going to ask him to do. And, anticipating that, Mani begins to shake his head involuntarily. Dolores looks at him and smiles.

"Don't be frightened, Mani."

Mani looks at her, a question in his eyes.

"That's all I'm asking you. There's no need to be frightened. There's never a need to be frightened, Mani. Of anything."

She pauses.

"There was never a need to be frightened, was there?"

Dolores looks at him.

She is so proud of this son of hers. She is proud of all of her children, but she is particularly proud of this son of hers because she knows he has a rare nobility in him, a gentle nobility she has seen lying down inside Mani's heart. A brave nobility she knows Mani is not even aware of. She caresses Mani's dark wavy hair again, combing it a little to one side so she can see her boy's handsome face: a godlike face that seems to have been chiseled out of the hardest granite by an angry sculptor filled with rage.

Mani looks at his mother, who is smiling at him.

And he, who can recall everything so well, suddenly sees on his mother's face the same smile with which she was looking at Gustavo the day he hung up his apron. And he also sees on his mother's face the same kind of pride he has seen only once before and has never seen since, a pride once aimed at Gustavo and that is now aimed at *him*. The immense pride of a teacher who sees one of her students graduate to a higher level of learning.

Mani is astounded.

He looks at Dolores looking at him, and all of a sudden Mani realizes where his powers come from. From her. From this frail tiny woman smiling at him.

He looks at Dolores looking at him, and sees that this frail tiny woman in the rocking chair with the white nightgown and the worn pink slippers is neither frail nor tiny but strong and powerful; a strong powerful woman able to command souls, just like him; a strong powerful woman with sparkling dark eyes who can anticipate—just like him—what souls will do even before they do it.

Because Mani has seen in the kind warm eyes of this frail tiny strong powerful woman looking at him that she has known of Mani's decision even before he made it.

That is why she is looking at him the way she is, with that immense pride of hers that fills Mani's soul with something he cannot yet understand, but something which feels immensely soothing, a kind of internal peace he never thought he could enjoy, a peace he has been needing, a peace he has unknowingly been praying for since those horrible doubts of his first entered his head.

And even though he does not realize it—but Dolores who is looking at him does—years of rage and years of fear lift off his face transforming it into a godlike face that seems to have been chiseled out of the hardest granite by a loving sculptor at peace with himself: the face of a courageous young man who is no longer frightened. Of anything. Because there was never a need to be frightened, was there?

Mani is speechless.

He is just able to say, "Mamá!"

And then, dropping his head into her lap and embracing this delicate woman with his powerful arms, the boy Mani begins to cry for the many many years he never cried, his shoulders shaking as he weeps for the many many years he never wept; for he has suddenly realized that this beautiful woman with the kind dark eyes he has been calling mother is and has always been his mother, just as this beautiful family he has been calling family is and has always been his family.

And now that the boy Mani is finally able to trust, now the man Mani can follow his own path.

And now the man Mani can finally go free.

Acknowledgments

I've been told that to get a first novel published requires not only a little bit of talent but a great deal of luck.

I must be very lucky then.

It was luck that brought me to a supermarket shelf where I found a paperback copy of James A. Michener's *The Novel,* a book that gave me the courage to sit down at an old typewriter and try something I had never done before: Writing.

Just as it was luck that brought me to Michael and Mary Tannen, who brought me to Maria Tucci and Bob Gottlieb, who brought me to Sarah Burnes and Robin Desser, who brought me to Martha Kaplan and Owen Laster, who brought me to Michael Korda, Chuck Adams, and Carolyn Reidy, who said Yes, and brought me to Gypsy da Silva, Victoria Klose, Carol Catt, Jim Stoller, Tia Maggini, Carol Bowie, Elina Nudelman, Meryl Levavi, John Wahler, Jackie Seow, Cathleen Toelke, Mary Schuck, Becky Cabaza, and Dan Lane, all of whom transformed my battered manuscript—by then filled with thousands of corrections—into this handsome book you now hold in your hands.

So, you see, I must be very lucky, for it was luck that brought me to you.

Just as it was luck that thirty-six years ago brought me, a young man forced to leave his own country behind, to this magnanimous country where countless people have extended their helping hands to me and my family; and where I found the best friend a man can ever have, Robert Joyner, who edited not only my manuscript but my life as well.

To all and every one of you, my deepest thanks.

De corazón, as we Cubans say.

From the heart.